I0691619

Forever

Tara Fox Hall

Published by
Melange Books, LLC
White Bear Lake, MN 55110
www.melange-books.com

Forever ~ Copyright © 2016 by Tara Fox Hall

ISBN: 978-1-68046-357-6

Cover Design by Caroline Andrus

For Danial...and for Theo

Chapter One

When Shaker and I got back to Hayden after dropping off a very drunken Theo at his home, I guiltily expected that Devlin or Lash would be waiting to ask us where we had been. Instead, our middle-of-the-night-foray had gone undiscovered. Further, no one had disturbed us during my venting of emotion with my personal demon afterwards in the kitchen. Though Shaker advised against it, I thought it wise to explain my teleportation and his presence, in case Titus had sensed me leaving or one of the guards had seen Shaker arrive. So I had a glass of wine, and Shaker grumblingly imbibed more of Titus's Black Arts whiskey, as we waited for inevitable discovery.

An hour passed this way, and no one came to find us.

Bitching that what we were doing was not only a waste of time but also completely unnecessary, Shaker finally mentally checked in with Titus and Sunrise. Shaker's demon brother brought his sleeping grandchild to the kitchen a few moments later, just to nod hello to me. For a moment he and Shaker studied one another, making me infer that the two of them were having a telepathic conversation. Titus shot me a look right after, as if he wondered why Shaker had come to see me instead of teleporting to Titus's home to say he was here. But he asked no questions aloud, either not wanting to wake Sunrise, or not wanting me to hear what was being said.

Devlin and Lash arrived an hour later. Lash was bitching about Thane, one of Devlin's Italian mob connections.

"Arrogant spaghetti bender!" he hissed. "I'm not from an island! I'm Southern!"

"Relax, you know how he is about anyone who speaks Spanish,"

1

Devlin said. "And you're being just as much of a jackass as he was tonight." He caught sight of me. "Love, what are you doing up? You should have been in bed hours ago in your condition."

Finally, the big chance to explain. "I had to go get Theo. He was drunk at Davy's. Shaker helped, as Theo was too heavy for me to handle."

Both my vampire and weresnake paramours begin talking at once.

"Theo? Why? He never goes to Davy's?" Devlin said suspiciously. "And why would Davy call you to come get him and not Jenny?"

"Fucking cat! I thought I smelled cougar. Why the fuck didn't he call his buddy Tears?"

I glanced at my weresnake mate, wondering why I had thought it important to tell him anything. "Terian was away, Lash."

"Why not his mate? Why is he fucking calling you? Asshole!"

"She's dead," I said flatly. "Or he would have called her, or maybe not even gone there. That's why he was drunk, he was upset she died." *But not too upset to try to kiss me…*

"What happened?" Devlin asked, sitting down. Lash sat down, too, angrily.

"Cancer, he said. Remember, Theo turned Jenny into werecougar to save her life, because she had cancer and modern medicine couldn't do anything. Becoming werecougar put the cancer in remission, but it came back."

There was a footstep, then out of the corner of my eye, the shadow of someone leaving through the garage.

"Danial," Devlin whispered. "He stopped by to visit me tonight on his way back from the airport. He said he had more news on Cain's brother, West, and possibly information to contact him. However, our talking can wait. Theo needs him more than I do tonight."

"I'm sorry for him," Lash hissed, remorseful. "It's terrible to lose someone you love."

"I went with Sar, to protect her," Shaker rumbled. "I was visiting my brother."

Lash nodded, and then absently thanked him. I felt guilty, my neck flushing. Luckily, I was so hot being near Shaker that my embarrassment went unnoticed.

2

"Come to bed," Devlin said, taking my hand. "Shaker, thanks for your help."

Shaker stood, his red eyes on me, waiting.

Shit, do I need to dismiss him? "Goodbye," I said as dismissively as I could.

He nodded and disappeared.

"Let's get into the Jacuzzi first," Lash hissed, the angry note in his words returning. "I need to wash off some Italian slime."

* * * *

The next morning, I sought out Rene. I found her in the gym, walking on my treadmill.

She gave me a half-smile. "You know, it's so odd, to be walking and not get anywhere. I never imagined there would be machines that would be created because people didn't walk enough to stay in shape—"

"What did you see?" I interrupted in a commanding tone. "You saw this happening! Tell me everything!

"No," Rene replied just as firmly. "I may be wrong. I was wrong before, and I did not see you helping me become human, I saw me ebbing into nothingness. Now I see another future, but it's not certain—"

"Tell me! I need to know if what Theo said was true, if Danial is going to try to force me to be intimate with Theo."

"Danial is going to call Devlin soon, and make plans." Rene said darkly. "That is all I know for sure. So we will likely need to go through with ours. That is all I'll say for now."

I left frustrated, but relieved that at least I knew something of what was coming.

* * * *

Sure enough, a day later, Devlin contacted Danial. During their talk, Danial mentioned that he had arranged for a night with Theo and him, and that my presence was requested.

Devlin came to me, and asked formally. I coldly accepted.

Danial, Devlin and Lash arranged the interlude a day later, with me present.

"Sar is pregnant now with another of Devlin's children, and Stephen

3

said there is more than one of mine, as well," Lash hissed at Danial proudly. "That is another condition, that you do nothing to endanger the babies tomorrow night, nothing rough, and take only a little blood from her—"

"So there is enough left for you?" Danial sneered back at him. "I know you feed on her, you vile monster!"

"It's her choice to give me her blood, just as it was when she was with you," Lash hissed coolly. "Stop being an ass, though I know that's difficult for you."

"Danial, as Ruler, and the father of one of her children, I stand with Lash," Devlin pronounced officially, his eyes red. "Sar's safety comes first in this, and the safety of her children. You will abide by what Lash has asked of you, or Sar will not be coming. You break these rules, brother or not, and your life is forfeit. Do you agree?"

"Of course," Danial said with disdain. "I am not going to hurt her or her children, especially your child. If she had been more than a month or two, I would have agreed to wait until after they were born." He cast an unfriendly look at Lash. "You are filth to even suggest that I would do such a thing."

Lash glared at Danial coldly, but didn't speak.

"Titus will teleport her at dusk tomorrow," Devlin said sternly. "When she wakes in the morning, she'll call, to let us know she is okay."

"If I don't hear from her by noon, I'm coming for her," Lash hissed to Danial. "And I'll be bringing a stake for you. Got it?"

Danial bared his fangs, and nodded. "I have a request of my own."

"Which is?" Devlin said.

"Sarelle is to come to me wearing her collar." Danial's tone was full of restrained anger. He approached, crooking his fingers at me, the gold fox head choker dangling from them and shining bright as a dagger. I repressed a sneer, and went to him with false obedience, letting him fasten it around my neck.

"It is to come off before she leaves," Devlin said flatly.

"Likely, she'll be able to remove it herself by then," Danial said with a possessive grin. "I'm acceptable to that removal, either way."

I can't abstain from sex with him and still get enough of the vampire virus into my system to allow me to make the magic of the collar work. It

4

won't register me as anything but human. Shit. Now Rene and I were really in trouble.

* * * *

Danial was not the only unwelcome visitor that day. I was in my sewing room when Caitlyn came to me, holding V's hand, both of them scared. One of the newer guards, Ranger, was with them.

"What's wrong?"

"You're to go to the main hallway," Caitlyn said.

I was surprised, as we seldom used the huge old entryway, or its oak double door formal entrance. It was the last existing part of the original house called Hayden, back when Hayden had been first built with wood at Devlin's arrival in America. Devlin has said the structure had survived much, including a fire that had engulfed the rest of the house. "Why? Who is here?"

"My orders are from Lash, and he didn't say. We're going below," Seth said from behind her urgently. "We'll take the dog with us, Sarelle. Ranger will escort you there."

I got up and went with Ranger, hoping I wasn't going to find what I guessed was waiting for me. My heart sank at the sight of a crowd of people there spilling out into the hall. I walked toward them, knowing showing fear and running weren't options.

Devlin leaned against a pillar, not really barring the way into Hayden while still maintaining a guarding stance. Lash stood in the middle of the hallway as a focal point, directly facing Samuel and Perseus. Zane was behind them, leaning against the wall as if trying to mirror Devlin. Another man I didn't recognize was with him, his features distinctly Asian. I guessed he was the new vampire leader of Asia, after Michael had gone into hiding. Outside the large front windows, there were many other non-vampire guards of theirs in the bright sunlight, though they were behind their respective second-in-commands, just as our best fighting guards were behind Lash inside and Kyle outside.

Devlin was speaking to Samuel, his manner cool but respectful. "I told you, Samuel, it was my choice to let Sarelle try with Lash. You know me, and that you think this unusual baffles me. It was part of the Oath she took to me—"

5

"We forbade her from having any more were children," Samuel said flatly. "If you want to share your Oathed One with your guard, that's your business. But it becomes a problem when something comes of that bedding—"

"You lied to us again, Dalcon!" Perseus snarled. "We are not going to let it slide, not this time! We are taking her from you."

Devlin glanced over at me wearily, then away. "You are not," he rasped. "And you have no rights to dictate to me any terms of a promise between myself and my Oathed One, according to vampire law."

"Yes," a Japanese-accented voice said, and Zane's "friend" came forward. He had a calm look about him, but he radiated danger, and his words were measured and forceful. "We are."

"Don't fuck with me, Kaizan," Lash hissed, baring his fangs wide. "You were fifth for a lot of years, and you got to be fourth by default, not by winning any fights."

"I am Ruler of Asia now," Kaizan hissed back, baring his own set of vampire fangs. "My status as a paid killer means nothing here. Though it should serve to remind you that you are not dealing with someone who'll hesitate to push back—!"

Lash shoved him, and then they were fighting. Devlin grabbed hold of Lash, and Samuel and Perseus grabbed hold of Kaizan, and dragged them apart, Lash still hissing swear words.

"No one is taking her," Titus rumbled, stepping forward. "She is my kin by blood, and my brothers stand with me on this." Blue fire erupted from his hand, darkening to the inky black of Hellfire.

Shaker and Rip were beside Titus, flanking him. Shaker sent me a mental "be calm," in my mind, and I nodded, though he didn't look at me.

"We brought enough men and other vampires to crush you with numbers," Samuel said calmly. "More wait to teleport in at my command. Just give her over, Dalcon. You should know that this time 'no' isn't an answer we are going to accept."

"I realize that," Dalcon said tiredly. "But Lash and I would kill her ourselves before we'd let you lay your hands on her."

"That's right," Lash hissed menacingly. "She suffered enough at Michael's hands. She's said before she would rather die than go through

6

that again."

"Enough," I said suddenly, and I walked in their midst, to stand in front of Lash. He looked at me like I'd lost my mind, but he gave me room.

"Perseus, you are eldest. Why do you really want me?" I said, resigned. I'd had enough of this endless pursuit. One way or another, it was ending here today.

"Because I have built too much in my years as Ruler," Perseus said finally. "I want to know there will be someone of my line to Rule after me, someone who would appreciate the things I've seen and done, who would rule, as I ruled—"

"Then you don't want a child really," I interrupted flatly. "You want another copy of yourself. A child isn't that, Perseus. They'd be only half of you—"

"Why are we letting her talk?" Zane said gruffly.

Both Lash and Kaizan turned and shot him. He hissed in pain, and sank to the floor cursing, though he was already healing the ragged bullet wounds in his thigh and shoulder.

"I had no human children, when I was mortal. My nearest descendants are dust, long dead, and buried. I have no family, Sarelle."

"Okay." I turned to Samuel. "You have two children already. Why do you really want me, Samuel?"

"Because I want more," he said emotionally. "I was never a father before, and I enjoy it, Lady Dalcon. Both Sharon and Elijah are growing so fast, they're already adults."

"Any other children would grow up just as fast."

"I know that, Lady. But I'd delay it this time as long as I could, now that the hunters are more under control in Europe." He gave me a smile. "If it was your baby, Lady, it would grow much slower." He turned covetous. "We would make a strong son, Sarelle. Together—"

"That's enough," I interrupted, taking great pleasure in cutting him short. I turned and looked squarely at Kaizan. "And you?"

"No Ruler is having something I don't have a chance at," he said arrogantly. "I love sex, woman, even if your looks are not to my taste."

I rolled my eyes. "And you, Zane?"

"Why should I tell you?"

7

"Tell me the truth now. Or leave, and I'll guarantee that you'll never get what you want."

Zane looked at me, and then away. "I am strong, and I rule a territory larger than anyone save Perseus. But I'm last in estimation, always, because my lands are not developed." He swallowed. "I want more for my lands, and the vampires who live there. But I need another partner, someone to watch my back, and help me, maybe take over, if I die, as Perseus said. Nevertheless, I need to be able to trust them, and I don't trust anyone. But I could trust a child I raised myself, which was my own child."

"Your own flesh and blood can turn on you," I said ominously. "It happens."

"Then at least if that happened, it would be some relation to me and worthy of Ruling."

God, these Rulers were a wacky bunch. But they did have their reasons, for the most part. I looked at them each in turn, then at Devlin. "What are your thoughts, Oathed One?"

"That they can all go to hell," Devlin said arrogantly. "And also that save for Kaizan, they all have good reasons for wanting offspring."

"I have a good reason—!" Kaizan snarled, and Lash shoved him again. This time the arrogant vampire wasn't expecting it, and he fell to one knee, before catching himself.

"Then you have my permission," I said. I turned back to Samuel and the rest. "Michael was working on a formula using my blood and some notes from a long dead witch. He managed to change a woman's blood enough so that it was medically similar to mine, though the effect was temporary." I paused. "The key is that you need more of my blood to keep the woman from turning through the pregnancy."

"Like Harriet," Samuel said, nodding. "But her children were not true dhamphirs; they are more vampire than human."

Don't actually be generous enough to call them "your" children, you asshole. "These will not be, they'll be as Venus is," I said confidently. "Michael did extensive tests."

"So did I, but I had no success—"

"You didn't have Monica's notes, Samuel," Devlin interjected. "She found the key. Her love for Danial made her search until she found an

8

answer."

"We'll give that answer to you," I said, not wanting to hear anything more about Monica. God, that woman had been dead for years and she was still haunting my life. "You can have all the notes and enough blood from me, you three, to each have one child of your own."

"What about me?" Kaizan yelled, enraged. "I have the right—!"

Lash shot him in the chest, and Kaizan sank to the floor, snarling in pain, even as he healed. "No one has the right to anything of Sarelle save Dev, her one Oathed vampire," Lash hissed. "This bullshit ends here. I'm sick of it, she's sick of it, and Dev's sick of it. Besides, Sar is finally turning."

There was a collective gasp from the Rulers. "She smells the same," Samuel said worriedly, looking immediately to Devlin. "Tell us, Devlin, is this truth?"

"Sarelle had a lot of trouble getting pregnant this time," Lash hissed loudly. "Michael theorized that it was from being partly turned, that even as she stayed young, her fertility would decrease, as her body used the virus to sustain itself. That seems to be happening."

"It's only been five years since she met Danial and me," Devlin added sadly. "But apparently, that's long enough. While I'll concede that the other main Vampire Rulers who were there that night at the Gathering in Toronto have a right at least to petition me for a chance, given how little time is probably left, none that comes after will be allowed to. That includes you, Kaizan."

No one said anything.

"Now give me an Oath, all of you, Ruler to Ruler, to let this matter end here tonight," Devlin said ferociously. "Sar may be pregnant now, and I'll not have her lose my child because of you assholes."

"Agreed," Samuel and Perseus said as one. Zane nodded.

Kaizan didn't, he regained his feet. "I won't agree," he said drawing his gun. "I'll take her by force, if I have to. I won't do it by trickery, as Michael did, I'll do it here and now. Most of the men here are mine!"

"Challenge me then, right now!" Lash hissed, drawing his knife, his gun still in his hand. "I'll be happy to end your reign."

"There are you and Devlin, and a couple demons," Kaizan said. "And your guards. But I can break you with enough men, Lash. You know it!"

"Don't think that this is all there is, you fuck!" Lash hissed. "You know me, Kaizan."

Kaizan smiled evilly. "I do know you, and your master. I know that you have few real friends, Devlin. Lash, you have none. I can hire fifty men to each of you, Lash. My continent is the hub of commerce and industry now! We Asians run the world!"

"Sarelle has friends of her own," Titus rumbled. "And we have friends, Kaizan. Lucifer has long waited for Devlin's soul. However, he'd be happy with any Ruler's soul I managed to snatch. I can take yours with a few words from your still breathing body. But you'll not last long once I draw it out—!"

"You were just dragged back in Hell by your real master," Kaizan laughed. "I'm not afraid of you!"

Suddenly, Kaizan was lifted off his feet. Though he struggled, he couldn't get free.

"Are you afraid of me?" a low voice rumbled.

Chapter Two

Shaker leaned closer to Kaizen. "Don't think you run this world, vampire. This world is the Devil's playground, according to rules set forth right after it was made. And I am one of his soldiers."

Kaizan went to spit something, but Shaker cut him off. "Silence." Kaizan struggled, but couldn't force his lips apart.

"You come near Sarelle, any of her children or Hayden, and I'll put one of my cloven hooves through your heart."

"You dare threaten a Ruler, Demon?" Perseus got out. "We've had a truce for the last five hundred years between our races!"

"I've killed Rulers, presidents, emperors, priests, assassins, children, mothers, virgins, and small baby animals, and eaten them alive with relish as they screamed," Shaker said easily. "I'll eat you too, Vampire, and leave your soul screaming forever in Hell. Stay out of this."

Shaker turned back to Kaizan. "You make a move, or attempt anything to ever take Sarelle from her rightful place here, and I'll come for you, Kaizan. And that goes for any other being you send; human, vampire, demon, faerie, ghost, angel, and werecreatures included. After they're all dead, I'll kill you with sunlight slowly, and take your soul to Hell. Then I'll kill anyone you ever loved, or cared for, any relation to you at all, no matter how innocent they are—"

I held onto Lash beside me, feeling like I was going to throw up. With effort, I held it in.

"I'll kill them all, until anyone with your blood in their veins is either dead or Lucifer's. I'll torture them, sear them with Hellfire, and then pile their carcasses in a heap in some dump for seagulls and rats to feast on. Then I'll harvest their souls for Hell, what's left of them."

11

"Damn you!" Kaizan hissed.

"Do we understand each other, Ruler?" Shaker said pleasantly.

"Yes," Kaizan hissed. "Now release me."

Shaker let him go, and Kaizan stalked off, without a backward look. The door had no sooner shut behind him, than Samuel turned to Devlin. "May we have the files?" he said eagerly. "I would like to return as soon as possible, to begin work. You are right, there is not much time."

"Yes," Devlin said, and handed him a thick sheaf of papers. "I expect you to use your lab to do the initial work. Once the woman is pregnant, I will want to see her, to taste a few drops of her blood. Once I determine it is as it should be, I'll give permission to Titus to give you the correct mixture of Sar's blood to use. Directly afterwards, I expect you to allow Perseus and Zane access to your lab, and to help them to achieve their own success, as quickly as possible. As I've said, time is of the essence."

"Agreed. Devlin, you may keep her, for the rest of her life," Samuel said. "I will not interfere again, on my word as Ruler."

"Nor will I." Perseus bowed.

"Nor will I," added Zane. "On my life."

The three of them nodded to me, and left.

"Titus, make sure they all leave the grounds," Devlin said quietly. "Rip, please get back to Danial. I know he is below guarding V, but until they are successful, I want everyone to be on guard. Words can be said in heartfelt Oaths, and straightforwardly broken just as fast."

Rip and Titus disappeared.

"Shaker, guard Sar, please," Lash hissed, giving me a hug. "I've got to go with Devlin. There's a call from the werebats he's expecting in a few minutes that I need to sit in on."

I didn't want to be alone with Shaker, after hearing what he did. But I couldn't well say that, I'd have to admit why.

Shaker walked me back to my sewing room. I sat down, hoping he'd leave, but instead he came and sat in the chair I sometimes read in. "What are you making, Mistress?"

"Please don't call me that," I said, trying to keep disgust out of my voice. I was happy he'd gotten Kaizan to back off. But my demon had also said that he'd killed children and animals and eaten them. *Alive.* My stomach clenched again.

"You're upset, because of what I said." He was not offended, but not happy either.

"Yes, of course."

"Why? I'm demon, Sar. Demons are supposed to eat their flesh alive, though conscious or unconscious is left to our discretion—"

I made it to the bathroom, and then I was on my knees, heaving up my breakfast. Shaker tried to help me up when I'd finished, but I shrank from him. "Please don't touch me."

"As you wish, Mistress."

I sat there for a while, feeling him watching me. I wanted to tell him to leave, but I knew he was supposed to be guarding me.

I heard creaking and looked out of the corner of my eye. He was leaning against the doorframe.

"I thought you were mellowing out, Mistress, when you gave me Jezebel. Now you seem to be uptight for some reason." He grinned at me. "Would you like a massage? I'm rather skilled at them."

"No."

"I've missed you," Shaker rumbled quietly. "Let me touch you, Mistress." He turned eager. "You were so soft and cool that night, so pliable."

I tried to ignore him, but suddenly got a vivid mental picture of us copulating. I saw myself orgasm as I rode him, my face slack with lust as he pushed deeply inside me, his body straining to give me release. I tried to block it out, but the image was inside my head. Shaker split, becoming two identical beings. Then the second of him was easing into me, his penis shrinking so as not to injure me as I moaned in joy as being doubly filled and the Shaker still beneath me began to move—

"Stop it," I breathed.

I could feel it as though it were happening again. God, his flesh felt so good inside mine, the fit perfect, and there was so much pleasure! In a moment, I was coming again, and he was rumbling in pleasure beneath me. Again, he split, and there were three Shakers with me. And the two still inside me began to move again in tandem, and my mouth opened as I moaned. And the third Shaker was there to fill it with his hot soft lips, his tongue reaching inside me as I sucked it desperately, already feeling another climax building—

"Stop IT!" I rasped out, my breathing fast and panicked.

I was awash in sensation, an idea, an emotion of desire without beginning or end. And when the third Shaker held his engorged member up to me as an offering, I opened my mouth, sliding him into me as he shrank to fill me perfectly, his mouth letting go a sharp cry of pleasure as I sucked him eagerly. He fell into rhythm with the other Shakers, and my orgasm hit me, making me spasm as I lost myself in pleasure.

Shaker waited until I'd finished, and then his three bodies came simultaneously with a fervent roar, his semen jetting into me as I swallowed the sweet milky fluid, sucking him as hard as I could. And when he gently withdrew from me, his three bodies moving to become one again, I stopped him with a touch, telling him I wanted that again, but more. All three of him grinned as he stiffened like magic, and began to move me into position on my side, becoming five beings. Two slid into me, my mouth opening in slack need to be quickly filled as hot mouths teased both breasts, and then they began to move—!

"STOP IT!" I shouted, and Shaker broke the connection, leaving me gasping for breath.

"Give in to me," Shaker rumbled softly. "I know what you desire most, Mistress. Of all your lovers, only I can give that to you."

"That's not true," I said raggedly, my chest heaving.

"No beings can move in tandem so perfectly in the waking world," Shaker said seductively. "I can scent your need for me, Mistress. You felt so good inside. I could feel everything my doubles were feeling, all of it at once. I loved feeling my member stroked by your body as you sucked my come down so eagerly..."

I shuddered at his words, my heart racing. Then it hit me he was right, I could scent myself. My panties were soaked from my desire for him.

Nausea hit me stronger than ever, and I ran for the bathroom, where I puked up what felt like everything I'd ever eaten. I held onto the toilet crying for a moment, disgusted with myself.

Shaker appeared behind me, and got me a glass of water, which he put on the floor for me. Then he handed me a towel, which I gratefully took while trying not to touch him.

"You aren't sick because of the children in you," he rumbled. "You're repelled at yourself, because of that one dream we shared after you miscarried, when I became what you most desired."

"Yes." I tried not to sound cold. "Please do not mention it to me."

"Mistress, we don't have to be intimate again in dreams, if you don't wish it," he said calmly. "Or in the physical world, either."

"I don't," I said, biting my lip. "I'm sorry if this makes you feel bad."

"I don't feel bad because you say that you want a professional relationship now," Shaker said, chuckling. "I think it's sweet that you can be so horrified at what I am and still so worried you'll hurt my feelings. I relish how much your body still desires mine. Shows I haven't lost my demon touch."

Now I was profoundly embarrassed. "Look, you got the Ruler jackasses to back off. I appreciate that. But I can't be close to someone who's done the things you've done, not even as a friend. So from now on, I don't want you to touch me in any way other than what is required for you not to go back to Hell. Anything else is off limits. And no more visions of us having sex."

Shaker smiled. "You know, Mistress, I admire your impetuosity. It's a favorite human trait among demons because it often leads to bad decisions."

My eyes narrowed. "That's a backhanded compliment if I ever heard one."

"It's not meant as a compliment, Mistress, it's meant as a warning. When I made plans to escape Cyrus, I researched your background. You are an easy mark for one who knows your weakness."

"And what is that?"

"You care too much," he replied. "You can't turn away from suffering, and are compelled to act. That caring led you to the very spot you find yourself in, through all your many varied relationships with supernatural males, and—"

"I stand for what I believe in."

"And are easily ensnared," Shaker finished. "Take this for the warning I mean it to be, Mistress. Demons are bred to seek out weaknesses, and exploit them. I tell you yours so you can take steps to counteract it."

"Thanks for the warning," I said aloofly, wondering inwardly if he was right. "Please leave me."

"As you will," Shaker said gently. "I'll be outside, if you need me." He left, shutting the door behind him, leaving me alone with my thoughts.

I tried to sew, but all I kept coming back to was the vision he'd shown me. And so finally I teleported to my bedroom, popped a Valium, and changed my underwear. Afterward I teleported back and took a nap in my reading chair, escaping into dreamless sleep.

* * * *

I emerged a few hours later, rested.

Shaker was sitting in a hall chair outside the door, reading. He got to his feet when he saw me. "Ready to go?"

I took a deep breath. "Are…is what we talked about…are you fine with that?"

Shaker grinned at me, baring his dagger teeth. "I said I was, Mistress. But are you bringing it up again because you want to reconsider?"

"No," I said flatly. "I don't know why I even said anything."

Shaker snorted. "Because you're human and decent. That type of human has rules of etiquette for their lovers—"

I blushed, but asking him again not to bring it up made me seem over reactive.

"—and you are adhering to them," he finished, his red eyes calm and removed. "But you have nothing to fear now you've told me what you want of me. Understand, I have been bound to many males and females over the years. There is no act I haven't taken part in, willingly or unwillingly. When I am ordered to do something by my Mistress or Master, there is usually no choice, unless it conflicts with some rule of Hell."

"What are you saying, Shaker?"

"That it was rare that a Master or Mistress didn't want some kind of sexual favor from me as part of my servitude, even if it was just to watch me with another being. A great deal of the time it was to be pursued and

16

seduced, for me to know they meant yes when they said no and to act on the former. What we did until now was the norm, Sarelle." He grinned widely at me. "Let me amend that: what we did in our dream was much gentler than the norm, at least for me. It was nice to be gentle for a change. Our time stands out from the rest because of that. But I won't bring it up, or allude to it again, because that's finished now. I won't tease you anymore, unless you want me to."

I watched him for a moment, trying to determine if he meant what he was saying. I finally decided that he did. "Good. Will you answer a question or two?"

"You have only to ask, Mistress."

"You mentioned ghosts. Is what I sometimes feel at Anna's grave her ghost? Or was it always just Rene? I sometimes think I still feel something there when I visit."

"A tiny piece of Anna is there," Shaker said. "I have felt her, though she knows what I am and leaves when I come near her resting place. You could say it is her ghost, yes."

"You mentioned angels, too. Have you ever seen one?"

"Yes," Shaker said emptily. "I was one once, Mistress."

I was dying to know, and still repelled. I settled for a middle ground. "Are you sad you're demon now?"

"Yes and no," Shaker said, walking off. I began to walk beside him.

"What does that mean?"

"I wasn't a big deal, when I was an angel," he rumbled. "I was kind of a pawn in a chess game. You could say I was disposable." He took a breath. "But I liked it, yes."

"I'm sorry."

"Don't be. Things happened, Mistress, and I became demon when I was relatively young. My...well, think of them as my parents, they became demon, too. We exchanged one leader for another."

"Titus said he'd never seen an angel."

"He probably hasn't. He was born after this transpired, and angels don't stray too far from Heaven, unless on His orders. The longer they stay away, the more chance there is they'll get corrupted and be banished from His divine presence."

"You are saying God's name and not grimacing."

17

"I was once an angel. My belief and love for my creator was stronger that any human's could ever be, no matter how fervent. It hurts, sure, but not much. Underneath my faith is still there. Some part of me feels good, to remember how strong my faith was," he said wistfully.

"So why does Titus act so 'good'—?" *And you're so bad?*

"He was born demon, but he's got something in him of God, from our parents. That's why he's not that bad, and Rip isn't, either. They have a hard time of it, because Lucifer's always watching them, waiting for them to trip up. He thinks given enough time in Hell and Devlin's service, they'll stop being good. "

"What did you mean, about serving Devlin?"

He glanced at me. "Most demons are out of Hell on average ten years before they're severed from their summoner and sent back. Titus has been out in Devlin's service for near two hundred, with only a couple voluntary return trips in all that time. That's no accident. You know your lover. You can guess what Titus has helped that vampire conspirator do."

Quick, new subject. "Were you banished from Heaven?"

"You could say that," he said, after a minute.

"I'm sorry."

"I'm okay. I'd never have seen all the things I've seen, or experienced making love with women, or tasted ice cream with Snickers pieces if I'd stayed in Heaven."

I studied him, unsure if he was serious or playing down his fall from grace. "Yes."

His red eyes met mine, and held on. "Don't think I don't know I'm on the wrong side. I was on the right side, and I'm not now. That bothers me." He shrugged. "But there's nothing I can do to change that." He gave me a grin. "Except enjoy the ride, while it lasts."

"I'll try not to die," I said, sad for him and angry that I cared.

"I'll do my best to see you don't," he said. "Summon me if you need me." Then he walked away.

* * * *

Not all visitors were unwelcome that day. Elle stopped by, looking happier than she had in a long time. She was positively glowing.

I asked her over a glass of wine how everything was, but she was

18

secretive, saying only that it was very good. She did tell me a lot of how she was managing on her own at my homestead. I told her she was doing far better than I had done alone, a compliment that made her blush deeply with pride. I also told her a lot of what was happening, warning her of Valerian and to be careful, which she assured me she would. However, when she heard that Lash and Devlin were on a conference call organizing some of the lab work parameters with Samuel, she abruptly gave me a hug and said she'd stop by in a few weeks for another visit.

I watched her go with curiosity, wondering what this all meant. Then I shrugged, and told myself it didn't matter so long as she was happy.

* * * *

The arranged night with Danial and Theo slowly approached. My nightmares intensified the closer it got.

The night before, I had a horrible dream. I was out walking at Hayden with Ghost. We met up with Darkness in the cemetery. Ghost and she played, racing around as she used to do. Then they abruptly raced off, disappearing through some trees. I ran after them, calling frantically.

I burst out of the trees, and into a meadow of wildflowers. They were there waiting for me, looking happy. I ran up to them, huffing out of breath, and then noticed a tawny tail in the tall grass. There was a loud purr.

Devon bounded out of the tall grass, purring and licking me. I shrieked with joy, embracing the familiar heavy weight of him on me. I kissed him, and he licked me vigorously. He abruptly stood up and bounded away. I ran through the grass after him.

Suddenly there was a shriek of pain. I ran to Devon's still twitching body, his head almost severed in a huge bear trap, blood pouring from the wound.

I undid the trap, ripping my hands, and tried to heal him, but his eyes were glazing over. I pleaded for him to hold on.

He looked up at me with dead eyes. "You didn't save me, Mom. Why didn't you save me? I needed you, Mom!"

I became hysterical as he repeated his questions, his voice hurt and questioning, his blood coating my hands, pooling on the ground as it drained out of him. Then I was screaming loudly, my mind shattering.

All of a sudden, Shaker was there. He ripped Devon in half, the small furry form becoming black and shiny, as my dogs became something like black centipedes, scuttling away. Shaker grabbed them, tearing them to pieces. I was on the ground, sobbing and shaking. Shaker picked me up, and suddenly we were back at Hayden.

He set me on the bed gently. "We are still within the dream. You are alone here. All Takers have been destroyed. Please get some rest, Mistress."

"I took a pill," I said hollowly. "A cross is around my neck and under the bed. And three of them got into my dreams anyway, Shaker."

"Your faith is not as strong as it was," he rumbled. "I can help." He wove a magical barrier, and placed it on me. "They will not be able to get through that to your dreams, no one will. Rest easy."

"Thank you," I mumbled, hugging him. "I was terrified."

"Do you want me to stay?" he said formally. "I can linger until you sleep. But I give you my word there will be no Takers in any of your future dreams."

"No," I said in a small voice. "You have things to do. I'll be okay. But thanks."

"Call me if you need me," Shaker rumbled. Then he was gone.

I lapsed into sleep. My dreams were of simple tasks like sewing, and planting. I slept deeply, awaking finally at five in the morning. Devlin was beside me sleeping, snoring softly. Lash was also beside me, his breathing even and his limbs twitching a little as he snored.

I lay back down and went to sleep again. This time I dreamed I was in the kitchen, doing dishes. Somehow, I was in a little slip that tied in back. And no matter how careful I was, my breasts kept popping out of it.

I fixed them once and a moment later, they were out again. I swore softly, but then I saw flushed hands reach from behind me to cup them gently, rubbing the nipples between thumb and forefinger. I let out a moan, feeling both nipples tighten. I let out another cry as the fingers squeezed gently, twisting my inflamed flesh.

20

"Your breasts are beautiful," a deep lustful voice said. "I'm happy to hold them for you, as you finish your work."

It was Shaker, but his words were not like him. Was this a real dream?

I nodded, and finished my dishes, letting out soft cries of arousal as he played with my breasts, stroking them gently with his hot hands. Soon I was done, and for a while, I just stood there, letting him touch my breasts, his fingers massaging them as they became more and more swollen. Then his lips found mine, and he was kissing me, his tongue gently caressing mine.

I broke the kiss. "I'm wet for you," I whispered. "Reach down and touch me."

He pushed up my sheer skirt, and then there was a careful intimate touch of his clawed hand. "You are, human." He stroked me gently. "I love that you want me so much."

He turned me toward him in a fluid motion, and then lifted me. He sat me on the counter, and he spread my legs gently, so he could move between them. He pinched my nipples, and I let out a sharp cry. Then he buried his face in my breasts, his tongue licking my skin. His famished mouth found my nipple, and I jerked, feeling him sucking my tightened flesh as he massaged my other breast with his hand. He turned his head to the other nipple, and sucked that one too, his body warming considerably. Then he kissed up me to my throat, licking gently. He sucked hard for a moment, and I moaned, and then he covered my lips with his in a deep kiss, his tongue winding around mine as he devoured me.

I was almost writhing by this time. So I reached down, pushed aside his loincloth, baring his partially erect organ to my eager eyes.

"I'm fighting my body to go slow," he rumbled gently. "But you're inflaming me no matter how much I fight."

I reached down and stroked him, squeezing the huge thickness of him, and he staggered a little, even as his organ filled out immediately to its massive size. I eased down to the floor, bringing him with me. I straddled him, and made to take him in my mouth when he stopped me.

"No," he said gently. "I want us to come together. And I want it to last as long as it can."

21

I tried to protest, but he cut me off with another long passionate kiss. For a long time we lay there kissing, his strong arms wrapped around me, our tongues entwined, his body pressed against mine, rubbing slightly but not penetrating. I slid on him in rhythm, making him groan as I lubricated us. When he shifted suddenly beneath me in mid stroke, sliding home with a thrust of his hips, I let out a jagged cry of need. In a second, I was moving on him purposefully, feeling his balls tight against my womanhood, his long hard length completely within me.

"You feel like Heaven," he rumbled, "Come for me. I want to hear you come. I want us both to know it was my body that made you cry out in pleasure."

I rocked on him, moaning, and he began kissing me again, his hands caressing and squeezing. I came a second later, screaming out my pleasure in a guttural wanton howl. Shaker joined me, pushing deeply into me, so deep there was some pain, his body tensing beneath mine, jerking, as he cried out with each new thrust. His orgasm seemed to last for minutes, the pleasure engulfing me, giving me another orgasm just by itself. When I eased down onto him, he slipped out and hugged me, cradling me gently.

"Again," I whispered. "I want you again."

"As many times as you want me," he whispered back. "I'm yours."

He slowly stiffened against me, and I slipped him inside me again, pulling a cry of desire from his lips. Then I devoured his mouth with mine as I began moving.

* * * *

I woke up alone, smelling of my arousal. I lay there for a while, thinking about my dream. Finally, I decided it had to be just a dream. Shaker had not acted like himself, but had instead been like the best parts of my lovers, reminding me most of all of Theo. I'd dreamed what I had because I would see him later on tonight. I thanked God for not sending me the dream on a night I'd been with Lash and thought no more on it.

I busied myself with chores, doing email and a lot of cleaning. Rene was off in her lab putting final changes on her spell for tonight, and Devlin had said he'd been gone all day, between conference calls, and his own email work. Lash had left word he had some job to do for Devlin that had to be done today, but he'd be back before I left.

Devlin had spoken of a few possibilities for a maid in the last few weeks and by all accounts, one was supposed to be coming tomorrow to audition. I laughed, as I remembered that Rene's magical female construct that took care of the single male bears would also be around. Her appearance changed depending on whichever werebear visited her, so it was impossible to tell what she looked like on any given day, or even half-day. I made a note to myself to remember to ask any woman to speak her name to me, lest I get them mixed up, and embarrass the new maid and myself.

Before it seemed possible, it was night. Time to go see Danial and my ex.

Chapter Three

I wasn't the only one who was ill at ease. Lash came in as I was dressing, nervous as a wild bird in a cage. "I don't feel comfortable letting you go to be with Danial and that fucking…Theo, so soon after you conceived," he said worriedly.

I don't need your anxieties now; I have enough of my own. "Theo has agreed to use protection."

"I remember what happened last time with Devlin and Theo," Lash hissed angrily. "I'll not be tricked into letting my mate bear another man's child."

He wasn't the only one who remembered. I took a deep breath, and thanked God for Rene again. "It's not the same," I said with relief. "You and Dev got me pregnant more than a month ago. My cervix has to be closed, and our children are already starting to grow. Even if Theo didn't use protection, nothing could happen." I managed a smile. "It was like those first times I was with you, Lash. Even if you'd been fertile back then, nothing could've happened to change my pregnancy."

Lash held my gaze, and nodded. "You're right," he hissed. "I'm just worried."

"I want this night of Danial's over with," I said softly, hugging him. "I don't want to put it off until I'd had our babies. I'd have it looming over me for the next year, knowing I'd have to go and be with Theo and Danial. I've already been dreading it enough just in the past week."

"I get it, Sar," Lash hissed gently. "I just don't like it. Make sure you feel the condom when he's in you and that he doesn't—"

24

"I'll make sure," I said, kissing him before he said anything more graphic. "If anything feels wrong, I'll stop him and teleport home, and that will be the end of it."

"Good," Lash hissed affectionately.

"Sar," Titus called from outside the room "It's time."

"Call me if there is any trouble," Lash hissed. "I'll have Titus teleport me straight there to fuck them both up."

I kissed him and then left, before I thought any more about how much I didn't want to go.

Titus performed the spell to block any kind of love or bond on me in a few minutes, and then he teleported me to the great room. With a smile of encouragement, he left. Right after, Rene winked into view. She melted away from sight almost instantly, and then I felt a warm hand grasp mine. I took hold of hers, and knocked on Danial's bedroom door. When he told me to come in, I did.

Danial was in bed surrounded by lit candles, the quilt covering his lower body. Rene gave my hand a squeeze, and I exhaled. I looked at him, not knowing what to say.

"You look good," I said finally.

"As do you," he said gently. His voice was gentler than it had been for a long time, since the night he'd remembered who I was. "But pregnancy has always become you."

I stood there, feeling stupid but also not wanting to go over to him.

"Come to me, Darling," Danial said softly. "I'll not hurt you. Deep inside, you know that."

No, I didn't. "Did you feel you had to say that?"

"I can scent your fear from here," he said, not moving. "I don't want you to be afraid. This is going to be lovemaking we're going to share, not anything else, not even sex."

"It will be sex," I said tiredly. "Because you don't love me, Danial. And Theo—"

"Theo loves you as much as he ever did. I know you still care for him, in spite of everything that's happened between you. It is in your voice whenever you say his name. It's why you protected him when you didn't have to, when by all rights you should've asked Devlin to end him."

25

I looked away. "No, that was for Elle."

"You do not have to admit it to me for it to be true," Danial said neutrally. "And I'll not make you. Because I do love you, Sar. I've loved you since you first lived with me, long before I gave you the diamond which graces your hand." He got up from bed and came to me, his sculpted body moving gracefully. He took my right hand in his. "It hasn't left your hand since we came together to raise Elle, and had Theoron, even during our difficulties of the last few months. Just as the band I gave you has also remained on your hand with it." He kissed my hand gently, and released it. "Just as the band I bought to show my love for you has not left my own hand since our honeymoon."

I was touched, remembering his right hand had worn that band since that time we'd first put them on, just as I had. If he'd not worn his fox head ring for almost four hundred years before meeting me, likely that band would have been on his ring finger instead. "I know."

"Devlin had his own ring made of identical materials so he could take part. He also wears his and has not ever removed it, as a symbol of his love for you. But his does not have an inscription, as yours and mine does." He tilted up my chin to look into my eyes. "Do you remember what that inscription says?"

I swallowed, feeling as if I were being seduced by him all over again. "It says 'Forever.'"

Danial nodded, his smile loving. "Yes. That means for all time, Sar. Eternally. Everlastingly. Without end." He kissed my hand. "That is the extent of my love for you."

My willpower was slipping away, even though I was trying to hold onto it with both hands. Desperate, I said something nasty. "Were you loving me when you were bedding Angelica? When you were bedding Monica?"

Instead of anger, or even shame, Danial calmly looked at me. "Yes, I loved you then. Both of them knew it and envied you. It was a mark of your love for me then that you were jealous of them, even knowing I didn't love them as I loved you. It's a mark of your love that years after both of them are gone, your voice is still suffused with jealousy."

It was stupid to try to hurt him with past transgressions. "I'm sorry for saying that."

26

"Do not be sorry for loving me," Danial said, holding me close to him, his right hand stroking my back. "I have never been sorry for loving you. It is you and you alone in my heart, Love. It will always be you and you alone, until death parts us."

I reached up with my hands and kissed him. Danial kissed me tenderly back, as I put my arms around him. "I love you," I whispered softly. "I was never sorry I did—"

Rene pinched the top of my hand sharply, bringing me back to myself. Thanking her mentally, I distanced myself a little from Danial. Shit, I was going to have to be careful, or he'd seduce me all over again, and Rene's plans would be for nothing. "Um, where is Theo?"

Danial smiled ruefully. "He's in the bathroom," he said. "He's nervous."

He wasn't the only one. I went into the bathroom. Theo was sitting on the toilet, fully dressed, looking at the floor.

"Theo, what is it? Do you not want to do this?"

He looked up at me, his eyes worried, but also sad. "Are you sure you're okay with this? I'll understand if you want to back out. I know you've been trying with Lash to have a baby, that you might be pregnant now."

His pain was like a primeval forest, it was so immense and dark. I went to him, because even after everything he'd tried to do and how we'd hurt each other, I still cared enough about him to want to comfort him. "I'm here of my own volition," I said, touching him on the shoulder with my hand. "And yes, though we didn't confirm it yet, I'm almost sure to be pregnant."

"I'll be extra careful of you," Theo said gently, as he got to his feet and hugged me.

His soft lips grazed mine lightly. When I didn't pull away, he immediately pulled me close to him, his mouth devouring mine as he kissed me. "I've missed you so much, Sar," he whispered, as he kissed his way down my neck. "I think about us at night, when I'm alone—"

That was enough being comforting. I pushed him back gently and he looked up at me irritated, opening his mouth to protest.

I put my finger to his lips. "Danial is waiting for us. We need to go out to him, Theo."

27

"Okay," Theo said nervously and he began to take off his clothes.

I got into my outfit, a short ivory colored silk slip with a tie in the back. I was surprised it wasn't more risqué, but Danial was probably trying to make me feel comfortable. I was oddly reminded of my dream of Shaker as I looked at my refection in the mirror. To my abject relief, my body did not escape the slip's confines with normal movement.

Theo turned to me, erect. "Ready?"

"Yes." I felt a faint naughty urge to reach out and squeeze him, but pushed it down. This wasn't my fantasy. *The sooner I get this night over and give Danial what he wants, the sooner I'll be sleeping, and then home at Hayden.* God, was this how Serena had felt in her two years in Devlin's service? I hoped not, even if she was done with that now.

I walked out to the bed, Theo following. Danial got up, pulling me close to him. "You look beautiful, Sar," he purred and began kissing me gently.

Theo sat on the bed and looked at us, his body shifting nervously. I watched him nervously myself, waiting and worrying over his inevitable touch.

"Theo, come around in back of Sar," Danial said quietly. Theo got up, and moved into position. "I'll kiss her neck and caress her from the front. You kiss her on the lips and caress her from the back."

"Danial, I'll try, but I don't know if I can get into it with you here," Theo whispered.

"Try it. You might be pleasantly surprised. For now, we're only going to kiss her, nothing more. Don't have her yet, please."

Theo turned my head to face him and kissed me, first hesitantly, and then with mounting passion. I felt his member, which had softened in his uneasiness, firm itself. Soon it was hard against my lower back, almost burning in its heat. I felt fear first, feeling how much he wanted me. I reminded myself that it wasn't going to happen, that Rene was here. I had to trust her. *God, help me to make this seem as real as possible...*

Theo was kissing me deeply, groaning, and I kissed him back with abandon, opening my mouth fully to him, licking him, as I tried to pretend he was Devlin. Danial kissed my neck, brushing me with his fangs. Then I felt Danial touch me intimately, gently playing with my clit. I focused on him, trying to get into the mood.

"Theo, lift Sar onto the bed. Then go get on a condom, they are on the dresser. The liquid contraceptive's in the bathroom."

Theo let out a growl of frustration, but he did as Danial asked, heading into the bathroom. Then Danial was on top of me, slipping into me as he passionately embraced me.

I have to hurry, before Theo returns! "Bite me," I hissed seductively. "Drink me, Oathed One."

"I'll wait," Danial whispered, his thrusts slow and measured. "I want to savor this, Love."

Not tonight, lover. I'm taking control, here and now. "No, Danial," I whispered seductively. "This time is just you and me." I thrust my hips up to meet his, then squeezed my vaginal muscles, making his eyes close and his mouth slacken as he let out a gasp. "I need you, I want you, and I've waited too long. Don't make me beg you." I kissed his neck, then bit softly.

Danial shuddered, the thrusts of his body into mine becoming more forceful.

"Make me come," I murmured, biting his neck again gently. He let out a groan, his fingers digging into my back as he pulled me closer, his mouth dipping to my breasts to tease first one nipple, then the other. I clasped him to me, feeling my own arousal heighten, my previous detachment gone in the blast of searing desire.

Danial slowed considerably, drawing back from me, his dark gaze as lustful as the wicked smile that graced his face. "Not until you beg me, Dearheart," he said seductively, then ran the tips of his fangs provocatively over my throat, the sharpness teasing my hot flesh. "I have to be sure you want all of me, my dear."

His response ratcheted up my need. My bodily essences, initially tame, burst forth to soak the rigid length of his cock as he pleasured me. "Can't you feel I want you?" I moaned desperately, my passion for him no longer imitation. "Can't you feel how much I love you?"

"Yes, Love, I can." Danial reared back, baring his fangs and sinking them in deeply. I let out a sharp cry, but he was already bringing me, and then I was climaxing, that utter gratification washing away the pain. Danial tensed, his breathing fast, as he sucked hard at my neck, his fangs

29

still deep inside me. He came in a few seconds, his grunts of sated need hushed. He withdrew from me, groaning happily.

"That was perfect," Danial said ruefully, gratified. "I couldn't last." He lightly kissed my neck and I relaxed, as his bites healed. "But I am surprised, after your initial reluctant mood, Love."

Tell the truth, just edit it. "I know this is your night with Theo," I said by way of explanation, taking his hand in mine and squeezing gently. "But I wanted us to have our own special time, Danial."

"We will, dear, but its Theo's turn now." Danial hugged me and moved aside.

Theo was crawling up my body, kissing me, trembling in his eagerness. "I've wanted to be with you like this for months," he said huskily, as he rubbed his body on mine. "Tell me you want me, too, Sar. God, it's going to be so good to be in you again!"

No! Shit! "Wait!" I said nervously. "Let me go to the restroom first, please."

Theo gave me an odd look, but he moved off me. I tried to move slowly, but still breathed an audible sigh of relief when the bathroom door shut behind me. I used the facilities, flushed, and then ran the water, washing my hands. Rene appeared, her form shimmered, and then I was looking at a double of myself.

Now for the hard part. I reached up, and undid the collar with only minor trouble, but I still had a hard time fastening it around Rene's neck. Finally, the links slid together, to my sigh of relief.

"Sar?" Danial called lightly. "Come out, Love. Or we are coming in to love you there."

Rene nodded and threw some yellow dust over me. I looked down to my hands, watching as my body faded from view. Then she opened the door, and I followed her back in.

I leaned against the wall, out of the way of the upcoming action. While I felt strange to be watching, if something went wrong, I needed to know as soon as possible, so she and I could escape together.

Rene walked brazenly up to Theo, and kissed him hard. His initial shock changed to lust in a split second, and he crushed her body against his. Then he laid her back on the bed, beside Danial, and pushed her legs apart.

30

"Tell me you want me, Sar," he said huskily.

"I want you, Theo," Rene said in my voice. I was surprised to hear she clearly meant it. Theo bore down with his hips and slid himself into her, letting out a loud moan. I saw as he entered her that he was wearing a condom. Theo stroked Rene's breasts gently and she moaned for him, clutching his body to hers as she drew him in deeper with each thrust. He kissed her, his hands running over her body that looked so exactly like mine that I shivered.

I'd gone over this with Rene, to make her lovemaking as me as realistic as possible. She ran her hands over Theo's muscular body, as I knew he liked me to. He stroked her repeatedly, sliding over that spot he knew I liked best, and soon Rene was panting for him. Then she was crying out, as the orgasm washed over her in a delicious burst. Theo felt her climaxing, and drove himself into her hard, grunting, and then he was roaring, jerking hard as he came.

Soon after, Theo pulled out of her carefully, making sure not to spill. He peeled the condom off himself and went into the bathroom to wash up. When the water started running, I knew he hadn't suspected anything. *Whew.*

Danial hugged Rene to him, and she reached over and squeezed his manhood in her hand. I was surprised to see he was erect again.

"I wanted this for too long," he said, kissing her neck softly. "It's the sad truth that I'm not going to be able to last much longer, my dear. This time will probably be our final one, though I'll enjoy watching Theo love you and kissing you between bouts."

I looked at him warily. If he'd wanted to, he could have gotten a potion to increase his stamina. A little demon blood would have done it. That he hadn't made me suspicious.

I wasn't the only one. "Did you do this for you, really, or for him?" Rene said flatly.

Danial looked back at her, nonplussed. "I did it for the both of us, mostly because I've fantasized about it for so long."

Without warning, Danial pulled Rene on top of himself, and began thrusting hard into her, groaning. I watched her close her eyes quickly, and mentally told her I was sorry. But she performed well, behaving as if she loved the feel of him in her. Again, Danial came in a few moments,

31

this time murmuring he loved her. I heard Rene tell him in my voice that she loved him, too. Luckily, he didn't bite her. I thanked God that I'd asked him to bite me our first time, because I was betting if he tasted her, she'd taste different enough he'd know it wasn't me.

"You didn't come," Danial murmured in surprise, giving Rene a tender kiss. "I'll have to owe you one, Love."

Theo came back with another condom on, and took Rene from Danial possessively, laying her down beneath him as he moved atop her. "Danial, we're going to need more than two."

"Sorry, I wasn't thinking. I'll be back," Danial said quickly and then he left the room, heading to the bathroom. I wondered for a second why he hadn't planned better, but then Theo was slipping into Rene again, caressing her, and I forgot about Danial in my watching of them. Theo came again in a few moments, and he withdrew from her. Danial came back soon after, but he just watched Rene and Theo with hot eyes.

Theo seemed to come to terms with Danial watching him, because he had Rene repeatedly that night. Sometimes Danial kissed and caressed her and sometimes he just watched Theo and her together. Rene seemed to enjoy herself, though I couldn't be sure.

On the third time, Theo slipped, and turned to her with a smile. "Again," he whispered lovingly. Then his eyes widened as he went beet red.

I'd coached her well. Rene reached up and caressed him gently. "As many times as you want me, Theo," she said softly. "Tonight, I'm yours."

Theo looked down at her with sheer lust, groaned in eagerness, and began making love to her again frantically.

Finally, around four am, Rene stopped him, and told him she was too sore to continue. He came then for the last time quickly. As he had all night, repeatedly, he carefully removed the condom, and then went into the bathroom to clean himself. By this time, I had relaxed, trading leaning against the wall for sitting in the far corner of the room where I dozed fitfully.

Danial snuggled close to her, and hugged her. "Sar, thank you for doing this," he said softly. "I won't ask for it again."

I was greatly relieved. As much as Rene had seemed to like this, I had enough lovers. This plan of Rene's and mine had worked, but it wouldn't work time after time. Besides, if Theo and the woman he thought was me were together more than this one night, Theo might think there was a possibility I'd come back to him. And I wasn't coming back to him, not now, not ever.

Theo came out of the bathroom, and crawled over to Danial and Rene, wrapping her in his arms, and sighing contentedly.

"You seem to have gotten over your fear of me," Danial said quietly to him.

"You were right, there wasn't anything to be afraid of," Theo said. "You never touched me. I was stupid to worry about it."

"I'm glad. I'd like you to sleep with us sometimes, when Sar spends the night. There won't be any sex between us like there was tonight, but you're welcome, if you want to."

Not going to happen. But I would deal with that later.

Theo was quiet for a long time. "I'd like that," he said finally. "And I wouldn't expect sex, just holding. Like it was in those months we lived here with you."

"You could kiss her, if you liked," Danial started.

Theo gave him a look. "If there's kissing, soon after there's caressing skin, and then there's sex," he said sarcastically. "I can sleep near her without having sex with her, but I'm not a stone, Danial."

"Fine," Danial said agreeably. "It's up to you."

"Let me go to the bathroom," Rene said with a yawn. "I need to freshen up a little."

Danial froze, and then slowly turned to look at her. "I have never before heard you utter that phrase, my Sweet Lotus Flower."

My breath caught in my throat. *Are we going to be exposed now?*

"You have never called me that before either, Love," Rene said teasingly. "You always call me 'Love', or 'Oathed One'."

Danial looked at her, and then his face softened. "True," he said lovingly. "But you are deserving of so much more, my dear."

I felt a chill at his choice of words, but I made myself move, as Rene headed to the bathroom. She used the facilities while I turned away, and then she was writing something on a piece of paper and handing it to me.

33

Something's up. I will not leave you here as I planned to. I will slip outside and wait for you in the great room when I get a chance. But tomorrow, do not wait for me. Leave as soon as you can.

I looked at her and nodded. She flushed the note down the toilet and then disappeared.

I went back out to Theo and Danial, and soon we were asleep.

I woke up the next morning in Theo's arms. I thought for one crazy moment we were still married, that Devon was sleeping in his little bed next to ours, and that nothing in the last year had happened. Then I remembered Michael, Ulysses, and Devon's death, and I began sobbing, as my heart broke all over again.

Theo woke up, and began kissing away my tears. "What is it?" he said worriedly, his blue eyes searching mine. "What's wrong?"

"I forgot for a moment that everything was like it is," I said brokenly. "I woke up and felt you next to me, and I was hoping to see Devon. I still miss him so much!"

Theo crushed me against his chest, shaking. I clutched him tightly to me, and for a while, we just held each other silently.

"I'm sorry, for what I tried to do to you that night," Theo whispered. "It was wrong, I knew it even when I was doing it, but I couldn't stop myself. Please forgive me. Please."

"I forgive you," I said, hugging him. "It was the backlash of the spell being broken. We both said some things we shouldn't have."

Theo gave me a tender look. Then he rolled over on me, kissing me passionately, getting into position to thrust into me.

But the night was over. I wasn't his anymore. Part of me still cared for him, but I loved Lash and Devlin far more.

"Stop!" I said loudly, pushing him away. "Get off me!"

Theo stopped, easing his body off mine. "Sorry," he said uncomfortably, running his hand through his hair. "It's hard to be here with you like this and not want to make love to you, Sar. You felt so good last night—"

"I need to shower," I interjected. I put into my words that he wasn't welcome in the shower with me, and he nodded once, looking away, to say he understood.

34

When I got back out to the bedroom, Theo was waiting there, dressed. I wondered that he wasn't showering, but guessed he wanted to smell like him and me for a while. I didn't blame him for that. It had been obvious last night he still loved me.

I went and sat down beside him, and took his hand in mine. "I'm sorry, if I hurt you when we were together. I did many things I'm sorry for, Theo. I wanted you to be happy. I hoped you'd be happy with Jenny, and I'm sorry she died."

"I'm sorry, too," Theo said softly. "I didn't love her, but she loved me. We were happy in those few months we had together. It wasn't like it was with you and I, but it was good."

"Thank you for coming for Lash and I, for tracking us and bringing the cavalry."

"I'm sorry I didn't find you sooner," Theo growled. "I was always a day late finding your location. If it hadn't been for Devlin sensing you—"

He swallowed hard. "I'm sorry you lost your twins."

"So am I."

"Are you happy with him? Being his mate?"

There was no answer I could truthfully give that wouldn't hurt him. Theo had always expected the truth, bad or good. "Very happy. He's not ever anything but gentle with me, even when he's angry with me. I know you've never seen that side of him—"

"I can't believe he has another side to see," Theo said gruffly. "But I knew there had to be more to him if you loved him."

I said nothing, not wanting a fight to start.

"You do love him," Theo said.

"I told you I did before," I said quietly. "My feelings for him haven't changed."

"I want you to be happy, Sar," Theo said gruffly. "If your feelings ever do change, please let me know." He got to his feet. "Do you need a ride home, or are you going to teleport? I'm heading out with Terian to a conference. We'll be going past Hayden on our way out of town."

"I'll teleport, but thanks for asking," I said, giving him a smile. "Take care of yourself, Theo."

"You too, Sar," he said, giving me one of his heart-melting smiles.

35

I looked at him for a moment, wanting to remember him this way. Then we both left, closing the bedroom door behind us.

* * * *

Danial was reading in the great room. Theo told him he'd see him later and strode outside, his truck starting up a moment later.

I went over to Danial, who hadn't looked up from his book. "Why did you disappear this morning?"

"You had things to say to Theo that should have been said a while ago," Danial said, eyes still on his reading. "I wanted to give you the privacy to say them."

"Thank you."

Danial looked up finally. "Are you heading home?"

I nodded.

He got up and gave me a hug. "Thank you, Sarelle. As I promised, I won't ask for this again. I'm very glad you enjoyed last night."

I forced myself not to fight him touching me. Last night, I'd been relaxed and calm being intimate with him. Last night I'd almost wanted to teleport he and I back to Letchworth and leave Theo and Rene to themselves, I'd been so enthralled with him. Yet this morning for some reason, I felt afraid of him, just as I had when I'd suspected he knew it wasn't me who he'd been in bed with all night. For some reason, my feeling of being in danger was sharply increasing.

I went to release him so I could leave, but he did not release me.

"And it is time also for me to say to you what should have been said long before." He paused. "I am sorry that we fought those months ago after we first made love. I am sorry for the things I said to you then. I hope you can forgive me."

I was silent.

"It has taken these months to finally see you as who you are, Sarelle." He was tender, his words soft whispers. "I could not for a long time, despite knowing it for certain. So much changed for you while I was unconscious. It was difficult for me to come to terms with." He took a breath. "In my fervor to regain you after being so long apart, I needed to possess you above all else." He cleared his throat. "It was not love, but desire that ruled me.

36

"I hope you believe me when I tell you I'm in love with you now as I once was. I hope it is not too late to repair the damage I did to our relationship." He laid his cool cheek beside mine and rubbed gently. "As I agreed, I will not make you come to me against your will. But I hope you will come to me, to spend time with me in the coming months, though I will not ask to be intimate with you. I hope that after the babies are born, we can sometimes be intimate together again, if you want to be." He paused. "I meant what I said, that my love for you is forever. I want you to know that there will not be any others in my bed, not ever again, so long as you live." He paused again. "And that will be true even if you never come to me again, Oathed One."

"I will come visit you, Danial," I said stiffly. "Perhaps I can meet you at Elle's home in the next few weeks, and watch you ride. I won't be riding myself, but I always enjoyed seeing your skill with horses. I ask only that you let me come to you when I'm ready to, with no pressure."

"Of course, Darling. That would be nice," he said agreeably.

I teleported the moment he let me go, arriving back at Hayden. Serena was in the kitchen eating breakfast. She gave me a smile. "So how was it? You look happy."

Don't elaborate. Be vague. "It went well," I said, shrugging. "I'm glad it's over. Are Dev and Lash upstairs?" I wanted to ask if she'd seen Rene this morning, but thought it best not to ask. "How was babysitting?"

"V is fine, she's still sleeping. We stayed up late watching horror movies. As for the two reprobates, yes, they're upstairs," Serena said, rolling her eyes. "They came in right before dawn. Lash had blood all over him—"

GREAT. Hopefully he hadn't killed anyone.

"—and Dev had some blood on him, too, but apparently they fought with an entire chapter of the Hell's Angels—"

Let me amend that: Fucking GREAT.

"—anyway, Lash was bragging to Nick that he won some money and the both of them went to bed about dawn."

"How are you?" I said, trying to be pleasant and change the subject. Serena and I had been a lot closer once, before Rene had come into my life and supplanted her. I hadn't been the best friend and I wanted to

37

make amends for that, even if it was too late for us to resume our friendship.

"I need to be getting back to Danial's." Her face softened in a smile. "You look exhausted, Sar. Go upstairs to bed. I'll get a hold of you soon; maybe we can see a movie or something."

I thanked her profusely, tried to give her some money for watching V, which she refused to take, and then saw her out. I gave her a hug goodbye, cheered with the thought that we might see each other soon. After checking on V, I went into Lash's bedroom, but it was empty.

Devlin's was not. I opened the door to find Lash and Dev in bed together, passed out on opposite ends of Devlin's huge bed. In that split second I opened the door, Lash woke up, grabbing for his knife instinctively. He sat up quickly to throw the knife, and then saw it was me. He relaxed, setting down the knife with a hiss of pain, holding his side and rubbing a little, as he grimaced. Devlin continued to sleep.

Worried and irrationally angry he'd let himself get hurt, I went over to him. "Are you hurt?"

"Was he safe with you?" Lash retorted, each word hard as nails.

I wanted to tell him not to worry, that Theo hadn't done anything to me but kiss me, but I only nodded. *No one must know.* "I made sure every time. He wore protection and he was careful."

"Good," Lash said, letting out a breath in abject relief. He scented the air with his tongue briefly, then pulled me close to him and kissed me chastely on the forehead. "You smell a little like him still," he hissed gently, all trace of his anger gone. "But soon you'll wear only my scent on your skin. It's good to have you in my arms again, Sweetness."

"It's good to be home," I said warmly and hugged him tightly.

He gasped a little. I released him instantly, feeling bad. "What did I do?"

"It's okay," Lash said, the pain in his tone at obvious odds with his words. "One of the last guys I fought hit me with a steel crowbar and it shattered some of my ribs. But they're mostly healed already—"

"Lay back down and rest!" I ordered him angrily. I wanted to add that he was an idiot for good measure, but decided to save that discussion for after he healed.

Lash lay back down. I lay down beside him, hugging him a lot more carefully.

He kissed my forehead again, and sighed contentedly. "I'm glad it's over. Danial agreed that this was the only time, yes?"

I don't care if he didn't; I'm never going through that again. I nodded, then said perversely, "He offered that Theo could sleep with us when I stay over there, but no sex, not even kissing."

Lash hissed, baring his teeth, and then reluctantly nodded. "That's okay, so long as he's not naked. You can be naked, Danial can be naked, but not him. You may forget who you're with, in your sleep. And no kissing him at all, I don't care what that fucking vampire tells you—"

Why had I said anything? "Uh, I'm not even going in for the sleeping in the same room part," I interrupted. "Danial can sleep alone himself, if he pushes the idea. I've had enough."

Lash relaxed. "He still loves you, doesn't he?" he said gently. "Theo?"

I nodded. For a few minutes, there was silence.

"You love him still a little, I know," Lash hissed finally, resigned. "It's okay, Sar. He was your mate really for years, no matter that you weren't married long. It's normal for you to love him."

As much as his sentiment was comforting, it wasn't the normal one for him, at all. "You're understanding this morning," I said, turning to study him. "I know your preferences. Are you really as okay with this as you're acting?"

"I've come to terms with what he was to you and it's obvious you don't feel for him what you used to before you loved me," Lash said, shrugging. "As for Dev, I love him like a brother. Danial's a prick, but even I can see he loves you, too." He grinned. "And I like how much he's pissed off he has to share you with me now."

Charming. "So you aren't jealous?"

"Why should I be? You need their protection and you have children with them. It's not casual sex for them or for you. Don't think that I did what I did over the years from some kind of honorable code, Sweetness. Most of my insistence on monogamy was so I could be with a woman and not have to use a condom, but still be assured I wouldn't catch anything. I detest condoms; I always have since their invention. They

39

feel unnatural to me, like skin that should have been shed long ago and is now too tight around me."

Ah. I'd always wondered at his preference for not using them.

"That's why I'm getting myself fixed," Lash said softly, kissing me. "I want you to not have to worry or take anything."

"I could have another operation. You've said the one you'll have isn't reversible."

"No," Lash said firmly. "You may live a long time, Sar, and you may want another child with Devlin one day, or even with that prick Danial. I don't want to take that possibility away because I'm too selfish to do what needs to be done. And according to Stephen, the pills are going to fail us for sure, if enough time passes." He paused. "I'm sorry about that, by the way. I got the strongest pills that exist, and I thought they would be enough. The doctor at triple R that I talked to assured me that was the case." He paused again. "Anyway, you've done enough over the years trying to prevent getting pregnant. You'll only be with me, save the two vampires. They won't give you anything, so we don't have to worry about disease."

"Will it hurt, what you'll have done?" I said, grimacing at his topic. "Your body will want to heal you."

"Stephen will insert some metal in me," Lash said haltingly. "My body will grow around it quickly, as it tries to heal it, and it will block my sperm from getting released when we have sex. Something he'll give me orally will inhibit my body from pushing out the metal, though I don't understand that part of it. But it's worked for weres for the last fifty years. It'll work for us." He managed a grin. "Then we won't have to worry anymore, Sweetness."

"I'm glad," I said seductively. "I like being with you, feeling you come in me, your skin against mine as you stroke me—"

Lash groaned, and covered my mouth with his hand. "Hush, Sweetness," he hissed. "I need to heal a lot more before I love you, and you're probably too sore to be with me until tomorrow anyway. Save your words for then."

"Fair enough. Hey, what's this?" I said, running my hand over a red patch of skin near his heart. "Another tattoo?"

"I had it done last night," Lash said, both nervous and excited. "I hope you like it."

I looked closer. There, over his heart, he'd gotten a tattoo of my name, "Sar." It was in black letters, only half an inch tall, and the whole thing was only about an inch and a half wide.

I didn't know what to say. I was absurdly touched and taken aback that he'd marked himself with my name in such a permanent way. *But we are mated for life. Unless he or I break it off, we are going to be together forever, until one of us dies.*

Lash was still waiting for my answer, but his excitement had given way to pure anxiety. He'd partially changed to snake, some scales rippling out of his arms and chest.

I gave an inward sigh of happiness. "I love that you did this for me," I murmured lovingly, kissing him. "I hope it didn't hurt much."

"It was nothing, next to the one on my back," Lash said happily, hugging me. "It was over in fifteen minutes."

"But why do it now?" I asked. "We've been together for a while."

"Because I thought it would bother you that you're having my babies, and despite we're mated, most everyone doesn't know that. We aren't married, either." He took my hand. "And it's safest for you if we don't ever officially marry. I can't wear a ring for you, but I can do this to show you I'm yours, the way you wearing my ring shows you're mine." His dark eyes were full of love and so much determination. "This is like the ink on my back, made especially for weres. It won't ever fade, or heal over. And removing it's a bitch."

"Did Cleave do it?" Cleave was the man who'd done the bear tattoo on my hip those many months ago when I'd first Oathed to Devlin. He was a tattoo artist for the supernatural, using ink that wouldn't 'heal' over in his custom designs or otherwise deteriorate.

Lash nodded. "We went there first. Dev told me I was acting like a lovesick teenager, that you probably wouldn't like it, etc."

"He said that because he doesn't like you showing him up." I chuckled. "He was probably just irritated he hadn't thought to do it first."

"Oh well," Lash hissed. He laughed, which quickly turned into a grimace of pain.

41

"Rest," I said, hugging him again gently. "I want you to heal, Tryst. Tomorrow's going to be a good day, now that we have the worst behind us."

Lash snuggled down beside me, and I carefully put my head on his chest. Swiftly, we dropped off to sleep.

Chapter Four

The next day, I went in search of Rene. I found her finally in my library, as she called it, sitting reading one of my horror novels.

"How are you?" I asked hesitantly. "I hope you're okay?"

She looked over at me, and gave me a smile. "I'm okay. And you?"

"Okay," I said, nodding. "I'm very grateful to you for doing what you did."

"Not a problem," Rene said with a leer. "I'd always wanted to try a werecougar for a lover. Theo was very energetic. I was not disappointed." She dropped her eyes. "I am glad that Danial did not touch me more than once," she added in a low voice. "It was hardest to act welcoming to him. Finally, I closed my eyes, and pretended he was Devlin. Thank the Goddess he was fast, and it was only the once."

"Why?" I said, concerned. "What did he do to you?"

"Nothing," Rene replied, her tone at odds with her words. "I was there to see his taking of Anna, and how devastated Devlin was by it. There was always darkness in Devlin. But there is equal darkness in Danial. It was his act of betrayal with Anna that started many bad things happening. I know that Devlin did much evil in retaliation through the years, even some of it to you. But I did not see that firsthand as I did Danial's evil. And I love Devlin, whereas I do not love Danial."

"I get it," I said. "It's over, at least."

"I don't know that it is," she said, fidgeting in worry. "Something has happened, Sar. My visions are again blocked, as they were long ago right before tragedy struck. And I am having no luck with any spells I try, none at all!"

Scared as her pronouncements made me, I put on a brave face.

43

"Rest, please," I asked, leading her to the small couch. "You were up all night and most of the days before and after, preparing. You're just exhausted, that's why nothing is working."

Rene didn't reply. She lay down and closed her eyes. When she was asleep, I left her there, shutting the door quietly behind me.

* * * *

Rene was right in one regard: something weird was going on. I had been pregnant with a dhamphir for two months now, yet still had no signs of The Lust.

When another week passed with no incident, Lash accompanied me to Stephen's office.

"Why has The Lust not presented itself?" Dev said in consternation over the intercom. It was day, but as usual, he'd found a way to be included in my doctor's visit. "Are you sure everything is well?"

"I can't say why it hasn't," Stephen said. "Things are developing as they should be. All Sar's signs are good."

"Could it be something with my child?" Lash interjected.

"Children," Stephen corrected. "And no, they are also fine. But I do have a theory." He paused. "Sar's virus levels are not low, as they have been in previous pregnancies. Dev, how much of your blood do you share with her, and how often?"

"I give her a little every week, to make sure she stays young, and so what Lash takes from her is as strong as it can be. It is only a few tablespoons, or so."

"It's enough to keep the levels steady." Stephen said confidently. "And because they are steady, there is no lust. Sar asked if the lust she felt for you when she was dying was related to the lust she felt when she was pregnant with her two dhamphir children. She said they felt similar. According to her blood, she was right. My theory is that both times, the lust she felt was because of decreasing virus levels in her system. Her body was telling her to get more of the virus, to balance out what her body needed, and when she was pregnant, what her growing half-vampire children needed. It has been well documented in women that are turning that they desire more of the virus and try to get it any way they can. In Sar's case the reasoning was different, but the actual cause was the same."

"Then why did it stop before?" Lash asked. "After the fourth month, her desire for me left her, though no one was giving her any more of the virus, according to Dev. She didn't want me after that. Why could I even raise it in her at all, much less sate it? I had to have only tiny amounts of the virus in my saliva and semen."

Stephen turned to Lash. "After being intimate to completion, did Sar ask for more?"

Lash looked embarrassed. "Yes. Once was…um, multiple times."

"Sorry, but it wasn't because of your lovemaking skill," Stephen said with a smile. "Sar's body saw you as vampire from your use of Devlin's blood, so she wanted you to bite her and have her sexually to increase her odds of getting more of the virus. However, you were not really giving her any of the virus, save trace amounts. So her body tried multiple times with you trying to get what it needed. And it must have gotten enough, eventually."

Devlin let out a snicker while Lash looked uncomfortable. I took hold of his hand and squeezed. He rolled his eyes at me, but grinned also.

"He's right," Devlin added. "The night Sar first went after you, you'd just had the longevity potion made from my blood."

Lash nodded. "I'd had it again in the morning of that next afternoon we were together." He squeezed my hand. "But that night you asked me for more at Davy's, I didn't, Sweetness." He made a face. "All this time I thought I'd been so amazing at fucking that you couldn't keep your hands off me, and now I find out it's because your body needed vampire virus. Fuck me dead…"

"You were amazing," I reassured him, coloring at his crude talk. I turned to Stephen. "But this raises a question: why did I go after Terian?"

Stephen gave me a shocked look. "When was this?"

"When I was pregnant with T."

"Do you remember what you were thinking?"

I thought back. "He smelled good." I blushed. "He smelled like Theo used to."

Stephen mused for a moment.

"Theo has no vampire blood in him," Devlin said heatedly. "Danial and Theo have been friends for years, but there was never anything between them besides friendship. And they never shared any blood, except when Danial needed some as an emergency measure."

"It's odd, to be sure," Stephen said reassuringly. "It may be just that Sar was missing Theo. It may have been something to do with the potion Danial took to become fertile, as it was made with Terian's blood. It may have been that Terian had already shared his blood with Sar, and she recognized the demon blood in him. I can't say."

As long as we were getting all our questions answered, I had one. "Why did I orgasm when I had The Lust with Devlin's child, and not with Danial's?"

Stephen looked thoughtful. "Devlin, a question; Do you sometimes orgasm when you drink blood without having sex?"

Devlin didn't answer. The silence stretched.

"Dev," Lash hissed. "Spit it out. Why are you embarrassed?"

"Because it's not only with women," Devlin replied grudgingly. "There has always been a sexual aspect to drinking blood for me. I've never wanted a man as a sexual partner, but often I get erect, when I drink blood, doesn't matter from whom." He turned embarrassed. "I often see to my needs, when my blood donors have left, Sar. I didn't want you to know, to think it was because I found them sexy or wanted sex with them."

"What's the big deal about that?" Lash hissed. "So blood gives you a woody."

"It's more than that," Devlin said haltingly. "When I drain someone completely, I orgasm: Every time, without fail, even if they are male. The same thing happens when I turn someone." He cleared his throat. "There is more than one reason I made it a requirement, that sex be part of the turning process for all would-be vampires. And that if I turn a male, a female lover must be there with me, to take care of my needs as part of the process."

Stephen was not the only one uncomfortable by this time; we all were. But he maintained his professionalism. "Sar was influenced by Danial's desires when she was pregnant with his child. His sex drive is much weaker. Devlin's is very strong, and it's a large part of his personality. His need for orgasm is much more intense, and more easily achieved."

"What about Lash's question of why The Lust ended?" Devlin said.

"My only guess is that after the fourth month, the babies must have stabilized in regards to how much virus they needed to be able to grow. Remember, her virus levels spiked after they were born. My guess is, the babies themselves gave her some of the virus somehow after the forth month, by having them within her, and her being half vampire."

That night after fighting with Dev over Catherine! That night, Danial had given me his blood, enough so my teeth sharpened. *That is why The Lust ended. Why Lash wasn't able to raise it, that day after, when he kissed me...*

"And that is why Harriet died, and why her twins were born unable to mask their vampire nature." Devlin said sadly. "Why she never had The Lust. She was not resistant naturally, and her temporary resistance faded in a few months. Titus's potion helped her carry them to term, and birth them, and heal the damage from the birth. But the virus overloaded her system, and so she turned anyway. She was not human enough in those last months to keep the balance between the species from shifting to the vampire side in her children."

"But they can walk in the sun," Lash supplied. "Samuel reports that Elijah and Sharon both can withstand daylight."

"For now," Stephen said gloomily. "But that may fade. Who can say how much humanity is in them?"

"Time will tell," Devlin said noncommittally. "Are we done, Camlyn? Any instructions for us and Sar?"

"We're done for today," Stephen said with a smile. "Keep eating plenty of meat, Sar, and call me if you begin to be too hot or too cool."

* * * *

Days turned into weeks, and inevitably, I got bigger. I would like to say I was glowing, and to wax poetical about the joys of motherhood, but really, as soon as I lost the ability to fit into my jeans, I got irritable.

Devlin and Lash were supportive, no matter how often I yelled at them. Danial was too, on those times I went to see him.

My visits to Danial's home were never for very long, but after

47

missing him for so many months, I couldn't stay away, not when I knew he wanted me to come, not after all he'd said to me of how he'd loved me. Most of the reason I couldn't stay away was that he'd changed.

Danial had always given me everything I asked for save his unconditional time or information about his past. But during that month, he did tell me some happy tales of his youth: helping hurt animals with his mother, helping his grandmother bake, and even a few tales of brawling with Devlin as youths. Whatever he was doing—painting or helping Theoron, even on conference calls—he always left it when I arrived, saying he would have plenty of time to get back to it as soon as I'd gone. To finally have that from him after so long of being made to feel like I had been second to his work was too addictive a drug for me to resist. Whatever had scared me so much that one morning with him had ceased to be.

To say we were becoming friends again would not have been strong enough. I felt as though I'd lost my lover and best friend, and walked through fire and still not found him. Then, taking that last step out of the flames, I'd come back into his arms.

Danial was very happy that I enjoyed my time with him. I stayed over a few nights at his home when Devlin and Lash were scheduled to be out raising hell. I'd missed sleeping in his arms. I'd loved him for the longest time, and knew him best. It was good to be comforted, and feel safe, even if only for a short time.

* * * *

I saw Elle sporadically, but she had her hands full living at my old homestead, and working over the internet doing tutoring for pay while still attending her online classes. I was proud of her, because Danial and Theoron would have supported her easily, if she'd asked them for money. I liked to think of her there, toughing it out, and being the strong woman that I knew she was.

Lash unfortunately missed all of her visits, as he was out either arranging some "construction" for Devlin, or getting me my almost daily order of sushi. He worried about me being poisoned by Valerian, as irrational as that seemed, and so had Titus teleport him daily to different restaurants at random to procure the food, something that took a good deal of time. The result was very tasty, as I got to try a lot of different dishes in addition to my favorite eel. I didn't protest, and just enjoyed the pampering.

I did worry a little about Elle being alone too much, but Devlin said cryptically not to worry, that Elle wasn't as alone as she seemed. I then worried that bone until he admitted that Elle had had Sharon for a houseguest soon after she moved in, and that Sharon visited now at least once a month, taking breaks from college. I thought he wasn't telling me everything, but he refused to tell me more, saying that was all he knew for certain, and to ask Elle, if I wanted to know more.

T wrote and called once a week from Europe. Though he'd been forced to go, he was making the best of it, and he'd done a lot of research with Samuel. The nature of the case was still not discussed to me, but he said he thought he was close to a break.

Shaker did confer with me mentally each week. Because he was polite, and never mentioned our former intimacy, I found it easy not to think about it. But his inevitable sexual remark before he cut our connection always made my nerves twitch.

Theo, I did not see, but Terian was also absent. As they were running the show now at Solutions, Inc. with Danial, I understood that. Sundown I also didn't see much of, but I heard from Cia that Sunrise was a handful even now that she looked about five. Although I liked Sun, I still hadn't forgotten her comments to Lash that night at the Haunt, and avoided her and her daughter.

V was excited to be getting a sibling, though also nervous. Some of that was because she saw how much her father wanted a son, and she was afraid she would be forgotten once he had one. I took Devlin aside one day, and mentioned it to him. He was embarrassed, and went that night to talk to her about it, returning after dawn. Afterward, V had nothing but enthusiasm for the baby.

Valerian had disappeared. Shaker could find no trace of him. Even though the bounty on him was huge, no one came to claim it, though Lash said he knew several big names in the world that continued to search. Michael was also still MIA.

The only one real problem was Rene. She kept to herself a lot, where she never had before. That resulted in Devlin being upset, sniping loudly that she had told him she was not going to be with him until I had my children, for her own reasons. I was also turned away, when I went to see her, or she wouldn't answer at all.

Finally, I went to her door with my lock picking kit, and picked the lock. The lock itself swore at me, making me drop my pick in fear, then reluctantly opened, the door swinging wide.

Rene was on her settee, looking at the fire.

"Why don't you come and spend time with anyone?" I said, going to sit next to her. "Dev is missing you, and so am I."

"I'm afraid," she whispered, not meeting my eyes. "And I haven't been afraid in centuries, Sarelle."

"Afraid of what?"

She looked over at me. "I'm pregnant," she choked out. "That's why my visions were blocked."

I couldn't form any words. "Is it Devlin's?" I got out finally.

"No, though I wish it was," she said, beginning to sob. "I'm scared to death it's somehow Danial's and to have his child would be such a sick joke on me, after disliking him for so long."

"It can't be his," I said calmly, clutching her hand. "He was cool, not warm that night. Please don't worry about that."

"And Theo used condoms every time! But I'm still pregnant, Sar! The spell I did should have ended with my monthly curse, but it didn't come! And now it has been months, and I can feel life growing inside me, and I'm scared to death!"

"Shh!" I said, hugging her. "There are options, Rene, like there weren't for pregnant women long ago. We can go to Camlyn—"

"I want to keep it," she said in a small voice.

I drew back from her, trying again to form words and failing. "Why?" I managed finally.

"I've never been pregnant before," she said, smiling tentatively. "With faeries it's very hard, if you're female, anyway. I wasn't the kind to marry, Sar, and I had many lovers in my long life. Even the potent ones...I never had any seed that I was given sprout. There were a few times I wanted a child, and nothing happened, no matter what spells I tried. Now that I'm going to have a baby, I can't bring myself to end it."

"I understand that," I said carefully. "But we need to get you to

Camlyn in any case. He should check you. You need to be on vitamins and to not donate any blood."

"I have not, since I knew for certain," Rene griped. "Devlin is pissed."

"He's going to be more pissed when we tell him," I said, rolling my eyes. "Unless somehow it's his, though the odds are small, if it's since the night with Danial and Theo. Somehow, it must be Theo's baby."

"I know," she replied. "That's another reason I've been putting off saying anything. But this was somehow meant for you, Sar. Danial must be behind it. I don't know what it would have done to you, whatever it was he used on me. But we must make sure he never suspects that it did not work on you. Or he will have grounds again to ask you back to his bed, for another try."

"Why would Danial do this?" I said angrily. "There is no reason! He has been loving, Rene, loving as he ever was! He can't be behind this! It has to be Theo, something he did!"

Rene gave me a look that told me I was naïve. "We will see."

* * * *

That night when Devlin returned home with Lash, I was waiting for them. They came with me to Rene's room at my request. When Rene turned to them, showing them her rounded body. Lash let out a surprised hiss.

Devlin gaped, then ran to her and hugged her. "You found a way!" he said joyously, smiling so wide he bared all of his fangs, upper and lower. "I knew there was a way we could have a child, with there being so much of Sar in you! I will be a father twice over!"

"It is not yours, my love," Rene said, tears slipping out of her eyes.

Devlin froze, and then he slowly put her down. His face was disbelief that was fast becoming rage. "Then who the fuck's is it?" he hissed angrily. "Lash's?"

Oh shit And I'm an idiot, completely. I'd just assumed because Rene's visions had been blocked right after Danial's "wild night" that Theo or he had to be the father. I'd never considered that Lash might be the father. But all that Stephen had said about how Lash was so potent came flooding back. I felt ill. And I wasn't the only one. Lash was looking like he might be sick.

"I was only with her that once, when we spent that day in New Orleans—"

"Rene?" Devlin said murderously. "Is it his? Is it?" He whipped around and snarled at Lash. "I should've known you'd be too busy getting your rocks off to even think about birth control!"

"I thought she was on the pill because you were fertile back then!" Lash's words were rising in volume, as he got more and more upset. "Why the fuck didn't you say something, Rene? It was your idea! God damn it, I'd never have done you if I thought this could happen!"

Devlin turned his attention back to Rene. "Answer me, Oathed One! The other men you were with all wore protection, all of them!"

What other men? "All of them"? God, had she been doing some of the guards at Devlin's request? I remembered her thoughtful musing over the guards in New Orleans as Devlin listed them and felt ill, realizing that had to be the case. *Still, better her than me, especially as she must have been agreeable.*

"Your choker's still on," Lash said gravelly, stepping closer to Rene. "You didn't fuck around on Dev. So it has to be mine, right?"

Rene was looking from one to the other, panicked. "I...I don't...I..."

"Why?" Devlin said in a softer tone, very hurt. "You have never spoken to me of wanting any child besides mine. Why did you do this without telling me?"

"And why the fuck didn't you tell me, the father?" Lash shouted. "God damn it, witch, you've had to have known for at least a month!"

Enough. It's time for the truth, whether she wants me to tell them or not. I eased between them and her. "She went in my place that night to Danial and Theo. I couldn't bring myself to be with Theo, Dev. So she assumed my form, and went for me. This happened after that night."

"You're telling me this is Danial's baby?" Devlin grated out, some of his anger leaving him. "How is that possible?"

"How can that be?" Lash said, anger fast building momentum again. "He was cool to the touch, Sar said. Theo used protection, right?"

"He did, I was there watching!" I replied crossly. "My money is on Theo, not Danial. But don't ask me how he did it, he wore protection."

52

"He did, I felt it," Rene said angrily. "Danial was cool, not warm. But I am pregnant, and that night was when my symptoms began. I did a spell to make it as if my body were already pregnant. Instead, I ended up pregnant for real! This must be one of their children! Do you understand what I'm saying? Do you understand that this was meant for Sar, she who was pregnant with your children?" Her words became black as pitch. "Do you understand what might have been meant to happen to your children?"

Devlin looked at Lash. Lash let out an angry hiss, and began dialing his cell phone. I heard him telling Dr. Camlyn to meet us in five minutes; he'd be sending Shaker to get him. Then Rene teleported the four of us to Stephen Camlyn's office.

Dr. Camlyn arrived with Shaker, irritated. When Rene explained what had happened, he became intrigued and worried. He said first he would make sure she was healthy, and then make sure she was indeed pregnant, and after, we'd take a look at the baby.

He laid her down, and then began to check her vitals. He pronounced Rene healthy, and a little later, pregnant, too. We were looking at the monitor, and Stephen was moving around the machine when he let out a gasp.

Lash gave him a quick look, and then he was looking back at the screen. He let out a loud hiss, his eyes flattening. "Tell me I'm not seeing what I think I'm seeing, Camlyn!"

"What is it?" Devlin said, worried. "I don't see anything."

I saw nothing either, but I was used to that. "What's wrong?"

"That's a tail!" Lash hissed, furious. "A TAIL! Four feet and a TAIL! THAT FUCKING COUGAR! I'll kill him! I'm going to fucking kill him!"

"Sar, you swore Theo used protection!" Devlin shouted, his eyes bleeding to red.

"He did!" I said, sliding into hysteria as I realized Rene's baby had to be Theo's. *Thank God she went for me, thank God, that could be me there on that table and THANK GOD that it's not me, as much as I feel bad for her.* "Every time! I saw it! I know Theo, he wouldn't have lied—"

"God damn it!" Devlin shouted. "IT WAS MY FUCKING

53

BROTHER! IT WAS DANIAL! HE DID THIS!"

Lash was already on the phone calling Titus. "Get here now, demon! This fucking minute!"

Rene was upset, but also very relieved. "At least it's not Danial's." She swallowed hard. "I need to teleport home; I think I'm going to be sick—"

"Shaker, can you take her home?" I thought quickly. "Watch over her?"

Shaker nodded in my mind as Rene disappeared.

"Act as though Sar's carrying the cougar," Devlin hissed to Lash. "We need to know if they were both in on it, or if it was Danial alone behind this. What Rene did for Sar, neither of them must ever know."

Lash nodded, still hissing. Titus appeared, Devlin grabbed me in his arms, and then the four of us were in Danial's great room. Lash strode right to Danial's bedroom door, and ripped the door off the hinges, throwing it aside with a crash into Danial's coffee table. He went in and a moment later, he dragged Danial out in his bathrobe. Danial was fighting him, but when he saw us there all together looking grim, he narrowed his eyes, a smile gracing his lips. "So it worked. Good."

Lash punched him in the face. Danial dropped like a stone to the floor, blood leaking from his mouth, just as Theo burst in.

"Back off," Theo said, his gun drawn and aimed at Lash.

Lash ignored him, looking down with murder in his eyes at Danial. "You fuck!" he hissed. "I'm going to beat you within an inch of your immortal life!"

"Back off, Lash!" Theo growled. "I won't ask again!"

"Why did you do it, Danial?" I said, tired and angry. "What did you hope to get out of this?"

"Lash is a horror," Danial spat, looking up at him with red eyes. "Whatever it takes, I want you away from him, Sar."

"He's my mate," I spat back. "Making me have another man's child isn't going to change that."

"What?" Theo said, his eyes bulging. He held his gun with effort, his hand shaking badly, as he glanced from Danial to me. "What are you saying?"

"Sar's pregnant with two weresnakes, a dhamphir and a

54

werecougar," Lash lied, furious. "Your child, Cat!"

Theo put his gun back in his holster, and went over and pulled Danial to his feet. "What did you do? I was protected, Danial! Every time!"

"I made holes in the condoms," Danial said quietly. "Not big enough for either of you to notice, but enough so that—"

"There was spermicide in the lubrication," Theo gasped out.

Danial shook his head. "There was none and no lubrication. Only her bodily fluids and yours, and a potion to make it possible."

"I didn't drink any potion—" I whispered.

"It was administered by me when I made love with you," Danial said and smiled evilly.

That's why he went first, before Theo...and why he made sure to have sex again, after I used the bathroom; he wanted to be certain to dose me again with whatever potion he used, if I had washed it off. I stared at him, speechless.

Theo punched him hard, knocking him back to the floor, and then faced Lash. "I'm sorry. I don't think I can apologize enough. I wasn't in on this."

"I see that, cat," Lash hissed, still angry. "Now get out of my way, so I can kick his ass."

"I told you once, Lash, you would rue what happened that day seventy-seven years ago," Danial hissed. "I just wish I could have made it so Sar was carrying only Devlin's and Theo's children!"

Theo moved aside fluidly. Devlin and Lash grabbed Danial, dragging him into his room. Danial was laughing at first, but shortly he began screaming in agony, swearing and growling gutturally. I stood and said nothing, listening to them hurt him, and wondering how I could have been so wrong about someone I had trusted so utterly and completely.

Titus went to the door and stood guard. "Don't interfere, Cougar."

But all of Theo's attention was on me, not what was happening in Danial's room. "I'm sorry. I didn't intend this to happen."

"I know that," I said tiredly. "It doesn't matter, Theo. It's done." *And the only reason I'm okay enough to speak to you is that it's not happening to me.*

He put his arms around me. "I'm happy you're having my child, even like this. Tell me if you need anything, anything at all—"

I resisted the urge to shove him away from me. "I'll keep you aware of how things are," I said, gently removing his arms from me. "You can call anytime."

"I'll be calling every day," Theo said warmly.

My icy heart melted enough to give him a wan smile. "Lash doesn't blame you and neither do I. Call as much as you want, but please give notice if you plan to visit."

My mention of Lash cooled his happiness, as I intended. "I'll do that. Now I'd better go save Danial, before they kill him." He got up, and pushed gently past Titus into the bedroom.

A minute later, Devlin swaggered out of the room, licking his lips. Lash followed him, also licking his lips. He headed to the kitchen.

Most likely, he'd bitten Danial and needed to wash the last traces of poison out of his mouth. *Danial deserves that and more.* "Can we go, Dev?"

"Yes," he said, casting a look back into the bedroom. "We're finished here for today."

Theo came out of the bedroom, grim. "He'll miss his meetings for the next week. He's almost dead, Dalcon."

"He's lucky you came in when you did," Devlin said, still licking his lips like a cat. "Lash wanted to give him every bit of poison he could and I would have let him."

"You would've killed him for real," Theo growled.

Devlin gave him a derisive look. "Danial will recover," he said bitingly. "He took that beating for you, Theo. He did what he did to Sar for you." He paused. "This is your fault, whether you planned it or not."

Theo stiffened, barely holding his anger in check. "I never wanted this, Devlin. As much as it makes me happy to be having a child with Sar, I would've stopped him doing it, if I'd known. This was about him hating Lash. Sar and I were just instruments of his revenge."

"Aren't you a bright boy," Lash hissed at Theo scathingly, as he came back in the room. "We're leaving, Cat. Stay away for the next week, or I'll bite you before you're through Hayden's front door. I'll be calm enough after that if you want to visit Sar, but stay away until then."

"Okay," Theo said slowly. "Please call me if there's a doctor's appointment—"

"She's my mate, not yours!" Lash hissed, furious. "You show up at any appointments and I'll make a rug out of you. I always wanted a cougar skin rug to coil with Sarelle on—"

"Stop it," I said quietly. "Theo doesn't need to go to any appointments with us, Lash. Camlyn can keep him in the loop. This isn't his fault."

Lash shot me an angry look with his snake eyes, then away. "He's going to have his hands full just covering for Danial."

"I'll get it done with Terian's help, and T's," Theo said with a sigh. "He's nearly finished in England anyway. Take care of her, Lash."

"I'll always take care of her, Cat. She's my mate, and I don't take that lightly like some idiots do," Lash hissed meaningfully. "Titus, get us home."

Chapter Five

When we got home, Lash, Devlin and I went to Rene's room. Despite that half of us were pregnant, we all had a glass of wine in the kitchen while we filled in Rene on what had happened.

"Nice acting," I commented to Lash.

"It wasn't hard to act pissed, since I am pissed," he hissed angrily. "Motherfuckers, the both of them."

"It was Danial," Devlin said, rubbing his eyes. "I'm sorry, Rene."

"I'm sorry, too," Lash hissed awkwardly. "I'm very grateful for you going in Sar's place with Theo, Rene. I know Sar is, too."

"I am," I said brokenly. "I'm horrified Danial did this."

"He wants to break us up," Lash hissed. "It wouldn't have hurt you. He wanted to hurt me, not you. He wants you back with Theo and him, as you were long ago."

"It would have hurt our baby, maybe," I said angrily. "That's hurting me. Hurting you is hurting me, just like hurting Rene is hurting me."

Rene shot me a surprised look, and then dropped her eyes.

"Please, don't be upset," Lash hissed, hugging me. "For the babies' sakes, please, Sweetness."

"I'm okay," I said, taking a deep breath. "I'm not the one who needs attention just now."

Lash got my prompt, let me go, and went hesitantly to Rene. "You protected my mate, and my babies," he hissed emotionally. "Thank you, Rene." He wrapped her in his arms, and she gratefully clutched him. He kissed her forehead lightly. "You need anything, you let me know," he said, affection in his words. "I want to be there for you, the way you've

58

been there for all of us."

"I'm here, too," I said gratefully, grabbing hold of her hand and squeezing. "We'll be going through a lot of the same stuff, being pregnant together. Though you shouldn't have the heating and cooling trouble."

Devlin crossed to where Rene stood. "Rene, do you want this baby? You do not have to have it if you don't."

"I know that, Devlin," she said irritably, turning deliberately away from him.

"I meant that I'll not judge you," he said carefully, bringing her into his arms as Lash released her. "I thank you for protecting Sar and my child. You do not have to carry the burden of consequences—"

"Do not treat me as if I were a mere child of thirty!" Rene said sharply. "I am as old as you are, Devlin! I am fully capable of making my own decisions!"

Devlin held her, and said no more.

"I need to think for a while," Rene said finally. "Please leave, everyone but Sar."

Lash and Devlin looked grumpily at each other and then left.

Rene took a deep breath. "I'd hoped not to have to say this to you," she said finally. "But I must. This is your child, Sar, yours and Theo's. I'll bear it for you, if you want me to. But it will bind you to him again if I do."

"You'll break his heart if you don't," I said, emotional for some reason I couldn't say. "But what do you mean, my child? It's your child. I was there to see it conceived. Your pregnancy has nothing to do with me."

"My body came from you and my eggs were created when this body was created," Rene said patiently. "My outside form has changed, and some of my features have reverted to full faerie, but my eggs have remained the same." She paused. "A female faerie carries no eggs, they must be made magically or taken from another being, in order for a female faerie to get with child."

She kept my eggs "as is" because she hoped to have a child with Devlin. Is her blood like mine, or full faerie? And will she tell me the truth if I ask?

59

"There will be nothing of me in this child: it's going to be half werecougar, and half human tainted with vampire. I did a test to confirm it while you were gone." She paused. "I wish it was mine, but it's not. I'm really just a surrogate mother."

"If that's all true, then why didn't you have a child of Devlin's by now?" I said sharply, folding my hands across my chest. "You are telling me that you have all the necessary means, probably even kept your blood as near mine as possible—"

"I tried to," Rene whispered. "I miscarried, Sar." She put her head in her hands. "I got pregnant less than a week after he began taking the potion. I was so happy—!"

She dissolved into tears. I shut up, went to her, and hugged her.

"I can't tell him," she sniffled, raw. "It hurts enough remembering how happy he was when he saw I was pregnant, and thought it was his. To let him know how close it came to happening would devastate him like it has devastated me."

"Shh," I said, hugging her tight. "Shh. It'll be okay."

"I don't know what to do," Rene said timidly. "Part of me wants to try with him again, after I have this baby, if I can somehow modify your eggs to carry some of my DNA. The rest of me is scared to death to go through that again and have my hopes fail." She paused. "I don't understand what I'm doing wrong, Sar. When we made me this body, we used your blood and flesh. You had already borne a dhamphir, and the mix of human, vampire and demon should have been exactly the same. But something is missing, because it's not working."

"Leave that dream until you've had this one," I said flatly, not wanting to think about all this now. "Please, Rene. If you've already lost one baby, you may lose another."

"You're right," Rene said, wiping her eyes. "Prepare yourself for an additional child, Sister. I'll need you to care for this baby as soon as it's born." She stared at me levelly. "You are its mother, biologically. You must be thought to be its natural mother for the rest of its life. Can you handle that?"

I felt so mixed up inside I wasn't sure what to say first. *How in the hell had she gone from wanting to have a baby to passing it off to me, no matter that she's right on our trickery needing to be secret.* "What do you advise?" I said finally.

"Love him," Rene said softly, hugging me. "He is innocent of any evil." She smiled. "Yes, it's a boy."

This is too much. Hold on, Sar. Just take one day at a time. "Okay," I said tearfully. "I'll do it, Rene."

* * * *

Later that night, I went to Devlin's bedroom to find only Lash waiting for me.

"He went to Rene," Lash hissed softly. "He feels terrible this happened and jealous too, as he hoped very much it was his own."

"I saw that," I said sadly. "She would give anything if it was."

"Could we not give her some of your blood when this is over, so she could have one for him?" Lash hissed. "Devlin would be so happy, Sar. She would be, too."

"I offered already," I said grumpily, unsure of how much to divulge. "Rene said it could not be done as she is faerie, not human. But there may be something else she can try, if she decides to." I reluctantly relayed to him what Rene had told me, of losing Devlin's child.

"Rene should know," he said, shrugging. "It's unfair, how the fates play with our lives."

"Very," I said wiping away tears. "Are you mad I didn't tell you?"

"A little. I understand you not wanting anyone to know. It's another secret that could be used to hurt you. The more people who know a secret, the more it's likely not to remain one." He hugged and kissed me tenderly. "I am very fucking happy that you weren't with that fucking cat again," he said, relieved. "It made me jealous every time I thought about it."

Time for more truth. "Rene said it's my baby, mine and Theo's, Mate." I explained as best I was able about how my body material had been used to make her body. "I agreed to be his mother, when she gives birth. She said it's a boy."

Lash gave me a bewildered look. "Does she know for sure already? How?"

"I don't know, I'm just telling you what she told me and probably forgetting something crucial," I said, shrugging. "This whole thing seems

61

ludicrous to me."

"Me, too," he said. "But if you're saying you're worried about my feelings, don't be. I love you, and I always liked all your children, Mate, even before I loved you. I'll help you take care of this one Rene's having, even if he hates me like his father does."

"You're a good mate," I said softly, swallowing hard and holding him tight. "You're maybe the best mate there ever was."

"I try," Lash hissed softly, grinning. "I try."

* * * *

In a week, Theo visited. Of course, there had to be trouble.

"Well, how nice to see you, Cat," Lash hissed, walking in on Theo and I sitting at the kitchen table. "What a pleasant fucking surprise."

"Call me Theo or O'Connor," Theo growled. "Enough with the "cat" shit already, Lash."

"I'll call you dog meat, if I want to," Lash hissed, his eyes flat. "Don't piss me off, or you'll be screaming shortly."

Usually I'd stick up for Theo, and I think he expected me to. Lash was taking out his anger on Theo because he was conveniently here. But I remembered a lot of times Theo had done the same to Lash and said nothing.

Theo shot a disbelieving look at me, realizing I wasn't going to defend him, and then turned to Lash with yellow eyes. "I wasn't going to say this, but you want to be an ass. So fine! How does it feel, Lash, when you are in my shoes? How does it feel when it's your 'wife,' to know I had her, and that she's having my baby?"

Lash had his knife out in a nanosecond and went for Theo. Theo expected it, and blocked him, drawing his own knife. Steel rang off steel, the two of them grappling. Theo threw Lash backward, and he crashed into the kitchen cabinets with a grunt of pain. Theo went after him.

I blocked him with my body, grabbing Lash's gun from his holster. "Back off," I said angrily.

Theo looked down at the gun I was holding. "Going to shoot me again?"

"If you make me again," I said quietly. "Back off. You know I'll really do it. Do you want another bullet in the heart?"

"What I know is you were pregnant with his baby, back after you healed him," Theo growled.

Lash almost crawled over the top of me to get to Theo, he wanted him so bad. "You FUCKING CAT, you did something to her to make her lose it—"

"I did nothing!" Theo roared, furious and bitter. "I didn't know she got pregnant. I found out when Dr. Camlyn recovered his memories, which you had Titus erase. Camlyn thought Sar and I were splitting up, that she didn't want to tell me. When he saw my face after he told me about her miscarrying, he knew he'd made a mistake. I knew it wasn't mine, that it couldn't be. But I knew whose it had to be: yours."

"It was Lash's," I said bluntly. "What's your point?" I was trying hard to be calm. *It isn't good for the babies, getting so upset. My heart is racing...*

"I want him to think about how he should've kept his dick in his pants and out of you. And how there's karmic justice!"

"Is there? What justice would that be?" I asked him in an icy tone.

Lash went quiet immediately. He knew that tone, though he'd only heard it once or twice.

Theo either had forgotten or didn't care. "There is! He deserves to feel like I felt, to know—"

"To know what?" I interrupted coldly. "That I'm having your baby only because I was tricked into it? That I was only in bed with you again because Danial made me do it? It's not the same, and you and I both know it!"

"You enjoyed me, Sar, enjoyed me making love to you," Theo growled. "You screamed loud enough when you came."

Lash hissed in fury, but I put my hand on him and he stayed still.

Better make this sound good. "It was sex, Theo," I said gently, but firmly. "Good sex, yes, but that was all it was. And it's over. Don't push this with my mate. Just leave, and come back some other day when you can keep your comments to yourself."

"Fine," Theo spat, his fangs extended in his anger. "Have a nice fucking day." He stormed out, the front door of Hayden crashing shut behind him.

I sagged into a chair, Lash cradling me. "Are you okay?" he said tentatively. "I'm sorry if I upset you. Seeing him here made me think of him and you, and it upset me, even if he really didn't—"

"Help me into the living room," I said with a sigh, leaning on him. "I'm exhausted and need to lie down."

Lash steadied me, and we lay spooning on the couch for a while, his hands stroking my stomach. "I'm sorry," he hissed, kissing my cheek. "I shouldn't have lost my temper. Especially as I know it didn't even happen, what he's so proud of having done."

"It's not your fault, Lash. You have every right to be angry. He shouldn't have said what he said to you."

"But he's right," Lash hissed sadly. "The shoe is on the other foot now. Back when I fell for you, I wanted you and didn't care at all you were his wife."

"No, it's not the same at all. I loved you and wanted to be with you. I came to you willingly. I didn't go willingly to Theo that night with Danial," I said forcefully. "If I'd had a choice, I'd have said no. I didn't want children with Theo; I gave in because he wanted one. But I want a child with you very much, Trystan." I kissed him lightly on his lips. "I'm very happy to be having ours."

Lash hugged me. "You're a good mate," he hissed affectionately. "You always make me feel better."

"I'm glad you feel better," I said, rubbing my cheek against his. "Please hold me and let me nap. I was getting kicked all night and didn't sleep well."

"Rest," Lash said, kissing me. "I'll watch over you, Sweetness."

I relaxed in his arms, and soon, I was asleep.

* * * *

Later that night there was trouble. It started when I felt so uncomfortable that I went to bed early. Lash was concerned but elected to stay downstairs for a while to finish his shift after Devlin said he'd watch over me. Dev's melodious lullaby soothed me enough that I soon fell asleep.

An hour later, I awoke to slight cramping. "Dev, something's wrong!"

"Titus, come to me," Devlin said. He picked me up and immediately headed for the stairs, yelling "Lash!"

Lash met us at the base of the stairs. Titus was already beside us, his clawed hand on my stomach as I panted, the cramps now steady waves of pain.

"What's the matter?" Devlin said frantically. "Titus, do something!"

"She's miscarrying again," Titus rumbled. "Hold still, Sar." He said some words over me, Suddenly, I couldn't move, and the cramping stopped, as well as all physical feeling.

"Give her to me." Titus took me from Dev. "Sar, please be calm and don't try to move at all. I put a hold spell on you, so we can get you to Dr. Camlyn's in time."

He teleported us immediately to the doctor's office. Devlin called Stephen, who said he would be ready in five minutes, and agreed to teleport in.

"What's wrong, Titus?" Lash hissed, brittle with fear for me. "She's been careful, we've done nothing, not been intimate, nothing! Why is this happening?"

"I don't know," Titus said grudgingly. "It may be that her being human and you being snake, she just can't carry your child to term."

Lash was stricken, his eyes anguished. He took a sharp intake of breath. I fought to be calm, scared to death that our worst fears were coming true.

"Damn you, that's not it!" Devlin said with red eyes, his fangs bared. "If she can have my child, a half vampire, she can have Lash's!"

"She is part vampire now, but not weresnake at all," Titus replied. "Sundown had a lot of trouble with Terian's child, even with the baby being only a quarter demon, because we are so different inside. Looking human is not the same as being human. The only reason Sar was able to have a child of yours, Devlin, is because of her being resistant to the virus and in a persistent partially changed state. Other women you were with over the years couldn't change enough without turning, which is why it never worked before her." He paused. "The same thing seems to be happening now with Lash's child."

"But she had a child of Theo's," Lash hissed, his eyes flattening to snake, his voice cracking. "And she had no trouble at all. It has to be me, that there is something wrong with me from all the years of potions and all the demon blood and my age, all the times I was hurt and needed magic to recover! It's my fault!"

Devlin shook his head. "That isn't it; it's just the species difference like he says! Warm blooded and cold blooded, reptile and mammal—"

"Can't you do anything?" Lash shouted. "God damn it, I want our children to live!"

"Enough," Stephen said firmly, coming into the room. "Lash, please leave. And Devlin, you leave, too."

Both of them immediately protested.

Stephen remained firm. "Go out and pray to whatever God you pray to that Sar hadn't lost them already. I'm going to check for heartbeats first. If they are still alive, I'll do my best to make sure they stay that way. That's all we can do."

Dev and Lash left, Lash shooting me one last agonized look before the door closed between us.

Titus faced Camlyn. "You're sure you want me to stay?"

"I don't want you to, no. But I need your help," Stephen said irritably. "Hold her magically as you have been while I check her."

"Proceed. She will not move, or feel any pain."

Stephen worked on me for what felt like a long time, though the clock said only a half hour had gone by. I felt nothing of what he did, due to Titus's magic.

Finally, Stephen washed his hands and turned to Titus. "The one weresnake baby is doing well. I had to sew her shut, as her cervix had opened. My thanks to you. Without your quick action, she would have lost them all."

Titus's hand clasped mine strongly. I was comforted, though I couldn't squeeze him back. *My babies....*

"We must do something to stop her uterine muscles from contracting. If she contracts enough, she'll either abort or damage the umbilical connective tissue enough the baby will wither inside her."

So that was what happened to my twins. I felt another wave of despair.

"Any ideas, Titus? I don't have any drugs that would be guaranteed to work on her, not with the regenerative power she has now."

"We can partially paralyze her," Titus said finally. "I have some poison that paralyzes locally, not completely, and has no other effects. A slight dose administered to her should do it."

"It won't harm the child?"

"It's not for killing, more for torturing, to hold a person still without restraints, like when their heart is cut from their chest—"

My stomach flip-flopped. I wanted badly to throw up.

"There is no loss of feeling, just paralysis." Titus added with a grin. "Otherwise it wouldn't be very useful for what it was designed for."

The sickening implications brought up my gorge, but it stayed where it was. *I am going to throw up as soon as this spell is off me.*

"But we must be quick or just the trauma of administering it will harm the fetus. I'll get it and be back shortly," Titus said. "I have some in my workshop." He disappeared.

Stephen came closer to me. "Relax, Sar. If he can do what he says, you should be fine, though we will have to give you a C-section when the baby is far enough along, as you won't be able to have normal contractions. But that can be done easily."

Titus appeared with a jar of pink paste. He said some words, making me numb in my stomach area. "Hand me a scalpel, Camlyn." Then he fastened his red eyes on me, tool in hand. "Look away, Kin-daughter."

I looked away, but still felt the pressure as he slit my stomach open, and then the feel of his hand reaching inside me. I broke out in a sweat, panting, telling myself to hold it together, that he knew what he was doing, that it would be okay. He touched me in sweeping gentle strokes as he spread a pink paste over the outside of my uterus. As he did that, the muscles relaxed, helping me calm down. The pressure suddenly disappeared, and then I felt my flesh knitting together.

"I'm finished," Titus said comfortingly. "You can look, Sar."

"Did it work?" Stephen asked.

"We must release the hold spell on her and see. But this is all I can do, Camlyn."

Titus unfroze me with a murmured word and three things happened: I jumped up, lunging for the sink, Lash came in the door with Devlin hot on his heels, and then I promptly threw up. I cleaned off my face, and rinsed out my mouth, feeling disgusting.

"Mate, are you okay?"

"Normal reaction," Titus rumbled. "I'll teleport her home to rest."

"Take her home," Stephen said. "No activity save walking very slowly on the treadmill and even then, Sar, limit your time on your feet to an hour each day. No work of any kind, especially no lifting, and she should never be left alone for more than a few minutes."

"I can be with her almost all the time," Devlin said quickly. "And when I can't be, Lash or Titus will be with her."

Titus nodded. "I agree with that. This should not happen again, but other complications might arise, and the sooner they are noticed, the sooner she can be treated."

Lash nodded. "Are the children okay?" he hissed.

"She lost one of yours, and Devlin's child, too," Stephen said as gently as he could. "But the other one is fine, thanks to Titus's quick thinking."

Lash gave Titus a look of gratitude, then looked away quickly.

A moment later Devlin, Lash and I were back at Hayden. Titus clasped my hand, and then vanished into thin air.

"Stay with her," Lash hissed as he stalked off.

Devlin led me into our bedroom and hugged me. "He's upset, Sar, just as you and I are. Right or wrong, he's very angry that his child is dead while Theo's is alive and well in Rene. He thinks this is his fault, because of what he is. He's going downstairs to work off his anger in the gym and have a few drinks, before coming back up here."

"I'm sorry I lost our baby too, Dev," I said softly.

"It was not your fault," Devlin replied sadly. "We can try again another time, Sar. Carrying Lash's child to term will be hard enough. I should have waited, and not pushed you for it. If it's anyone's fault, it's mine."

I hugged him and didn't speak. There was nothing to say. There had been so much pain for him, and so much joy for us, and it had all been for nothing.

* * * *

I woke up to feel someone behind me. *Lash rejoined us in bed.* He was behind me, spooning me. I snuggled backwards into his arms, then recoiled. Lash's skin was much too cool, almost cold. I turned to see

Danial, his eyes full of tears.

"Love, I'm sorry."

I wanted to be nasty, to ask him if he was happy that one of my children with Lash was dead. I just swallowed instead, because just thinking it hurt too much. And the truth was it wasn't his fault. The spell he'd done had only touched Rene. I turned my back to him. *If it is anyone's fault, it's Theo's for fighting with Lash and upsetting me. But it's probably no one's fault, as Camlyn said.*

"Forgive me, Sarelle," Danial whispered, his tears falling like rain to wet my shoulder. "I'm so sorry. The witch said that there was no possibility of miscarriage! I would never have used it, never have put you through this horror, Love, if I'd thought there was even the slightest chance! I'd never have hurt any child, especially your children, not ever! Please believe me—"

"It wasn't you that caused it," Devlin said quietly, hugging us both. "Sar most likely would have lost at least one of Lash's children in any case. Camlyn said it was so."

"When?" I gasped, staring at him in horror. "When did he say this?"

"He cautioned of the possible effects of species difference back when Lash went for his fertility check. That is why Lash had Titus brew the potion, Sar. He wanted to make sure to...create more than one, so that he could have the best chance of having one survive to term."

"Why did no one tell me?" I demanded.

"Lash said he hoped it wouldn't happen, that instead they all would live. He said if you thought there might be a miscarriage it might make you upset enough to trigger one."

"You should have told me," I whispered. "I would have stayed in bed."

"There was nothing you could have done differently," Devlin soothed. "This is no one's fault."

"It is mine," Danial said, sobbing. "I have cost you your son, Devlin!"

I turned to Devlin. "Was it a boy?"

"Yes," he said, letting out a breath. "As was Lash's baby you lost."

"I would take it back if I could—" Danial sobbed.

"Oh, Danial, hush," Devlin sighed. "It was not of your doing.

Carrying on will not bring back the dead. You want to do something for me, bury your hate of Lash along with my son when we inter his remains tomorrow night."

Danial put his hand over Devlin's. "I swear it from this moment on. I will apologize to him as well."

"Fine, but do it in private, not at the crypt," Devlin cautioned. "For we will be interring his son's remains after mine, and he wants only Sar and me there for that."

"Are you naming him?" Danial asked.

"No," Devlin said almost inaudibly. "I am having the marker say only 'Beloved Son.' Lash gave his father's name to his son. The inscription will read 'Jared F. Valeras, beloved son.'"

"What is the F. for?" Danial whispered.

"For his brother, Franco," I guessed.

Devlin nodded.

"I did not know he had a brother." Danial said, surprised. "I did not think of him as a man who ever had a family."

"You never looked at him as a man," Devlin said, his golden eyes sad. "For a guy whose childhood was as similar to his as yours, Danial, you were always looking down on him."

"I was wrong," Danial said. "Some of it was jealousy that he was close to you, that you had a close friend. And some of it was what happened with Brianna."

"I know, he told me," Devlin said, hugging Danial again. "That was not his fault, what happened."

"Who is Brianna?" I asked.

Devlin started and looked at me. Then he looked at Danial.

"Answer me," I demanded.

"She was a woman Danial loved and Devlin stole," a hissing voice said sadly. "A woman I envied both of them and took advantage of, when chance gave me an opportunity." Lash entered the bedroom and stood before us. "I am sorry, Danial, that she ended as she did."

"It was the fault of each of us, equally," Devlin said, glancing at Danial, then at Lash. "We all had a hand in it. But she is long dead and it is time we put her to rest between us."

"I am sorry," Danial said to Lash. "For what I did to you, both now

70

and then."

"I am sorry as well," Lash hissed, his eyes flat. "If I'd refused to take her to that train station, you might have—"

"Stop," Devlin said gently. "Might-haves are long over. We have only the future. It's time to stop letting the past haunt us. There is no point looking back, only forward."

Shaker had said something similar. He is right, it's time to let go of old grudges and pain.

"I'm showering," Lash hissed as he eyed Danial, Devlin, and I in bed. "When I get back, there had better be room for me in there with my mate."

He stalked into the bathroom. Devlin chuckled, hugging me tighter.

Danial made to leave, but Dev stopped him. "Stay," he said tenderly. "There is room for you, at least for tonight."

"Where?" Danial asked, disgruntled. "She only has two sides, Dev."

"I'll lie beneath her and a little to the side," he said, piling pillows on his other side. "She has been hot at night anyway. Come, Love."

Soon, Devlin was positioned under me and I was lying with my head on his chest on my side, propped up on pillows. Danial came closer, his body resting against my back, and his hand on my hip.

Lash came out of the shower, looked at us, and rolled his eyes. He climbed in on my other side. "Are you comfortable, like this?" he asked me.

"I'm fine."

"Sleep," he hissed affectionately. "I will be right here." He looked over me at Danial. "I'd better not feel you touch me in the night, Dan."

I expected Danial to growl, but he just gave Lash a look. "You sleep with Dev all the time."

"But I know from talk that you're a kinky boy and I'm telling you now, any touching me at all, you'll get my knife in your hand."

"I think I can manage to restrain myself," Danial said drolly.

"Good," Lash hissed. "See that you do."

I fell asleep, still sad but with a faint smile on my lips.

* * * *

The next morning, I woke up to find positions had changed. As he always did, Danial had pulled me into his embrace as he slept. Lash and Devlin were absent.

"Good morning," Danial whispered, kissing me lightly on the cheek. "How are you feeling?"

"Where are—?"

"Devlin took a call a few minutes ago," Danial reassured me. "He and Lash got up. They grumbled a good deal when they woke up clasping the pillows instead of you."

"Never again," Lash hissed with a grin from the doorway. "Three is a crowd, at least, when they're men. So when you next spend the night, Dan, I'll be sleeping in my old room."

Danial looked up, shocked. "You are giving me your place, willingly?"

"Loaning, not giving, Dan. And only because you finally concede that it *is* my place," Lash hissed softly. "You and she are Oathed. You have a place in her heart; you should have one in her bed sometimes."

"I misjudged you badly," Danial said brokenly. "Please forgive me."

"Many have," Lash said gruffly. "It says something that you admit it to me."

"I do…Trystan."

"Then consider us no longer enemies," Lash said. "Maybe someday we can be friends."

"Let's not rush into anything."

"Asshole."

"Snake."

Lash hissed, laughed a little, and walked out. And my smile that had been faint broadened slightly, as I finally let myself relax in Danial's embrace.

Chapter Six

That night, we interred the remains of my lost children in Devlin's crypt. I stood there sniffling with Lash and Danial as Titus took the urn containing the ashes of Devlin's baby and placed it in a room containing many jars of ashes.

"Rest easy, Son," Devlin said sadly. "Be at peace." He turned to Danial. "Let me walk you out."

As Devlin bid Danial goodnight, I waited with Lash and Titus, staring at the many other urns on granite shelves all around us.

I didn't want to ask, but I had to know. "Are all those other urns, um…Devlin's?"

Titus nodded. "He tried often in those first years after Anna. Back when we thought it was he that was special, that he was the one the magic resided in and not Anna. Devlin was handsome, powerful, and rich, Sar. Many women offered to have his children, knowing well the risks. Those that got pregnant, you see their remains here, and those of the children inside them. Two hundred years worth."

"This is so sad," I said softly, turning away. "Would it not have been better to scatter their remains in the forest, instead of having a crypt full of lost babies?"

"I could not let what they did go unremembered," Devlin said in an old, old voice, as he returned to the crypt. "They sacrificed their lives trying to make me happy, trying to bring forth my children. I didn't know what else to do to honor what they did." He closed the gate to the crypt with a creaking sound. "Donations to charitable organizations they favored were not enough. And as the years passed, I forgot most of their names, Oathed One." He took my hand. "Most emotions fade, over time,

73

especially when loved ones die. And I must not forget them, Sar. Not ever."

I didn't understand, really. I'd have wanted to forget in his shoes. But I nodded anyway.

Titus teleported us to the cemetery's edge, where Lash scattered the remains of our son next to the black granite marker.

"Feel the sun, little one," he hissed gently. "Listen to the wind and the water. Be at peace."

Titus teleported us back almost at once to the main house and excused himself abruptly. Lash and Devlin went to the kitchen, where we joined Rene, who was eating a large bowl of ice cream.

"Are you feeling well, Love?" Devlin said, rubbing her shoulder.

"Hungry again," Rene said grumpily. "I just had dinner not four hours ago. Where is it all going?"

"Werechildren are hungry at all times," Lash hissed with a faint smile. "Sar, do you want me to get you a bowl?"

"No, but sushi tomorrow," I said, easing off my swollen feet. "I'm going to turn into an eel soon."

"Good, then I can coil with you easier," Lash teased, handing a glass of wine to Devlin. "Do you want a tablespoon of wine?"

I nodded. He handed me his near empty glass and poured another one for himself. Then he looked pointedly at Devlin, who picked up Rene and her bowl and carried them without a word into the living room. A few minutes later, the TV started up at high volume.

"Please tell me," I asked politely.

"You saw the black marker near the pond," Lash hissed in an old voice, as he moved his wine glass around nervously. "I wanted to talk to you about it, if you want to know."

I reached out and took his hand. "Did you have other children?"

"I..." Lash began and stopped. Then he began again. "It wasn't like Devlin," he said finally. "The only one I know of who miscarried my children ever was you, Sar."

I wasn't sure what to say, so I just watched him.

"I was with a lot of women," Lash said, his eyes staring to the left of me. "This was before condoms and before I took the potion that made me sterile. Most of them...well, they were whores and they had methods they used to make sure they stayed able to work."

He stopped talking and drank some more wine.

I squeezed his hand. "Take your time."

"I told you about how I got that one girl pregnant, and she ended the pregnancy. She wasn't the only one, Sar. There were a few women I knew who got pregnant. And the babies would have been mine."

I squeezed his hand again. "Go on."

Suddenly something snapped in him. "I felt them move," Lash hissed furiously. "I knew they were mine and I loved them just for that! Then they were dead. That stone is to remember them."

"I'm sorry," I said comfortingly. Though I didn't understand what exactly had happened to his children, all that mattered to me was that he was in pain.

Whatever had made him so angry seemed to leave as swiftly as it had come. "So am I," Lash said gruffly, pulling me into his lap. "Sorry I didn't meet you a long time ago, Sweetness, before I had all these bad memories." He kissed me lightly. "I wish you'd been my mate all of my life, though it's true I was kind of an ass until I got to be about forty."

I guffawed, my laughter breaking the solemn nature of our conversation.

Lash smiled. "But at least I have you now, Sweetness."

"Yes, you have me," I said lovingly, as I hugged him. "And we'll have a real family soon."

* * * *

Theo came back the next week. This time he caught me alone.

Devlin had just left me to take an emergency call, after calling Lash's cell to tell him to come take over for him. In retrospect, I'm sure Theo saw Dev go, and then waited for him to get out of earshot before approaching me.

My back was to the door, my ears filled with iPod music and the noise of the treadmill. When Theo sidled up to me and touched my shoulder, he startled me so much I fell off.

Theo moved quickly and caught me. "Careful!"

I looked up at him in shock "What are you doing here?"

"Visiting my child and its mother," he said, his tone implying that

75

he was thinking hard about kissing me.

I asked you never to show up without calling. I pushed him away gently, disentangling myself from him so he stepped back. "Then come upstairs. I'm just getting done. After exercise I need to lie down on the couch for a while and get off my feet."

We walked slowly to the living room, Theo steadying me on the stairs. Though I wanted to tell him to let me go, I played the shaky pregnant woman. Nothing mattered but us getting into a less isolated place and finding a few guards for company. To my surprise, there were no guards on the main floor, not even our new housekeeper. *Shit, where is Rene's construct when I needed her?* I put out a mental call for Shaker, but got no answer.

Theo sat down on the couch beside me and pulled me into his arms.

I put up my hands against his chest to stop him, annoyed. "What do you think you're doing?"

Theo tilted my head up, trying to kiss me.

I pushed him off and scooted away until we were at opposite ends. "Knock it off!"

"Sar, come home with me," Theo purred softly.

I froze, remembering. He hadn't often purred for me, the great rumbling contented sound he'd first made for me as a cougar years ago. *I always liked that...*

Theo saw my hesitation and grabbed my hand. "Danial misses you," he purred. "T would like to see you more too; he'll be coming back soon."

"Don't use them to try to get to me."

"I miss you," he purred. "Give me another chance."

I gave him an appalled look, resisting the urge to laugh. Was he kidding? "You had all the chances you'll ever be getting. But I am sorry things got as bad as they did at the end."

"Come back to me," Theo purred gently, taking my hand and putting it on his heart, so I could feel the vibration of his body. "I'll make you happy, Sar, I swear I will."

"It's too late for that," I said flatly, trying to draw my hand back. "I'm sorry."

"It's not too late!" Theo said quickly. "I still love you, Sar."

Time to not be nice. "I don't love you, Theo. The spell Terian did years ago was what made us be together, that made us love each other. And it's broken."

"No, I loved you before that spell. I was attracted to you from the first time I saw you, I wanted so many times to tell you—"

"But I wasn't attracted to you, not until the spell was on us! I wasn't in love with you; I was in love with Danial."

"Don't give me that shit, you loved me! What we had was real, you know it was!"

I felt my anger leave me. All that was left was pity for him. "It wasn't. And even if it was, it's over now."

"No," Theo purred, caressing my cheek with his hand. "We're soul mates, Terian said so! We were meant to be together, Sar. You were meant to be my mate, not anyone else's!"

There was a sharp *crack*! Theo cried out, jerking his hand back from me, a deep whiplash mark on his arm, the blood already clotting as he healed up the wound.

Theo turned, bared his fangs and growled. "Always, it's you."

Lash stood in the doorway, whip in hand and mad as hell. "That's it," he hissed furiously. "I've had enough. I'm killing you this time, Cat."

"Come on and try it, Snake." Theo grinned, his eyes hard. "I'm happy to have you challenge me! And to the winner goes not only the title of being the best, but also Sar."

"Stop," I said harshly, and got between them. "There isn't going to be any fight, because I'm not a prize, Theo." I paused, thinking quickly. "But you want a chance, fine, Theo. You answer me three questions here and now, and get them right, and I'll go with you."

Lash let out a surprised hiss, as Theo sheathed his knife, waiting expectantly.

"What's my favorite movie?" I said quietly.

"The Hobbit, animated," he answered triumphantly.

"What's my favorite book? Favorite passage?"

Theo gave me a blank look. "I never heard you mention one."

I gave him a sad smile. "That's because you never cared enough to ask."

Theo growled. "That isn't fair."

77

"Fine, I'll give you another one and we'll do two out of three. Who's my favorite music artist? My favorite song, the one that makes me happiest?"

Theo growled again. "You listened to a hundred different songs in the time we spent—"

"Lash, what is it?"

"Artist varies depending on your mood," he hissed, unsure. "You have a lot of favorite songs, but not one that I ever heard you say makes you happiest."

Theo let out a purr of satisfaction. "He doesn't know either. Some game, Sar."

Finish this, once and for all. And hope to God that Lash's memory isn't faulty on this one. "No, Lash is right, Theo. I don't have a favorite song. But I'll give you one more question, to be fair. What did I want from my life? The one thing I wanted most?"

Theo's eyes narrowed. "To have a family, and live at your farm and be independent. Hell, I don't know."

I felt Lash's hand take mine and squeeze.

"Lash, tell him."

"You wanted to love someone deeply, and be loved that way in return," he said softly. "To be completely and utterly happy in that, for as long as it lasted."

Theo let out a room-shaking roar. "So because I can't remember some words you said to me just once years ago, I lose you? That's bullshit!"

"No. It's a lot more than that. You can't really love me," I said simply. "Because you don't even know me."

"I know you intimately," Theo purred, locking his storm cloud eyes on mine. "I know every curve of your body like my own."

"But you don't know me, the me inside, the me that thinks and feels and prays and hopes and dreams. You know my body very well, and sure, I know everything you like in bed. But though I know you very well; what your fears were, what your dreams were, what you wanted out of life, you have no idea what and who I am."

"You are my soul mate!"

"Really? You never once asked me what I wanted out of life. You never altered your life or gave up anything that you wanted in order to help me make what I wanted a reality."

"And Lash did?" Theo roared. "Give me a fucking break!"

"He did," I lied, locking eyes with Theo. "But what's more, he wanted me for me. He's never made me feel guilty for the things I want out of life, or the things I think or say. So many times we fought Theo, and why? Because you didn't like how I thought about certain things. You wanted me to think what you did, and you hated that I didn't, that I wouldn't just go along with you! Because down deep inside of you, you don't really even like me, the me I am!" I paused for breath. "You like the idea of me that you molded and shaped me into. And I let you, because I was stupid, telling myself it was okay because you loved me, that you were my husband. But I'm not that woman anymore. I never was! That damn spell is off me!"

"You'll never share a dream with him," Theo said with pleasure. "Not even if you dream forever! You can say what you like about how he knows the real you, and how much you love each other. But you are my soul mate, not his!"

I wanted to say something cutting and nasty, but thought he might be right. Lash squeezed my hand in support, but stayed silent.

"That's why you are carrying my child again, Sar. Because any time we make love without protection, your body knows what I am to you, and naturally wants to—"

I almost told him it was all a farce; the child, the night together, all of it. With grated teeth, I held all my rage in. "I'm having Lash's child because I want to. I'm his mate, not yours. I'm in love with him, not you. And I'm never leaving him and coming back to you. Never."

"All you did for me and for Elle wasn't because of a spell," Theo said calmly. "You cared enough to come alone across the country to marry me once." He eyed Lash contemptuously. "He's not the marrying kind, Sar. I give you and him six months, tops." He smiled cruelly, his blue eyes glittering. "You'll end up with a broken heart, or maybe another disease—"

ENOUGH! "Don't call me Sar, Theopolis," I said coldly "Get out and don't come back. You are nothing to me. I never want to lay eyes on you again. You come near me again and I'll ask Lash to kill you."

79

Theo seethed, baring his cougar fangs. Without a last word, he slammed out of Hayden. A few minutes later, his truck started up.

Lash's arms snaked around, hugging me tightly. "Mistress of Hayden, you want him dead, all you ever have to do is ask." He nuzzled me. "Kidding aside, I'm glad you finally have. I'll make sure all the guards know to bring him to me if he shows up."

I blanched from hearing him call me 'Mistress' and his blatant eagerness to kill. "Please take me upstairs. I'm exhausted from his bullshit."

I felt a sudden kick and quickly put his hand on my belly so he could feel the slight flutter. "I think your son wants attention."

Lash went motionless, feeling the movement. "I feel him," he hissed lovingly "God, he's so strong."

"You'll love him even more than me," I teased.

"No," Lash hissed softly. "But I'll love him just as much and that's saying something."

"Indeed," Devlin murmured from the doorway.

He came over to me with a proffered hand. Quickly, I let him feel the kicking. A moment later, he took his hand away and picked me up.

"I'll take this lady up to bed," he said rakishly, shooting me a grin. Then his manner became cold as ice. "Go alert the guards that Theo is not to be admitted any longer. He is to be shot on sight inside these walls and explosive bullets are to be used. And they are not to shoot to wound. Understood?"

I opened my mouth to protest, and then closed it. Theo had come close to kidnapping me today. His eyes when I'd refused to leave with him had been as angry as the night he'd tried to turn me against my will. He hadn't left me any recourse but this.

Lash nodded and gave me a chaste kiss. "Got it. Get some rest, Sweetness." He walked off quickly as Devlin carried me upstairs.

Soon we were settled in bed, the lights off.

"Sar, are you comfortable here like this? Do you have everything you want?"

"Yes," I said curiously. "Why are you asking like that?"

"Just making sure," he said gently, yet there was an odd note in his melodic tones. "Please go to sleep, Love. You've had a trying day."

I snuggled into him, but didn't sleep. My mind was racing, wondering at why I had said what I had to Theo, and lied for Lash. *It isn't a mark or test of true love, knowing someone's favorite things. The test was unfair, to say the least. And maybe you did lie, but so what? Theo couldn't just accept that it was over, probably because there had been so many chances he'd blown previously. He needed to know it was over, that there was no chance of reconciliation. That's what matters.*

* * * *

That next week the local shelter called to say that a puppy that was part German Shepherd had been brought in, asking if we wanted to adopt it. "It's a female," Devlin relayed to me later. "They asked we come today, if possible, to pick her up."

"Part?" Lash hissed, annoyed. "We wanted a German Shepherd, period."

"I can go," I said, trying to get to my feet. "Titus can teleport me,"

"Sit down," Lash said, pushing me back gently. "You aren't to move. I'll go. And I'm only bringing it back if it looks like your dogs, Sar."

"Lash," Devlin began. "You know Sar has wanted to rescue a dog. It's a direct way to help so many of those animal charities she likes to support—"

"Dev, it's going to be my dog, too. I want it to be big and menacing, so it will protect my mate and our child. I always liked Darkness, that she was solid black."

"Lash, if it's a puppy its color might change when it's an adult," I interjected.

Lash was already putting on his shoes. "Mate, I'll handle it. Don't move from that couch."

An hour later, Lash was back and he wasn't alone. A small ten-pound puppy was with him who looked too cute to be real. She was fluffy, with long light brown hair, dark bright eyes, and a black tongue. Her feathery tail was wagging uncertainly, and she didn't look menacing in the slightest.

"That's not a German Shepherd," I said as tactfully as I could. Devlin just blinked his eyes in disbelief.

81

"I'm calling her Honey," Lash said tentatively. "She seems to like it."

Seth came to the door. "Lash, there's a call for you from Mad." He looked down. "Whose fluffy little dog is that?"

Lash decked him. Seth hit the doorframe with a yelp. "She's my dog, and don't refer to her as either little or fluffy. Got it?"

"Got it." Seth left, rubbing his jaw.

I waited a moment until Seth left and then burst out laughing. Devlin joined me. Lash just looked at us and glared.

"So what about your big talk?" I said, reaching out a hand to pet Honey. "Not that I mind; she's adorable and Ghost will love her. So will V."

"She was in a cage," Lash hissed, upset. "It was loud and it was bright and she was whining. I couldn't leave her there, Mate."

It was obvious he was remembering his stint in prison. I got up with effort, and went to him. "That's all you had to say, Mate. I'm glad you brought her home."

"Welcome to Hayden," Devlin said seriously to Honey. "I guess you'll be staying."

* * * *

Ghost did indeed love Honey. Though he was much older than she was, they played together and slept near one another. Phantom loved her too, oddly enough; she was almost as a surrogate mother to him. One day soon after her arrival, Lash and I were sitting watching TV, when Phantom began to knead Honey's stomach. Honey gave him an anxious look, but stayed still.

"Dev, that fugly cat of yours is bothering my dog!" Lash yelled. "Come down here and get him."

"Don't be calling my cat 'fugly'!" Devlin said in a prickly voice from upstairs. "He was here first. Your dog will have to adjust."

"Enough," I said wearily. "Take Phantom upstairs, Dev. Lash and I'll take Honey for a walk. I need some quiet."

Lash knew better than to argue. Soon we were slowly walking the path to the pond, Ghost and Honey beside us.

"The weather is nice now that it's July," I said, drinking in the sight of the many-hued flowers blooming in Hayden's gardens. I'd waited a long time to see them in midsummer.

"You'll deliver soon and so will Rene," Lash said eagerly. "Camlyn said you're both going to come early, probably in late August. We'll have good weather until late September, with any luck. Now that we've got that new maid, Vera, working for us, you don't have to do as much as you used to, so we can get some rock time in before fall comes."

Lying on the big rock beside the pond in the sun sounded great to me. "Any news on a werebat guard?"

"Drake gave me the name of one of his cousins, Ben. He's coming for an interview tomorrow. I know the bloodline, and I'll tell you now, we're going to hire him."

"Good. It'll be interesting getting to know a werebat."

"Don't get to know him too well," Lash said gruffly. "He's single."

I rolled my eyes. "I'll keep that in mind, Tryst."

We reached the pond, and I took a moment to visit Darkness's grave. With dismay, I noticed the flowers we'd planted hadn't come up. The grave was barren, except for straggly wildflowers, grass and rock.

"I'm sorry," I whispered, kneeling down with difficulty. "I wanted you to have flowers."

Lash hugged me. "I'll come out and put some in tomorrow, Sweetness. Don't worry."

I stood with effort. "I'm just sad we planted so many and nothing came up."

"When you come back again, there will be flowers here. Come inside, you need to rest."

I let him lead me away, bereft despite his touch and my two other living dogs by my side.

Chapter Seven

August passed without incident. On September third, Camlyn induced labor in both Rene and I. Sometime during the morning of the fourth, I gave birth by Cesarean section.

When I awoke that night and remembered what happened, I immediately looked around. My eyes located Lash. He stood behind Devlin, who was sitting in a chair near the open window holding a bundle, staring at it with wonder.

I propped myself up groggily. "Where is Rene and—?"

"She is at home, recovering after healing herself. The birth was a difficult one," Lash said seriously. "Theo arrived right after and took custody of his son." He gave me a guilty look. "You were still in surgery and Rene told us to let him take the baby cougar." He paused. "It was a boy, Sar. Theo is calling him Harrison, after his father."

"I would have liked to see him," I said quietly, remembering Devon. *I never got a chance to see my son by Theo as a human, before he died.* "Did he say anything about visitation?"

"He said to stay away," Devlin replied. "Theo took a leave of absence from Solutions, Inc. According to Danial, he's already left to go west. Harris is with him."

Maybe it was better this way. Theo'd been robbed of Elle's childhood. I knew that if I'd seen Harris and how much he probably looked like Devon, I'd have refused to let Theo take him. Right or wrong, Harris was werecougar. He belonged with the man who would be able to teach him about how to be werecougar. *And no matter what Rene said, he's not really my son. I have no right to take him from Theo.*

"Theo said he would be in contact," Lash said uncomfortably. "But there's someone else here who's been waiting to visit with you, Sweetness."

I beckoned with both arms, smiling excitedly. "Let me see our child, Tryst."

Lash grinned and then knelt down next to Devlin. "Give him to me," he hissed. "Sar wants to see him, Dev."

"He looks so happy," Devlin whispered. "I can't believe how much he looks like the both of you—"

"Give him to me right now," Lash hissed with irritation. "You can look at him later."

Devlin gave him up reluctantly with a sigh. "Okay."

"Hold our son, my love," Lash hissed lovingly. He handed me a bundle.

I'd birthed three children in my life so far and loved them all. But for the first time, I looked into my newborn child's eyes and human eyes stared back into mine, studying me seriously. My son's eyes and hair were dark, like his father's, and his skin was darker too, a shade about halfway between Lash's skin and mine.

Devlin snapped several pictures with his phone as I inspected my son, Lash posing beside me.

"Dev's right, he looks like you," I said finally, giving Lash a big smile.

He put his hand on my shoulder and squeezed. "I hope he grows to look like both of us."

In a few moments, Lash took him from me. "I'm going to change him now to snake. It will be safer for him to be in that form until he's older. Now that he's got your scent, he won't bite you if you handle him in his snake form."

Lash went into the other room. A half hour later, he was back with a three-foot long snake coiled around his lower arm. He walked to me and held his arm out over my lap. "Go to your mother, son. Open your arms, Sar."

I watched my son again; apprehensive at how he would react as I opened my arms. I needn't have worried. He let go of Lash's arm and immediately dropped himself on me, hissing a little as he landed. He quickly coiled himself up on my chest.

I held him in my arms, feeling very odd but also very content. "From the sounds he's making, he seems okay. Is he?" Our son was making a continuous soft hissing as he rubbed his head on my skin, his tail curled around my hand. However, it wasn't recognizable words to me, just noise.

"Yes," Lash said, easing himself down on the bed beside us. "He knows you are his mother, and I, his father." He ran his hand down our son's back, bringing a louder hiss out of the child. "He's content and warm. He'll communicate his feelings first, and then pick up words slowly. I'll change him back for you sometimes over the next months, so you can see him growing. But he's safer this way, Sar, at least until he's the size of an eight year old or so."

I nodded reluctantly. "I know. What do we feed him?"

"He can eat meat of any kind, insects, and any small live animals he is big enough to swallow whole, and probably eggs," Lash said, by his face calling up some forgotten memories. "I'll teach him to catch fish. But that's it, while he's snake."

"Is he, um, the right size?"

"He's big, actually. He should be only about two feet long, or two and a half, and he's three. Usually with snakes, there are at least two babies born per birthing. You being human, you usually have only one at a time, so that's to be expected. Harrison was larger than normal, too, Stephen said. It's cross-species mating, probably."

"Do you want to rest, or are you ready to go home?" Devlin said lovingly as he snapped another picture of us.

"Ready to go home," I said, yawning. "I want to sleep for a week."

Stephen came in at that moment. "Before you go, I need to talk to you."

"What is it?" Lash hissed, before I had a chance to ask.

"Sarelle," Devlin said softly. "There won't be anymore children."

I gave him a look. "I've heard that before."

"But this time it's true," Titus rumbled from the doorway. "That potion which paralyzed your uterine muscles is permanent, Kin-daughter. I'm sorry. I'd have prepared something else if I'd had time."

I gave Dev a look, then Stephen. "What?"

"You still have the equipment, but not the power to use it," Stephen

86

said delicately. "And according to Titus, this will not heal, Sarelle, no matter how much vampire blood, or demon blood, or other magic is used."

"Even with the precautions Lash will take next week, there was a serious risk to you if you ever conceived," Titus continued. "Enough of one that I asked Lash and Devlin for permission to administer a sterility spell, which they gave. It's a hundred percent effective. And non-reversible."

I gave Devlin an anguished look. "That means—"

"Love, it was not to be," he interrupted with a worn tone. "But leave these thoughts for now. This is not a night for sadness. Can you walk?"

"Yes." I moved to get up from the bed, setting down my son.

Dev immediately stopped me. "I'm not letting you walk so soon after giving birth," he said lovingly. "I just wanted to know if you felt you could. Come."

Devlin picked me up, Lash picked up our son, and soon enough, we were back at Hayden courtesy of Titus.

Devlin helped me take a sponge bath while Lash got a heated tank ready for our son and fed him his first meal. We'd agreed that until he was older we didn't want him roaming the house alone. He might hurt our pets or bite a guard, not knowing any better.

Soon, I was in Devlin's arms, cuddling, and Lash was coming out of the bathroom from taking a shower. Our son was already asleep, coiled in a small pile in the corner of his tank. I felt bad for him in his confinement, and then reminded myself that it was only for a little while, until he knew what was expected from him, and wouldn't hurt anyone.

Lash lay down beside me and Devlin moved back enough so he could hold me, too.

"What are we going to name him?" I threw out.

"How about 'Devlin'?" Devlin said with a little longing.

Both Lash and I looked over at him with a little irritation.

He had the gall to look indignant. "What? It's a good name."

"I want to name him 'Trystan'," Lash said hopefully. "What do you say, Mate?"

"We're going to have the same problem T and Theo did, you and he having the same names," Devlin said grumpily. "And we can't even call

Tryst Jr., 'T'."

"I can go back to 'Lash'," Lash said, resigned. "You all call me that anyway. Besides, I want my son to have my name. We'll call him Tryst Jr."

"That sounds fine," I said nodding. "We'll give him the middle name of Devlin."

"You mean it?" Devlin whispered emotionally.

"Sure," Lash said, grinning over at him. "You're right, it's a good name. And you are my best friend."

"Thank you," Devlin said, wiping at a tear. "Thank you."

"Trystan Devlin Valeras," Lash hissed with pride. "I've got to say, it sounds like a future badass."

I gave him a look, but he just gave me a winning grin of complete happiness. Unwilling to ruin his joy, I relented and smiled back. Soon after, we were asleep.

In dreams, Shaker came to me. "Greetings, lovely Mistress of mine."

"What do you think you're doing here?" I said crossly.

"Hoping to see you," Shaker rumbled. "I am here to congratulate you, Mistress. I'm glad you delivered safely." He gave my hand a gentle kiss.

"Thank you. Now you need to go, Shaker."

"Can I not tempt you?" he rumbled, caressing my bare arm with a hot, clawed hand. "I'd give much to feel your hands on me again."

"We talked about this," I said firmly. "No more dreams. No touching. Now, do you need sustenance?"

"In a few weeks," he rumbled, sounding forlorn, then he suddenly grinned. "Rene is taking care of that for you. She is quite accommodating."

I was not going to ask what that meant, not under any circumstances. "You've been good? No killing innocents?"

"On my earthly body, no." He grinned. "I killed a few men, drug dealers, as I remembered you preferred that they be evildoers. They were tasty."

My stomach rolled. "What other evil have you done?"

"I laid a couple females, no humans," Shaker said impishly. "I'm not sure that was evil as they seemed to enjoy it, on the whole. I did most of the drugs I got from my 'meals' last time I got together with Lash and Dev. I figured you'd think that was good, as I made sure the drugs didn't fall into innocent hands."

I rolled my eyes, then shook my head. "And the cash?"

"Deposited in the places you requested," Shaker said. "Spread across a few charities. Total take was almost ten thousand."

I felt a little evil, but this was the best I could do, given his demon needs for human flesh. "Very good. You have pleased your Mistress, Shaker."

"Then touch me, Mistress. Soothe me with your cool hands."

Part of me still wanted him, remembering how good he'd felt that night I'd let him have me. But I knew better than to give in to temptation. "No, Shaker. Lay here beside me and rest. You've worked hard and I appreciate—"

"I am hard," he rumbled. "You make me hard, Mistress, every time I think of your soft hands on my—"

"Leave," I said crossly. "Now."

Shaker grumbled, and disappeared. A moment later, I awoke.

* * * *

The day after, Devlin came to me as I was holding Tryst on the balcony in Lash's room, and told me Danial was here to see me.

I'd not seen him since that night I'd miscarried when he'd come apologizing for his actions. "He's here? Why right now?"

"He wanted to see your son. He wants to see you. He misses you, Love. Is that so hard to understand?"

I wasn't sure how to feel. Most of me wanted to stay there on the balcony feeling the sun raining down on me and hold Tryst, who was in a warm pile on my lap, hissing in happiness. But the smarter part of me wanted to get this visit over with, because if I didn't see him now, I knew he would just return until I did. Danial was not the type to give up. He might even don protective gear and brave the sunlight if he was in one of his stubborn moods.

"Did he come by car? I didn't hear anyone arrive."

"He teleported via demon in order to see you. You know how much he hates that. See him, please, for me."

Reluctantly, I got up. Tryst let out an irritated hiss as we left the sunlight, but I shushed him. We walked downstairs and into the living room, where Danial waited for me.

He was dressed in an expensive suit, looking handsome. His back was to me. On the table beside him were roses of all colors that he'd just finished putting in some water.

"Did you come from work?"

"From a meeting, yes. Solutions, Inc. is again back on track, even though Theo's abrupt departure is still giving Theoron, Terian, and I some headaches. I've had to do some day work."

Enough pleasantness. "Why did you come?" I said, holding Tryst, who was watching Danial intently.

"Because you have not come to me, or asked to see me, or called once in months," he said, turning around to face me. "I wanted to come see you before things got worse between us than they already are."

"I don't know what you mean," I said, trying to hold onto Tryst, who was struggling hard to slither over to Danial to investigate.

"You do, Love. Devlin has forgiven me. Lash has forgiven me. But you have not."

"I have," I said, holding Tryst with a death grip. "I told you I did."

"Let him down," Danial said, sitting on the couch. "I've come to see him too."

"I'm afraid to," I replied watchfully. "I'm afraid you'll hurt him."

"Likely it is Tryst who'll bite Danial," Lash hissed softly from behind me. "You know he doesn't like strangers. His venom is the strength of my own now, Mate. It's all right."

I reluctantly let Tryst go, and he slithered quickly over to Danial, coiling up at his feet and scenting the air. He ventured closer, pushing down with his body, making it rigid so he could climb onto the couch. When he got up there, he coiled up right beside Danial, until his head was an inch before Danial's, his forked tongue close enough to lick his face.

"This is Danial," Lash said. "He is Devlin's brother, Tryst. So he is something like an uncle to you. He's come to see you, so behave yourself."

Tryst looked over at Lash, and then back at Danial.

"May I give him some meat?" Danial offered, producing a bag. "I got some fish on the way over here. It's haddock."

"If you'll give me a piece first," Lash replied. "Even though you meant well, others could have known why you bought it. I'd rather something happened to me than him."

Danial tossed him a piece, and Lash ate it. After a few moments, he said it was okay for Danial to give some to Tryst.

At first, Tryst was suspicious of the proffered meat, scenting it and turning his head this way and that. But after eating the first piece, he began gulping them down as fast as he could until he had a bunch of large lumps inside the length of him. When the bag was empty, Tryst looked in vain in Danial's pockets for more, and it was comical, to see his entire head rooting around inside the cloth, the rest of him outside twitching in excitement.

"Sorry," Danial said apologetically, patting him awkwardly. "You ate them all."

"Come here, Son," Lash hissed to Trystan. "He wants to see your other form, too."

Trystan immediately went to his father, and Lash shifted him to human form, his appearance that of a year-old baby. Lash swaddled him in a blanket from the couch and handed him to Danial.

Danial held him for a while, Trystan studying him. "He reminds me much of Theoron," Danial said finally. "He's a quiet baby. He has your darker coloring, just as Theoron had mine. But he looks a lot like Sar, also."

I didn't see that, but Lash was nodding. "Hand him back," he said after a moment. "I'll take him for his nap. You two have things to discuss."

Danial handed him Tryst, and Lash left immediately, walking upstairs.

"Will you sit with me?" Danial asked.

I went over and sat in the chair near him, absently touching the roses. "They're beautiful."

"Will there ever be a time you'll want to resume our relationship?"

I gave him points for being direct. "I don't know. But forever is a long time, Danial, as you made a point of saying. Think you can give me longer than a few months?"

"I know what I said; you do not have to remind me. Nevertheless, tell me what I can do to facilitate our reconciliation. I meant what I told you and Lash months ago, as I've tried to prove by coming here today. I was wrong not to accept him as part of the Oath. I want peace."

"Does that mean you've given up on pushing Theo on me?"

Danial narrowed his eyes. "I've given up on you and he reconciling, if that's what you mean."

"Has Devlin told you what he tried?"

Danial let out a breath. "Yes and that it's a death sentence if he comes here. He's still my friend, but I agree you shouldn't see him for a while. He's not himself. I hope that the time alone with Harris will help him come to terms with how things are now. When he returns at Christmas—"

I blinked in surprise. "He's going to miss the Hallows party? What about your security?"

Danial nodded. "Terian's taken Theo's position and it will likely remain that way even when Theo returns. Theo's told me he wants to do my home security, so he can be near Harris. Bear in mind he may not return for good, Sar. He's also talked of opening up a satellite of Solutions, Inc. in the Midwest and working from there. He's checking into it with that State's Ruler. I don't anticipate a problem, if he takes that course."

That was possible with Terian's teleporting skills. Thinking I'd never have to run into Theo again made me weak with relief. However, if I were really Harris's mother, I would react differently. *Play the part.* "Has he mentioned visitation for me with Harris?"

"No. He was killing mad the day you told him never to see you again, and he's still angry with you. I suggest you let him alone until he returns, and broach the subject with him face to face."

"Will Harris be with him when he returns?"

"Yes, of course," Danial replied. "His son is more precious to him than anything. He wanted these months alone to stay with Harris at all times, until he's old enough to protect himself."

"What does Elle think about this?"

To his credit, Danial didn't ask why I as her mother didn't already know. "She's upset he left like he did, but she's relieved too, I think. She has her mind on other things."

I seized on that like a Godiva truffle. "What other things?"

"Is she coming to see Tryst, Jr.?" Danial asked, giving me a sidelong glance that told me he knew something I didn't.

"Yes, tomorrow."

"Make sure Lash is here for her visit and not out on one of his jobs."

"Of course he'll be here," I said defensively. "He's not, um, working right now."

Danial nodded, and got to his feet. "Let her tell you, Sar." His face broke into one of his careful smiles. "It's good news, not bad. I'd tell you if it were bad, you know that."

"I do," I said slowly.

"I'd better be going," he said politely. "Things are going better than I anticipated, and I'd like to leave on that note. I'll take you to dinner sometime soon, if you'd permit me to."

"Come back in a month," I said quietly. "Come back and we'll go to dinner then. Okay?"

"It's a date," Danial said. "About seven?"

"Sounds good."

Devlin suddenly appeared beaming, announcing he would walk Danial out. As they left, I rolled my eyes for not suspecting he had been listening.

"He wasn't the only one eavesdropping," Rene said from behind me. "I confess I was, too."

I turned, ran to her and hugged her. "How are you? I've been busy taking care of Tryst. Devlin said you were resting—"

She nodded. "The birth was difficult. I almost bled to death. But I stopped it with Titus's help and I'm fine now."

"Have you seen Tryst Jr.?"

She nodded. "Devlin carried me in to see him in his tank the morning after you came home. He's beautiful, Sar."

I didn't know where to look, I felt so awkward. "I understand Theo took Harris."

She nodded. "I miss him, yes. But he isn't really mine, and it's

93

better this way for everyone, including me."

"Have you foreseen anything?"

She looked away. "Yes."

"Just 'yes'?" I commented, annoyed. "Talk, tell me what to do, Rene!"

She looked at me, oddly annoyed. "What do you want to do, Sar? The truth."

"Take care of Tryst and sit in the sun," I said guiltily.

"Then do that," she said, relieved.

"Why are you relieved?" I said angrily. "Tell me what you saw!"

"I saw death and pain and loss," she whispered. "I saw you in the middle of it all, defiant."

"What should I do?"

"Do what your heart tells you to do, Sar. This is not a time for duty or for work, this it a time to do what you were meant to do."

"What is that?" I said angrily. "Stop the cryptic crap and tell me!"

"I've said all I can," she said regretfully. "I love you, Sister. Don't think badly of me."

She left abruptly as I sat down fuming, pondering her words.

* * * *

A day later Elle arrived, looking happier than I could remember seeing her in years.

Lash and I hugged her, and then he went to get Trystan. Devlin came back with them. He gave Elle an awkward hug, but his happiness to see her seemed genuine. Stranger still, she seemed happy to see him too, if uncomfortable.

The trouble started when Lash tried to let Elle hold Tryst. Our son scented the air, jerked, and then lunged for her silently, fangs extended. I let out a shriek and so did she. Lash grabbed for Trystan, but only got his tail. But Devlin got in front of Elle in time to take the fangs in his lower arm with a hiss of pain.

Lash quickly pried Trystan's mouth off Devlin, hissing at him furiously for attacking his stepsister. Trystan curled himself in a tight quivering pile, hiding his head. Devlin was sitting on the couch where Elle had helped him.

94

Titus appeared suddenly. "What is it, Devlin?"

"Snakebite," Lash hissed furiously. "I'm very sorry to you, Elle, and to you, Devlin. My son should know better."

"You should know better," Titus said sternly, giving Devlin a vial to drink. "Instinct is all werechildren know. She's a predator by her smell and he's only a week old, Lash."

"I reminded him not to strike as we were walking down the stairs just now." Lash picked up a still quivering Trystan, not mollified. "Since he can't behave, we'll leave you alone to visit." He started from the room.

"Wait!" I said, remembering Danial's words. "Stay here. Let Devlin take him to his tank."

Devlin gave me an astonished look, but he nodded and took a still quivering Trystan from Lash, heading upstairs.

Titus looked over at me and grinned knowingly. "I'll go too, just in case." He followed Devlin out.

Lash folded his arms angrily. "Why'd you stop me from disciplining Tryst, Mate? He needs a stern talking to—"

I gave him a stare to shut up, grabbed his hand, and faced Elle. "You have something to tell us?"

She gave me a shocked look. "Who told you? Dad?"

"Told us what?" Lash hissed quickly, his eagerness to mete out discipline forgotten.

"I'm pregnant," Elle blurted out.

My eyes popped out as my mouth dropped open. "What?"

"Didn't waste any time, did you? Let's see your neck," Lash said happily, going over to her. "There'd better be something there, because I don't see a ring on your finger."

Elle moved her hair out of the way, revealing a gold choker with an eagle dangling. Sapphires sparkled in its eyes.

Lash hugged her hard. "Good. I'm happy for you. Is he here?"

I found my voice. "'He' who? Who are you Oathed to, Elle? You never even told me you had a boyfriend, much less that you were seeing a vampire!"

"Me," Elijah said as he strode to stand next to her. "We were Oathed right before Christmas. We just found out she's pregnant."

95

"Samuel must be pleased," I said, then went crimson from head to toe, and started apologizing.

"It's okay, it's well known my father dislikes weres," Elijah said uncomfortably. "But he's accepted Elle, and he's excited about the baby."

I'd bet. There was something in the way he said it that told me everything wasn't rosy as he was painting it. But Elle was in love with him and he had committed to her. That was all that mattered to me. I hugged her hard. "I'm happy for you, I'm just in shock. When are you due?"

"Next spring," she said happily. "You'll be a grandma, Mom."

I swallowed hard, trying to process that and failing.

Lash came to the rescue. "I'm looking forward to seeing your young, even if I get bitten," he joked. "What do you want for a present? Where are you going to live?"

"We're going to stay at mom's house," Elle said haltingly. "That is, if you'll agree to rent it to us."

I looked at her standing there, my grown up daughter who was about to be a mother. She was so young and yet there was a sureness about her that made me see her as a woman for the first time, and not my little girl. "I won't rent it to you. I'll sign it over to you, with the understanding that if you decide to move you'll give me first dibs to buy it back from you."

"I'm never moving," Elle said with tears on her face. "I want my children to grow up there, to live there with Elijah for the rest of my life."

I hugged her hard again. "I hope you'll be happy there."

"I have been this spring and summer," Elijah said, coloring a bit. "Hope and us, we go for walks at night—"

"Who?" I said.

"I got a dog, Mom. It's a long story, but she's very loyal." She hugged Elijah. "I've been happier this year than I ever remember being."

"Young love is a beautiful thing to behold," Devlin purred from the doorway. Then he crossed to Elijah and shook his hand. "Welcome to the family."

"Like you didn't know all this time," Lash hissed grumpily. "I'm beginning to think everyone knew but us."

"Her pregnancy is news to me," Devlin replied crossly. "Come. Let's have a glass of wine to toast the occasion."

"Just a small one," Elle said firmly. "Dr. Brenda—"

"Of course," Devlin said with a placating gesture. "Come." He led Elle and Elijah out.

Lash hugged me around the waist, and together, we followed them into the kitchen.

"So much good news," I whispered happily.

"We were due some good news," Lash hissed, hugging me.

Chapter Eight

A month later, Danial was there on the dot for our prearranged date. In spite of my apprehension, I was ready and waiting, having left Tryst in Devlin's capable hands as Lash was on guard duty. Ben cordially told me to have a good evening as he shut the front door behind us. Another few moments saw us leaving the gates of Hayden.

I waited for him to ask where I wanted to go and then remembered I was with Danial, not Lash. "Where are we going?"

"The restaurant we had dinner in many years ago when we were first dating."

That meant about an hour drive. I settled into the seat.

The silence lasted for almost a half hour, until Danial abruptly said, "Tell me of Trystan."

I tried to keep the irritation out of my voice. "What do you want to know?"

"What foods does he like? Does he get along with Venus? How about the pets?"

"You must know all this from Devlin. You don't need me to tell you."

"I want you to tell me, Sar. You say Lash makes you happy. I want to hear that the child you had with him makes you as happy as the one we had together."

"Take me back," I said sharply. "There's no point to this, Danial. I don't want to spend the evening listening to your sniping."

"I'm not taking you back," Danial said, his eyes on the road. "You are spending the evening with me. I'm not going to be shut out of your life."

I tried to teleport and couldn't. A rush of fear enveloped me. "Take me back, Danial. Right now!"

"No," he said calmly. "Stop acting like a child and relax."

I took my phone out and began dialing Lash.

He picked up on the first ring. "What is it, Sweetness?"

"I want to come home. Have Titus activate the tracking spell on me—"

"No, Sweetness. You are staying there and talking to him. Things need to be said."

I was shocked. "You...you're not going to come?"

Lash hissed uncomfortably. "You aren't in danger. Devlin asked for this as a favor. Don't worry, Titus knows where you are. He'll come to you if he feels you're afraid."

"You are pissing me off, Lash."

"I'm sorry about that. But this is best. I'll see you when you get home—"

I hung up on him, fuming.

Danial gave me one of his wry smiles, then turned back to the road.

I thought about calling Shaker. Just like that, he was there in my mind. *Mistress?*

I may need you, I thought back to him. *Be on watch, okay? If I call, come immediately.*

Of course. Just call.

I sat back in my seat, soothed to know I had a way out if I needed one.

We got to the restaurant outside Alan's Creek ten minutes later. I stretched as I got out, trying to ease my knotted muscles.

"Come, my Darling," Danial said, offering his arm. "We're a tad late."

"Why don't we go for a walk?" I said flatly. "I'm in no mood to eat. And you can't eat anyway."

"I got a potion from Titus, so I'll have a little," Danial said calmly. "Stop being difficult."

I glared, but reluctantly took his arm. We went inside and were shown to a nice table with a view of the fountain. Seeing it cascading sparked in my mind that this was the same table we'd sat at, all those years ago when we'd come here on one of our first dates. But it wasn't surprising that Danial had remembered and requested it.

When the waitress came, I gave her my order for a glass of wine and for an entrée, trying to hurry the night along. Not to be stymied, Danial ordered a bottle of wine, an appetizer, and an entrée, telling her to take her time, that we were going to have dessert, too.

When she left, I glared at him. "Stop this, please!"

"No," Danial said, unfolding his napkin and utensils. "Either fume if you like or calm down and enjoy yourself. It's your choice. But you are going to spend this evening with me."

"Aren't you tired of forcing me to do things? How is this fun for you?"

"It's not fun," Danial said patiently, as if to a small child. "But I'll not be put off either. And you would be happy to put me off, Sar, for the next ten or twenty years. I'm not waiting that long to heal the rift between us."

"You must be trying to emulate your brother," I said nastily. "Will you be forcing me to go to a hotel with you after dinner? I mean, why stop at food?"

Danial gave me a sad look, and then he gently touched the back of my hand so fast I didn't have time to withdraw it. "Because you know that's never been my way. I've never forced any woman in my life, after how I was conceived. And after what you endured from Michael—"

"Don't say his name," I said desperately, shutting my eyes. "Please."

"I'm sorry, Love. May I touch you?" Danial asked softly.

I nodded, not opening my eyes. I felt him take my hand in his cool one, and then felt him raising my chin. I opened my eyes to look into his.

"Sit with me here. Sit with me and eat, and tell me of yourself. I miss that most of all, Sar. It was one of the things that drew me to you all those years ago."

"What do you want me tell you?"

"About your empathy, to start. Surely you must have rescued some small creature lately?"

I took a breath, and then a breadstick. "All right." I told him the story of a bird I'd rescued from inside of the birdfeeder at Hayden last spring, when he'd crawled inside to get the last seeds and become trapped. When I was done, I did feel better, and more relaxed.

Our appetizer came, and I ate most of it. Then our entrées came, Danial eating only a little of his as we talked. Before I knew it, we were on dessert and I was wondering where the time had gone.

Danial took a sip of his wine. "So V is learning to defend herself, too. I'd thought Devlin too protective to let Lash hurt her, even with her looking in her late teens now. I'm glad he's allowed it."

"She's learning," I said, eating my last bite of cake. "She doesn't have a natural talent for it, like Tryst does, or even as Theoron did. Lash says it'll take some time for her to learn just the basics, which is all he's teaching her. Titus and Leri have offered to give her some lessons in magic too, something Rene's not too happy about—"

"How are she and Dev?" Danial said softly. "I wondered if they were trying for a child. But Dev has not said anything to me."

Then he doesn't want you to know, doof. "She's doing some research," I said vaguely. "She's waiting to tell him until she knows it will work. It's harder for her than for a human, she says, and she doesn't want to dash his hopes. So please don't mention it to him, okay?"

Danial nodded. "I will not. But are you okay with it?"

I nodded. "She loves him. So do I. That's all there is to it."

"Let us go," Danial said, rising to his feet. "They are closing. It's time we left."

I took his hand, and together we walked to his car. Instead of taking the road back to Hayden, Danial took the road toward his own home.

I looked over at him, curious. "What are you doing?"

"We are going to my house. I have something to show you."

I had an inkling of what he had to show me, but just nodded. Before long, we were sitting on the stone bench Theo had carved in Danial's entryway, taking off our shoes.

He led me into the great room, which I was relieved to see was again overloaded with books. "I got rid of the TV; gave it to the foxes along with the video games," Danial said disdainfully. "It was so…commonplace."

I laughed aloud and he gave me a smile.

"Sit with me." He poured me some wine, and we sat on the couch.

After a few minutes of silence, I looked over to find his face was melancholy.

"What is it, Danial?"

"Tell me of what happened, Sar."

"When?" I said, taking a sip.

"With Michael, when you were his captive."

"No." I put down my wine glass with a clatter. "I'm not going to talk about it."

"Yes, you are," Danial said, taking hold of my hand. "You are going to tell me all of it tonight. Because I can see it is festering inside you like a cesspool: all the fear and helplessness. I saw your terror as soon as you knew I had complete power over you tonight—"

He hadn't asked me with him tonight to talk about him and me! "You're wrong! You have no power over me," I snapped, yanking my hand back and getting to my feet. "Stay here. I can drive myself home."

In a blur of movement, Danial grabbed hold of me. I pushed backward, he pulled me forward, and we fell still grappling to the couch. He was struggling hard to hold onto me, as I tried in vain to get away. But his greater strength prevailed and he pushed me to the couch, holding me helpless beneath him.

"Calm down, Sar. Stop fighting me."

"Let me go! Let me go, Danial! I just want to forget it!"

"Devlin said you'd refused to talk about it. Talk to me. You're not alone in this—"

"You're damn right I'm not! Shaker! Come to me!"

In a split second, Shaker was beside me. He grabbed Danial's hands off me, and pushed him hard. He pulled me to my feet, then stepped in front of me and sent Danial and the couch toppling over on its side with a kick of his hoof.

Danial put his head up over the couch's edge, regarding Shaker in shock and horror. "What are *you* doing here?"

I opened my mouth to tell Shaker to say nothing, but I was too late. "My Mistress called, and I answered," he said, looking down at Danial coolly. "If she wishes to leave you, she'll be leaving now."

Shit. I sighed, rubbing my forehead with my fingertips.

Danial looked like he'd been slapped. "Sarelle, you're his mistress?

Since when?"

Oiy. "Since my captivity."

"Are you lovers?" he asked, clearly afraid of the answer.

Shaker rolled his eyes and snorted. "No. She's a pious one."

Danial gathered himself. "Release her and I'll give you my soul in exchange for hers."

Shaker looked at Danial in surprise. "You're a brave one," he rumbled. "I'd love to accept. Alas, I can't take your deal. I do not have rights to Sarelle's soul. My deal is much like Titus's with Devlin."

Danial sort of oozed down into the couch, his relief was so vast. "That's good," he said weakly. "Thank God."

Shit. As much as I'd wanted to leave, now I was going to have to talk to Danial. If I left now, he would be on the phone to Devlin before I pulled out of his driveway or even teleported home with Shaker. He would tell Devlin all of this, and he'd tell Lash. Within the hour, I would be facing three men who would demand I talk to them instead of just one. Danial had always been good at keeping secrets. The question was could I convince him to keep this one for me.

"Mistress, where do you want to go? Back to Hayden?"

"No, Shaker," I said, resigned. "I've got to talk to Danial. But you may leave now."

"No, he can't!" a furious voice rumbled. Titus stepped out of the shadows. A moment later, he hit Shaker with a fireball that blasted him through Danial's great room wall and into the dining room to crash through the table.

"You lying bastard!" Titus shouted. "You told me you'd been in Afghanistan, looting the dead. You were the demon working for Michael! You let him hurt Sar, one of your own Kin!"

"It wasn't my choice," Shaker said with effort, getting to his cloven feet. "I had to."

"You should've gone back to Hell," Titus said bitterly. He hit Shaker with another fireball, knocking Shaker to the floor again. The Hellfire incinerated the table and chairs instantly and scorched the floor, though Shaker didn't burn. "I should send you back right now."

"But you won't," Shaker said painfully, slowly getting up again. "You're my goodie-two shoes brother."

103

Titus punched him in the face and Shaker fell back to land on the floor, black blood glistening on his smashed nose. "I'd do it in a heartbeat," Titus said, standing over him. "But Sar might be hurt if I did, being bound to you. I don't know all the conditions of your deal with her, though I'll know them shortly, all of them. And you'd better believe I'm going to tell Lash about this."

"Don't," I said, putting my hand on Titus's arm. "He's right, he didn't have a choice. And for better or worse, what's done is done."

Titus hugged me. "You're naïve, Kin-daughter. He had the choice to free you and Lash, but instead he saved his own skin. He chose you being hurt over him going back to Hell. I'm not going to forgive that."

Before I could blink, Titus and Shaker disappeared.

Danial had vanished also. A moment later, he came back from the kitchen, dustpan and broom in his hands. Silently we swept up the wreckage. There wasn't much left, just the huge scorch mark on the floor, a few tiny pieces of kindling, and some ashes. When we'd finished, I followed Danial outside and watched him toss the dustbin contents at the edge of the woods.

"Theo carved that for you."

"It was his first piece of completed furniture," Danial replied. "He was so proud of it. He felt so bad after giving it to me, comically realizing only then that I'd never eat at it. But it did get used by Theoron, Elle and you."

"I'm sorry."

"I'd rather be standing here with you now with the table destroyed than be sitting at it alone with its beauty and no memories of us and our loved ones," Danial said gently. "Tables are replaceable. Memories are not." He paused. "Your soul is not."

"He doesn't have my soul. Like he said, the deal was all business."

"Was it? Titus and Devlin have never been intimate, at least to my knowledge."

I shot him a look, and then went to walk away. When he grabbed hold of me, I struck him as hard as I could in the face, enough to knock him backward a step.

"Stop this!" he said sternly. "We have hurt each other enough. Stop."

"How could you do it?" I whispered brokenly. "I loved you. I trusted you. When Rene told me not to, I told her she was crazy, because I knew you, that you'd never hurt me!"

"I could've said the same of you," he said tiredly. "I'd never have thought you'd choose a crude murderer over me, not after everything I've done for you over the years. But love makes us do terrible things." He reached out with a hand, raising my eyes to his. Fear swam in his dark eyes. "Do you love him, your new protector?" He gathered himself. "Are you going to leave me?"

"No," I whispered, wiping away sudden tears. "I didn't want to hurt anyone. It just happened and I feel terrible—"

"Shh," Danial said putting his arm around me. "Come inside." He brought me into his bathroom and handed me a pair of pajamas.

I took them. "Thanks, but I should be going home."

"Put them on. You are staying tonight. And this is a night for us to talk, not make love."

Mystified at what he wanted to talk about now, I put them on. When I came into the bedroom, Danial was waiting for me before the woodstove, also fully dressed in a robe and what looked like long johns. He offered me a robe. "In case you're cold."

I was hot from being nervous and upset. I took it and put it aside. "I've never known you to wear nightclothes."

"I have not slept alone stark naked for centuries," Danial said with a faint smile. "I get cold. Before there were electric blankets or your warm body to comfort me, I used stove irons and nightclothes like these. Please sit with me."

I sat down beside him and he handed me a glass of wine. In his hand was a glass of blood.

"Does it bother you?" Danial said, glancing at me, then away. "It's spiked with a drug to calm me. I needed it, but—"

"No, I don't mind. But I've never known you to take anything. Why are you so upset?"

"You need to talk. I need to listen." He sipped. "Devlin, you were attracted to. It's not the same—" He cut off abruptly, and took another swallow. "A man hurt you. I know only you got pregnant with Lash's babies and lost them, when Cyrus tried to kill you. And that Michael thought they were his children, which means he had cause to think that." He took another swallow. "Just knowing that little piece of information has been enough for me not to be able to sleep without drugs since I realized who you really were."

"Can you spike mine, too?" I said, offering him my glass. "I need more than alcohol to talk about what happened."

"Just a little," Danial said, sliding out a packet from his robe pocket. "Brenda prescribed them for me. But there's a human dosage listed on the label, so it should be safe enough." He tapped a tiny amount of lavender powder into my glass.

I swirled it, then sipped, hoping to sag in chemical relief. But I felt nothing.

"I know you were taken with Lash the night Peter attacked Hayden. You can start there if you want to."

"I don't want to relive it, Danial. It was bad enough going through the first time."

"I understand—"

"Bullshit, you understand! How could you understand?"

"Do you think women are the only ones who are raped?"

I felt sick, sipped again, and then slowly let my eyes drift over to him. He was gazing into the fire. By his voice, he wasn't talking about his mother.

"When?"

"It was a long, long time ago," Danial said in an old voice. "When I was human, before I married. I'd left the village I was born in to find my way in the world. But my pretty face was more of a curse than a blessing." He sipped. "The world was different then, when not everyone had rights. As a peasant, I had none." Danial glanced at me. "Devlin does not know of this, nor does Theo. And I'd appreciate you not telling Lash."

"Of course," I managed to choke out. "I won't tell anyone. I'm sorry."

"So am I," Danial remarked bitterly, turning back to the flames.

"Did you get vengeance? Did you kill the man?"

"Yes," Danial said after a moment. "But killing him didn't make my feelings of being victimized go away. I could not tell my wife of the time. I couldn't bring myself to tell my priest. I could tell no one but God. He didn't seem to care, as some time after I was made vampire, it happened again. And this time, it wasn't for a night." He sipped his wine. "This time, it was for years."

Shit, I didn't know what to do, hug him, or try not to touch him, as he recounted this. No wonder he'd never spoken of his past. "I'm sorry, Oathed One."

"I killed him, too," Danial said hollowly. "He was older than I by a hundred years, but he was careless, despite that he was much stronger and faster. It took a decade for me to plan, and another year to carry out. In addition, he had friends, a lot of friends. They hunted me all across Europe, sending demons after me, until finally I sought a monastery for sanctuary. It was some years later that Devlin found me there. It killed me then that he was happy and had everything yet again when I had nothing but agony. That was why I seduced Anna." He smiled faintly. "But the joke was on me there, too. I ended up loving her myself. It haunted me for many years, the last words she heard me speak. I'd give a lot to go back and leave her with kinder ones."

"I'm sorry," I said, wiping away tears. "I'm sorry, for all the times I wanted to know of your past and wouldn't let it go."

"You couldn't have known," Danial said, still looking into the fire. "And I didn't want you to. I didn't want anyone to know, Sarelle. But I should've told someone years ago and unburdened myself. I feel a great weight lifted, not trying to carry that secret with me anymore."

He slipped an arm around my shoulders. "Tell me, Love. Tell me everything."

I did as he asked, though I was careful to vague up the details of Lash's immunity to magic, and his plans to give the source of that immunity to me in my story, saying only he'd planned to buy my freedom with his death, if not kill Michael. But Danial wasn't really interested in that part, anyway. When the tale was done, I was exhausted, though I did feel a lot better. It was nearly four a.m. Danial put our empty glasses aside and led me to his bed. We held each other tightly after we got under the covers.

"I'd like to promise you that what happened will never happen to you again," Danial whispered softly. "But forever is a long time, Love,

107

and I cannot, just as I can't promise Devlin won't ever stray, or that I will not be staked by a hunter and burnt to ash, or Lash won't be killed in some duel to the death some year—"

I struggled in his arms, frantic, but he held me tightly.

"I can only promise that no matter what happens, I'll do my best to be here for you. That so long as I live, I will be here to listen, to comfort, and to hold you like this, no matter what destiny or fate hands either of us. And I pray to God that our lives will be filled with happy times, and watching your children and ours grow up, and have their own children, and grandchildren. I pray that the worst of our trials are over, because you and I have had enough bad things in our years so far to last us the rest of eternity."

"I agree," I whispered back. "I believe you, that some things can't be adverted. And I promise you the same thing: that I'll be here for you, to listen, and hold you, until my end."

"Good," Danial said softly, kissing my forehead. "I was hoping you'd say that."

"Unless you stray," I said in a warning tone.

"You know me better than to think that," Danial said chidingly. "There is only you and Theoron and Elle—"

"And Solutions, Inc."

"Well, of course," Danial said quickly, turning sly. "I need something to do when you are off with my brother or Lash, don't I? Especially as you don't want me straying."

"Shh," I said, giving him a kiss. "Go to sleep. It's going to be dawn soon."

"It is dawn," Danial said, yawning. "Time for bed for all good vampires and naughty Oathed Ones."

"I'm not naughty."

"You bedded a demon, my dear. That's not nice."

"I explained that."

"I think you glossed over something, as you sound guilty. But it's not my concern. Your choker remains on, which means Devlin must have okayed it."

"It was a mistake, one I'm not going to repeat."

"I've made more than a few like that," Danial replied. "I'll keep your secret, as its obvious you want me to. How long do you think you can keep you being bound to Shaker from Devlin? He would not have kept that from me, so he must not know."

"As long as I can."

"Why? He and Lash will not be on anyone's side but yours."

"Neither of them were going to save me." I remained bitter, even as I tried to lighten my tone. "I had to save myself the only way I could." I glanced over at him. "Look how you took the news."

"I understand," he sighed. "Get some rest. In the evening we'll talk more."

* * * *

When I woke up, the bedside clock said seven. Looking closer, the clock wasn't mine. Where was I?

Then Danial stretched beside me, and last night's events came crashing down on me like a brick. "Are you hungry?" he said, rubbing sleep from his eyes. "There's nothing here but meat for the guards, but I could send one of the guards for pizza."

"Are you hungry?" I whispered seductively.

"Of course," Danial said, nuzzling me. "But that's going to wait until we talk further. Let's clean up, and resume our conversation, Oathed One."

Grumble.

Having showered and dressed in some of my clothes I'd left there some time ago, we sat down together in the great room.

"I'll order a new table tonight," Danial said, eyeing the scorch mark on the dining room floor. "If I move a rug in there, no one should be the wiser. The hole in the wall I can pass off as remodeling." He gave a faint smile. "I always wanted the entry to the great room a little wider, anyway."

"Yeah, except for the lingering stench of sulfur, you've got everything covered, I remarked nastily. "Now what did you want to talk about?" I reclined back on the couch. "It wasn't a replacement table."

"You admitting to Devlin what Shaker is to you now," Danial said patiently. "And about you forgiving me for what I did."

"We've been over both. There's nothing to talk about."

109

"I'll give you that in regards to the former, but not the latter," he said neutrally.

"I forgive you. I understand why you felt you should do it. If Lash forgives you and Devlin does, than I can, too."

"But you don't trust me."

"I trust you not to hurt me. I don't trust you not to hurt Tryst, no. In addition, I might not ever feel different about that. I remember you a few months ago in this room, telling me you'd have killed him except you were worried for Devlin's child—"

"I didn't mean that. What I said that day I said out of anger—"

"And what you did you did out of anger, too, because of your old grudge against Lash."

Danial's eyes bled to red in a second, and then slowly returned to dark. "He's been an enemy of mine for all the time I'd known him, some sixty odd years. I was used to Devlin taking my loved ones from me by that time. Hell, I expected that to happen when you met him! But to go through everything we have together, and then have you want Lash…It made me lose all reason." He cleared his throat. "I'm not a monster, Sar. The potion was not supposed to hurt the children already in you, just allow you to conceive an additional one with Theo. That was all I wanted."

"Why? I'm not with him anymore."

"Because he loves you and he'd lost everything in the last year. He lost Elle to me, and she's never really thought of him as anything but a distant uncle, if that. He lost you to Devlin, even when he fought with everything he had. But more than anything else, he lost his son Devon—"

"He wasn't the only one who lost a son."

"It was his only son, Sar. You have five living children, including Elle."

"I'll repeat it, as clearly you didn't hear me the first time: he is not the only one. I have a son I've never seen, except in pictures. I don't know where they are, except they're out west."

"Harris will have questions about you. Soon, Theo will be calling you to arrange a visit. The question is, when he does, are you going to be able to resist falling in love with him again?"

110

"I'll restrain myself somehow," I said sharply. "You're getting off track, Danial."

"So I am," Danial said, getting to his feet. "I've taken enough of your time away from your son. I'll walk you out. One of the foxes can drive you home, if you'd prefer not to teleport."

I stood there staring at him, utterly shocked that he didn't want to be intimate.

Before I could cover it, he caught my eye. "What is it?"

"Do you not want me, now I'm bound to a demon?"

He hugged me. "No," he said gently. "It is me who wasn't sure if you'd accept me now, knowing what you do about what happened to me. I thought you might need some time." He added softly, "I thought you might even not desire me anymore. What I admitted…for a long time it made me feel less than a man, that I didn't find a way to avert it. What is attractive about that?"

I kissed him gently. "I have never once not wanted you or found you anything but sexy. Nothing you could tell me about yourself would change that I love you." I hugged him. "Do you find me not sexy, because of what happened to me?"

He gave me a smile. "No." Then he covered my lips with his.

* * * *

A few hours later, we lay holding each other, dozing. I reluctantly looked at my watch. "I should go, Danial. It's almost noon—"

"Stay with me," he whispered. "I've missed you very much, Sweetheart."

How many times had he asked me to stay and I'd put him off, or had to leave? *Too many times.* Another few hours wouldn't hurt. Devlin knew where I was and so did Lash. I settled back down next to him. "I'll stay."

"Tell me our story," he whispered.

"What part?"

"From the beginning," he said. "I remember so much of what we were, but my memories have another woman's face over yours, another woman's body, and voice. Some of what I remember is from another time period, so that woman must be Brianna or another one of my lovers.

111

As a result, I cannot trust my memories of us, any of them. Though I've asked Devlin to tell me, he said he could not, as I hadn't shared much of those first years we were together with him. Theo no doubt remembers, but he's not inclined to tell me. Terian I can't speak to either." He paused. "You are the only one who knows it all. Please tell me of what happened."

"Tell me where to begin. You said that you remember us on my couch, so—"

"From the night you found me, from the beginning. Leave nothing out," Danial said, letting out a deep breath. "And please tell me the truth. Even if you would rather I'd not remember a certain event happened, I need to know if it did." He produced a notebook and pen. "With the record I'll make of it, enough time, and a lot of memorization, I can hopefully reshape my memories into something resembling reality."

It took most of that day, the notebook's twenty pages, a bottle of wine, some water, a pizza, a bag of chips, a box of chocolates, and a few small drinks of my blood, but I told him everything of us from the beginning. We cried together over some of the bad parts where we'd hurt each other, and apologized again. Several times, we made love, because hearing how easily we might never have found ourselves here at this place and time was enough to make us reach for one another, desperate for the reassurance of physical closeness.

"—and you know the rest," I finished. "How I was saving Frank in Lash's Jacuzzi and you walked in and realized who I was."

Danial made a final note, and laid the notebook aside. "Thank you, Love. I know it wasn't easy to do, but you've gone a long way towards restoring my sanity." He kissed me gently. "But you are overdue. I admit, I have a meeting in four hours I must prepare for."

I grinned. "Go ahead. I'll see you sometime soon."

"Dinner next Friday?" he offered. "I'd love to take you out again, and then have you spend the night. My schedule is tight for most of the next five months, but I still wish to see you at least once a week."

"Sounds good," I said, giving him a kiss. "Watch your back."

"Indeed," he said, grabbing me tight. "We need a few months of peace, if not years. I'll be careful."

Forever

Chapter Nine

A week later, I heard a scream, and then a thump.

"Sar, come get your son!" our maid Vera yelled, annoyed.

I ran upstairs, but didn't see Tryst Jr. "Where?"

"In my laundry basket," Vera fumed. "He was coiled up in the warm clothes."

I went through the basket, and sure enough, there my son was, basking in the heat of the clothes fresh out of the dryer. "Come here, you," I said, picking Tryst Jr. up. He hissed happily and twined up around my neck, resting his head on my shoulder. "Didn't I tell you twice this week not to do that? I told you if you did it again I was going to tell your father." Tryst Jr. immediately tried to let go of me to slither away, but I grabbed tight hold of him. I turned to Vera. "Sorry about that."

Vera nodded, but she didn't look happy. "When I took this job, ma'am, it was with the stipulation that there wouldn't be critters roaming free. I know what kind of dangerous things...um, werecreatures that vampires keep for guards. I know he doesn't mean any harm, I was just startled."

"It won't happen again, and he's sorry," I said frostily, making sure she knew referring to Tryst Jr. as a thing had better not ever happen again, either. "Thank you."

I took a squirming Tryst Jr. into Lash. He was dozing in his bedroom as he'd been up most of the night. Per usual, even as quiet as I was, he awoke instantly when he heard the knob turn, and his knife was in his hand before I spoke. "It's just me."

"It's okay," Lash rasped, putting down the knife. "I was having a nightmare anyway. What is it?"

"Your son needs a talking to. He was in the laundry and Vera's upset."

Lash hissed dangerously. Tryst Jr. cowered, hissing fearfully. Lash took him from me carefully, hissed a short lecture to him in snake, and finally Tryst Jr. nodded.

Lash handed him back. "He said it just feels really good, he's sorry, and he won't do it again. Likely it's because he's been inside for two weeks with all the rain. But the forecast says this week will be sunny, so we can sunbathe."

That was a relief. I'd been depressed from the rain and damp myself.

"I've been meaning to ask you," Lash said very hesitantly. "Would you consider changing with me, and not having sex? Just lying with our son on our rock as snakes? I'd like to do that very much. It'll be another month or so before my need to mate in animal form returns."

"Of course." I hugged him. "But I'll need to grab you a little later on for some human lovin'."

Lash hugged me tight and let out a long hiss. "God, I love you, Sweetness. I don't know what I did without you all these years. My life before you seems a wasteland."

"I'm happy to have you, too," I said, kissing him.

"Not as happy as I am. You're the perfect mate; loving, a good mother, smart, strong, and you always want me."

I rolled my eyes. "You've told me that a dozen times in the past week. I never understood the last part, Tryst."

"I love that you always want me."

"Because you want me," I said with a grin. "Women are turned on by seeing how much a man desires them, and you always desire me so much—"

"No," Lash said, depressed. "No human woman ever liked the feel of my forked tongue, though a few tolerated it to be nice to me. But really, they felt the same way for me. Not a one of them wanted me, all of me, not until you." He kissed me again. "That night, when I first kissed you back...well, I did it because I expected you to recoil when you felt my tongue. I didn't know what else to do to get you to back off, and I was sure that would do it. When you liked it, I was amazed, so amazed for a moment I forgot myself and put you on the bed so I could have you—"

"I wanted you so bad that night," I laughed, hugging him. "That tongue of yours hooked me, it felt so good."

"I know," Lash hissed with a grin. "That's why I went down on you that night at Davy's, I knew you'd like that if you liked my kisses." He paused, lost in thought. "It was such a shock, you wanting me." He turned bitter. "I've never been sought after. My whole life, I've had women sticking their noses up at me—"

"What?" I said, shocked. "Why?"

"When I was younger, because I was so mean-looking. Later in my life, it was because I was so old. Weres are half-animal. Mating is usually between the youngest and strongest, because they are the most fertile. I might have been strong, famous, and notorious, but I wasn't young or fertile at all, and they could smell it. It was a turnoff for them."

"But these weresnakes, they didn't want children and they were going to be..."—*how to say "paid for it" in a nice way*— "... um..."

"Yes," Lash said uncomfortably. "But women of the streets are discerning, too, especially weresnakes. They made it clear that once I was done, I'd better pay up and get lost, because they got no pleasure out of being with me, no matter what I did or didn't do."

"Lys seemed to like you well enough, she was jealous of Cin. And Cin herself—"

"Cin wanted Lash the badass to fuck her brains out, the rougher the better," Lash said crudely. "That was all she wanted him for, ever." He paused. "Lyssa was an exception. She really did want me for more than sex. We had a good thing, a few years back. I think she's still out west partying, I got a postcard a month ago—"

I'd heard all I was going to hear about fucking Lys. And from now on, I would be checking the mail, too, every time I got an opportunity. "Lash, it's okay. I'm your mate. I love you and the past doesn't matter."

He didn't take my offered comfort. "I didn't fit anywhere. I wasn't welcomed among humans for being snake and not among my own kind for being too much demon—"

"What?"

"I was too warm," Lash said with a sigh. "The demon blood in that

116

potion I drank for so many years made me warmer, warm enough so that I could be with a human. Weresnake women hated it, said I felt like a half-breed. I always had my fangs, forked tongue, flat eyes, and scales, so no human wanted me. Worst of all, I had the desire of a demon. They like sex more than any being. So I was horny a good deal, snakelike, and too warm. It was a disaster." He laughed mockingly. "Thank God for prostitutes."

"You fit with me," I said, kissing him. "You always will, no matter what you look like or if you are warm or cool. Besides, I like how you feel. You aren't cold at all."

"Humans don't notice the difference, like I said. Sun didn't seem to anyway—"

Shock hit me like an ice water bath. I turned to Lash, who'd gone still, looking at the floor. "What?"

Lash didn't say anything.

"When?" I choked out.

"Before I met you," He wouldn't meet my eyes. "Back when you were with Danial and had first brought back Theo. Before you were with Devlin, when she wasn't with anyone, either."

"How many nights?"

"Two."

Sun had wanted a repeat performance and Lash had, too. "Did you love her?"

"No. I've only loved one woman, you."

"Do you still think about her?"

"She loved Terian even then, not me. Sar, I—"

"Do you still think about her?" My tone was brittle.

"No. You're my mate; I think about you. That part of my life is done."

But is it done for Sun? I remembered her flirting with him hot and heavy that night at the Haunt. *Fuck, I knew there was something to their dancing and mouthing the words of that song to each other.* "Why didn't you tell me? You said you hadn't been with a human in decades!"

I expected Lash to say many things. In retrospect, I should have anticipated just what he said. "She said she didn't want anyone to know she'd been with me," Lash said flatly. "So I told her I wouldn't say

117

anything to anyone, that it would be like it never happened."

Sun had been embarrassed for being with him, though she'd obviously liked it and they'd both been single. I felt scathing dislike of her for using him and then just telling him to pretend it never happened.

"I didn't love her. She was a friend, we were both lonely, and when she kissed me—"

Sun made the initial advance? I got even angrier.

"Don't be angry with me, please—"

"I'm not, I'm fucking furious with her."

"Don't be angry with her. I didn't want you to know, either. It was a lifetime ago, her and me. Nothing's going to happen now; we're both happy with other people. Whatever chance there was for me and she is long gone."

"She never gave you a chance—"

"It was me who didn't give her one. That was meant to happen so I could find you, Sweetness. I want to be right here with you, not with her. There's only you."

"But—"

"There's only you."

I relaxed back into him as he rubbed his face against my neck.

"Are we okay?" he asked quietly.

"Yes," I said, letting go of my anger for the moment. "We are."

* * * *

The next day I went looking for Sundown. I found her sunbathing on the deck of the werecompound in a tiny bikini. *I should be glad she has any clothes on at all.*

"Sar," she said with a smile. "Why don't you lay out with me, it's so warm—"

"Warm as Lash was, the nights you and he got it on?"

Sun went crimson from her heat to her feet. I got angrier with her, if that was possible, because some of it wasn't that she was embarrassed I knew. She was embarrassed anyone knew.

"Sar, I—"

"Yes, Sun? You what? Fucked him and told him never to breathe a word of it, because you were ashamed?"

118

"No, I—"

"Yes," I said with gritted teeth. "That's exactly what happened."

"No, I cared about him," Sun said, her eyes filling. "I asked him to stay here, and he said he couldn't, but really it was that he wouldn't. He was the one who told me you were in love with Theo and not with Tears—"

She was either a good actress or she was telling the truth. "I was never in love with Tears!"

"I thought you were! I called here one day to talk to Theo, years ago, to warn you about Devlin, that he still wanted you! But Terian answered, told me Theo had disappeared a year ago and that you were pregnant, and I thought you were together! I met up with Lash one night. He'd been a friend when I needed one, months before—"

What the hell does that mean? My mate apparently had left out a good bit of detail.

"—he said he was leaving. One thing led to another, we were together—"

"It doesn't take much for you to sleep with someone, does it?"

"You're the one with children by four different men, not me," Sun said pointedly, getting angry. "After a night with him, I wanted more. Lash was very giving, as I'm sure you know—"

"Two nights *is* more."

"More than sex, you bitch! I wanted to see if it would work, to at least try! Next to Terian he was the one man who seemed to care about me, more than just to make himself feel good."

I felt sick for her. It was in her voice that no one besides Tears had ever really loved her.

"—but he wouldn't stay and I couldn't go with him! Do you know why? Because of you! Because he couldn't risk taking me with him because Devlin had a thing for you still!"

"I'm sorry about that—"

"Fuck you, Sar! You're SORRY? Do you know what your vampire did to me? Do you know what he let that guard Kev do to me? I couldn't move without pain for days afterward!"

I went to her. She struggled, but I hugged her anyway and she began to cry in my arms. "I'm sorry. I understand a lot better why you've always treated me like you have."

"I don't know how you can stand to be with him," Sundown said, chilled. "He's a maniac. What he did to me was just practice for you."

"Dev isn't the same as when you knew him."

"You're lying to yourself," she said flatly. "He hasn't changed."

"Being a father changed him. I didn't do it, V did. He finds ways to control the darkness inside him. And having Rene in his life again made the difference." I briefly thanked Rene again mentally, feeling a slight touch of her mind before she severed the connection.

Sun didn't reply.

"I'm sorry for coming here and yelling. I just love Lash and was upset, because I'd thought you hurt him."

"I would never hurt him. It was me who called that night from Davy's, when he'd broken up with you, and he was going to kill himself—"

I looked at her with horror. *That can't be true.* "No—"

"He said he'd had enough, that he couldn't take being without you. So I called Devlin, though it was the last thing I ever wanted to do. I called, told him you had fought, and what Lash was planning. He said he'd come in time—"

"He did," I croaked out, hugging her as tight as I could. "And not just for Lash, Sun."

She stared at me, aghast. "You also planned to—?"

"I wasn't thinking clearly that night, I was upset, too. I'd drunk a bottle of wine and was trying to play vampire savior."

"I know how that goes," she laughed, and gave me a smile. "The drinking a whole bottle, not the vampire-saving part."

"Trust me, it sucks," I said flatly, and both of us burst out laughing.

"If you want some time, we could sunbathe," I said hesitantly. "I could bring a suit, when I visit Danial."

"Maybe a movie instead," she said quickly, a shadow crossing her face.

"Sure," I replied just as fast, not wanting to ruin a good thing. "Just give me a call on my cell, Cia knows it."

"I will next week," she said, grabbing her towel. "I'll get Cia the wonder foxsitter for Sunrise. I always keep some partridge in the freezer

120

in case I need to bribe her."

I laughed, wondering why I'd never realized she was this funny. "Sounds good."

As I walked away, my guilt over my dream with Terian threatened to overwhelm my good sense, telling me to run back to her and admit how he had come to me in the guise of Lash and had me. She'd been honest, and here I was hiding this big lie. Instead, I made myself keep walking. I hadn't been the instigator of what happened, just the victim. Bringing it up now would only ruin Sundown's faith in Terian, which by her face was still shaky even when it came to small things like him seeing me in a bathing suit. It was Terian's place to tell her, and he hadn't. I'd leave it at that.

When I returned home, Rene was waiting for me in the kitchen. I gave her a hug, excited to see her. "Where've you been, Sister? You've been gone two weeks."

"Helping Mad," she said grumpily. "With Leri gone, all of her sorceress duties have fallen to me." She poured us some wine. "I love magic, don't get me wrong. But I really hate the political bullshit these State Rulers spout constantly. It wears on the nerves."

"Have some chocolate." I handed her a box, and she popped a truffle in her mouth. "Now what happened?"

"Peter doesn't like Mad because he's a chauvinist pig. Hector doesn't trust Peter now he's a vampire. Neither of them likes Lash. Mad tries to get them all to work together, and most of the time it backfires, and one of them walks off with their men." She rubbed her eyes. "I'd like to meld them into one being for a week, so they'd have to work together or die."

I laughed uneasily, thinking it was 50-50 she was kidding. "Can I help? You've taught me most of the healing there is, or so you've said. I've almost mastered the drawing out poison spell, so we could move on."

"No, Sister," she said gently. "You keep your magic for emergencies only. Besides Titus and me, you're the only one here who can do healing well. If Titus was in Hell and I was gone on some vampire business, it would be left up to you."

I'd been feeling miffed she'd refused my help. Now I was slightly

121

panicked that the well being of everyone at Hayden might someday rest in my novice hands. "I'll practice."

"Are you making dinner?" she said, popping another truffle. "I'm hungry. I'll need to teleport back in a few hours. "

"Vera is, I think," I replied. "She should be down soon, it's close to six."

Vera walked in, giving me a hurried smile. "Sorry I'm so late." She took down a pot, and began putting water in it. "How's pasta sound, Ladies? I made some sauce earlier."

"Make extra," Rene said. "Lash will be back before dawn, and he said he'd be hungry."

My mouth watered. "Pasta sounds great. V's in her room, I can get her when it's ready. You didn't have any trouble with Tryst today, did you, Vera?"

She shook her head. "No. But I did finally tackle Lash's room. My God, there were cobwebs the size of yarn balls in that bathroom—"

I looked at her in horror. Then I bolted for the stairs, Rene behind me. I ran up, threw open Lash's door, and dashed into the bathroom.

The Jacuzzi tub was sparkling clean and smelled of citrus. And the little nook where Frank always crouched was empty.

"I'm sorry," Rene said gently, hugging me.

I rounded on her in irrational fury. "Sorry for what, Rene? You know for what, don't you? Because you foresaw this and didn't warn me! You let him die!" I pushed her away roughly.

She gave me a last pitying look, then abruptly left, the door of her room closing with a click. Tryst Jr. curled up my leg, his body still hot from the heated rock in his tank. He nudged me with his nose, and then squeezed me gently with his body, trying to comfort me.

"Thanks," I said sadly, picking him up. "I needed a hug. Because it's really my fault for not telling Vera to leave the tub alone, not Rene's."

He squeezed me again gently.

"Let's get you dinner," I said tiredly. "You must be hungry."

* * * *

I waited up for Lash, wanting to tell him the bad news about Frank.

122

Sure, it was silly, but we'd thought of Frank as a kind of pet now for months. Mostly I wanted to hear him assure me that another spider was bound to crawl in and make his home in the same place. But it was Devlin who finally entered Lash's room a little after midnight.

I put down my book. "What's wrong?"

"Nothing," he soothed immediately. "Lash isn't coming home. He's got a large nest of vampires to clean out of an urban part of Philadelphia. They've been subsiding on pets, squirrels, and rats." He wrinkled his nose. "Why would anyone consider that a good way to spend a year, much less decades?" He shut the door behind him.

"Are you staying here, then?"

He picked me up. "No, you are joining me and the rest of the family in my room."

"I can walk," I said, easing out of his arms.

"I was trying to be romantic," Devlin grumbled. "But walk yourself if you want to."

A few minutes later, I'd said another goodnight to Trystan Jr., and the dogs, and was under the covers, Devlin lying beside me.

"Love, I have news for you. Samuel has achieved success with your blood sample. I need to go tomorrow to check his women."

"Women, plural?"

Dev nodded. "He's taking no chances with a miscarriage. The initial sampling I did was a dead ringer for your blood. Now that she's pregnant, I need to make sure that she's not close to turning."

"Isn't Samuel old enough to tell that himself?"

"He's not turned many vampires, in spite of living so long. Those he has turned have usually been men. It won't take long, but I'll be gone most of tomorrow. Rene will go with me as guard, as Lash will need to sleep. Titus and Kyle will be here to watch over things."

"That should be fine," I said easily. "Be safe."

Chapter Ten

The next morning, I spent with V. She did some of her charity work, which I helped her with, and then we went for a three-mile hike around Hayden with Honey. After we returned, we'd planned to go out for a nice lunch. Instead, I ended up teleporting her to Danial's after the walk, when she got a last minute call asking her to babysit Sunrise.

"I don't know why she asked for you, either," I said as I dropped her off. "Cia must be busy. I know from Danial that since Theo left, the guards are stretched thin watching things here and for all the Solution's, Inc. meetings. It's good of you to help out."

"She did sound desperate." V shrugged. "She said she'd get Terian to take me home, but it wouldn't be until late tonight. We'll have to have dinner another day."

"Sure." I gave her a hug. "See you later."

I arrived back at Hayden, exhausted and starving. The first thing I saw as I walked into Hayden was Tryst who slithered up to greet me.

"Let's get some lunch," I told him. "C'mon."

"I've just had lunch," he hissed back in snake. "Dad's back and he's awake."

The second thing I saw was Sun sitting at the kitchen table, drinking scotch. She saw me, and gave me a hate-filled look.

Shit. "Go upstairs, and take a nap," I told Trystan. "I'll call you, when its time for dinner."

Tryst nodded and slithered up the stairs out of sight.

As soon as he was gone, Sundown spoke, her words slurred. "Tell me the truth, Sar. Did you ever have sex with Terian?"

I sat down at the table. "Yes, because I thought he was Lash. But it

124

was only in dreams."

"Explain, Sweetness," Lash hissed furiously in my ear, grabbing hold of me and squeezing me so tight I almost couldn't breathe. "When was this?"

I tried not to panic. "Back, when you were in jail. It was in dreams only, as I just said."

"You lied to me," Lash hissed, angrier. "You said he never was in your dreams!"

I began to get angry. "I didn't remember! Not until Cyrus did a spell, which restored my memory of it. And it wasn't my choice to dream what happened, Lash!"

"God damn him," Sun spat out, downing another shot. "God damn demon!"

"Why didn't you tell me?" Lash hissed menacingly. "Why did I have to hear this from someone else more than a year after Cyrus is dead?"

"What was the point in mentioning it? Terian and Sun were happy. I was ashamed, Lash! I didn't know anything was odd until he called me Baby in the dream. I confronted him and he revealed himself. I told him our friendship was over, that I was furious. He sent me to another dream, and when I woke, my memory of what had happened was gone."

"Bastard," Sun said, downing another shot. "God damn you, Terian!"

"I'm going now to kick his ass." Lash let me go, and started for the door. "And I want a few words with you, Sweetness, when I get back."

"No," Sun said, wiping away her tears and standing unsteadily. "I'll go tell him I know and see what he has to say." She swallowed. "Kicking his ass isn't going to solve anything."

"Sun, I'm sorry," I murmured. "I didn't want to tell you."

"Sar, it's not your fault. You didn't know it was Terian. He used a forgetting spell on you, by the sounds of it."

"He gave me a potion to give me good dreams. It was around the time I was leaving Theo, and upset. The potion let Terian ride my dream."

"For all his fucking words about being so honorable," she said bitterly.

"Terian made a mistake." I paused. "Forgive him, Sun. Go home and forget you know this. It's not worth ruining what you two have now."

"I can't." Sun gave me a sad smile and walked out. "Goodbye."

"Should we really let her drive?" I asked, turning to Lash.

"She'll be fine, Sar," Lash said, pouring himself a large shot. "She's only had four shots. For her that's nothing."

I restrained myself from saying something cutting to him about how well he knew her. I sat down instead.

"You should have told me." Accusation was heavy in his words.

"I wasn't with him when I was with you, Lash. Why are you so upset? I've never asked you about any of the other women you were with over the years."

"I'm upset because I didn't know. And I didn't know because you didn't tell me."

"Look, I didn't tell you for the same reasons I just told her to forget it! This wasn't an affair I had, it happened before we were mated. Plus I didn't want you fighting him, Lash! Sun and he are trying hard to make their marriage work! They have enough strikes against them, with him going to live so much longer than her and stay young!"

"You sure you thought he was me, Sweetness?" Lash hissed sarcastically.

Bastard. "Yes, you ass! I didn't want him, and I told him that, that I was disgusted with him and that our friendship was over! He has never come back! If he had, I'd have told you at once!"

"So you've never pined for a demon's touch?"

All my guilt crashed into me like a tractor-trailer going seventy. Because I had asked a demon into my arms, it just hadn't been Terian. It had been Shaker.

"Sarelle!" Lash faced me, his eyes furious. "Who were you thinking of?" he hissed low and dangerous. "I can smell the lust coming off you. Are you thinking of Terian?"

"No."

"Then who are you thinking of? Answer me!"

It would be so easy to lie, to say I'd been thinking of Devlin. But I hadn't been. I'd sworn to myself never to lie to him. If I wanted to stay

126

his mate, I needed to tell him the truth. "Shaker," I said, sitting down and pouring myself a triple shot. "He also was intimate with me in dreams."

"What?" Lash said, visibly shocked. "Him? Why? When? You've never spent any time with him except when I've been there, too."

"He was the one who gave me the idea to use your resistance to magic to subvert Cyrus's negation of the tracking spell on me. He helped me contact Devlin."

"So you slept with him as a reward?" Lash said, appalled.

"He had no way to tell me except in dreams and my dreams were monitored by Cyrus. So he pretended it was a fantasy, which involved sex. As soon as we weren't being watched, he told me and then I woke up and bit you—"

"Shit, I knew you were dreaming of sex that day," Lash said irritably. "You were way too into me for just waking up."

Why does he always have to be so hurtful? "I'm his Mistress. That was his price for helping me and you, and leaving Rene alone." I shot him a scathing glance. "And stop being so goddamned crass!"

Lash rolled his eyes. "Nice of him to be so generous. So that was the only time, Mate?"

Blood suffused my face. "There was one other dream, right after we came back—"

Lash swore, and then abruptly put his fist through the kitchen table, splintering it in half. I leapt back, avoiding the splash as the whiskey bottle shattered, and pushed myself tight to the wall, trying to make myself small as possible.

Lash kicked the table remnants again, breaking them further into shards as he swore again. He stood there with his back to me, his form vibrating with anger.

I watched him, scared of him and also wanting to go to him to try to calm him. But I remembered what he'd done to Leri and stayed still.

He didn't turn around. "Have you been with him in the flesh? The truth."

"No, just in dreams. It—"

"I need some time to myself," Lash said gruffly, kicking the table again. "Don't teleport off the grounds, okay?"

"Okay. But please—"

127

Lash walked out without another word, slamming the door behind him.

I sat there for a while on the floor, rubbing my eyes and feeling like a slut and a bitch. And like I should buy some stock in tables. *It's done. At least it's not a secret anymore.*

Finally, I called one of the guards who were hovering outside the door, and had them take the table remains outside to the burn pit. Then I went to my laptop in the living room, got online, and ordered a new table and matching chairs, billing them to my credit card. After that, I got a glass of wine and sipped it, thinking I should have handled the situation better, all of it.

I'd known Shaker had been a mistake since the moment I'd woken up from the dream with him. All I'd wanted to do was forget I'd given in to temptation. But that had been hard to do when I'd ordered him to make it memorable. I'd been stupid not to tell Lash. He'd always forgiven me when I'd admitted things to him. He'd told me worse and I'd forgiven him.

Had I been with Shaker out of anger at Lash, even a little bit? My mate had always told me he'd be there for me, to save me. But he hadn't. I'd still be with Michael if I hadn't made that deal with Shaker. Lash would be moldering in some unmarked grave, and our son would never have been born.

There was a noise above from Tryst's room. I went upstairs, glass of wine in hand. Tryst was there in human form. He'd smashed a glass orb that I'd bought him that glowed in the dark. He was looking at me with regretful eyes.

"What happened?" I said, expecting he wouldn't answer me. He was fluent in snake, but he hadn't spoken English yet, just a few words in Spanish.

To my surprise, he did. "Is dad a killer?"

I eased myself down to the floor to sit next to him, my heart racing. "Tryst, why are you asking this?"

"I heard two of the guards talking a few minutes ago outside. I had heard you and Dad fighting, and I was...I was..."

I gently pulled him into my arms. "I'm sorry we scared you—"

"I wasn't scared!" he almost yelled, his eyes angry. "I'm not scared of anything!"

There was no point arguing with him that he clearly had been. "Okay, so you weren't scared, you just went outside to give us some privacy. Then you overheard someone talking about your father?"

Tryst nodded. "They said he'd killed some government man, someone in another country last week. They said he'd gotten a fortune to do it." He looked at me. "Is it true?"

The first words I'd even heard my son say in human form, and this had to be the conversation we were having. I wiped my eyes a little, not knowing how to answer.

"Mom?"

"Let me call your father," I said, relieved to have a reason to and worried Lash wouldn't answer. "This is really an answer he needs to give you, Tryst."

I dialed my cell, calling Lash.

He answered on the second ring. "What is it?" he said low and angry. "I asked you to leave me alone—"

"Please come to Tryst's room. He needs to ask you something and it's a question I don't want to answer for you."

Lash was quiet for a half second. "I'll be there in ten minutes." Click.

While we waited, we cleaned up the remains of the ball. "Can you buy me another?" Tryst said hopefully. "I like it at night, when I'm falling asleep."

"I'll order another this afternoon," I said, slipping the broken glass into the wastebasket. "Just try to be more careful, okay?"

"I'm sorry," he said, looking at the floor. "I was upset, and it was the nearest thing to throw."

"Don't throw things and break them out of anger," I said gently. "There are better ways to get out your emotions."

"Like what?"

"Like yelling or screaming," I said, blushing. "You know where the gym is, and it's soundproofed. It's got a punching bag too, if you need to hit something."

"Your mother is right," Lash hissed from behind me. "I don't want you breaking your toys or making holes in walls. Destroying things in anger is not a good habit to get into. Now why were you angry?"

"The guards were talking about you, acting like you were some kind of mass murderer. And it pissed me off—"

"Don't use that word," I said sternly. "Say you were angry, Tryst."

"Why can't I say it? Dad says it all the time."

"Don't patronize your mother," Lash hissed in his low scary voice. "She's right, you are too young to swear. You've just learned to talk in human."

"I didn't know that word was bad."

"Don't give me that...crap, you did so," Lash said sarcastically. "When you're ten actual years old, you can swear all you want to, Tryst. But there's a time to swear, and a time not to swear. I want you to be able to speak without swearing for those times and to do that, you need to restrain yourself."

"I don't see the f...um, the point, Dad."

"I learned to swear young," Lash hissed, rubbing his eyes in apparent exasperation. "My father encouraged it in me, or at least, he didn't discourage it. I have a crude way of talking that comes naturally because of that. I didn't learn how to speak more eloquently until joining with Devlin and spending a lot of time reading. I want better for you, for you to sound like more of a gentleman than I usually do. So you need to practice. Got it?"

Tryst nodded. "I got it."

"Was that your question, if the guards were telling the truth?" Lash said, looking down to face Tryst.

Tryst nodded.

"Then why don't you ask it of me?" Lash hissed, still looking hard at him. "If you have the courage to ask me something, I'll always give you an answer. And it'll always be the truth."

"Do you kill people for money?"

"I'm what's called an assassin," Lash hissed, looking Tryst in the eyes. "I take money from people to kill other people. They're called hits. I'm famous for it and I've been doing it for the last ninety years."

"You don't look that old," Tryst said quickly. "You can't be that old. Are you—?"

"That's another question for another time," Lash hissed, still staring at his son. "We're talking about killing people. Now, are you done with your question?"

"Are they all bad people, the ones you kill?"

"Not always," Lash said, still maintaining eye contact. "Mostly it's government people or businessmen that want other men out of the way. It's usually boring actually, not at all like the intrigue you see in your TV shows or movies. And the rest is usually over sex, some partner wanting another killed for being unfaithful to them."

I swallowed, wondering if he was adding that bit to hurt me.

"But once in a while it is someone famous, or someone hard to get to, or someone who has some skill with killing their own selves. Those are not boring. Those pay a lot of money."

"Enough for another glow ball?"

"Yes," Lash hissed affectionately. "We'll get you another, don't worry. But don't break any more on purpose, either. Okay?"

"Do you like it, Dad? Is it fun, to be an assassin?"

"It's not fun," Lash hissed, sounding very, very old. "It's something I was trained for, though, and I'm good at it. I'm the best there is, Son. So I don't want you to worry about me, okay? I'm not going to end up dead."

"I didn't think about that," Tryst said, upset. "What if you die? What if someone kills you, instead of you killing them?"

"It won't ever happen."

"Can't you do something else?" Tryst said hopefully. "You're smart, and you—"

"This is what I do," Lash hissed, crouching down to sit on his haunches before Tryst. "This is who I am, who the world knows me as. I can't be anyone else, Son. Do you understand?"

"No," Tryst said, biting his lip, his eyes moist.

"One day you will," Lash hissed a little sadly. "Now give me a hug, because I need one."

Trystan hugged his father tight. Lash squeezed him back, and then gave him a kiss on his forehead, which Tryst grimaced at.

Lash released him, and stood up. "Was that everything?"

"Yes," Trystan hissed eagerly. "Will you teach me to kill people too?"

I opened my mouth to speak, but Lash was already answering. "I'm already teaching you, Son. You've been learning to defend yourself since you could hold a knife. But defending and attacking are two different things. Doing what I do takes a long time to learn."

"Will you teach me everything you know?"

"If you want to learn it," Lash hissed softly, sad. "But there are a lot of other things that I want you to learn about too. You'd have to learn them all, Son."

"Cool!" Tryst said, beaming. "Can we do another training session now?"

"Not now," Lash hissed, moving to the door. "You have other things you need to learn, like I just reminded you. I believe Caitlyn's waiting to teach you some history."

"I don't want to look at any more books," Tryst hissed grumpily. "I want to do things!"

"History is one of the things I want you to learn. No history, no training—"

"Okay, I'm going," Trystan said loudly, getting up. He grabbed a stack of books and headed to the ballroom.

Lash came to stand beside me, watching him walk away. "He's a lot like I was, when I was younger. But he surprises me, too. I'd have loved to have books of my own when I was younger, even dull history books."

"Thanks for coming and talking to him," I said hesitantly. "When he asked me, I wasn't sure how to answer him."

"Thank you for calling me," Lash said abruptly. "It was my question to answer."

"You did a good job. You made what you do sound...you handled his curiosity well."

Lash moved away, walking down the stairs.

"Please come back," I called to him. "Come back and talk to me, Mate."

Lash stopped, and turned his head to look back at me. "Don't call me that, Sar. Not right now."

"It's what we are," I said, trying hard to keep my anger in check. "We didn't stop being mated just because you're angry with me."

"If one of a mated couple has sex with someone else after they said they wouldn't, the mating is broken," Lash hissed sharply. "It's were law. There is no separation, no period of waiting until you can call it quits. It's just over."

I stared at him, sick. He held my gaze for a long moment, and then walked away.

* * * *

Later that night he finally came in, while I was reading in bed. Devlin was with one of his blood donors in the silver room. Tryst Jr. was in his room, asleep, Honey curled up next to him.

"I'm sorry," I said, setting aside my book. "I can release Shaker from my service, if it makes you uncomfortable for me to see him. Rene must know a way."

"Forget it," Lash hissed, sitting down on the bed, and pulling off his shoes.

"Mate," I pleaded. "Please, talk to me."

"No," he hissed. "Not tonight. Tonight, I need to think. I need to get past my feelings, so I can decide what I'm going to do."

"Okay. I have something else to talk to you about anyway." I took a breath, steeling myself. "I don't want you to teach Trystan to be an assassin, Lash. I don't want him killed. He's in enough danger being your son."

Lash nodded. "I don't want that for him, either. However, he may gravitate to it all the same. And if that's what he wants to be, I want him to be as safe as I can make him, which translates to skilled."

I faced him. "No, Lash. I'm not standing by and watching him become a murderer."

Lash stiffened, and slowly turned to look at me. "I am not a murderer, Sarelle."

"You kill people for money according to whoever pays you the most."

Lash tensed as if he would strike me, and then rubbed his eyes. "I have never killed anyone who was innocent. But it shows how much you know me that you could think I would."

You are such a fucking bastard. "You've told me what you've done over the years. What am I supposed to think? You are who've you've

133

always been. That's what you always tell me, that you can't be anyone else. You told Tryst that very thing today."

"How can you think I'd want this life for him?" he hissed back, upset. "There isn't anything I can do about me being what I am now. You're right; he's in danger just from being my son. So he's going to learn everything I know. I'd rather him be a murdering son of a bitch than be a sweet moral child who never sees his eighteenth birthday."

"I want you to teach him enough so he can take care of himself, that's not the point. I'm afraid for him, afraid that he's going to want to follow in your footsteps."

"So am I," Lash sighed, putting his head in his hands. "I'll do everything I can to discourage it, Sar. But telling him he can't do it is only going to make him want to do it more."

"I understand that," I whispered. "Thank you. I'm sorry, if you were hurt by what I said."

Lash didn't reply.

"I'm sorry if I hurt you. Please forgive me."

He didn't reply. I gently lay my hand on his arm and he pushed it off with an irritated hiss.

I got up and walked downstairs, and put on a jacket. It was warm enough; I could go for a walk. I had on only pajamas, but they covered all of me. Lash needed more time, and I could give that to him.

Ghost looked at me hopefully as I put my shoes on, so I motioned to him with my hand and he came outside with me. We walked out into the forest, and down the path towards the pond. It was a clear night with a small breeze, making the long grass ripple in the wind with a faint swishing sound. I walked with Ghost to Lash's rock, and sat there while he rested, looking at the water, and remembering happier times.

Maybe I should have told Lash about Shaker, and Terian. But there'd been no simple way. I hadn't asked for Terian to do what he had. I hadn't wanted to have to save myself by binding myself to a demon. Hell, I'd never touched Shaker outside of a dream. I'd never wanted to after that one night...

More's the pity, Shaker said teasingly in my mind. *If I didn't know better, I'd think I was a bad lover.*

Leave me, I thought to him.

134

Have I offended you? he thought. *If I have, I did not intend to.*

Lash knows about us, I thought. *All of it.*

I see, Shaker thought back to me, after a pause. *Is he angry?*

Yes, I thought back. *He found out about Terian and I, as well.*

That wasn't your fault. You were duped, and—

Look, I need to be alone, I thought back to him. *Please, Shaker.*

Call me, if you need me, Mistress, he thought back to me, and then his presence disappeared from my mind.

Ghost whined a greeting, alerting me that we'd been found. I was surprised that it was Devlin who sat down beside me.

"Lash told me everything this afternoon," he said, after a few moments. "I'd have come to you earlier, except I had to see my donors." He paused. "I spoke to Danial right after speaking to Lash, and he told me he knew already. Why did you not tell me?"

"For what? So you could kill Terian?" I said bitterly. "I've had enough of revenge."

"No, about Shaker," Devlin replied evenly. "You did not have to tell Lash, Oathed One, as I understand you'd rightly think he'd be jealous. But I leave your dream lovers to your own discretion, and you know that, else you'd have awoken after your dream with your choker off. I'd not have withheld permission, if you'd asked me to let you bed Shaker a few times in the physical world, so long as I got to watch. So what reason did you have not to tell me?"

"So you're not mad about Terian, or about the Mistress thing?"

"Terian made a mistake," he said, taking my hand. "Your revolted face as you confronted him after is likely all he remembers of the dream. He'll remember it forever, and that punishment is better than anything I could do." He sighed. "As for Shaker, I'm guessing Rene's been helping you fulfill his needs for flesh. If she knows and did not tell me, then it must be what is supposed to happen. She would not let you come to harm. But I ask again for all of this, why did you not tell me?"

"I don't know," I said, picking up a pebble and throwing it into the pond. "At first, it was that I was protecting Shaker, as Titus and Rip were angry that he'd helped Cyrus. I was so grateful he'd helped us get away. But later, I don't know why I didn't tell you or Lash. It just felt like it was never the right time."

"Do you care for him?" Devlin said curiously.

I looked over at him, inquisitive that there was no jealousy. "Shaker?"

"Yes."

"No," I said, guilty. "We were together only that one time in dreams, right after I lost the twins. I was just using him, and I think we both knew it. But he didn't care. We haven't been together since. I told him not long after that I'd made a mistake, that I wanted our relationship to be just professional. It has been ever since."

Devlin slipped his arm around me. "I'm sorry again you went through that," he said quietly. "Don't feel bad that you were weak for a moment and found a little comfort with him."

"You know, you always surprise me," I said, resting my head on his shoulder. "Things that I'm sure will make you angry, you just forgive me."

"I love you," he whispered. "You've given me a lot in these past years. You're forgiven me far more. I'm not going to condemn you, Love. I know you now like I didn't when we were first together. I doubted you loved Shaker and knew you didn't love Terian. You aren't like me; you want sex only with those you love, so there had to be circumstances that made it happen. I know your heart lies with Trystan, Danial and I. That is all that is important to me."

"I love you," I said, hugging him. "I love you very much."

"I know, Love." He rose to his feet. "Come to bed."

We walked back to the house, Ghost following.

"Is Lash still upset?" I said as we neared the house.

"I haven't seen him since this afternoon. I'm guessing he's working out in the gym," Devlin said. "He'll likely be up after." He paused. "Your son is upset. It was Tryst who came and got me, telling me you'd left with Ghost. He would have followed, as Lash told him to protect you, but he knew he couldn't keep pace with you in snake form and you outdistanced him before he'd had time to dress."

Worried, I quickly walked into the house. Tryst Jr. immediately slithered down the stairs, making sounds of distress, fear, and worry.

"Told you I'd find her." Devlin turned to me. "I need to finish with my donors," he said, kissing me on the cheek. "I'll be another hour." He strode off.

"Shh," I said, looping Tryst around my neck and supporting his head. "I'll come tuck you in. You need to get some sleep."

Soon, I had him back in human form in his pajamas, his dark eyes focused on me.

"Mom?"

"Yes?" I said, kneeling down beside his bed.

"Why is Dad angry?"

"I didn't tell him something I should have," I said carefully. "He was right to be angry."

"Did you say you were sorry?"

I nodded.

"Did he forgive you?"

"Not yet."

"Why not, if you said you were sorry?"

"Because sometimes that isn't enough. It's the wronged person's right not to forgive."

"He'll forgive you, don't worry, Mom. Goodnight."

I gave him a wan smile, though my heart was locked in despair.

Chapter Eleven

When I awoke in the late afternoon, Lash had not come to bed. I checked his room, and that bed was empty, too. Trystan's tank was also empty, as was V's room.

Feeling guilty, I went downstairs to make myself a late breakfast. To my absolute shock, I found Serena there happily making pancakes for Nick. I smirked, unable to repress it. Their on-off relationship had flipped on again after all this time. *Good for you, Serena. Nick, you had better not hurt her again.*

"Lash is outside with Trystan," Serena said, after greeting me. "They went swimming."

I walked out with Ghost and Honey to the pond, where Lash was teaching our son to swim. Tryst was doing well, too. Maybe that was instinctive if you were a water weresnake.

I watched them play and splash for a few minutes. Trystan suddenly noticed me and immediately came out of the water, changing form. Like his father, he had no shyness about being unclothed. Though I was getting used to it, a faint flush still crept over my face. He pulled on his clothes quickly when he saw my unease. "I'm going back to the house," he said, giving me a hug. "I'll take Ghost and Honey with me."

"Do you want lunch?" I said quickly, getting to my feet. "I can make you something—"

"No, I caught a fish. Besides, Dad wants you to stay," he said, giving me a quick smile. He took off running, his sneakers kicking up dust as he ran towards Hayden, Honey like a shot after him and Ghost trotting along in their wake, barking excitedly.

I glanced back toward the pond. Lash slithered out of the water. He paused for a moment, and then moved fast, coming toward me as snake. My first instinct was to run, but I stood my ground. A few seconds later, he was twining up my legs. He wrapped his body around my middle, then his tail around my other leg, tightening his coils suddenly in a deft motion. I went sprawling in the dirt, the majority of my weight landing on his solid muscle, cushioning my fall.

I gave him an annoyed face. "What are you doing?"

He began to shift back. A moment later, he was lying on me as human, looking absolutely exhausted. "You hurt me, not telling me what Terian did," he said, his dark eyes serious. "I'm your mate. Why couldn't you have shared your hurt with me?"

Relief flooded me, to hear him refer to me that way. "I'm sorry I didn't."

"I understand why," Lash said, getting to his feet. "But it makes me uneasy, that you didn't tell me for so long." He offered me a hand, which I took. "And that you didn't tell me about Shaker, any of what you had to do to get him to help us escape or afterwards. Did you think I'd be angry? That I'd judge you?"

"Yes," I said honestly.

"I don't know how to say this delicately, so I'll just say it. I want you not to f... um, to be with him again, even if it's just in dreams. Not ever, Mate." He collected himself. "You do it ever again, and I'll take Tryst and leave, like Theo did with Harris."

"I'm not going to. That was finished over a year ago. It was a mistake I'm not going to make ever again. Shaker knows this."

Lash gave me a confused look. "Just like that?"

"Lash, I don't love him, I love you—"

"Call me Tryst, Sweetness," he said emotionally. "Please."

"Tryst, we're friends, kind of. We haven't been anything more for a long time. I'm happy keeping it that way. I think despite how he likes to tease me, he is, too."

Lash breathed a sigh of relief. "Good. I was worried you'd say no."

"Why on earth would I say no?"

"I don't know," he whispered, gripping me tightly. "I'm just glad you said yes. Lay back for me, please—"

He hurriedly slid off my jeans. "Tell me I'm your mate," he said

139

desperately, spreading my legs quickly as he pushed inside. "Tell me you love me. Tell me you're mine."

"I love you, you're my mate," I said, kissing his throat. "I'm yours, Tryst."

Lash made no sound as he moved on me frantically. Several minutes later, he collapsed on me, his body going limp as he spent himself. I was surprised he hadn't waited for me to climax first, but didn't want to mention it. I was sore enough from the rocky ground under me right now.

Lash abruptly tensed up. "Shit," he said coarsely. "My gun is back at the rock. I wasn't thinking." He leapt to his feet. "Here, grab your jeans. We can't be lying here naked and unarmed."

"Wait," I said, still sitting in the dirt trying to gather my wits. "I'm sorry. I'm sorry for not telling you."

"It's not okay," Lash hissed softly, bringing me to my feet as he grabbed my jeans in his other hand. "It's going to take me a while to trust you again, Sar. I want you to tell me if you see Shaker, even if it's just in dreams."

"I'm not going to be with him."

He began to lead me toward the pond. "I know. But do that for me. In fact, if you dream of anyone I want to know about it, even if it's me. I also want you to go with me to see Titus tonight. I want him to check you, to maybe put something on you, so we know if any of your dreams are more than just your mind wandering in sleep."

"Ok. I haven't had any dreams of sex for months, just so you know."

"From now on I also want to know where you go, even when you're on the grounds here. I want to know who you're with at all times."

"No," I said gently, to his surprise. "You want to monitor my dreams, that's fair. But I've never slept with anyone else here, save Dev. You know that I wouldn't, either."

"I thought I did," Lash hissed softly. "I'm not sure now. It's not as if I don't have reason to doubt you, Sar. You've given me reason to."

Anger and bitterness welled up within me. "I had a weak moment. I was raped, held captive for months, and then I lost our children. This wasn't some fling I had out of boredom."

"They were my children, too, Sar. It's not like they were the first of mine to die—"

"They weren't the first for me either, you insensitive bastard!"

I slid like nothing into hysterics, my loss crashing into me just as it had when I'd lost the twins. It was worse now, because I'd lost another two babies since then. Compounded in that was losing my original child with Lash, Danial's first child with me that I'd miscarried years ago, and Devon's death. Harris, he was gone too, just in a different way! Then I remembered Stephen's words, and it hit me all over again that there wouldn't be any more children, ever.

"Sweetness, I'm sorry! Please don't cry, please—"

I couldn't answer him. I sobbed hysterically, my tears pouring out of me like a river, drowning me in sadness and utter despair. Worse, the more I cried, the more I wanted to keep crying, as if somehow I could cry all my tears out, so all this hopelessness and sorrow that had been festering inside me for so long could finally ease.

Lash squeezed me tightly, hissing frantically, "Please stop crying, Mate, please, I'm sorry."

Shaker was suddenly in my mind, trying to soothe me with soft words of comfort. *Mistress, please stop crying. I am here for you. Do you want me to come to you?*

I didn't answer him, crying harder. Their words quickly jumbled together in a cacophony, adding to my feelings of helplessness and grief.

"Sar, please stop crying. I shouldn't have said—"

Mistress, let me come to you. I will comfort you, wipe away your—

"—it's okay, we have Tryst, Sweetness, and he won't be killed, I'll make sure he's safe—"

You are safe, Mistress. Let me come to you. I can bring you some chocolates, I know you—

"I know you, Sar. I know you wouldn't do anything. I'm sorry I—"

"Shut up!" I suddenly shouted. "Both of you, shut up!"

Lash gave me a look of shock, and then let me go. "Tell him to come here," he hissed angrily. "Tell him right now."

Shaker, come to me, I said in my mind, as I slipped on my jeans.

A moment later, Shaker appeared before me. He looked at Lash standing naked near me and the edge of his mouth curved upwards a fraction of an inch. "I take it you made up?"

141

"Stay out of her mind, unless she's telling you she needs help," Lash hissed furiously. "We had enough of that shit with Rene."

"With all due respect, Lash, Sarelle is my Mistress, and it is she who sets the rules, not you," Shaker replied evenly. "I do not like hearing her upset. I'm fond of her, as Titus and Rip are. She is Kin, after all."

"Kin who you fucked," Lash hissed nastily, baring his fangs.

Shaker was unruffled. "So what if we did? How many women have you fucked in your life, Lash? A thousand? Two thousand? Five? How many were related to each other, grandmothers, and mothers, and their daughters knowing you down through the years."

"That's not the point," Lash hissed back. "I asked you to stay away from her, as a favor to me. We've known each other a long time, Shaker. But I should have remembered you're a piece of shit demon."

"I am a demon, and if you think I was going to refuse sex from any luscious female ever, you're wrong." Shaker laughed. "But it was a command she gave me, Lash. I could not have refused if I'd wanted to. And I didn't want to; I'd have taken any excuse she gave for a little action from her. She was just as yielding within as I'd hoped she'd be."

"Shaker, shut up!" I said loudly, closing my eyes in dismay. "You are not helping!"

Lash looked over at me in disbelief. "Is that true, what he said?"

"It's true."

"I thought he seduced you," Lash hissed roughly. "I didn't know you ordered him to. Mother of God, I've been stupid, believing you were the victim here when all along you instigated the whole thing! You've just been dying for him to fuck your brains out all along, haven't you?"

I went to leave, but Shaker grabbed my arm, sitting me down hard. Then Lash tried to leave, and Shaker shoved him down beside me. Lash shifted to snake and Shaker grabbed hold of him before he could slither away. Lash whirled fast and tried to bite him, his whole length thrashing madly. Lash lunged repeatedly trying hard to hurt Shaker, but Shaker just held him, murmuring words. As he finished speaking, Lash shifted to human and Shaker threw him down beside me. Lash lay there breathing hard, his eyes murderous.

"Sit there, Snake," Shaker rumbled. "And don't get up."

Lash bared his fangs, but didn't move.

"I've seen this all my life," Shaker said abruptly. "I've seen a lot of people make stupid mistakes, and lose everything they had because they couldn't forgive someone they loved. So let it go, Lash. She regrets it, even if I don't. That's what should matter to you, that if she had a choice, she'd undo it. That every time I've approached her since, she's refused me."

"I can't," Lash hissed angrily. "I thought Sarelle made exceptions to her morals for me. Instead, the truth is she just doesn't have any. I mated a cat to me, not a human." He snorted. "An alley cat, one who fucks anything the moment fresh dick is offered."

That was the moment my guilt snapped like a stretched rubber band and I let go of it. I was old, tired, and used up. Most of all, I was worn out. *It's time to stop this bullshit, for the last time.* "Shaker, you know my Oath to Devlin?" I said tiredly.

"Of course, Mistress."

"Then I command you right now and forever after to hold me to it."

"Yeah, you're going to tell him never to fuck you again," Lash hissed scornfully. "And that will work until the next time you get a longing for demon dick. And then you'll command him to forget what you said, and take you, and he'll fuck your brains out again."

I ignored him, though his words hurt me terribly. "I give you permission right now to take my soul if I ever break my Oath, Shaker. Or if I'm ever intimate with any male without Lash's permission, even if it's one of my lovers within the Oath."

Lash stopped in mid-sentence, giving me a stricken look.

So did Shaker. "The devil heard your offer," he said sadly. "And he marked it, Mistress. So be careful of your words and actions from now on, because I'll be bound by what you've said here. I'd not like to take your soul to Hell, if I could help it. Not only would I go to Hell with you, but likely Titus would make sure I never left again."

"I know," I said. "Now come with me back to the house. I need to pack a few things."

"Pack what?" Lash hissed, getting to his feet, and reaching for me. "Where are you going?"

"You said you needed some time. I need some, too," I said, wincing as I brushed dirt from my jeans. "I need some time by myself. When I'm

143

ready to talk to you, I'll call." I took off the ring he'd given me and tossed it to him. "You can hold onto that for me while I'm gone, since we aren't mated anymore, anyway. If we both decide we still want each other after we'd had some time alone, you can give it back to me then."

"You aren't fucking leaving!" Lash hissed, reaching for me. "You're my mate, and—"

Screw packing anything. "Shaker, take us somewhere warm."

In the next moment, we were in the Everglades. Mosquitoes quickly besieged me, until Shaker put a shielding spell over us.

"Was this okay?" he said. "I wasn't sure where you wanted to go. This is where you went before to be warm."

"This is fine. Now please go get a room for me with twin beds, so there's one for you. I'm not stupid enough to stay without a guard near me. I trust you'll respect me, and not try to take advantage."

We began to walk towards the hotel, down the path towards the visitor center. No one approached, though a flock of roseate spoonbills took off, flying deeper into the tropical forest.

"I will, as I've no choice now really," Shaker replied. "I do need to know, do you want not to be disturbed? Lash will go right to Titus as soon as he dresses to get him to locate you. Once he finds him, he'll teleport here right after."

"Yes, please. I need a day or so at least to think. Stop him from teleporting here."

"You know he loves you," Shaker said. "Don't judge him too harshly. He's not like Devlin is, who has learned how to forgive. His life has been a hard and lonely one, Mistress."

"I know. But mine's been rough, too. I need some time alone to decide what to do."

"Then you'll have it," Shaker promised. "The most I can guarantee is a day or so, and that's if we move every other hour to a new location. Lash will get everyone looking for you."

"Contact Titus, tell him I'm safe, and you're with me. Ask him, Rip, and Rene not to teleport Lash. That'll work." Lash might be many things, but there was no way he'd ask Terian to help him, or that Terian would, anyway.

Shaker nodded and walked away out of sight. I wondered a moment on how he'd get us a room dressed in nothing but a loin skin, not to mention the hooves and horns, then decided I didn't want to know.

I walked to the bay, and stood and watched the ocean roil, the breeze increasing to a steady wind. I went over the conversation again and again as I waited, my anger increasing. Belatedly, I thought of the diamond ring Lash had given to me, and wished I hadn't thrown it to him, so that I could throw it now into the ocean.

Just as well you didn't. It was his ring, and it was better to return it to him. There came the sound of hooves on concrete. I turned with a sigh.

"The hotel is gone, Mistress," Shaker said apologetically.

I blinked at him, shocked. "What?"

"There was a hurricane here, in the year or so previous," he explained. "It was a small one, but the hotel was flooded, and partially destroyed. Instead of rebuilding, they demolished the ruins."

Lash and I had such good times there together. Just one more thing that doesn't last. "Let's get a bite at the Buttonwood Lounge then, and then—"

"That is also destroyed," Shaker interjected gently. "As was the hotel restaurant. And the café that replaced them is not currently open."

I bit my lip, feeling tears threaten and wondering why the loss of a place I had been to only one night mattered so much to me. *Because it was one more thing that had irrevocably changed while being Michael's captive. I may not look any older, but I sure feel it.*

Shaker took my hand, then teleported us. We arrived on a beach, the wind steady but warm and inviting. "Come," he said, gesturing to a large hotel looming before us right off the white sands. "This place is much better. And you can likely eat anything you'd want here in its restaurant, as well."

I followed him up the concrete steps, mindful of my now sandy-bottomed jeans, and the socialites that were walking past me in high heels, tuxedos, and designer clothes. "What is this place?"

"This is The Breakers, of West Palm Beach," Shaker said. "We are still in Florida, just to the side coast instead of the bottom."

After showering in our luxurious room, I spent the rest of the day lying in the sun with Shaker invisible nearby, thinking about all that had happened. God, I'd made a lot of mistakes. What should I do now? What was the right path to take? What was best for my sons?

Rene arrived in late afternoon. After Shaker saw it was she, he let her come over to me.

"Are you okay, Sister?" she said, giving me a hug. "I heard what happened."

"I'm getting there. I just needed some time."

Rene nodded. "I understand. Devlin sends his love, and to tell you to come back when you're ready. He said to tell you that if you're gone longer than a few days he's going to come to you to spend some time, no matter if you're in a tent or a hotel."

"Tell him I'll be back by then," I said, smiling wanly. "And there's no tenting for me, not when a hotel room has all the amenities and no mosquitos."

"Danial also sent a message. He asks you to be careful and to call him every night from a phone," Rene continued. She handed me a bag. "Here is a cell phone, a credit card, your ID, and some cash from him."

"Good," I said gratefully, taking the bag. "I'll tell him thanks tonight personally."

"Titus said don't worry, he and Rip will honor your wishes," Rene said. "Be aware, Lash is already on his way here, as Devlin refused to keep your location from him. He'll be here in another day or so at the most, even though he's driving."

"I expected that," I said, resigning myself internally. "It's okay."

"Want to swim?" Rene asked impishly. "I brought my swimsuit."

I looked at her in surprise, and then laughed. "Sure. Let me go get one."

I bought a very overpriced swimsuit at the hotel store. The rest of that afternoon, we spent tanning and swimming. The salt water wasn't warm really, but to be in the sun and the waves felt wonderful, easing some of my depression.

That night Rene and I had a few drinks in the hotel bar. I spent most of the time sipping a drink and thinking of Lash, while Rene flirted with some young stylishly-dressed men at the bar.

Right after Rene left for home, I called Danial from my room. He answered on the first ring. "Are you okay?" he said gently. "I understand from Devlin that the fight was a bad one."

"It was, but I'm okay. I'm taking some time to think about what to do."

"I assume you'd like me to wait for you to return," he said gently. "Otherwise you'd have come here for solace."

He was asking if I wanted him to come "save me" from Lash. "I need to handle this myself, Danial. After I do, I'll come back, I promise."

"Fair enough. But call me every night when you're gone. And please make sure Shaker is near you, though I'd be careful about letting him get too close." He paused. "I love you."

"Point taken. I love you, too. I'll call tomorrow night." I said goodbye and hung up.

Later that night, I lay in bed, thinking on what I should do. I was tired of plans and trying so hard to make things work with Lash. *For what? Everything just goes to hell anyway. Theo gave Lash and I six months. Maybe he was right. Maybe he wasn't. Do I want to make up, when all we ever do is fight again? I'm tired of him making me feel like shit.*

Nightmares haunted me when I finally slept, but I resisted asking Shaker for a spell, or for him to procure me some valium. Instead, I practiced breathing and calming myself down after, and wrote the subject of the nightmare down to think about tomorrow. It was time to stop covering up my problems and start dealing with them.

The next day, I spent most of it laying in the sun, thinking. My nightmares had been about Devon dying, about putting Darkness to sleep, and about losing Danial and Devlin to sunlight. They'd been vivid, but not terrible. I talked myself through it all again, telling myself that I'd done the right things for Devon and Darkness in their lives, and that Danial and his brother could take care of themselves. We'd see how tonight went. If the nightmares didn't get better after doing this for two weeks, I'd go see Rosalyn. It was a start.

Chapter Twelve

That night after dinner alone in the restaurant, I went again to the bar, Shaker shadowing me, invisible. When Lash threw open the bar door with a crash about a quarter to midnight, Shaker got up and left, telling me to call if I needed him.

Lash spotted me at once and strode to my table. He looked at me for a moment angrily, as if he wasn't sure how to start.

"Sit down," I said easily. "Have a drink. Try not to wreck any lights. This is not a backwater dive no one cares about; it's a premier hotel with a lot of witnesses."

He went to the bar, got a whiskey, and came back, sliding into the opposite chair. "That was a fuck of a long drive," he hissed angrily. "I haven't slept in two days."

"You needn't have rushed," I said nastily. "You knew you'd find me here alone with Shaker guarding me. I don't want to go to Hell."

"You didn't have to do that," Lash hissed awkwardly. "Promise him what you did."

"Didn't I? I think I did. You were ready to call it quits between us."

"I wasn't," Lash said, downing his drink. "But I didn't know how to feel, hearing that you asked for his dick. You always said—"

"Stop talking about it and being so fucking crass," I snapped. "I'm sick of your crudeness! I did what I did so you could let it go, because I want to let it go. It's past. I'm tired of you calling me names, and saying shitty things to me every time we fight. I've never judged you for the people you slept with, or any of the bad things you've done in your life. And I know a lot of them, Mate, even the worst ones that made me wonder if I could still love you after knowing them. But I never bring

148

them up to you or throw them in your face to hurt you when we fight."

Lash was quiet. Then he reached over the table, and took my hand. "I know you don't. I'm grateful for that." He paused. "I'm sorry for what I said. Come back with me, Sweetness. Tryst is worried we're going to break up, though he hasn't openly said that. He needs you. I need you, too."

I was sick of his "sorrys" and his needs. "For what? What exactly do you need me for, Lash? For someone to take out your anger on? Or for someone to ease your sexual woes who never says 'no', no matter how fucking rough you are, or how hurt I am afterwards?"

Lash shut his eyes, took a breath, looked back at me, and then looked away. "To be with me and make it all bearable. To talk to me, love me, and to help me raise our son. And yes, to have sex with. But that's not a bad thing that I want you—"

"It's a bad thing that you tell me I'm your mate, and we're going to work things out, and after we have sex until you're sated and I'm sore, you suddenly decide that we can't, and start right back in saying shitty things to me."

"I shouldn't have done that. I'm sorry, Sweetness." He paused. "No matter what you did, or didn't do, I love you, Mate."

"Are we mated?" I said nastily. "You told me we weren't, because of what I'd done. Why don't you get your fucking story straight and stick to it!"

"Stop being like this," Lash hissed desperately. "I had a right to be angry, Sar."

"But not a right to be vindictive, when all I wanted was your forgiveness."

Lash took a deep breath. "We're still mated. Even if you had sex in real life with some other male snake, it wouldn't end our mating, not if I said it was all right with me. I'm not willing to break our mating over what happened. I'm upset about it, and I will be for a while. But I want to work with you to get past it. I'll try not to mention it again in anger." He reached into his pocket, brought out my ring, and slipped it on my finger. He clasped that hand in both of his gently as his moist eyes looked into mine. "I just never thought you'd do this to me, Sar. I thought it was different what we had, because it was real; it wasn't a

149

blood-binding, or because of a spell, or for any reason other than we loved each other. I thought what we had was better than anything. And I thought you did, too."

"It was," I said, dissolving into tears again, even as I fought not to cry. "But things have to change. Stop being sorry for your actions, Lash, and actually make an effort not to do them."

I wondered if my words would be the final ones, if he would get up and leave, or say something to end us. I was almost sure that he would. Instead, he nodded. "I will try harder," Lash murmured. "And I am sorry."

"I'm sorry," I murmured back. "And I'll try harder, too. I don't want to hurt you. I love you."

Lash's arms went around me. "I'm the same way, Sweetness. I'm sorry I hurt you. I love you. Please say you'll come back with me. Tell me you still want to be mine."

"I'll teleport us tonight," I whispered, my tears hot on my cheeks and I pressed my face into his neck. "I want you, to be with you. I'll never not want that, Tryst."

We paid the bill, and walked out. A few moments later, we were frantically embracing in the elevator, kissing desperately. Getting out, we hurried to my room, where I opened the door. Shaker had left a note on the bed, telling us to "Make up and fuck." I tossed it out before Lash saw it.

Lash turned me to face him. "Tell me if I hurt you," he said, troubled. "I don't want to hurt you, Mate. So the instant my body isn't feeling good to you, you tell me, okay? I don't ever want what I do not to feel good to you. I'll stop, I promise."

"You didn't really hurt me, having sex on the path," I whispered, hugging him. "I just said that out of anger."

"Was there ever another time that you didn't like what I did?" he hissed anxiously. "Tell me the truth."

"Only that night before we were snake together for the first time," I said after a moment. "And I should've just said something to you then, just like I should've about this whole mess."

We took off our clothes, and settled into bed, spooning. It was two in the morning by this time and we were both dead tired.

I woke up to find Lash snoring softly. I turned to face him, studying his face as he lay there still asleep. He must have been dead tired, to not have awoken when I moved. I'd never moved before and not had him wake immediately.

An idea sprang into my head. Why not? I was never going to get this chance again.

I moved his knife out of reach, then parted his legs gently, moving slowly so not to startle him. When I was between his legs, I gently licked him with my tongue.

He let out a murmur and thrust up with his hips, his penis already stiffening. I put my mouth over him as he elongated, making a loose seal. Lash let out a long moan, and thrust his hips up slowly, now as hard as rock. I sucked him lightly, working him in and out of my mouth.

Lash began to jerk on the bed, his moments almost desperate to get inside me, his loud intakes of breath tortured. I sucked harder, tonguing him, and squeezing his balls gently.

Lash cried out, then with a start, his eyes snapped open, and he looked down at me with fear. Then he was groaning loudly, as he gave himself up to his orgasm, his organ squirting into me in great gobs. I swallowed, but he kept coming. Just when I worried I'd have to push him out of me to breathe, he gave one last jerk and pulled out, shrinking and softening.

"God, I love you," Lash hissed, pulling me up into his arms to hug me. "If I forget to tell you later today, I love you, and you're the best lay of my life."

"Thanks," I said, rolling my eyes.

"I've had fantasies about that, about waking up like that," Lash hissed affectionately. "I was dreaming about you mouthing me. Then to awaken and actually find you doing it—God, that was amazing!" He looked over at the clock, remorse erasing his happiness. "Shit, we need to get dressed. We need to be out in a half hour. We're both going to need a shower."

We showered quickly. After checking out, I teleported us home. Devlin happily welcomed us back, though no one else mentioned my absence. Trystan was glad to see me and Lash, and we spent the rest of the day watching movies with Devlin and V, our dogs and cats curled on us or at our feet.

That night, lying spooning with Devlin and Lash, I felt like nothing could go wrong.

* * * *

But the next morning, something did.

I was making breakfast for Trystan, congratulating myself on a night with no nightmares and no drugs, when I heard a knock at the front door. Knowing that whoever was there had already cleared the gate guards, I went and answered it. To my surprise, Lyssa stood there on the step. She looked as surprised to see me as I was to see her. "Hi, Sar…elle. Is Lash here?" she said carefully.

She knew my name, and my nickname. The guards had cleared her. That probably meant one thing. Part of me felt terrible. The other part of me was fucking furious. "He's on duty. But why don't you come in?"

She came in, and I shut the door, trying hard not to slam it. Suddenly Tryst was there, winding around my feet, looking at her curiously.

"He's beautiful," Lyssa said, crouching down to look at him. "Tryst looks the image of Lash—"

I wanted to kick her, knowing how she'd seen Lash in snake form and what they'd likely been doing when she had. No wonder he hadn't asked me to be snake for him in Florida! In addition, Lash'd told her our son's name. *Fucking bastard…*

"Come here, Sweetie, I won't hurt you—"

…and fucking bitch. "Don't touch my son, *Lys.*"

"Look, I didn't expect to find you here, *Sar*," Lyssa said roughly, her eyes narrowing at my use of her nickname as she sinuously stood. "I don't want to get in the middle of anything—"

"You are in the middle," I said harshly, dialing my phone. "But don't worry, we'll sort this out real quick."

Lash answered on the first ring. "What is it, Sweetness? Did you make me cookies?"

"There's someone here to see you. It's urgent you come right now." I hung up before he could say anything. Then I teleported my son to Titus's house.

I arrived to find him playing with Sunrise in his living room,

152

levitating small globes of colored light for her amusement. The bigger surprise was that Leri was with them.

"What the fuck?" I shouted. "When did you get out of Hell?" I cast my mind out for Rene, shouting telepathically that Leri was back.

"Who's that woman we just saw?" Tryst hissed shyly. "She's snake, like Dad and me."

"Her name is Lyssa," I said, trying to sound calm. "She's an old friend of your father's."

"Sar, I'm sorry," Leri said quickly, as Titus said, "Just yesterday, Kin-daughter. Rip helped me rescue her."

"Rescue her? You fucking put her there! What the hell is wrong with you, letting this...this..."

"This bitch free," Rene supplied quickly, appearing in our midst. "What is she doing here, Titus?"

"I'm reformed," Leri said quickly. "Titus has many spells of binding on me, and I'm under house arrest, Rene. There won't be any trouble."

There would be when I told Terian that his baby girl was in the company of his evil mother. But I could only deal with one bitch at a time. "Rene, can you deal with this? I have to get back—"

"I know," she said, her eyes telling me she knew who waited for me in Hayden's kitchen. "I'll deal with this, Sister. Take your son to Elle, instead."

"Elle? He tried to bite her last time."

"Go now," she hissed. "Hurry!"

I nodded and teleported to my old home, aiming for the driveway, the one landmark there least likely to change. We arrived to see a nice modular home, my old garage, and a small dog barreling straight toward us.

"Hope! Come back here!"

I told Trystan not to bite, and held him up, away from the lunging dog. Elijah arrived in a moment and grabbed her. "Sorry, Sar. Elle didn't say you were coming. Hope, no! Down!"

"Trystan, this is Elijah. You need to stay with him for a little while. Don't bite him, okay?"

Elijah looked at me calmly, though he was clearly worried. "For how long?"

"Hi, Mom," Elle called as she waddled over. "Come to see how big I am?"

"I need you to watch Tryst," I said quickly, noting she was indeed big enough for twins. "I need to get back."

"Please come in," Elijah said. "I'd love to show you the nursery. Elle's done a lot of painting and stenciling. We were going for a beach theme with sandcastles and shells."

I ignored him, hating how mean it felt. "Tryst, I mean it. You have to be good, and not bite anything, okay? Promise me."

"I promise," he hissed sullenly. "I wanted to meet that woman. She was like me."

Elle shot me a look as if she understood, then averted her eyes. "He'll be fine," she said, reaching to take Tryst from me fearlessly. "Come over here, brother."

Trystan hissed in distress, but he went to her, coiling a few times around her arm.

"I have a few old clothes he can put on," Elle said firmly. "We'll have a good time. You like horror movies, Tryst, right?"

Tryst nodded enthusiastically.

"We'll see you later, Mom," Elle said with a nod. "Good luck." She turned, and walked with Trystan to the house, Elijah following her with a confused look on his face.

I teleported back to Hayden's kitchen in time to see Lyssa sitting at the table applying fresh lipstick. I was just going to comment that the color wasn't her shade when Lash strode in, his eyes relieved when he saw I was okay. "You hung up before I could tell you it was going to take me ten minutes. What's so important? Who is—?"

Then Lash saw Lyssa. He closed his eyes, and leaned against the door, taking a deep breath and holding it a few moments before he let it out slowly.

His response to her was all I needed to know. "She's here to see you," I said flatly. "She's confused, and you need to figure out a few things, too. I'll be out."

Lash didn't try to stop me from teleporting, not that he could have. I thought about where to go to get away. All I could thing about was I wanted to get away from them, from him and her, from what it meant for

154

us. Then I told myself to stop acting like a child. Running away wasn't going to solve anything. I had to stay right here and solve this. The sooner I did, the sooner I could get on with my life. *Tryst Jr. is what's important. He has to come first, before anything else. You have to stay and talk to Lash, after he talks to Lyssa.*

Instead of teleporting off the grounds like I wanted, I went out by myself in the sun and walked the cemetery. I visited Anna and Abraham, and walked for hours not really seeing my surroundings. I might have walked the entire cemetery that day, I'm not sure. Rational and adult as I was acting, this was the best place for me. If I didn't see anyone, I'd be less likely to make things worse by fighting with Titus over Leri or being sent to Hell because of a revenge screw.

No worries, Shaker said in my mind. *I'm on good behavior.*

I gathered my will to ask what I didn't truly want to know. "Did you know?" I said aloud.

No, came Shaker's reply. *Whatever is going on with him and her, it can't have been—*

I'm not asking about Lyssa and Lash's relations, I interrupted, forcing out each word. *You told me that night Theo got drunk about how I was doing the best I could, that the future would work out okay. And you mentioned everyone important in my life then, except one: Lash. Did you know then that this was going to happen to us, that we would end up like this?*

It took Shaker a few minutes of silence to answer. *The future is not set,* he thought finally. *But I didn't need Rene's talent for sight to know that trouble was coming. I knew about him and Sundown, and I knew about you and Terian.* He made a noise of disapproval. *Lash lets things matter that shouldn't matter, and reacts and speaks before he thinks. It is why none of his relationships has ever worked. And it's why you and he likely won't work, either. I'm sorry, Mistress.*

Leave me, for now, I thought to him, trying not to let my hurt show. But of course, Shaker already sensed my hurt feelings and departed immediately.

Lash found me there at dusk beside Anna. He sat beside me on the stone wall, and didn't say anything for a long time. When he put his hand over mine, I let him.

155

"Do you love her?" I whispered.

"No," he hissed softly. "I did once, though. We have a lot of history."

We were silent for a few moments.

"I'm sorry," he said finally. "I was angry and I knew how jealous you were of her—"

"I already know why and what happened," I said with difficulty. "I just want to know when it started."

"After you told me you'd been with Shaker. That first night after you told me, and you left." He swallowed. "I thought you were going to him, to be with him, now that I'd told you we weren't mated anymore and refused to talk to you. I went crazy." He paused. "I knew she was visiting her sister here, she always sends me postcards letting me know when she's going to be in town—"

And you fucking saved them, you bastard. "How many times?"

"Just one night," he hissed softly. "Nothing started, Sar. There's no relationship. I made a mistake, one I was and am sorry for."

I didn't respond. Lash took that as asking for more information. "I have no idea how many times. I wasn't in a frame of mind to care at the time." He paused. "The truth is, I was so drunk I don't remember any of it. But I know how I woke up."

He is lying again. He remembered what happened, at least some of it. *Just breathe, and get to the minute after this one.* "Why didn't you say anything?"

"I didn't want you to know I'd fucked up," he hissed. "Not after I'd been true to you so long." He paused. "Like I said, I was too drunk to really remember most of it, but I know it wasn't just as snake, Sar." He swallowed. "I went right from her to Camlyn's and got tested by Brenda, even though Lys swore she was clean. I got the results before starting my drive to see you. And there was nothing, um, I was clean."

So you fucked me in the dirt the next day before you even knew if you had something, you utter bastard. "You should have told me when you came to me about her," I whispered in an old voice. "I'd have forgiven you, if you'd just told me the truth then. Instead you lied again to me."

"Please forgive me," Lash hissed. "It was a mistake. I told her after I was sorry, that it'd been a mistake, that I'd used her to hurt you. She said she didn't care, that she—"

"STOP talking about HER!" I shouted.

He fell silent.

"Did she like my name over your heart?" I said nastily. "Or didn't you bother to take off all your clothes when you fucked her?"

"I'd scored it with my knife and some poison earlier, trying to get it off. I told her it was a scar," Lash hissed regretfully. "I was so angry, thinking of you with that demon, of him inside you. I wanted to cut it out of me, cut you out of me, but I couldn't, even though I carved myself up good trying."

I felt very old and just didn't care anymore. *How did I get to this point, when I can't stand to look at someone that months ago I would have died for?* "Do you still want to be with me, like you told me you wanted yesterday? Or was that bullshit?"

"Yes," Lash hissed quickly. "I only want you. I didn't go to her because I wanted her."

"Then why is she here?"

"Hoping to break us up by telling you what happened," Lash said, kicking at the ground. "She made it clear she wanted me, and would do whatever she could to get me back. I asked her not to say anything, to stay away from me, but you know how well that goes."

No, I don't, actually, Lash. "Maybe we should break things off," I said, putting my head in my hands. "Our mating is broken anyway, with what both of us did. I'm tired of crying over you, Lash. Though I like making up after, it's too much stress. This isn't love: how nastily we fight, how jealous we both feel, and how badly we treat each other. This isn't how people are supposed to show their love for one another."

Lash got up, stood in front of me, and unbuttoned his shirt, showing me his chest where my name was still etched over his heart. "It's still there, Sar. It's going to be there forever, because I love you. This is love, Sweetness. It hurts so much because it's the real thing. We just need to get better at it and work harder. I admit I'm at fault, I keep letting my anger get the best of me—"

"Nothing is forever, not really," I said bitterly with a shrug. "Not love or a tattoo. You can get it removed, and I'll give you your ring back.

You can be with her and have more children, and I'll stick to Danial and Dev. We'll be okay living here if we avoid each other. I'm not leaving our son, and it'd be wrong to ask you to leave his life. But I'm not sure how best to break it to Tryst."

Lash looked at me sadly. "You really believe it's that easy to say goodbye?"

"It's not easy," I said bitterly, wanting to slap him for minimizing my broken heart. "It hurts like I'm fucking dying. But it'll hurt less this way, because it's clean and quick. I remember what you said, how it was hard for weres to stay faithful when a younger one of their kind offered sex. You didn't save those postcards of hers for sentimental reasons. All your bullshit talk in Florida about how we had something so special was just that: bullshit. Lys is younger, she's still fertile, and she wants you bad. This was going to happen sooner or later, Lash."

"No," Lash hissed brokenly. "It wasn't, Sar. I never would've gone to her, not—"

"I don't believe you. This isn't the first time you lied to me, Lash. I do believe that Lys thought she had a good enough chance at you to come here. She probably knows you better than I do. You told me I didn't really know you, remember?" I closed my eyes, and looked away from him. "Go back to her, Lash. Go back and tell her you're all hers."

"Please, Sweetness, please don't do this."

"Don't call me that, Lash." I swallowed. "Not ever again. We'll work something out with Tryst, so you get to see him every day. I don't want him to see us fighting anymore. He gets upset and he has your temper. I don't want him to grow up to destroy things or people, like you do so casually." I looked him up and down slowly and deliberately. "I don't want him to be anything like you."

He took a deep breath. "So you want it to be over between us?"

"Yes."

Lash unsheathed his knife with a snap and handed it to me. "Then remove your name, Mate. Dig it out, my blade is sharp enough. Consider that breaking our mating."

As I took the blade from him, he steeled himself and it suddenly clicked. "There's poison on your blade, isn't there?"

Lash nodded. "It's the normal I use now. I started using it again, after what happened in New Orleans. It'll make me bleed out in a matter of a minute or two. If you actually hit my heart, it'll be faster."

I threw down the knife. "I'm not killing you, you asshole. You want to die, do it yourself!"

"I'm not living without you!" Lash hissed, grabbing me in his arms. "I'd rather die by your hand than have to go back to being alone!"

"Stop the melodrama! Go be with Lys, she obviously loves you!" I shouted, pushing him away. "Just love her back, Lash! It should be easy!"

"Not for me," he whispered, a tear sliding down his cheek.

I stared at him, surprised.

"I've never loved anyone like I love you," he said, another tear falling. "Please love me back. Please don't leave me. I want to be with you and our son, or else die, because Hell's got to be fucking trouble-free next to living without you."

"You threatened to leave me a few days ago with dry eyes, Lash. What changed?"

"Nothing changed, except I'm not bluffing anymore. I'm not taking Tryst away from you, you're right; I lied when I said I'd do that. He needs you, needs your love to make him grow up so he's not a monster like me." He swallowed. "He needs you more than he needs me." He wiped his eyes angrily, despite they were filling again. "If you can't do it, it's okay, I can. Just leave me here, if you don't want to see me do it. Tell Tryst I was killed on a job. Please don't tell him I fucked up, and that you told me it was over. Please tell him you loved me, that we loved each other. I don't want my son to remember me as a bastard or a coward." He swallowed. "I want him to think of me as a good man who sometimes did bad things because he thought he had to."

"Look at me," I said, pausing a moment until our eyes locked. "I'm not covering up your misdeeds, not ever again. You are everything Danial always said you were, to the letter. You are not a good man. And you don't deserve me." I threw the knife down, and began to walk away. "Goodbye."

Lash picked it up, and with a hiss of pain, he sunk the blade into his stomach and began to rip upward with both hands.

With a scream, I dashed to him and pulled it out, but he was already

159

toppling backward, blood gushing out of him. I quickly pulled off my shirt, wrapped my hands, and put them on his streaming wound, desperately murmuring the spells Rene had taught me. His flesh slowly healed, as I painstakingly drew out the poison, letting it flow drop by drop to soak into the ground by his side.

As soon as all the poison was out, I threw aside the shirt quickly, checking my hands nervously. I breathed a sigh of relief to see they were undamaged. The barrier spell had worked. *And this is why she taught it to you, and the healing: to save him.*

I ripped Lash's shirt the rest of the way in the front, peeling it off him, being careful not to touch any poison or blood, and lay it over the spot of poison-soaked ground, covering it.

Lash lay there on his back, gasping, looking at me with pain-filled eyes as his body continued to heal. "Let me die," he hissed weakly. "Don't save me. You should have let me die and not saved me those years ago—"

"No, you bastard," I said angrily. "You're going to live, not take the easy way out. You're going to spend every Goddamned day of the rest of your life making me happy that I saved your stupid ass. You're going to get your shit together, and stop being an asshole, too. Understand?"

Lash looked at me in surprise, and then he began to sob. I hugged him to me, loving him but not forgiving him, wrapped around each other in the tall grass, him telling me I was his mate, that he loved me, that I was everything to him. We held each other, crying, bloody, and not caring, because at least we were still together, even if we were both fucked up and crazy and deserved each other.

"So what's this death wish shit?" I said finally. "Sundown told me you were planning this last time we broke up, that she stopped you by calling Devlin."

"Should've known it was her and not Davy that let you know where I was that night," Lash said, embarrassed.

"You should thank her, she saved your life. Now tell me what the hell you were thinking, sticking yourself with a poisoned blade."

"I've lived a long time," Lash said, sounding for the first time his real age. "I never wanted to give up, no matter how bad things got. Things always can get better when they're bad. Things were never

160

stupendous for me anyway. But they're really good with you. Even despite everything we've been through, these years since knowing you have been my happiest." He paused. "So what have I got to look forward to after life's been the best it can be?" He shrugged. "That's why."

"Why didn't you stab your heart? I don't know if I could've healed that, I'm still learning the more intricate spells for healing."

"You're there, over it," he hissed tenderly. "I wasn't going to put my knife through your name, not even if you left me to die." He hugged me tightly. "I won't fuck up again, Sweetness."

"We won't fuck up again," I replied. "But I don't want you to ever try that again."

"Shaker can have my soul, too," Lash hissed quickly. "If I ever cheat on you again, he can have it, then and there."

"I accept," Shaker said, popping into view. "But only give me permission, both of you, and I'll be happy to join your garden party right here and now without taking any souls."

"Stop," I said, rolling my eyes. Lash was busy trying to cover my bra with my long hair, hissing swear words in irritation. "Please leave, Shaker."

"Good fucking," Shaker said cheerily, and disappeared.

"Demons," Lash hissed. He got to his feet. "We should go, Sweetness. Tryst is upset."

"I left him with Elle. Why is he home?"

"From what Elle said, most of the day went fine. However, Tryst kept asking to come home, and got angry when they refused to let him call Hayden. He was wrestling with Elijah in fun, but somewhere the line blurred and they both began fighting for real. There was no lasting harm done, but Elle decided that Tryst should come home for dinner, as he was clearly upset. I gave him some fish before coming to see you, and told him to stay in his room, that I might be a while getting you. He ate it, though he said he wasn't hungry."

I leaned on him. "Let's go talk to him."

We found Tryst in his room, a few broken toys around him. When he saw me, he ran and hugged me. "Mom! Where were you?"

"Out walking. I'm okay," I said, hugging him. "Everything's okay."

"It wasn't, that's the truth," Lash hissed darkly, hugging Tryst. "But your mother is right, it is now. I see some toys broken here, son. What happened?"

"I broke them because I was angry and worried you weren't going to be my dad anymore, the way that Theo stopped being Elle's dad—"

Where did he hear that? From who? Elle, today?

"That would never happen," Lash hissed flatly. "You're my son, and I'm always going to be your dad, always. Sar's always going to be your mom. Neither one of us are going anywhere, because we love you and each other. We just have had trouble relating that love to each other a good deal of the time lately." He hugged Tryst and me. "Your mom and I are going to work on that. I admit, a lot of it is my fault, for not having experience."

"And some is mine, from having too much," I said sadly. "Your father's right, you don't have to be afraid. We'll fight again, Tryst. But we'll make up after. It doesn't mean we don't love each other, or love you." I reached out and grabbed Lash's hand. "It doesn't mean we're not going to stay together."

"Who was that woman, Dad? I asked and you didn't answer me before."

"She was a female to my male years ago," Lash hissed finally. "She wanted to be your mother. I explained to her you already had one. She won't be coming back, Trystan."

Trystan gave his father a long look. "Okay. That's good, I already have a mom."

"Let's go see if Dev and V want to go out and catch a movie tonight," Lash hissed to me gently. "We could use the break."

"Sure," Devlin said, strolling into the room. "But perhaps we should save the movie for tomorrow night?" He handed me a card in flowing script. "We need to celebrate and make some plans. We've all been invited."

"What's this?" Lash hissed, looking the card over. "Danial is throwing Elle a shower/wedding?"

"Elle told him yesterday about being pregnant. He immediately called Samuel and asked him if he wanted to go in on a big bash." Devlin rolled his eyes. "I of course would've been happy to co-host, but alas, I'll have to wait for V to settle down."

162

"Not going to happen anytime soon," V said with a snort as she passed by. "I have too much to do to think about men, Dad. There's a new racetrack opening soon, and I need to help organize a protest for the poor greyhounds—"

"Which I told you I'd be glad to help with," Devlin finished. "As will your Mom. I want you to remember that Elle is your sister. That means you'll be asked to be a bridesmaid, if not maid of honor." He gave her a pointed look. "This is your chance to mend fences with her."

"She did call and ask me to be a bridesmaid," V mumbled. "I said I would."

"Good!" Devlin said in approval. "It's a start. Don't forget, the Hallows party is coming up in another week. You'd better start looking for a dress."

"I know," V said sarcastically. "I'll be there to dance the night away both nights. But right now I need a snack." She gave a dazzling smile, and then flounced away. Tryst ran downstairs after her, yelling at her to make him some liquefied steak.

Devlin gave Lash and I a satisfied look. "Did you hear that? We may make a family out of this tangle yet."

That was a nice sentiment, but we had more important things to discuss. "Dev, did you talk to Rene? Leri's back."

"Yes. Rene is handling it."

"Damn bitch," Lash hissed. "I knew she wouldn't be gone long. Titus is such a pussy."

"Leri is under house arrest," Rene said, appearing in our midst suddenly. "I put a few binding spells on her myself, in addition to Titus's. She'll do little but tend his house and his personal needs."

"Good, he'll be more accommodating," Devlin said. He turned to Lash, curious. "Are you up for a conference call with Mad? You're missing your shirt, and I smell dried blood."

"Sar got pissed and stabbed me," Lash lied, his eyes asking me not to call him on it. "I deserved it. She healed it after I apologized. No big deal."

"If you weren't such an idiot, you'd learn to keep your blood on the inside," Rene said jovially, giving him a big smile. "Next time apologize first, and keep the knife out of reach."

163

I began to laugh with the others, and then noticed her eyes looking at Lash sadly. Then the double meaning of her words hit me.

She knows he's lying. She knew what he'd tried to do.

Chapter Thirteen

As soon as Devlin and Lash went down the hall, I grabbed hold of Rene. "You knew he would try what he did!" I snarled at her. "That's why you suggested teaching me healing! That's why you led me to believe I might have to deal with an emergency! To get me to practice, so I'd be ready when the time came!"

"And you were," she said coolly, her words measured. "Now I suggest you go play with your children, Sarelle McGarran."

Ice water bathed me at her use of my full name. "What?" I said weakly. "Why?"

"Bad times are coming," she said, a shadow flickering across her face. "Tonight is safe, Sister. They are safe. Enjoy it."

She strode off to her room, me gaping after her, tears in my eyes.

* * * *

The next week was a flurry of activity. Danial had Tatiana arranging his Hallows celebration as usual, but she was also arranging the bridal/baby shower for Elle. There was still much to plan: what to wear and what presents to buy or make. I'd signed the house over to Elle already, so wasn't sure what else to give her. In the end, I made her a baby outfit, and put one of her favorite childhood books inside it.

Lash and Devlin were busy making preparations also, both for the Hallow's party and for our trip the following week. Because the biggest surprise was that Elle's party wasn't going to be held in a convention center, she'd decided it was going to be held on a beach at night. Her formal marriage to Elijah was going to take place just after dusk in a nearby church, in the small town of Homestead, FL.

165

I teleported in to the small town of Sylmar's Beach the next morning. My mother accompanied me, as did Rene. They were standoffish at first, but by lunch were talking like old friends about shoes and many other things.

"Devlin can be an ass, it's a fact," Rene said as she put a fry in her mouth. "But so can I, Tina. Don't worry, Sar and I have him well in hand." She smirked. "Well, hands."

I blushed, but my mother was riveted. "Tell me about being a witch, Rene. Is it hard to learn?"

"Not at all. Your daughter's well on her way to being a good witch," Rene said proudly. "She's a gifted student."

My phone rang, and I excused myself to answer it. It was Shaker.

"Why aren't you just talking telepathically to me?"

"I can't," he rumbled. "Something's blocking me. Tell me where you are."

"Tell me what we did in dreams, so I know it's you."

He laughed, and began to describe the first hour of our dream in vivid detail.

"Enough, it's you. Sylmar's Beach, near the entrance to the diner," I said. "Come to me."

He appeared, instantly becoming invisible. "Mistress, let me shadow you," he murmured in my ear. "Something old and evil is lurking nearby."

I ran back in the restaurant, and sat down quickly. Shaker following me.

"Did it get hotter in here?" my mother said, drawing her coat off her shoulders. "I'm glad they turned on the heat. Why Elle wants her party on a beach at night in November, I can't figure."

"This is Florida, it'll still be warm," I soothed her. "We really should be getting back. Chris probably has his hands full with Trystan."

"I'm sure they're having a great time," she said, giving me a grumpy look. "I thought we were, too. But you girls probably want to get back to that scoundrel."

"We do," Rene said with a wink. "He needs watching. Let's do lunch again soon, say next week? I enjoyed talking to you."

My mother agreed with a smile, clearly pleased.

166

After we dropped her off and returned home, I told Trystan he could go swim if he wanted. As soon as he took off for the pond, I turned to Rene heatedly.

"What was the big deal, telling my mother we'd see her every week? You had no right to do that. She's in enough danger just seeing us publicly once in a while."

Rene gave me a calculating look. Then suddenly her features shifted, becoming mine. "I have every right," she said in my voice, giving me a shark smile. "I'm like a daughter to her, Sar, or I soon will be. Who said you were even invited?"

I lost control and slapped her hard. "Don't you dare go near her," I hissed. "What is wrong with you?"

"You going to stop me?" She laughed. "Please!" She gave me a murderous look. "Stay out of my way, Sar. You get in the way and you'll be dead." She stalked off to her bedroom, and slammed the door.

I gaped after her. Shaker appeared next to me, also looking stunned.

"Tell me, was that really her? It sounded more like Leri."

"It was Rene," he rumbled. "Don't worry. She's no match for me, Mistress. I'm in your corner."

"But I thought she was," I murmured, rubbing my eyes. "I thought we were friends."

"Come," he said, leading me to the kitchen. He poured me a glass of wine, and then one for himself.

I sipped it, not knowing what to think about what had just happened. "I thought Rene was my best friend. I'm going to have to reconsider that now."

"So she showed you her dark side," Shaker said, tossing back his drink. "You knew she had one. That witch has had an agenda her whole life. You want my advice; take her words to heart. Do what she says. In other words, stay out of her way, and you'll be fine."

"What if I'm in her way right now just being alive?" I murmured, moving my wine glass around. "She threatened to kill me."

"It was talk," Shaker said flatly, pouring another glass of wine and knocking it back. "I know enough to recognize a bluff when I hear one. She wants you cowed for some reason."

"What reason could there be for her behavior?"

167

"I don't know." He knocked back a third glass. "So you're easier to control? That's the usual reason for scare tactics."

Rene did seem way over the top. Hmm. "So you think this is some kind of manipulation?"

Shaker nodded, finishing the bottle. Then he took my untouched glass from me, and drank that. "It's an old trick, maybe the oldest. I should know, I've been an instrument to scare good and evil beings both since Lucifer's fall from Heaven."

I gathered my courage. "What was he like, really? Um, or is he like?"

"I didn't know him, really," Shaker said, grinning. "I'm a midlevel demon, not some big archangel. I haven't seen or heard from him directly in hundreds of years. But he was known as the wisest of all creatures. He believed in what he was doing. It was hard not to follow someone with as much faith in himself as in God."

"How did Titus get Leri out of Hell?"

"There's an old rule, Mistress: Heaven can pull strings to get souls from Hell, if other souls in Heaven need them saved in order to find peace."

"I don't understand."

"He bribed someone in Heaven to put in a call for Leri's soul. Titus has harvested more than a few souls in his time. Likely, he traded one of his stash for hers, one Heaven wanted back. Then he pulled her out in transit, where she'd be easiest to grab—"

Titus had a stash of souls? The good father figure who called me his daughter? My flesh got goose bumps. "Do you have a stash of souls?"

Shaker looked at me, gave me the evilest grin imaginable, and said nothing.

Quick, next subject. "Why don't you have more powers?"

Shaker gave me a dumbfounded look, and then cracked up in laughter. "Like what?"

"Like flying or something?"

"I offered to teleport you to the Bahamas," he said teasingly. "But we could've flown instead, though it would take days. I have many powers through magic, Mistress. Flight is one of them, as it is for Titus. What kind of powers are you interested in?"

He was making it sound like powers were my sexual turn-on. "Can you see the future? Can you possess people?"

"Some of us can," he said grumpily. "All I used to hear for most of the second century was summoners asking me to divine their future, quoting that idiot who wrote Acts 16:16. But I can't."

"And possession?" I said impatiently. "I know that's mentioned in the Bible, and I've seen a lot of TV shows."

"Forget your TV shows," Shaker said, rooting around the cabinets looking for more alcohol. "It's not anywhere that glamorous or tawdry." He turned to me. "Ever wonder why the Old Testaments don't talk so much about demon possession, but the New Testaments are rife with it?"

"Um...no."

"Of course you don't, because no one ever points that out." He slammed a cabinet, frustrated. "You'd think we demons just appeared after the year 0 the way it's written. Fucking angels are all over the place...Where's the good stuff, Sar? Lash must keep a bottle in here for emergencies. Titus has moved his Black Arts, damn him."

"I don't think so; his best scotch is under lock and key in our room. Why are you changing the subject—?"

"Why aren't you ever asking me about Jesus?" Shaker said loudly, slamming another cabinet door. "I thought you were big into Him, yet your questions never mention Him."

"I didn't know you knew Him."

"I don't," Shaker howled with laughter. "But I saw Him once, when He came to Hell to free souls. He freed a favorite torture-ee of mine, a monk who was a great beer brewer. I tell you, he was a blast to talk to, even with him being a virgin—"

"What the hell?" Lash walked in. "Did you call me? I got a message to come here fast."

"No," Shaker said, shaking his head. "But come in and sit down. Sar and I were discussing the merits of monks. I'll open another bottle, if you'll tell me where the scotch is. Titus has hidden his Black Arts, the bastard."

"I called you," T said from the doorway. "Hi, Mom."

He was almost unrecognizable. His eyes were sunken, yet they flashed with pride and anger. His clothes were rain-soaked, his long dark hair back in a bedraggled ponytail. I went to get up to hug him, and then noticed he was holding a chain in his hand.

T gave a vicious yank on it. A figure in rags fell into the room, sprawling at our feet.

"Tell her you're sorry," T growled, his fangs long and white in his face. "Tell Lash you're sorry, Michael."

Chapter Fourteen

It was indeed Michael. His beard was back, and he was a good deal thinner, his eyes rolling in their sockets. He didn't speak. Lash was moving before I had time to process T's words. He grabbed the ragged figure by the throat, and pushed him up against the wall. "You miserable fuck," Lash hissed maniacally, slamming Michael hard into the wall. Several cracks appeared radiating above his head. "I'm going to beat you to death. What do you think of that?" He put his hands around Michael's neck and began to squeeze slowly.

"He can't answer," T explained, pulling up a chair and sagging into it. "I cut out his tongue."

"Smart move," Shaker said, nodding as he poured T a shot of whiskey from a bottle he'd somehow procured. "He knows a fair amount of magic."

Lash continued to strangle Michael, who struggled, gasped and wheezed, but didn't die.

T drank the shot down, and Shaker poured him another.

Devlin strolled in, followed by Rene. "What's this, an impromptu party? Good, hand me a glass—" He cut off sharply, his mouth dropping open to see Lash still choking Michael.

"Stop, Lash," Rene commanded suddenly.

Lash ignored her, making Michael's eyes pop from his head as he gasped for breath.

Rene strode up to Lash, crackling lightning forming in her hands. She flexed her fingers, and two bolts hit him square in the back, dropping him to his knees.

"Rene!" Devlin shouted, staring for her. "What are you doing?"

171

I screamed, lunging for her.

She kicked Lash out of the way, grabbed Michael and disappeared.

"Go after them, Shaker!" I screeched. "Kill him! Kill him now!"

Shaker disappeared abruptly, as Kyle rushed in, gun drawn. I fell to my knees beside Lash, who was grunting in pain, dual wounds on his back smoking. I put my hands on him, murmuring words of healing as I tried not to cry.

"Assemble the guards now, Kyle," Devlin said quickly. "We are going to Titus. Leri must have subdued Rene earlier, and assumed her form to rescue Michael. I'm going to need all of your demon-fighting skill; he's going to resist us taking her—"

"No, I won't," Titus said abruptly, striding in with Leri in tow. "Because Leri is right here next to me."

"You're lying," Devlin hissed. "Rene would never betray me. She would never betray Sar." His red eyes latched onto Leri. "Where did you teleport him, witch?"

Leri raised her brows. "I didn't." Then she looked down at me, and knelt next to me, taking hold of my hands. "Sar, don't bother, really. Lash doesn't need healing. He's just stunned." She got to her feet and helped me up, as T propped up Lash in a kitchen chair.

"She can't have done this," I sniffled. "Not willingly. Not purposely."

Devlin quickly embraced me, gathering me up in his arms. "Shh. We'll find out what happened, Love. Shh."

"Motherfuck," T said, knocking back another shot. "It took me the better part of a year to track that shit down, and I no sooner get him here than he escapes. Son of a bitch!"

"Easy," Danial said sternly from the doorway. "Your mother is present, son. And your siblings upstairs can also hear you."

"Kyle…" Lash rasped, staggering to his feet. "Get the guards….mobilized. Scan the house, all of it. Check everywhere. She may have just done this to get him alone to torture him first, or to find out information."

Kyle nodded, and ran out, barking orders into his phone.

"Titus…can you locate her?" Lash asked.

"No," Titus rumbled. "She is near my level of magic, Lash. Shaker can best her, but he will likely lose her as she teleports repeatedly. She would not have tried this unless she was sure to succeed." He turned to me. "Sar, can you reach her telepathically?"

I concentrated hard. "No. Shaker says he is still tailing her. They are near Queens."

Lash groaned. "Sar, you contact Shaker regularly and let us know his progress. T, how did you…find him the first time?"

"A lot of checking into everything he's known to have enjoyed doing or seeing in his decades as Ruler. A lot of fruitless legwork checking out old crumbling mansions in jungles and arid mountains, his favorite spots to reside." T knocked back another drink. "I finally found him lurking in a tomb in Mexico. He was feeding off drunks." He sighed. "So much work and it was all for nothing!"

"You getting drunk won't solve anything, either," Danial said harshly. "Pull yourself together, T. Michael is unimportant and no threat. Rene is. We need a plan and to figure out what she means to do next."

"To do that, we need her motive," Devlin added. "And we don't have it."

Lash let out a loud hiss, and slammed his hand down on the table. "Then we operate without one. We go to the highest defensive level. Cell phones for everyone at all times, on at all times. No unnecessary trips outside the walls and necessary ones are to have four guards at least to every non-guard. The children are not to leave the house, and neither are you, Sar. Titus, you and Leri seal every inch of this house from magical attack and from Rene teleporting in. Rene is to be detained by any means necessary if seen on the grounds. Shoot to incapacitate her just short of killing her outright. Does everyone understand?"

We all nodded.

Lash got to his feet with a groan. "Let's get moving. We have a lot to do before the sun rises."

"What do you want me to do?" T said, getting to his feet.

Lash eyed Danial, and then looked back at T. "You offered me your help, T, if I ever needed it. Well, I need it now."

"What do you need?" Danial said, standing beside T. "I'll help as well."

Lash held his eyes a moment, and then gave a single nod. "Get that

173

white witch and half-demon of yours to find Rene, whatever it takes, Danial. Use whatever influence you have with the State Rulers to get them looking for Rene and Michael, but only say we want him dead and her questioned. Keep it to yourself that they aren't working alone."

"You're saying Valerian's alive, that he planned this?" Devlin interjected.

Lash nodded. "I'd wondered why he hadn't surfaced in months. I think all along he was waiting for Michael to be located and brought here to us." He let out an annoyed hiss. "He either loves Michael, or he wants to torture him to death instead of letting us do it."

Terian appeared in the doorway. "Danial, T, I'm here for pickup," he quipped with a grin. Then he saw us all standing there, and his concerned eyes gravitated to me, then to Lash. He dropped his eyes, as Danial moved past him. A moment later Danial, T and he disappeared.

"Go and talk to Tryst and V," Lash said, giving me a quick hug. "Make sure they know what to do, Sar."

I nodded. He kissed my cheek, and strode away, Devlin and the rest following.

* * * *

That night I barely slept. Part of the reason for that was V, Tryst, Devlin, and all of our animals were crammed into his bedroom. I was taking no chances.

Devlin and I had talked for hours on why Rene had suddenly turned on us, and been unable to come up with any reason. Even after I'd told him of her odd behavior weeks earlier, he steadfastly remained certain that there must have been a reason. "Love, she could've killed Lash instead of stunned him. Just wait, she will likely contact us soon and explain her actions."

"Whatever the reason was, it doesn't matter," I'd replied. "I can't trust her, Dev. And I can't be friends with someone I can't trust."

The others had agreed with me. To that end, Lash was standing guard outside our door with Seth tonight, their presence heavy on me even though they made no sound.

I shifted, moving V over closer to Devlin, and tried to get some sleep, reassuring myself that if something were going to happen, it would be tonight. Rene had acted aggressively, and so more aggressiveness was likely to follow, according to Lash.

But nothing happened that night.

The next week, T, Terian, Tatiana, and Danial teamed with Leri and Titus and did an exhaustive magical and physical search of everything within a thousand miles. They found no sign of Rene or Michael.

Shaker returned reluctantly, admitting he had been able to singe Rene's hair short with a burst of Hellfire, but not kill Michael. "She escaped me with him. What punishment would you like to administer to me, Mistress?"

"None. Continue looking. Go to Devlin if you need what Rene used to give you."

"Yes, Mistress."

Days became weeks. Reluctantly, Devlin admitted that his faith in Rene might have been misplaced. "She could contact me easily," he mused one night. "I don't like to think of her betraying me. It's as if you betrayed me, Sar. It shakes my belief that there is order in the universe. But I have to face that she did."

"I believed in her, too," I said, shrugging. "She was like a sister to me."

Devlin hadn't replied, his golden eyes focused on something else only he could see.

* * * *

The night of the Hallows Party arrived.

Sipping drinks and smiling that night near Danial, I was struck by how surreal this all was to me now, this elaborate dress up party I'd agonized over only a few years ago. Scenes from the last one also haunted me, as I waited for Emma to appear, or someone to ask me where Rene was. But no one did.

I played my part and kept smiling, watching Devlin dancing with V. At least someone was having fun.

Lash was again working security, Terian collaborating with him. Lash had made it clear he'd as soon pound on Terian as work with him, but so far, things were okay. Ben, our burly newly hired werebat was also on the job. I wanted to ask him to change for me as I was curious what size a werebat would morph into, but resisted. *Lash will think I'm flirting.*

As the clock tolled eleven, the last human guests filed out as the first vampires came forward. Shortly after the various Rulers arrived, save for Kaizen. This time, they weren't alone with only guards. Zane and Perseus had two women with gold collars trailing them in elaborate dresses, their distended stomachs clearly revealed. Samuel had four in various stages of pregnancy, the largest looking as if she might give birth at any moment. All had gold collars.

I was slightly disgusted, but masked it as I greeted them.

"You've started a new trend, my dear," Devlin remarked jovially to me. "Everyone I've seen lately of the newly Oathed upper class is wearing gold collars instead of silver."

"It's good to be admired," I said nicely, shooting him daggers with my eyes.

"It's good to see you, Lady Dalcon," Samuel said, kissing my hand. "I thank you again for your gift of blood. You see the exciting results behind you."

Charming. "Yes, I'm very happy for you...all."

Samuel and the other Rulers talked to Devlin, Danial and I for the better part of an hour. Making conversation with them was easy, which surprised me. But all of the charged pressure that had surrounded my interacting with them over the years was gone. I was no longer earth-shatteringly special or coveted, just very respected. It was a huge relief.

Unfortunately, not everyone was pleasant. Around ten forty-five, Devlin excused himself for a moment. Two minutes later, a bloody brawl ensued.

The details came later: how Kaizan showed up with ten guards and began an argument with Akira almost at once. By the time Devlin had been alerted, Kaizan had his sword drawn and Akira was drawing his. When Devlin interceded on Akira's behalf, Kaizan sheathed his sword and threw a punch at him. He grazed Devlin, knocking him back a step, then Lash grabbed hold of Kaizan to escort him out. Kaizan turned around and promptly knifed Lash in the arm, which started the battle.

I missed all this. I made it to the sidelines just in time to see Terian hauling Lash off a bloodied, unconscious Kaizan. Most of the demons present were holding Kaizan's guards, in addition to our werebears and werefoxes. Lash was cursing, asking Terian to let him give Kaizan just a little venom.

The entire thing lasted no more than two or three minutes, but it terrified most of the demure "brides", and one of Samuel's fainted. He picked her up and strode off, his demons and other guards herding the rest of his harem after him through the doors. Perseus and Zane also abruptly took their leave, filing out with a swift and barely cordial farewell.

By that time, Kaizan had been teleported to his own domain with his guards by a few demons, still unconscious. Most of the vampires were in small groups, watching eagerly and talking amongst themselves. Devlin was talking to T as if the fight hadn't happened. But Danial wasn't nearly as calm.

"What is the matter with you?" Danial asked a bloodied but healing Lash. "You know better than to fight here. This is not some bar or brothel."

"Don't get your fangs twisted," Lash hissed easily. "This wasn't Ruler business, it was a challenge. He is still fifth in the Ranking, and if he starts a fight, I have to fight him. I can't walk away, or I forfeit my Rank."

"Let's get back to work," Terian said gruffly, coming over. "I admit he's right, Danial. That is one of the unwritten rules."

"You used it as an excuse to fight, Lash," Danial accused. "That isn't your job."

"It's my profession," Lash hissed back arrogantly. "And it's my life, if I back down instead. "

"Still, you could've taken it outside," Devlin said, rubbing his jaw. "Titus could've teleported you somewhere where you could've finished him off quietly. Now I'm going to hear about this from Samuel and the others, plus Kaizan's going to be an adversary every chance he gets."

"He already was our enemy," Lash hissed, grabbing his knife from the floor. "But he won't try any more of his shit with me again, I guarantee you that."

I excused myself to go to the bathroom, Dev asking Ben the werebat to accompany me. We'd reached the doors when I heard Lash telling Rip to watch hard, that he'd be gone a moment to clean off his knife and some of the blood.

"I'll go set up a perimeter against teleportation," Terian replied to Lash. "It'll take ten minutes or so. I don't want Kaizan teleporting back in here with more guards to up the stakes."

Lash ignored Terian, walking away. I saw him come through the double doors as I went into the women's bathroom.

"Watch the doors," I told Ben. "I need a private moment to speak to Lash."

Ben nodded, and took up a position near the doors, watching into the conference room. I went into the men's bathroom after Lash. He was shirtless near the sink, using wadded wet paper towels to wipe off some of the blood from his half healed wounds. His knife was already cleaned and back in its sheath.

"What's wrong?" I said, leaning against the door. "Why'd you fight him really?"

"He said some things about you," Lash hissed angrily, mopping up his bloodied chest. "Even if he hadn't, what I told Danial was true: I had to fight when he threw the first punch or forfeit my Rank." He turned smug. "He didn't have a chance. I wanted to pound on him anyway, so screw it." He finished mopping up his chest, and slid his blood-soaked shirt back on.

"Do you need some blood?"

Lash turned to me, his face softening. "Tonight, Sweetness. Go back before you're missed. I'll wait for a moment before coming out to give us distance."

I nodded and left the bathroom to go back to the party.

As I cleared the bathroom doors, I noticed Ben was missing. I was abruptly grabbed from behind before I could scream.

Chapter Fifteen

I struggled, but the arms holding me didn't loosen. I was dragged down a hallway and into a room. After being shoved inside, the door slammed after me. I waited, trying not to breathe loudly, listening for movement.

A bright light switched on above, making me blink. Michael stood before me, his rags now a suit, his face clean-shaven. "Hello, Sarelle."

I reached into my purse and produced an exploding bullets gun, aiming it at him. "I've been hoping you'd be stupid enough to do something like this."

"Please!" he put up his hands. "I'm not here to—"

A gunshot deafened me, and a large hole appeared in Michael's forehead. He dropped without a word to the floor.

"I thought I smelled vampire," Lash hissed, holstering his gun as he walked in. He strode to Michael and pulled his knife out of its sheath, sinking it in Michael's heart. Michael's body jerked, then lay still.

"Stupid fuck," Lash hissed, getting to his feet. "Stay here, Sar, I'll be right back. Don't get too close, he's not dead—"

A blast of fire caught Lash in mid-sentence, roasting his left arm even as he pushed us both to the floor with a hiss of pain. A swarthy being strode in, his flushed skin almost entirely covered in polished black leather. He threw more fire at us, but Lash got us out of the way, reaching into his coat for a vial. He threw it in the figure's eyes with an exultant hiss, and it crumpled, screaming as pockmarks formed from its melting skin.

"Stay back!" Lash pulled a knife from inside his coat, and leapt onto the blinded writhing figure. He stabbed down into its neck as the thing

179

howled, blasting him with fire again.

The being collapsed, and the absolute fear I'd been spellbound with dissipated in a rush.

"Fucking demons." Lash got to his feet, his back to me. For the most part his clothes were fine, except his black shirt was now blood-soaked and ripped to shreds that were mostly burnt. He took it off, throwing it aside with a hiss as specks of blackened skin flaked off in a cloud. "Fucking Hellfire." He wetted some more paper towels, scrubbing angrily at his arms and chest. "I should've guessed he had a demon. That's how he got in here." He let out a quick hiss of pain.

"Are you okay? Your voice sounds funny."

"My lungs got a blast of superheated air. It's hard to breathe." He turned to face me.

I let out a gasp. He'd been burned, the right side of his face blistered. His right arm was seared to the shoulder, his left mostly blackened muscle and bone. None of it was healing. "Can you heal Hellfire burns?" he asked hopefully.

I shook my head. "No. Rene left before teaching me that."

He strode toward me, grimacing. "Then I'll need some of your blood, please."

I nodded, easing down the left strap of my gown.

He embraced me, my stomach turning at the smell of his roasted flesh. A moment later his fangs slid in and he began sucking gently.

It'd been a long time since he'd bitten me without us having sex. I squirmed a little, trying not to think about how much this hurt.

Lash quickly slid his fangs out, and brushed his arms hard with his hands. Another flurry of burnt skin fell off, revealing new skin beneath. He faced me. "How's my face?"

"Partially healed," I said, inspecting him carefully. "But your one arm is still raw."

"And my chest hurts like sin," he hissed angrily. "I'll need to take more." He lifted me suddenly, setting me on a nearby couch. "Here, lay down. You shouldn't stand, you might faint."

I sat down, brushing specks of skin ash off my dress so it wouldn't stain. "Watch my dress. This silk will show everything, especially blood."

"I'll be careful." Lash pushed down my other strap, baring my breasts. I felt him kissing my neck gently, then a sharp painful thrust of his fangs deep into my unbroken flesh. I jerked, letting out a cry of pain.

He withdrew at once. "I'm sorry. I'll stop."

I swallowed hard. "No, you need it. Take it. I'll be okay."

He let out a breath and dug back in, making me cry out again. He clutched me around my waist, swallowing me down as I tried hard to hold still.

Suddenly came the sound of a zipper, as I felt one of his hands pushing up my dress.

"Hey, what are you doing? I didn't offer—"

My words ended in a soft cry as he eased my legs apart and pushed his stiff cock inside me. He began to move on me purposely, his lips still at my neck, drinking.

"Stop it," I moaned. "We can't. They'll scent you on me, all the guests—"

Lash gently withdrew his fangs, kissing my neck, his body still moving on mine. "So what?" he breathed.

"They'll put it together that I came to find you because I was worried you were hurt—"

"I don't care." Then he kissed down my front, taking one of my breasts in his mouth, teasing me with his coiled tongue. He moved up and kissed my neck passionately. "I need you and you need this. Nothing else matters."

I moaned, trying hard to fight what he was doing with skillful sure strokes. "Stop...ah!"

"No, Sweetness." He teased my other breast, then hissed forcefully in my ear, "I'm not giving you pain when there's another way. I love you too much for that. And the only thing that satisfies me more than coming in you is hearing you come and knowing it's me making you."

Lash kissed me deeply, his tongue coiling around mine as he drove into me. My orgasm burst in me suddenly with a shiver. I moaned loudly, clutching him to me, shaking.

He dug his fangs back in and drove harder, his arms squeezing me tightly as he climaxed.

Abruptly he went rigid and then moved off me, groaning as he

181

pulled out. As he did, his semen spattered my dress, staining it right in front.

My eyes widened as my mouth fell open in horror at the spreading stain. "Oh my God!"

"Oops," he hissed with a broken smile. "Guess you'll have to do your ceremony with Danial with a dirty dress. I'm sure he won't mind."

"You son of a bitch," I whispered, shocked. I ran to the sink and tried to wash it off, but only succeeded in smearing it and soaking the front of my dress, making a bigger mess.

Ignoring me, Lash brushed his arm again, flaking off more burnt skin to reveal he'd healed fully. He turned to me and said casually, "Ready to go back, Sweetness?"

I promptly kneed him in the balls. He went down hard with a hiss of pained surprise. I gathered the shredded remnants of my pride and stalked out, my only thought that I had to teleport home and change. *But everyone will know if I show up in different clothes that something happened, and there's no time to shower...*

"Thank Goodness," Ben said, appearing in the hallway before me. "I'd looked everywhere else but this section for you." He looked down at my dress. "What happened?"

"Please tell Dev I had to go home to change," I said quickly. "Tell him I'll be right back."

"Devlin asked me to find you and bring you back in at once," Ben said, taking my arm. "He was worried. I've already been looking for you five minutes now. The ceremony needs to be performed. Everyone is waiting for you."

This couldn't be happening: it had to be a nightmare. "Tell him I'll just be a moment, I have to change."

"He said now," Ben said apologetically.

I tried to teleport and couldn't. I called to Shaker, and he didn't answer. *Shit, what is happening?*

"Please come with me. I'll carry you to him, if you make me."

Goddamn it, Terian's set up his perimeter. I blinked back tears of frustration, jerked my arm free, and strode to the double doors, banging them open. My face and neck were fuchsia as I entered the ballroom ahead of Ben. The first vampires I passed scented the air, and immediately began whispering. All eyes were watching as I walked to Devlin, who was talking to Danial.

He sniffed once curiously, and then he saw my dress. Shock mixed with horror passed across his face. His red eyes found Lash strolling in behind me bare-chested and he bared his fangs. "I allow you many liberties, Lash. This is not one of them."

"So I did her," Lash hissed nonchalantly, hands on his hips. "Everyone knows I do."

"Not here," Danial growled. "Not *ever* here. Get out, Lash. You are banned from this annual party from now on. I was a fool to let you in."

"Make me," Lash laughed. "Try and make me leave. Call your guards and try it!"

"Leave now," Devlin growled. "Or you'll leave my employ as of this moment and our long friendship is over. Do as he says."

Lash looked hurt for a split second, and then his eyes flattened. "Sure, Dalcon. Whatever you say." He strode out, banging into the double doors so hard they slammed into the outer walls with a squeal of metal.

"This party is over," Devlin said loudly. "Any who were waiting to talk to me, please send me an email or letter. Come, Love." He took my arm and walked me quickly outside to the parking lot.

Danial came after us. "Sar, are you sure you want to go back to Hayden tonight?" He hugged me. "You do not have to."

"Danial is right," Devlin said viciously. "Go home with him tonight, Love. Lash and I need a few words on what is and is not appropriate, and they're going to be loud bloody ones." He kissed me quickly. "Take V with you."

"What about Tryst?" I said anxiously.

"Yes, he should not hear this either. Teleport home, and pick him up. I'll be there shortly."

Vampires were already coming out, asking petulantly if they could speak to him or Danial for a moment before leaving.

I nodded and teleported home with V, ending up in the kitchen.

"Get Tryst and pack," I told her. "Take only a few minutes. I'll grab some of my clothes from the dryer and then wait here for you."

V looked as if she wanted to say something, but she just nodded and walked upstairs. I slipped downstairs, walking to the dungeon. Lash was waiting for me beyond the cellar door, his face embarrassed.

I stood there, arms folded and glared at him. "Well?"

"I'm sorry for embarrassing you," he said, rubbing his eyes.

I debated slapping him. "That's all you have to say? I had to walk out there feeling like the world's biggest whore."

"I thought I heard something. It was an accident."

"Why did you do it at all? I told you not to."

"I needed to finish healing, and taking your blood was hurting you. Initiating sex seemed like a good idea at the time."

His logic had holes the size of warehouse doors in it. "You couldn't have found some other way? Sent me for Titus, or something?" I said sarcastically. "Devlin is as livid as Danial."

"I know," he said angrily. "Funny how he can sneak off and ball you at a party, yet I'm not allowed to."

"He's angry for the same reason I am; he was embarrassed."

"Look, for what it's worth, it gave us a big scene to get us all out of there, with me leaving first with Michael. Everyone will be talking about this, but the motives for what happened are easy and supplied. You're embarrassed, but safe. Michael's mine to torture with no one being the wiser. That's not all bad."

Said like that, it did make a warped kind of sense. But that didn't mean Lash didn't have his own reasons for his actions. I just shook my head and walked out, still feeling used.

V and Tryst were waiting for me in the kitchen when I returned, duffel bags in hand. "Where are your clothes, mom?" Tryst asked.

"Someone took them over already," I lied, shrugging. "But even if they aren't there, Danial will have some. Come on."

I teleported to Danial's. After I got V settled into Danial's spare bedroom upstairs, Tryst ready for bed, and tucked in to his sleeping bag in front of the woodstove, I took a shower. When I emerged, Danial had returned, and was just taking off his suit. "What a debacle," he said angrily. "Many of them made snide comments veiled in sympathy. I'll not repeat them to you." He slammed his hand down on the dresser. "I wanted to smash their simpering faces in."

"I can imagine," I said, flushing. "I've never been so embarrassed."

"It won't happen again," Danial said assuredly. "Thank God the Rulers had already left, not that they won't hear of it."

"I'm sorry," I said quietly. "It wasn't like what happened before with Devlin."

"I know," Danial said quickly. "I saw your outrage on your face. Don't think for a second I blame you, Sar."

I didn't reply, slipping into nightclothes.

Danial went into shower, and I lay down, falling asleep almost instantly.

* * * *

When I woke, Danial was holding me. I ran my hands over his, and then last night's events came crashing down on me.

I blinked back tears, and swallowed hard.

"Don't think about it," Danial said soothingly. "You were not at fault."

I turned and gave him a disgruntled look. "I never thought I was. I'm angry at Lash. I don't know why he does the things that he does."

"I am angry as well," he growled. "This was aimed at me, though Devlin took offense too, to my surprise."

I thought he was right, but didn't say that. *Enough talk of Lash and his failings.* "Why the party for Elle? I'm very happy you're doing it, but I'm surprised at its suddenness."

"I wasn't sure Elijah was a good match," he replied. "I thought it might be puppy love, not the real thing. I thought it might not last. But seeing them together, I believe its right."

"Have you visited them?"

"Yes. I was overcome at first to see them living where we started our relationship. They've made a real home there. It eases my heart to know she'll be watched over."

"You're a good dad," I said affectionately. "And our son? Serena was with Nick only a month ago. I haven't really talked to T since before he left."

"Serena and T are long over," Danial said with a shrug. "He made the mistake of trying to get too serious too fast before trying her blood." He sighed. "Once he had, he found it repugnant. As for Nick, I can't say.

185

Serena's okay though, she's taken up with Red, one of the newer foxes."

"I always knew it was all about the blood," I teased.

"It is," Danial said seductively, nibbling my neck. "I never said otherwise." He paused, his eyes mock serious. "Did I?"

"Many times," I said mock forlornly. "Lucky for you, I'm resistant to your charms."

Danial didn't reply.

"What is it?"

He sighed again. "That's just it: T wants a woman whose blood is resistant. He doesn't want to bed someone and never drink from her, only from others." He kissed my cheek. "I admit keeping the two separate was very tiresome. Finding you was a godsend."

"We have the formula now," I said confidently. "Devlin reports that they're only a tiny step away from being able to recreate my resistance with a series of injections. Then any woman T loves can be resistant."

"But he's afraid to love a human woman, Dearest. Hearing Terian's stories of how cruel they can be have jaded him. And finding one who is naturally resistant is close to impossible."

"Has he been seeing anyone?" I said meaningfully. "Maybe he's depressed."

"No, he's not in therapy," Danial said. "But he's my son, Love; he's not driven by hormones to bed just anyone. I've been keeping an eye on him, making sure he's occupied and not depressed. Don't worry, he'll be all right. He won't be alone forever."

I hugged him, saying nothing. He was right, that T would have to figure this out for himself. When I got home to Hayden, I'd give Lash the heads up to watch out for T, after I kneed him again for last night.

* * * *

When I returned home with V and Tryst the next afternoon, I was told Dev was resting. I went upstairs to find him dead to the world, his skin shining, freshly healed in places. I went downstairs to find Lash, but the dungeon cells were empty and he wasn't there. I finally found him by the black granite marker near the pond in the cemetery, sitting quietly.

I was surprised he wasn't drinking, but remarking on it sounded nasty, so I just sat down beside him.

186

"Michael is dead," he said, throwing a small rock in with a splash. "I had Rip teleport me to Europe right after I talked to you, where he helped me burn him in sunlight." He looked at me, then away. "I know it doesn't heal you to know he suffered a lot at my hands before he was ash. But I wanted you to know it wasn't easy, like it was for Ulysses. It took me most of last night."

"I'm relieved he's dead," I said finally. "Otherwise he didn't matter to me. It's Valerian I'm worried about."

"Oddly enough, Michael hadn't seen him. Rene transported him to one of his fortresses, and left him there without a word. He hadn't seen her since either."

"Could he have been lying to you?"

"Not with what I was doing to him," Lash hissed with finality. "I can't figure it out."

We sat in silence for a while.

"I saw Dev was resting. He looks like he's healed."

"We got into it when I got back," Lash said, throwing in another rock. "He was waiting for me, enraged. I let him get in a few good ones before I fought back. Titus healed me, and Dev had a few of his donors come. We're okay now." He paused. "Though I'm banned from future Hallows parties again for 'the rest of my existence'."

I didn't reply.

"I'm sorry," he hissed. "For embarrassing you."

You're always sorry for something. I didn't reply.

"Aren't you going to say you're sorry for kicking me in the nuts?"

"I'm not sorry."

Lash let out a hiss, then turned away with a roll of his eyes. "Well, okay then."

"You gave me reasons for doing what you did," I said flatly. "But none of them was why you did it. So why did you?"

"Because I'm tired of the charade," he said angrily. "I'm tired of being your mate and having to act like we're nothing to one another except fuckbuddies. I'm tired of Devlin and Danial getting to touch you wherever, and me not getting to unless we're at home."

"That's nothing new. Why'd you suddenly snap?"

"Because I was hurting you taking your blood and having sex

would've eased it. It made me mad I needed your blood at all, and then doubly so that I was letting you be hurt because I was following orders from a stupid jealous vampire, instead of what was right by you."

"I told you not to, jerk. How is going against my wishes right?"

"We're mated. It's right for us to be intimate whenever we want to, that's why people get mated. It's not right for someone else to tell us where and when we can…um, make love."

I gave him a shocked look. "I'm surprised to hear you refer to it that way."

"I like to make love," he hissed softly. "I haven't ever done it with anyone before you. I love to do it with you, like I told you last night. I resent someone telling me I can't. What's hard to understand about that?"

"Nothing. But we didn't make love, Lash. We had sex on a couch in the middle of a party." I held his eyes with mine. "Tell me this wasn't about Danial."

"He sees me as one thing," Lash said, throwing a rock hard at the water. "One thing and nothing else: a thug who tricked his gentle innocent Oathed One into a mating. I admit I enjoyed the thought of sending you to him smelling of me." He faced me with cast down **eyes,** his face flushed purple. "But the truth is your dress was an accident." He flushed a deeper shade of red. "I was embarrassed and angry about it and said what I did to cover it." He swallowed. "I'm sorry."

His admission surprised me, but it was easy to see he was telling the truth. He was too mortified for it to be anything else. "You could've just said that." I took his hand. "Next time tell me the truth, okay?"

"Okay." He slipped his arm around me. "So are you sorry now you kicked me?"

"Maybe a little. You're healed, right?"

"I'm not sure. I feel some stiffness there. Maybe you should take a look."

I shoved him into the pond. He landed with a splash and didn't surface.

I waited a full two minutes, and then he raised his head, gasping. "You were supposed to come in after me when I didn't come up for air! Were you even worried?"

"You're a water snake, so no."

Lash gave me a disgruntled look, and then laughed. He pushed wet hair back from his face as he walked out, his clothes and shoes drenched. "Come on, loving mate. Let's go home."

* * * *

The next few days passed without incident. Then it was the night before Elle's ceremony with Elijah. Devlin was at home with V, getting the final touches put on her strapless metallic gold Cinderella-style dress. I was a little worried she was going to upstage Elle, but after hearing that Elle had told V to wear whatever she wanted, I told myself it wasn't my problem.

Trystan and I were at the local amusement park riding the rides. He was still an inch too short to ride most of the bigger ones, but I was bribing the college kids ten dollars apiece to let me on with him. Bribery for rides might have seemed excessive, but he was only two months and he already looked five years old. I wasn't going to let him miss this chance to have fun. Plus, I'd already said no to a tattoo earlier that day. Twice.

Shaker was watching me telepathically, as agreed. Lash was finishing the game plan for tomorrow night with Danial and Devlin, going over the final plans for security with Terian and Titus. T was staying over at Elle's, as she wanted her last night before the wedding to be without Elijah. Harp and Song were there, along with Sharon, so I didn't worry about her. My thoughts were on Theo, who was supposed to arrive tomorrow afternoon with Harris.

Would I know my son when I saw him? *Will he know me? What has Theo told him about me?*

"Mom!" Tryst said loudly. "I asked you if I could get some ice cream."

"Sure," I said, "let's get in line."

We got in line. Tryst had just received his chocolate dipped cone a few moments later when Lash strolled up to us. "Having fun?" he said to Tryst. "I see you're eating nutritiously."

"Done already?" I asked. "I thought you might have to be there all night."

Lash shook his head. "No, we're set. Samuel is bringing many of his own guards, and importing a number of weres as well. Demons of course can't be in the church. Terian is upset, but he understands. Titus is setting something up so they'll be able to view the ceremony from outside."

"Good," I said absently.

"Can I ride the coaster next?" Trystan asked.

"Sure, go get in line," Lash hissed. Trystan ran off, and we stood by the fence to watch him as he moved towards the car.

"What's on your mind?" Lash asked. "You worried about Theo?"

"And Harris. I'm not sure how to act, Lash. Rene's not here to tell me."

Trystan climbed into his seat, and the car began rolling, ascending the first slope.

"I'll be right there, Mate," he hissed, putting his arm around me. "You should act how you feel like acting."

Tryst let out a delighted shout as the car raced down the slope, wheels clacking. It ascended another slope, picking up speed. We watched him, for a moment, the bright lights making us blink.

"I'm sure it'll be fine, I'm just nervous," I said.

"You should be, you're the mother of the bride—"

Trystan shouted again, this time more loudly. We both looked up to see him staring at the dusky sky, panicked.

Lash looked up and his jaw dropped. "Oh shit."

I looked up. Three funnel clouds were in the distance, their long tails swirling water as they headed inland toward us.

Chapter Sixteen

"Tryst!" I screamed.

Lash leapt the fence, and stood on the platform, shoving the college kid out of the way. He grabbed Trystan out of the seat before the ride locked in place, and ran toward me with our squirming boy under his arm. "Run!"

"Where?" I shouted, as he set a wriggling Trystan down. "There's nowhere to go!"

Lash took off running and I ran after him, pulling Trystan with me. Everyone had seen the clouds by now, and people were running panicked in all directions, knocking others down in their haste to escape. The wind had picked up, swirling papers all over. A far off roaring was steadily getting louder.

Lash headed for the funhouse and ran inside. I followed him with Tryst.

He went to a steel door. Producing a set of picks, he picked the lock, pushed us in, and shut the door behind him.

He produced a lighted ball from his pocket and handed it to me. "Does this lead down? I hoped this was a basement access. Take a look, Tryst."

Trystan moved off, looking into the darkness. "Yes. There are stairs."

"Go down them. We've got to go to the lowest level."

We went down the stairs and crouched on the concrete floor, Lash's body protectively over Tryst's and mine. The roaring was nearly deafening now.

The stairs began to shake. The building began groaning, the sounds

191

of cracking wood and rending steel a clamor above us. The tiny safety lights suddenly winked out. I heard shrieking and screaming, but couldn't tell if it was people or the storm. A few moments later, it quieted. By then the ball's light had gone out.

"It needs to be recharged," Lash said sheepishly, pocketing it as he got to his feet. "But we can leave now, anyway. We've got to get out if we can."

He climbed the stairs, then remarked that the door had buckled in, becoming wedged. With Tryst's help and mine, he managed to move it enough to slip out. Within five minutes, he had the doorway cleared.

"Careful where you step," he said, helping me out. "There's blood here, enough to know some people must be dead. It's not going to be pretty Sar, so prepare yourself."

I steeled myself, stepping into the black night. "I can't see anything."

"I can," Tryst said, his voice wavering. "There's people everywhere dead. I can't smell anything but metal and grease and blood."

"Get moving," Lash hissed. "A demon's coming, maybe more than one. It'll take them only a few moments to sense the souls that just were released. Sar, can you teleport?"

I tried to no avail. Shaker was also missing from my mind. "Someone's blocking teleporting. I can't reach Shaker."

"Then we'll try another way." Lash spotted a flipped Chevy Blazer, and righted it with a few rocks of the chasse. He hotwired it in a few seconds, Trystan looking on in awe as I grimaced.

Lash pushed us in. "Get in. We have to leave now. Those demons might be after more than just souls."

We all got in, and Lash gunned the engine, rolling over bumps that I tried to tell myself were just fallen trees. "Where are we going?" I asked.

"Somewhere safe," Lash hissed. "Those clouds weren't natural. Keep trying to teleport. I'm betting this is just a perimeter too. So as soon as we get beyond it, take us to Hayden's driveway. Give me a warning, so I can slow down."

I nodded and began concentrating.

"Tryst, put on your seatbelt."

The miles flashed by. Almost an hour later, I made the connection and teleported us.

I'd forgotten to make Lash stop the SUV. We instantly smashed into the side of a parked semi, the windshield shattering over us as Lash swung the wheel hard right. The SUV rocked hard, and then stabilized.

I shook myself. "Tryst, are you okay?"

"I'm okay," he said from the backseat. "My seatbelt was on."

"So was mine," Lash hissed in a garbled voice. He spit out a tooth and winced. "But I didn't expect a semi in our driveway."

"We're not home," I said worriedly. "We're in a hotel parking lot. It looks like that Comfort Inn in Pennsylvania. Why aren't we home?"

Lash looked around, sniffed, and struggled hard, freeing his hands from the truck. "Get him inside now, Sar. Now!"

I fought with the door, prying the lock open. Lash pulled Trystan into the front, and handed him to me. "Go!"

He grunted in pain, trying to tear himself free, as I ran for the nearest door. To my horror, it was locked.

I knelt swiftly. "Tryst go around to the front. Sneak in; pretend you're with someone else if you have to. But get inside. Then come down and let us in."

Tryst nodded and took off running for the entrance.

I went back for Lash, who was still trying to get free. The left side had caved in around him when we'd crashed, the metal twisted over him like a cage.

Lash stopped struggling, and looked up at me. "Turn away, Sar. I'm going to have to cut myself out."

I turned away. I heard wet noises, and his heavy breathing. Then I felt his hand clasp mine.

I turned in time to catch him as he staggered, supporting him. He'd been hurt badly. Blood was all down his gashed left leg, ivory that must be bone showing through. "We need to get inside," he panted. "Is Tryst inside?"

I nodded. "He's going to let us in."

I supported him as we retraced my steps. Tryst was already there, opening the door to let us in. "I picked a hotel room like you showed me," he said proudly. "This one, here."

Lash nodded. "Good. Get me to the bathroom."

I helped him in and shut the door. Tryst got some towels, and Lash began to wash off the blood.

"Do you need more blood from me?" I said hesitantly.

"I do, but you'd better keep it," Lash said darkly. "You may need it before tonight's over."

"What do we do? Devlin's got to be worried."

"Flip on the TV," Lash hissed. "Check CNN for those tornadoes."

I flipped it on. A beautiful reporter was there, her sad face relating the death toll at Sylmar's Beach amusement park was over a hundred.

"Tryst, tear me up some sheets like I showed you. Sar, can you contact Shaker?" Lash hissed.

I tried, and again got nothing, no matter how loud I screamed mentally. "Shaker had trouble contacting me before in Sylmar's Beach. He said there was something old and evil there."

"There's something old and evil after us," he hissed, binding his leg wounds. "We can't stay here. There's likely already more than a few cops out there near the car. They'll follow the blood trail in here."

"Shouldn't we call Devlin? He can send Titus for us."

"If Shaker's been separated from you this long, I've got to believe it's by something over Titus's power level. Titus won't be able to teleport to us, even if you could get through to Devlin. Us fighting alone won't work. No, we need to outrun it, regroup, and then fight."

"Where?"

"Out of this motel," he said, getting painfully to his feet. "Tryst, are there any clothes in that bag to be cleaned?"

"No," Tryst said, upset. "Sorry, I should've picked a room that smelled of a male."

"Forget it. Just stay near my side and hold onto me as we walk. You've got to hide my bandages with your body, both of you. We'll head out the opposite direction that we came in."

We walked out carefully. An executive nodded to us, and we smiled nervously at him. Then we were out the door, facing a police officer in a car.

"Sir, Ma'am? I need to ask you a few questions."

"Shit," Lash hissed, stopping. "That's the sheriff. He and I go back."

Why am I not surprised? "He won't recognize you. Come on."

194

We walked over to the car. "Yes?" I said.

"A car accident happened here a few moments ago. Hear anything?"

I shook my head. "We were watching HBO and we had it pretty loud."

"And your names?"

Lash gave him some fake names, complete with home address and phone number. "We're in town just for a family visit."

"May I ask why you aren't with them?"

I flushed, sure we were caught.

Lash grinned. "Her father hates me. I got in a fight with him, so we went to this hotel. At least here, I have my favorite channels. My in-laws didn't have cable."

The sheriff laughed, putting away his paper. "Thank you. We'll call if we need more."

He drove off, and Lash kept walking slowly, using my body to steady himself. We went down the main drag, and then took a side street, then another.

"Where are we going?" I asked worriedly.

"Tryst, see that Toyota truck, the red one?"

Tryst nodded.

"Go pick the lock. Look for keys above the visor. We'll wait here."

Tryst ran off. He was back in a minute. "There was a spare under the visor. How'd you know?"

"Because that's the sheriff's house and this is his truck," Lash said with a grin. "Get in, we're taking it. Your mom will drive."

We all got in, and I started the truck. "Where am I driving?"

"Go straight until you reach the stop sign, then right. You can get on the highway there."

I pulled out, hoping that good neighbors weren't taking down descriptions of me. "Then where to?"

"They expected us to go north, to try to make it to Devlin or Danial. Whomever it was lost us at least temporarily for some reason when you teleported. They have a demon or a sorcerer: someone knocked us from our intended destination to that hotel you were familiar with, something I've never heard of."

"We should call in, let Dev know we're okay."

195

"Not until we are, Sweetness. They're hoping to head us off. They might even think we'll try backtracking, and spilt their forces. So we have to do something unexpected: go east." He leaned back in the passenger seat. "Get on the highway. I'll give you directions."

We drove most of the night east. Close to dawn, we made it to Montrose, to the country home of the vampire Rulers Van and Erik.

* * * *

Their getaway retreat was a beautiful cabin surrounded by trees, the full moon shining down as if spotlighting it. Lash hid the truck in brush, while Trystan and I made our way up many steps to the front door.

A handsome human answered the door, his eyes looking at me quizzically. "Yes?"

"I'm looking for Erik and Van," I said. "Tell them Sar and some friends came to visit."

The man nodded. "Wait here." He shut the door.

Van came out a few moments later, beaming. "Sar, how good of you to come." He kissed my hand. "You brought your son." He tilted his head, a shadow crossing his face. "And likely Lash too, if I'm not mistaking the scent of blood on the night air."

"Are you gay?" Tryst hissed curiously.

Erik strode out, laughing. "When I was raised, that word meant happy. So yes, we are gay, especially to have you here. Please milady, come have a drink. Van, if you'll go check on Lash? He probably needs help disposing of some bodies."

Soon I was gratefully sipping a Shiraz, and Trystan a glass of ice water in an interior room with no windows, made of lovingly polished wood. Lash came in a moment later, followed by Van. "I can get rid of the truck tomorrow," Lash was saying. "We just need to rest here until I heal."

"If you need meat, we're happy to supply some," Van replied. "Even if this isn't a social visit."

"I wish it were," I said, getting to my feet. "We might be bringing trouble to your door."

"We have our own share of enemies," Erik said gruffly. "Don't think your arrival caught us unawares: our sorcerer warned us as soon as

196

you turned up the drive. We're happy to be of help, but Lash is right, you should recoup your strength and try to get to Dalcon."

"Have you tried to call him, Sar?" Lash said. "My phone is offline."

"There's no cell service here," Erik said apologetically. "And we don't have a land line. That's the whole point of getting away here, to be unable to be disturbed."

The human who'd answered the door popped his head in. "Erik, Van, I'll be in my room, if you desire me."

"Thank you, Charles," Erik said politely. "Leave your door unlocked."

Lash's eyes widened. He looked over quickly at me, and then away.

"I'll get you that meat," Van said curtly, and headed for the kitchen.

"May I have some, too?" Tryst said politely, jumping up. "I didn't have dinner yet."

"Of course," Van said. "Come with me."

Trystan went with him into the kitchen. The moment he left, Erik became all business. "What was tracking you? We heard of the tornadoes. That place being struck so close to Elle's wedding is no accident."

"We don't know what. I can't figure why they didn't wait until tomorrow night," Lash mused. "They got a bunch of humans, but not any of us."

"Where's the alternate wedding reception site, in case of storms? Did they perhaps know it, and want to ambush you there?"

"There isn't one," I interjected. "Terian said his present was a guaranteed calm starry night." I ran my fingers back into my hair. "Elle's going to be devastated. She and Elijah had the whole church already decorated, except for the flowers."

"Dad, your meat is ready," Tryst called from the kitchen.

Lash looked uneasily at me, then at Erik.

"You can leave me here with her," Erik said coolly. "I don't bite." He gave a wide grin, baring his fangs.

Lash slipped out his knife and handed it to me. "I'll be in the kitchen, Sweetness. You need me, just call." He got up and left.

I sat there awkwardly, his knife in my hand, unwilling to put it down and possibly get poison from the blade on the furniture.

197

"Sorry for my humor," Erik said cordially. "I couldn't resist. Lash has always been leery of Van and I."

I faced him. "I'll make you a deal; you tell me what Van is to you exactly, and I'll give you a taste of my blood. Fair?"

Erik looked astonished, and then laughed aloud. "You must want to know badly, to offer to break your Oath."

I flushed. "Damn it, I forgot that sharing blood without leave was as bad as adulterous sex under my promise. Please excuse me. My mind is rattled from tonight's crazy events."

Erik chuckled. "You're excused, Lady Dalcon. Besides, I would not partake unless Van was also allowed to join in. We always share our donors, as our young houseguest already told you. But you don't have to bribe me." He let out a breath. "Yes, Van and I are lovers, and have been since we met each other decades ago. He's the other half of me. But most of the vampire clique is either opposed to men loving men, or they are so ancient they believe that boys your son's apparent age are fair game. So we don't advertise our love, or wear our chokers publicly."

I wasn't sure what to say. "I didn't know vampires could take the Oath to other vampires."

Erik sighed. "It's seldom done, as it usually makes hunters target you. They figure if they kill one, the other will likely give up their life." His eyes locked with mine. "And they'd be right. I wouldn't want to go on without him."

"I know. When Danial was drained, both Devlin and I were devastated."

"It's good strategy," Erik said, getting to his feet. "One that Devlin used on Ebediah. It was his love for Sola that doomed him."

Now I really wasn't sure what to say, so I was blunt. "Danial always trusted you and Van. Because of that, I trust you. But I don't know you at all, Erik. You've always just been a mysterious figure at the annual Hallow's party, like Akira and Chi. So please don't—"

"Please don't compare Van to that wench," Erik said coolly. "I don't take kindly to it."

God, what had I said now? "I apologize. I'm not sure I follow you. All I know of Chi is that she left Akira to return to Japan, as Michael had been dethroned, and Kaizan was made Ruler."

"She's become a province Ruler in name and Kaizan's mistress; one of many, I'm afraid. That news was what caused the fight at the Hallow's party this year. I forgot you missed most of that."

I flushed, dropping my eyes. "Yes. I...um..."

Cool fingers touched my chin, tilting up my head so I met his eyes. "Do not be ashamed of your love. Because it is love, isn't it?"

"Yes," I said, relieved. "It's nice to be able to admit it without being judged."

"I know the feeling," Erik said, chuckling again as he removed his hand.

"How did you know? About Lash and me, I mean?"

"Despite the reports of tawdry behavior, stained clothing and other assorted nastiness, I've never known Lash to have a live-in lover, ever." He bared his fangs in a wide smile. "And you hold his knife, his single most prized possession. You braved everyone's wrath to have his child, despite not being a weresnake yourself. It must be love."

Lash came out of the kitchen, Tryst and Van trailing him, all business. "Thank you for the meat for my son and me. Do you have somewhere we can rest for a few hours? We'll leave at noon; I just need a few hours sleep."

"Erik, you go to bed," Van said. "I'll watch over them. I'll get you when they leave, and then I'll sleep the rest of the day. Even after they leave, we should be vigilant."

Erik nodded, then grabbed hold of Van and gave him a passionate kiss, which Van returned while we all stared agape. With a goodnight to us, Erik left the room.

"This couch folds out," Van said, moving cushions as if nothing momentous had happened. "If you go to the hall closet, you can grab some linens there. I'll bring you in some clothes." Van left the room.

"Tryst, help your mother with the bed," Lash hissed, peeling off his shirt. I was relieved to see he had both his explosive bullets gun, and his whip, along with some other vials in his holster getup.

While Tryst and I made the bed, Lash checked all his weapons, laying the gun within reach, along with the whip and his knife. He put another gun from his ankle under my pillow. "Reach for it if you feel demon," he said to Tryst and I. "The bullets will kill it."

"Holy water?" I said hopefully.

He shook his head. "A blessing was said over the bullets by a priest, the same one who blessed the knife. Kyle got them for me, as a favor."

Van came back in. "Here you go. The black ones are for Lash, of course."

"Thank you again, Van. We appreciate it very much."

"We appreciate you, Sar," Van said bluntly. "You've done a lot for the vampire race. Rest easy, we have you and your family's back." He left the room.

I got Tryst into his nightshirt, then into bed. He was almost instantly asleep.

Lash got into his borrowed clothes, and I got into mine. The shirt was long on me, but it wasn't too bad; Danial's shirts fit me about the same. But Lash looked comically lost in Van's clothes. Rolling up the sleeves helped the shirt's fit, but the pants were excessively long. Lash ended up using his pocketknife and cutting the leg ends off. "There."

I gave him an appraising look. "You look like a pirate or a beach bum, I'm not sure which."

"They don't like me. If I'd come here for help, they'd have refused."

I got into bed beside Tryst. "Why is that, do you think?"

Lash got on my opposite side, to my surprise. "Tryst will watch your back, Sweetness. You're safer in the middle of us."

I settled down. "You didn't answer me."

"Danial's long-standing feud with Devlin, most likely. They are Danial's friends, as you told Erik earlier."

"Did you hear everything he said to me?"

"Of course. I choked on my meat when you offered him your blood. I'd have been in there if he hadn't refused. What possessed you to do that?"

I shrugged. "I wanted to know. And now we do."

"It's a relief, I admit," Lash said, snuggling in closer to me. "I'm glad they accept me, even if they dislike me."

"I just don't understand why Devlin hasn't contacted us. My tracking spell is still on me."

"Rest. Tomorrow we'll find out."

* * * *

Promptly at noon, Val knocked on the door, and told us blearily that the stolen truck had been taken care of, and a new car found. We dressed quickly, Lash leaving on his pants and borrowed shirt. Five minutes later, we were in the entryway, saying goodbye.

"Send the car back when teleportation comes back online," Erik said, stifling a yawn. "Your phones should work again when you reach the New York State line. Good luck."

"I owe you for helping us," Lash said gruffly. "What do you want in return?"

"When things calm down, come and see us for a meeting," Van said formally. "There is a Philadelphia politician making trouble for Erik and me. It's nothing exceptional, just business."

Lash nodded. "You want a warning, that's free. You want more than that; I'll need something for my time. But your price will be half what everyone else pays."

I waited for one of them to take offense, but Erik just nodded as if that was expected. "More than fair. We'll need more than a warning."

Van added, "No rush either, so long as it's done this year."

Lash nodded. "I'll be down to see you sometime in November."

"That works for us. Travel safely."

We got in the car and began driving north.

It took me a while to think of how I wanted to phrase my question. "What did he mean about warnings?"

"A lot of the underworld knows who I am," he replied, his eyes on the road. "So I make good money off giving warnings, as well as hits."

"You just tell them to stop doing what they're doing? Does that work?"

"Depends on how smart they are," Lash said, snorting. "Most human men aren't smart. Women usually take the warnings to heart. I rarely have to kill a woman anymore."

"Are these unfaithful women?"

Lash nodded. "Most of them, yes. But some are just ruthless bitches every bit as bad as men. Whomever said women were the gentler sex was crazy."

"What's a bitch?" Tryst said from the backseat.

"Good going," I said sarcastically. "Answer him."

Lash opened his mouth to answer, and my phone rang abruptly.

"Who is it?"

"I don't recognize the number. Should I answer?"

"Hand it to me."

I handed it to him. He listened for a few seconds, said okay, and hung up, his face grim.

"Erik and Van were attacked at their home a half hour after we left. They made it out through a tunnel, but their houseboy is dead, as is their sorcerer. They both got singed with Hellfire." He stepped on the gas, rocketing us forward. "It's back on our trail."

* * * *

Lash went north, and then turned west, then east. I fell asleep soon after he turned north again. The next thing I knew, Lash was shaking me awake.

"Where are we?"

"Some tourist trap close to Niagara Falls. I got us a room, Sweetness. Come with me."

Exhausted, I followed Lash inside, Tryst's sleeping form in my arms. I laid him on the bed, and then saw Lash check the window.

"What is it?"

"Nothing," Lash said, shutting the drapes. "I figure we have a couple hours before it tracks us down again. Get some sleep."

"I can't sleep. I'm so nervous I feel like throwing up! We've been running for more than forty-eight hours, Lash, and we still don't know what we're running from."

"I'd like to say it was Valerian," Lash said reluctantly. "But I'm guessing instead it's some relative or pal of that demon I killed for Kyle. There was one who was hunting him that would teleport any time Kyle did to the same location? Do you remember?"

I nodded. "Yes. But why now?"

"Because it's out I have a son," Lash hissed, touching Tryst lovingly. "Erik and Van knew, so it's getting around." He turned ruthless. "How we handle this is going to set the mold for any who attack us after. We have to do it right."

"What do you mean?"

"I mean we need to finish this on our own. Erik said they were heading back to the city, that he'd call Devlin to let him know what's happening. I'm going to get you to safety. Then Tryst and I'll stand and fight."

He was absolutely crazy. "You can't. He's a child!"

"I'm not a child," Tryst piped up, blinking his eyes awake.

Lash ignored me. "Change to snake and guard your mother. I'll try a pay phone down the street to see if I can get Rip here."

"He's too young, Lash."

They both ignored me. "You know what to do, son. Don't hesitate."

"I won't," Trystan said solemnly. He began taking off his clothes as Lash closed the door.

I wasn't sure what to do. However, I felt disgusting from not showering for close to two days, so I went into the bathroom to wash up. I'd just removed my shirt and begun washing when I heard a gunshot.

Chapter Seventeen

I ran to the other room to see two vampires fighting their way inside. Tryst was hanging from one's ankle, his fangs buried deep, blood oozing from his back. That vampire was convulsing, his arms flailing as the poison flooded his system. The other was aiming his gun for my son's head—!

I dove into him, knocking the gun from his hand. We landed on the floor, grappling. He tried to bite and I grabbed his neck, holding him back, screaming for Lash. The vampire hit me hard in the side. I tried to take another breath to scream and couldn't get any air.

The vampire punched me again, the impact of his fist radiating intense pain through my ribs. I sagged, my body going limp even as I told myself to get up, to keep fighting.

The vampire's head exploded in meat and bone, and his body fell onto mine, bringing a burst of color into my head along with a new flash of pain. Lash threw the body aside, his arms cradling me. "Sar! Sar, answer me!"

"Is Tryst okay?"

"His back's broken, but it'll heal in time. Can you walk?"

"No," I whispered. "I feel weak. What's wrong, he didn't bite me—"

"Listen, you have to get up. You have to walk, because I can't carry you and Tryst and cover us. We have to get to a church; I can feel a demon coming."

Maybe it was Shaker. God I wanted to just stay here and not move. "No, I can't—"

"Get up now, damn it!"

I got to my feet, swaying.

Lash had looped Trystan around his neck, where he was hanging limply. "Come on!"

We staggered down the street. A large Catholic church rose before us, its steepled spire black against the sky's first beginnings of dawn. Lash left me on the steps, and went to the door, kicking it in. He laid Tryst inside, and then came back for me.

"Easy," he hissed. "Put pressure on your side, Sweetness."

"I can't. It hurts so much. Why does it hurt so much? He punched me."

"He stabbed you," Lash uttered worriedly. "They aren't bad, but they're deep. Keep walking."

"I can't." I collapsed. "I feel like I can't move."

Lash picked me up, and tried to carry me in. But he couldn't cross the threshold with me.

"Leave her," a black voice intoned. "She is ours, Snake."

I looked over my shoulder, terrified to see a vaporous being, horned and grotesquely muscled, its skin brick red, its bull's tail lashing in excitement.

"Fuck you," Lash hissed, setting me down and drawing his gun. "Come on. I'm right here."

Two more thickly muscled demons came to stand at the side of the first one. "Go inside, before we take your soul, too. It's fair game."

Lash sat me up, and then stepped in front of me. "Come and get it."

The three rushed us in a wave. Lash shot one through the heart, and it exploded, shrieking. The other tackled him, and he went down, his blessed knife flashing as he stabbed for it. Black blood blossomed, and then a massive chest of brick red blocked my view. "You're just tainted enough," the demon rumbled hungrily. "Delicious. They call you Sar, I understand."

"Fuck you," I hissed through gritted teeth. "It's Sarelle to you."

The demon leaner in closer, widening its dagger filled mouth. I braced myself for the bite.

Gore showered down on me as explosions rocked the air. The demon's head exploded, then its arms were blown off, and its chest blew apart.

I sagged down to the concrete stairs, fading in and out of consciousness.

Lash staggered up to me, his body a mass of blood and claw marks. "Shh, Sweetness. They're dead."

"Good." *Why is my voice so faint?*

He hugged me. "Can you teleport?"

"I can't concentrate."

"Let me get Tryst. Wait here." He was back in a moment, grabbing me tightly. "Try Sweetness. Try once for me."

With the last of my will, I tried to teleport. The building faded, to be replaced by the side of a blue barn and a starry sky overhead. I lay there on my back, thinking this seemed familiar. It was peaceful, too.

"Sar?" a voice called out.

Abruptly, I sat up. *Where are Lash and Tryst? Shit, am I dead?*

"Sar?" Rene materialized before me, her face worried.

"Where am I? Where's Tryst and Lash?"

"We have to focus on you first, Sister. Can you stand?"

I took her hand, and she helped me to my feet.

"We have to get you inside. You're hurt."

"No, we have to find them, I was holding them, but they're gone—"

"I know," she said in delight. Her arms tightened, and then she twisted my hair sharply, making me scream as she sunk her teeth into my throat.

I kneed her, and she promptly threw me roughly to the ground, making everything hazy. But I was coherent enough to watch her lovely features morph into those of Valerian's.

"You."

"Me," he said smugly. "It's wonderful having fairy blood in your veins."

I tried to get to my feet, but he kicked me gently, toppling me back into the dirt. "Don't worry about Trystan showing up, either one of them. They're at least a mile away. I dropped them in some cattle before taking you here. With luck, they'll be stampeded."

"You bastard."

"Not at all," he said curtly. "I'm just taking what's owed me. I care about making you suffer. I care about making Lash suffer most of all. Your son's just frosting."

"You'll be hunted for this. Even if you kill us, Devlin will hunt you."

"I've been hunted for the last hundred years," he said bitterly. "I've become very good at hiding in plain sight." He looked up at the sky, as if savoring the sight. "I can be anyone except myself."

My side was hurting less as I healed. *Can I heal fast enough to escape him?*

"You know, we didn't have to be enemies," he said finally. "You had empathy for Michael; at least he said you did. You have empathy for my race. It didn't have to end like this; you bleeding out onto the earth you spent so much time working."

His words clicked. *I must be home. That means Elijah must be nearby.*

"I see by your face you realize your surroundings. I thought it the least I could do." He knelt beside me. "I am grateful for you dethroning Devlin. I planned to slip in and kill him, when enough of his men left him. But you Oathed to him before I could get plans in place. And the next thing I knew, you'd fallen for Lash." He got to his feet. "I thought it was the good girl wanting the bad boy thing, not something that'd be a problem. But when he began to love you, I knew I'd been waiting all those decades just for this. So I scrapped my plans and started new ones."

"Did you ever love Michael?"

"You don't really care, so I won't answer." He kicked me sharply, and I let out a scream. "Don't interrupt. I've waited years to stand here and relish this moment. I'd hoped to watch you burn here in your house years ago. That would've been something to relish; your flesh cooking along with that of your pets—"

My jaw dropped open. "You were the sorcerer who helped Ulysses."

He nodded. "Stupid moralistic idiot. He refused to give you to me the night he captured you and Devlin, something he came to rue. I loved listening to Dev scream for him. I only wish I'd recorded it—"

"You were going to let him kill Dev and then kill him?"

207

"Of course. Ulysses was powerful in his vengeance, but not cagy or cunning. He was happy to assume all the risk, not really knowing the kind of men he faced in Devlin and Lash. I've always wanted the States for my own, as no doubt Devlin told you?"

Gunshot slammed into the earth at Valerian's feet, a crater forming.

Valerian closed his eyes. "Azaroth."

Instantly a huge deep green figure appeared, its winged form blotting out the stars. It opened its mouth, but I heard nothing.

The horses in the barn began to scream, their kicks shaking the barn walls. Then I heard an agonizing scream that belonged to Lash.

I tried to get up, to move in his direction, but Valerian pushed me down. "Stay, please. I'm not finished."

"Lash!" I screamed.

"Valerian," Shaker intoned, appearing in the air. He threw blue fire at Valerian, but Azaroth blocked it.

Valerian laughed. "You'll have to do better than that. Kill him."

The demons slammed into each other with a screech, their clawed hands rending skin as they burnt each other with fire, their flesh sizzling. Shaker punched Azaroth, but he slammed his hand into Shaker, punching through his stomach. Shaker screamed, and then bit into Azaroth's hand. Azaroth shouted a curse, and then withdrew his hand, clutching intestines, which he ripped out.

Shaker went to one knee, lightning forming in his hands. "I'm not done, not by a long shot." He hurled the lighting with a snarl. It hit Azaroth, toppling him over as it rent his wings. But as he did a burst of black energy burst from his hands to hit Shaker square in the chest. He screamed and went to his knees, the energy binding him as he writhed on the ground.

Valerian bared a fang at his demon. "You are master of sound, so do something about that noise."

Azaroth again opened his mouth. Abruptly, Shaker began to twitch and spasm, his mouth open but no sound issuing forth.

"Very good. Azaroth, please bring the erstwhile Lash to us. His mate wishes to say goodbye."

The massive green dragonish demon walked off, its footsteps shaking the ground. I heard more gunshots, and then scuffling. Then a figure hit the ground with a sickening thud a few feet away, embedding into the dirt.

It was Lash. He remained motionless.

"Come," Valerian said, pulling me to my feet. "I've expounded enough. It's time for the coup de grace: your death. I want Lash to witness it, as I understand it's his greatest fear." He sank his fangs into me deeply, and began swallowing, his arms holding me tightly.

I struggled weakly, but my body was too wracked with pain, too hurt to resist. *He's going to drain me. I can't escape.* Camlyn had seen this coming years ago.

I'd bound Shaker thinking he'd be able to stop anything that ever came after me, so I'd never be at anyone's mercy again. But there was always someone stronger. There always would be. In the end, it came down to me. I couldn't rely on anyone else. It was time to save myself.

It's time to become a vampire.

I bit Valerian as hard as I could. He yelped, then sighed softly, feeling my teeth in him. As I nursed from him, my hunger for his blood went from repulsion to sudden desire. Valerian groaned, feeling my teeth began to get sharp inside his flesh, and he released his fangs from me. I put up my hand to move his head slightly away, and bit deeper, drinking, wanting nothing but more of his blood, more than anything.

Suddenly, the sweet flavor turned sour. I kept drinking, his sweet blood becoming more and more bitter to me.

Valerian rapidly realized I wasn't going to stop. He fought hard, pushing at me, but I had strength now. I burrowed deeper into his flesh with my fangs. He tried to bite me again, but I'd gotten my hand between my neck and his fangs, and he couldn't reach me.

Azaroth roared, reaching for me with his taloned hands. Shaker ripped free of his manacles and grabbed his scaled foot, the both of them vanishing.

With a massive shout, Valerian pushed me, and I felt my strength give under his. Then he screamed, and I saw Lash behind him, his left eye a ruin, his face snarling as he stabbed into Valerian's heart. Valerian grabbed for me, but Lash twisted the knife, hissing swear words, and I pushed up, and crawled away, trying to gasp for breath, and cutting myself on my fangs.

Lash reared back, and bit down into Valerian, and Valerian convulsed, screaming. I tried to crawl to the dying vampire, to save him, because I needed him, and he was my reason for being. I ran my tongue over my fangs with force, slicing it to ribbons, and the pain cleared my head, making me scream, but giving me the strength to resist the vampire blood I'd drunk.

Lash released Valerian, but he was already dead, his eyes glazing over. Lash cut off his head, and drop-kicked it into the night. Then he took some powder from his pocket and sprinkled it over Valerian's body. "You fuck," he hissed darkly. "This ends here and now."

Lash said some words, and Valerian's body burst into white flames. He was soon a slagheap of clothes and roasting meat. Lash came over to me, and hugged me with his one good arm. "Sweetness."

Where is our son? I grunted at him, trying to get my worry across.

"Are you okay? Don't talk; I can't hear you even if you could. Fucking demon burst my eardrums. Just nod if you are."

I nodded.

"Don't kiss me," he hissed. "I've got poison and venom all down my face, and it can still kill you even as vampire. Can you walk?"

I nodded, and then tried again. I weaved my hand through the air like a snake, and then looked at Lash expectantly.

Shaker appeared suddenly. "Mistress, are you okay? I've tried to reach you for days."

I'm okay, I thought to him. *Where is Tryst? Find him.*

Shaker nodded, and disappeared.

"Come, Sweetness. There's got to be something to write on in your old garage."

With effort, Lash and I walked to my garage. I opened it, and got into Elle's truck, getting some paper and a pen from the glove compartment. I wrote down what I told Shaker and handed it to him.

He nodded. "He's unconscious on the other side of the barn. A cow trampled him before I got us out from under them. He's hurt bad, but in time, he'll be fine. He just needs meat."

Shaker appeared, and handed me Tryst's limp form. "Here he is."

Take us home, Shaker, I thought back.

A moment later, we were outside the gates of Hayden. Seth let us in, on his phone already announcing our arrival.

Titus appeared and picked me up. A moment later, he was settling me on Devlin's bed. "Please wash, Kin-daughter. Leri is seeing to Lash. Then come out, and I'll check you for wounds, though yours should have all healed by that time."

When I came out in my bathrobe ten minutes later, Devlin was there. To my shock, Rene was with him.

I recoiled from her, baring my double set of fangs in a hiss.

"Shh, Love," Devlin said. "Rene has told me everything. She is on our side, just as she always has been. Have no fear."

I gave Rene a look to tell her I didn't trust her. "Tryst is fine. I've healed his broken spine, and a few broken ribs from hooves," she said. "He's resting, Sister. He should be fine in a day or so." She walked out.

Before I could think a thank you to her, Dev's arms went around me. "I'm sorry," he said sadly. "I'll help you, Sar. It does not have to be all bad, living in the night." He leaned back from me. "Are you hungry? I can call some of my donors, or get one of the bears."

"She needs some blood," Lash said, Kyle supporting him as he came in. "She hasn't had any yet."

Devlin gave me an odd look. "Why did you not drink from Lash? You should be starving for blood, any blood." He offered me a paper and pen.

I shook my head. "No blood. I want meat," I wrote. "I want liquefied steak."

For a split second, Lash and Kyle looked afraid, and so did Devlin. Then they masked it with fake smiles, and took me into the kitchen.

I drank five steaks, and then they put me to bed. As I lay there it registered I could hear them, even though they were outside Devlin's closed bedroom door, and it was as soundproofed as ever.

"What is going on, Titus?" Devlin whispered.

"By the time I'd helped Shaker kill Azaroth, Sar was healed. I'd assumed it was vampire blood, from her turning. Now I'm having second thoughts."

"She smells like a vampire to me and she's got the fangs," Lash hissed softly. "Isn't she?"

211

"She may be becoming demon," Titus said outside the door. "Shaker said she was bathed in demon blood, that she reeked of it."

"She was," Lash hissed worriedly. "Two bled all over her when I blew them apart."

"Most of it soaked into her. Enough demon blood is just as transformative as vampire or werecreature blood, and she has no immunity to it—"

"We will wait," Devlin interrupted firmly. "And we will give her whatever she needs. She is still Sar, no matter which she becomes."

Becoming vampire was okay, but demon? I grabbed for the bottle of Valium desperately. *Screw it, tonight I have a pass.*

Sudden steps thundered up the stairs, then Danial's worried voice said, "Where is she? In there?"

"You can't see her," Devlin whispered urgently. "She's resting."

I heard a crash of a body hitting the floor. "I'd have been here to welcome her home, if you'd have but called me sooner than a few minutes ago to tell me the events of the last few days."

"Don't you watch CNN?" Lash hissed sarcastically. "Your daughter's wedding was called off from the massive destruction—"

"I assumed Sar was here with you, Dev, safe. You led me to believe that."

"She is safe now," Devlin soothed. "But you can't go in there. Rene herself told Lash and I not to, not until morning. She said no one was to go in."

"Get out of my way, Lash," Danial ordered.

"I don't care if you kill yourself," Lash hissed angrily. "But you aren't going in."

"Danial, listen to reason! If she turns to demon, she'll want your soul!"

I heard a loud gunshot, and a screech from Lash.

The door opened, Danial's silhouetted figure in the doorway, his back to me. "She already has my soul. She can have my blood and flesh as well."

He shut the door and locked it, then turned around to see me watching him, gun in his hand. He crossed to the bed, and laid it on the

212

nightstand. Then he took off his clothes, and sat down next to me. With one hand, he reached to mine and clasped it.

"I'm here," he said softly. "Are you hungry at all?

I clasped his hand back, and shook my head, blinking back tears.

"Let me see your teeth, Sweetheart."

I bared my vampire fangs for him, as he'd bared his for me so many years ago.

Danial touched them, and then nodded. "Do you need anything of me?"

I nodded my head, and opened my arms. He pushed back the covers and climbed in, cradling me against his chest, my head near his throat.

For a long time, we lay there holding each other. Sometime around dawn, I fell asleep.

* * * *

I still couldn't talk by morning. But I had another three steaks, and felt well enough to watch some TV downstairs. Lash kept me company, his missing eye covered with a bandage that didn't stop him from making lewd remarks. Everyone else stayed away, except for the guards posted near us "for safety". Whether they were there to keep me safe or keep others at Hayden safe from me wasn't elaborated on.

That night, Danial alone joined me as he had previously. This time when he offered himself to me, I lunged for him passionately.

We made love frantically for an hour, my only desire to have him as much as I could. When he nibbled my neck gently in mid-stroke, I pushed up suddenly, impaling myself on his fangs. Danial started, and then he bit down and began drinking in long pulls.

I'd never felt such ecstasy. I writhed, moaned, came, and came again. And when he pushed his shoulder down into me, I latched onto it, biting deep. His blood tasted the same to me it always had: of spices and the tang of aromatic wood.

Danial arched his back with a sudden intake of breath, then relaxed, still drinking and moving. A moment later we simultaneously slipped our fangs from flesh as we came, clutching each other.

I moved back, looking at Danial expectantly, willing him to tell me how changed I was. *Which am I becoming, vampire or demon?*

He touched my cheek gently. "Your blood doesn't taste of summer," he whispered gently. "It tastes predominantly of demon, with some faerie and vampire mixed in."

I grabbed a pen and paper from the nightstand, writing, *Your blood tasted as it always did to me. I don't understand why it's not bitter. And how can you stomach mine now?*

Danial read it and hugged me tight. "I spoke to Tatiana before I came, telling her what had happened. She advised me to drink if you let me, to try to get some of the demon essence out of you through your blood. That my blood tasted the same is a good thing, Love, a very good thing. You are on the road to recovery."

* * * *

By the next morning, Danial checked my teeth again. I almost passed out from relief when he proclaimed my teeth had begun getting smaller and duller.

Later that day, Lash brought in Tryst to see me. He was groggy, but he coiled the tip of his tail around my finger, hissing he was sorry he'd not stopped both vampires in the hotel.

"You did well," I hissed in snake carefully, stroking his tail. "I couldn't be prouder."

"She's right," Lash hissed proudly. "You did very well. Those vampires were old, and you killed one of them. Now let's get you settled on her lap. You need to rest."

"Mom's not going to bite me, is she?" Tryst hissed softly. "She smells like Uncle Dev and Danial."

"No," Lash hissed back to him. "If she needs blood she can bite me. Go to sleep."

Lash and I slept the rest of that day, Tryst on my chest. That night as before, Danial joined me. Again, he took my blood, though this time, I felt no urge for his. We fell asleep clutching each other tightly.

* * * *

By the next afternoon, I could speak again, if I was careful. Devlin and Lash held me for a long time that evening, telling me they were very happy I was still me.

"I'd have loved you as demon," Lash hissed softly. "But it was going to be awkward, telling Tryst. I'm glad you aren't."

"Me, too," I said. "I was afraid of going to Hell."

Lash flicked out his tongue and tasted the air. "Your scent is back to normal, Sweetness."

"I can't believe you didn't turn," Devlin said. "I feel like God Himself intervened."

"Maybe He did," I said musingly. "He may have something else in store for me that I'd need to accomplish in the sun."

"I made an appointment for you with Dr. Brenda," Devlin added. "I believe Danial is right, that you'll be as you were in time, but—"

"Where is Danial?" I asked suddenly. "Why isn't he here tonight?"

Devlin shot a look at Lash, but neither of them spoke.

"Where is he?"

"He's at home resting," Devlin said finally. "He's ill."

I teleported in the next second, arriving in Danial's lighted bedroom. There was a shape huddled under the sheet.

"Danial?"

A moment later Terian appeared, a ball of Hellfire in his hand. "Get out, demon—"

"It is Sar," Danial said weakly. "Go ahead, Terian. We'll be all right."

Terian rolled his eyes and disappeared.

I came to Danial's side. He looked flushed, as if he were sick. "What's the matter?"

"Demon blood isn't good for vampires, not the amount I took. I should've thrown it up after drinking it, but I didn't want to leave you, or have you hear me do it."

"Can I do anything?" I said, clasping his hand. His hand was warm, warmer than mine was.

"No. I have donors coming in an hour. Once I feed, I'll be fine, or so Tatiana said. I'll come visit you in a few days."

"You're sure?" I said worriedly.

Danial managed a smile. "I'm sure. Terian is watching over me, as you saw. But I will need your help, Darling. The demon blood will have aftereffects, or so Tatiana tells me."

215

I gave him a confused look. "Such as?"

"The same effect taking it in the past had on me. So be ready, Oathed One. Be ready for me."

* * * *

As he'd said he would, Danial came to me near sunset, his eyes tinted red as he clasped me to him, devouring my lips with his. When I took his hand and led him in to find Rene, Devlin and Lash waiting for us, he was surprised enough to stop in his tracks.

He turned to me. "You want this?"

I nodded. "You need this, Danial. I—"

My words cut off as he kissed me passionately, bringing me to the bed.

* * * *

I woke up in Danial's arms, Lash on my chest, and Devlin in Rene's arms a few feet away Seeing everyone here and remembering all we'd done together last night was kind of mind blowing to me. *Then again, almost becoming demon or vampire was, too.*

"How are you, Sweetheart?" Danial whispered softly. "I hope you enjoyed last night."

"You were great," I said confidently. "I'm happy. Did you enjoy Rene?"

For the third time I'd ever seen it, Danial blushed. "Yes. She is talented, as Devlin said she was. Did it bother you to watch us?"

"No," I said truthfully. "I loved how much you seemed to enjoy it."

"Good," he said lovingly. "I loved watching you enjoy yourself also. Yet I'll likely decline any more orgy invites, just so you know."

I laughed. "I'm going to, also. Rene and Devlin do okay on their own."

"That's because they're deviant," Lash hissed from my chest, stretching. "You saw what they did on the loveseat last night. I'm never sitting there again."

"I'm not deviant, I'm just a woman who knows what she wants," Rene said, yawning. "And I want some breakfast."

216

"Good. Make me some, too," Lash hissed, and she threw a pillow at him, which he caught, and threw off the bed, snickering loudly.

Devlin yawned, and opened his eyes. "This needed to be done eventually anyway to consummate the Oath with all parties here, if not for the sheer pleasure of it. But be mundane if it pleases you, brother. Is it dusk, Sar?"

I looked at the clock. "Close. Another hour."

Devlin sighed. "I've got to get up. My donors are coming."

Danial yawned. "Devlin, do you mind if I crash that? I'm starving."

"Sure. I always have a few extra. Help yourself. Do you feel cooler?"

Danial nodded. "I feel like myself again. It's a relief."

"Let's get showered then. We'll use the guest rooms; we're just going to be in time if we hurry. I'll give you Jill; she's got a nice taste—"

They both put on robes, grabbed some clothes, and walked out, speaking of blood flavors.

"So girls, what about that breakfast?" Lash hissed.

We both hit him with pillows, which he ducked, but then Rene zapped him with a little lightning. Lash let out a hiss, then grabbed her and tickled her, making her shriek as I laughed. He let her go with a kiss on the cheek, slipping on his jeans.

"No more zapping me, Rene, or I'll spank you. I'm going to go check the guards. You have thirty minutes to produce breakfast, or I'm coming back in here to have you both for breakfast."

He dashed out the door, laughing as another bolt of lightning zapped where he'd been standing.

Now that I was alone with Rene, I felt uneasy. "We'd better get some food ready," I said quickly, "I'll use Lash's room."

Rene nodded. "I'll meet you in the kitchen in a few moments, Sister."

When we met in the kitchen, I turned to her with my festering thoughts of the past five days. "What was your kidnapping Michael, all an elaborate ruse? Why did you do what you did? Where have you been these past months?"

"I foresaw certain events," she said vaguely. "I did what I did to avert them, Sister. Because I acted, I was able to avert the worst of them."

Her words were distant, her expression and tone agonized, her eyes moist. But that didn't move me, as it always had before.

"I'm very sorry you went through what you did. I tried to help where I could—"

"Okay," I said just as distantly. "Let's leave it at that, Rene."

She nodded and we began cooking without talking again.

Lash did come back, and we had a good large breakfast of meat. I volunteered to clear, Rene went to work on her blood transmogrification, and Lash went back to the gatehouse.

When I was finished, I went for a walk. When I was alone, I summoned Shaker.

"What do you wish, Mistress?"

"Where do you stay?" I said softly.

"Stay?"

"Live. Sleep."

"A small house in a deep forest. I can build well enough, when the materials are of stone."

"Take me there."

Shaker took my hand, and soon we were before a small stone house that was much like Titus's home.

He opened the door. It was cozy, if messy. Shaker made us a fire, and we sat down.

"What do you need?" he rumbled.

"Come and warm me," I said gently. "I can't give you anything more, Shaker, and you have others for that, anyway. But you served me well. I'd not be alive if it hadn't been for you. My son might not be alive. I'd like to caress you, if you still want my hands on your skin."

Shaker came to me, and laid his head in my lap. As before, I stroked his face and his hair, even his horns. He let out rumbles of pleasure as I touched him.

"Why do you like this so much?" I said curiously.

"Every being likes to be touched," he rumbled. "A demon is no exception."

"I understand. But you have lovers, as you make a big point of telling me. So why would you want my touch?"

"No one has ever touched me as you have," he rumbled. "I'm a being for lustful desires, a being for power, for grand designs and wild nights of orgies." He looked up at me, and grinned. "Gentle touches do not fit into that, Mistress. Neither does kindness."

"I'll always try to be kind, so long as you respect me," I said honestly. "I appreciate your saving me from Azaroth, even if it's not something you wanted to do, but just something you did in the name of duty—"

"It was nothing but duty." He gave me a look out of the corner of his eye. "Don't kid yourself, Sarelle."

We sat in silence for some moments, me still gently touching him.

"A little more where my horns meet my skin...ah, yes, right there..."

"Tell me the truth," I commanded. "Your word."

"Ask," he rumbled.

"You let those Takers into my dreams, didn't you? It wasn't just being bound to me that did it. You invited them, told them a way in past the crosses."

Shaker's skin flared with heat, then it abated. "Yes."

"Did you help them find me the first times?"

"Yes."

"I thought you had," I whispered, taking my hands off him. "So you could save me, right?"

"I'm demon," Shaker rumbled. "It's my nature to cause suffering and fear."

"Even in your mistress?"

"Especially in my mistress," he replied. "Satan gives me extra points for that."

"Tell me why. The truth, not your propaganda bullshit."

Shaker growled, and then he said, "Because I knew of how you let men have you after they saved you. And I wanted another time with you, and you'd said no."

"Apologize. And mean it."

"I'm sorry," he rumbled. "I didn't mean to get you as upset as you were."

"Answer this truthfully, Demon: were you invading my dreams that night I dreamed of you in my old kitchen?"

"I didn't invade," he rumbled gently. "I picked up your mental images from your brain partway through. I rode the dream with you, much as Terian did. But the dream was your own—all of it." He cleared his throat. "I'd not have said such things if I'd have had control, Mistress. I sounded like an idiot human who was head over heels from some romance novel."

I didn't respond.

"Please touch me," he rumbled. "Did you expect me to ignore the opportunity to lie with you again? I've stayed out of your dreams since then."

"I can't trust you," I said finally. "You may hurt me in the same breath you're telling me you'll defend me."

"If you ask me for something, I'm bound to obey," Shaker rumbled. "You have only to ask." He gave me a meaningful look. "Those are the rules."

"I forbid you to hurt me ever again, Shaker, in any way. You are to protect me at all costs, even your life. If you do not, you are to return directly to Hell. Is that understood?"

"I shall not raise a hand against you, nor invade your dreams. And I'll protect you with my life, forever. Fair enough?"

I nodded. "For now."

"Will you touch me again?" Shaker persisted.

"Tell me you love me," I said, feeling perverse yet enjoying the power. "And mean it."

"I love you, Mistress," Shaker rumbled. "I don't love easily, but I do love you. It's an odd sort of feeling for me, to care about a human as more than a fuck, or something to be tortured."

"Tell the truth. Are you lying?"

"A little," Shaker rumbled, grinning. "I am allowed loopholes sometimes, when my master or mistress asks the impossible of me. I am fond of you, Kin. I find you sexy. I also enjoy doing just this with you, and that's new for me. No, it's probably not love. But it's as close as I come to it, so you'll have to be happy with that." He paused. "And I meant what I said about protecting you. Anything that wants to harm you will need to go through me first."

"Ok."

"Touch me?"

I began stoking him gently with my hands in his hair, and he groaned softly. We passed the rest of the afternoon that way.

Chapter Eighteen

A week later, I was getting ready to head down to the pond with my potion. Lash had paid Titus to give us a week's worth of sunny skies and above normal temperatures, and we were set to make full use of it.

Terian burst into my bedroom. "Sar, please come with me. Theo's asked you to come and see Harrison."

I gaped at him. "Now? I'll be seeing him in less than a week at Elle's wedding—"

"Come now, please," he said urgently. "It's your son's life if you don't."

A moment later, I was breathing the dry air of Wyoming, standing before a house I knew well. It was the house I'd found Theo at all those years ago. I wasn't surprised he had come back here. He and I only had good memories here of finding each other and getting married.

Terian began walking, and I followed him hesitantly. He called for Theo, but no one answered. The house looked almost the same as it had the last time I'd been here, with Theo and Elle. Theo had been busy carving. There were two more chairs here, or perhaps those were the ones he'd carved long ago. But there was also a carved table, and set of chairs, much like the set in Danial's house, and a huge flat screen TV. A room I'd never noticed before, off to the side by the bathroom, was now a boy's room. *My son's room.*

Terian was still yelling for Theo, but no one was answering. *Why hadn't Theo been waiting for us?* It suddenly occurred to me that my coming here wasn't expected, and probably very unwanted. "Theo didn't ask you to come and get me, did he?"

Terian grabbed hold of me. "Stay here, Sar, you need to see

222

Harris—"

"Tears, I thought they expected me! I can't just show up here like this!"

"Why not?" a voice asked.

We both turned to see a little boy looking at us. His face was the spitting image of Theo. But his hair was dark blond, almost brown, like mine, and his eyes were a blue green color, like the ocean. He was looking at us very curiously.

"Who is that, Tears?"

"Harris," Tears said, going to one knee. "I need you to meet someone. This is your mother, Sarelle."

Harris looked at me as I crouched down. "Is that true?" he said bluntly.

"Yes," I said, extending a hand toward him. "I am your mother."

Harris growled at me. I took my hand back, a little surprised.

"That's a lie. My mother's dead. My father told me that."

"It's your father who has misled you. Where is he?" Terian said angrily.

"It's five p.m. He's outside mating," Harris said bluntly. "He should be back soon."

On cue, a door slammed. Theo barged in, a gun pointed at Terian and I.

"Tears, why are you—?" He saw me and swore. "Why did you bring her, I told you not to!"

"She needs to see her son," Terian growled. "And her son needs to see his mother."

"She didn't want to be his mother," Theo growled. "She missed her chance."

I said nothing, too much in shock at the sight of him. Theo had always been muscular, but he was larger than life now, not an ounce of fat on him. Sadly, he was just as menacing looking now as Lash once had been. All trace of his one sunny disposition was gone. His cold blue eyes were as like the surface of a frozen lake, his icy voice the howling winter wind.

"You didn't give her a chance to be his mother," Terian said quietly. "Whatever happened between you then, you need her now."

"I'm not letting her take him," Theo growled angrily. "Not to Hayden, not ever—"

"Remember Devon?" Terian said, "Harris is safer with her. You have your hands full."

"Will someone please explain this to me?" I said, raising a hand. "All I heard from Tears was that I had to come, that there was a problem—"

"There is."

"I can handle it."

"Stop yelling!" Harris shouted, his eyes yellow. "Stop fighting!"

I went over to him. Even though he growled at me, I grabbed hold of him and hugged him. He shifted uncomfortably in my arms, then suddenly froze, breathing in short bursts of air almost frantically. "You are my mom, like the mom I dream of," he whispered. "You smell like I remember, of leaves, sun and earth."

"What you smell is snake scent on your mother, mixed with vampire," Theo growled to Harris. "She is mated to a snake, your enemy and mine, and a vampire too, the one she left me for."

"You told me that snakes were evil," Harris said, turning to look at Theo. "But this scent smells comforting, not evil. It smells good."

Theo gave Harris a quick look of surprise, then turned back to Terian. "Take her and go."

"Theo, you have two challengers next week. Even training hard, you are going to need my help. Plus, you need someone to look after Harris."

"I can take it—"

"You have another two challenges the next week after!"

"Why so many?" I gasped. "Robert—"

"That's the problem," Terian said darkly. "Robert."

Theo sighed, holstered his gun, and sat down. I took Harris's hand, and led him over to sit down next to Theo. Terian sat on his other side.

"Explain, somebody," I said.

"I'm second," Theo said wearily. "I've been second for a while, with not too many challenges. Robert was the one who got most challenges, and kept them from ever getting to me. Until he got tired of being third, anyway, and wanted more. After Robert died, a lot of fighting occurred in what you might like to call the 'top ten' of us. More than a few of the old guard, those who'd been good but were aging, were killed off. You know I'm nearing forty now, Sar."

More like forty-two, I thought, but I just nodded.

"There are a lot of twenty-something young guns looking to topple me."

"Lash is older, too," I said, fear welling up inside me. "Much older than you."

"No one wants to go after Lash after what happened to Ulysses and his men, as well as to the other people after you and Dev these past years. What Lash did to Michael's corpse is still being talked about. Someone got film of some of it, and it's made the rounds. Rumor embellished that legend that he took that lightning bolt from Cyrus without a scratch, then killed him singlehandedly. Everyone knows he is young again." He sighed. "I'm not. I'm looked at as easy prey."

"So take a potion," I offered. "Slow your aging, or reverse it."

"No, thanks," Theo said with a curled lip. "I'm not becoming a monster."

"What other option is there?" I said flatly, looking from Terian to Theo. "Just training hard to fight men half your age while hoping like hell not to get killed?"

Terian gave Theo an I-told-you-so-look.

"I'm better than they are," Theo growled. "I can do this, but I need to know that my son will be okay if I fall. Terian, just say you'll look after Harris, if something happens."

"I'm staying with you here, to watch your back, like I should have with Robert those years ago," Terian said, folding his arms across his chest. "Sar is taking Harris home with her."

"No."

"Harrison," I said loudly. "Would you come home with me, for a few weeks? You just heard what's going on. Your father is fighting for his life. I'll take care of you."

"Can I come back, when it's over?"

Theo and Terian looked at me expectantly.

I never wavered. "Of course. Though I'd like to come visit you sometimes here."

"I don't want to leave. This is my home," he said stubbornly.

I saw a lot of myself in him. "I understand that. But it's not safe for you here right now."

"She's right," Theo said suddenly, looking at me in defeat. "You should go with her, Harris. I need to know you're safe to fight my best. My opponents may come for me before the fights, they all know I'm being challenged, and where I'm living."

Reality hit me in that moment. These men thought Theo was old, but still skilled. So they were going to attack when they thought they had the best chance of success, either separate or all together. They knew Theo had his son with him, but no guards to watch his back, and no powerful vampire, either.

Harris pushed me away, and ran to his father, who hugged him hard. "I'll miss you," he said tearfully. "But I'll go if you tell me to, Dad."

"Go with your mother," Theo said, letting Harris go. "She'll bring you back to me like she said she would. She keeps her word most of the time."

I shot him a dirty look. He wasn't looking at me, but into some distant memory.

"I'll have him call here, if you want."

"I'll call Hayden to speak to him every night," Theo said with a growl. "Hear me, Harris?"

"I hear, Dad," Harris said nodding.

I took Harris's hand and a moment later, I was back at Hayden's kitchen. I asked Harris if he was hungry, and he said he was. So I heated up some of the soup I had made yesterday, and we both ate a late lunch. "This tastes like the soup Dad makes," Harris said in surprise.

"This was his favorite recipe," I said, giving him a smile. "He liked pumpkin pie, too."

"I love that!" Harris said in excitement. "Can I have some?"

"Sure, for dessert." I enjoyed being the indulgent parent for once instead of the discipline master. "As much as you want."

After half of the pie was gone, Harris helped me clear the table, and I asked him to follow me upstairs. "Wow," Harris said, looking around. "This is a nice place."

"Thanks," I said proudly. "Come, there's someone I want you to meet."

I knocked on Devlin's door. "Dev?"

"Come in, Love," he purred seductively. "I'm in here waiting for you."

"Are you decent? I've got someone I want you to meet."

I heard him get up, then him putting on clothes. A minute later, he opened the door. "You must be Harrison," Devlin purred, looking down at him. "You look much like your father. But there is a good deal of Sar in you as well."

"Are you 'that bastard Devlin'?" Harris asked innocently.

Devlin's eyes flashed red, but he controlled himself. "That is not polite, Harris," he said coldly. "Do not think to be insulting, and pretend you know nothing of swearing, with Theo as a father. Now apologize to me immediately."

"I apologize," Harris said in a small voice. "I know this is your home, and I'm going to be living here, at least for a while. I promise not to be rude again."

Devlin did a double take, and then looked at me. "What?"

"Theo needs to fight challengers, four of them," I said with a shrug. "It's for a few weeks only. But if you—"

"Of course Harris is welcome to stay." Devlin looked down at Harris. "As my Oathed One's son, you are welcome here, cub. You are to be polite to everyone here, especially me and your mother, as well as Lash and your brother and—"

"I have no brother."

"You do, a half-brother," I said ruffling his hair. "Would you like to meet him?"

Harris looked up at me in astonishment, and then nodded.

"Lash and Tryst are near the pond, Love, on the rock. Expecting you, I believe?"

Ah shit. I was about an hour late. "Thanks." I grabbed Harris's hand, and ran out the door.

We hurried to the pond. Even being late, there was still more than half the day left. I brought Harris to the rock, and grabbed the forgotten potion from my pocket. It still looked okay.

"Stay right here," I said quietly. "I don't want you to startle Lash or your brother. They are most likely in snake form."

"My brother's a weresnake?" Harris said in revulsion.

"Yes," I said forcefully. "There is nothing wrong with snakes, Harris. They are just another type of wereanimal."

"That's not what my dad says."

"Your father had a bad experience once," I said delicately. "He and Lash do not get along. But that doesn't mean you have to hate all snakes. Give your brother and Lash a chance."

"But they are my enemy if they are snakes."

"Your father and Tears once were enemies, too, and they are best friends now. You should not hate a species, demon, vampire, weresnake, or any race, just because one person of that race hurt you once."

"I guess that makes sense," Harrison said, more to placate me than that he understood.

"I thought I heard your voice, Sweetness. Is that who I think it is?" Lash hissed to me, coming into view as he tugged on his shirt. "Your son, by Theo?"

"Yes," I said. "He needs to stay with us for a few days while Theo faces challengers."

Lash looked at Harris thoughtfully, and then walked over to him. I was sure Harris would back away, but he stood his ground. "I want your word right now that you will do nothing to harm anyone while you are here," Lash hissed to him in menace. "I love my son and mate very much."

"Who is this?" Tryst Jr. asked, walking up behind Lash in just his jeans.

"Your brother," Lash and I said together.

"He doesn't look like me," Tryst Jr. said, looking Harrison over.

"You had me for a father," Lash hissed. "He had another man."

"Why didn't you tell me about him?" Tryst Jr. said, angry. "You never said anything about me having a brother! Why wasn't I told?"

"You learned to talk only a month ago," Lash hissed with annoyance. "I hoped you'd meet him one day, Tryst, but that day seemed far off. Harris lives across country from us. Theo took him hours after he was born, before your mother even woke up after giving birth. He asked us not to visit or contact them."

"Is that true?" Harris said, looking over at me quickly.

I nodded. "Yes. I've missed you, Harris."

"Come over and lay down with us, Sweetness, now that I see why you were late getting here," Lash said to me soothingly. "We have a few hours of daylight left to sun ourselves. Do you have the potion?"

"Should I, now that—?"

Lash nodded. "I'll stay in human form until Harris is comfortable with yours."

I went into the bushes, and took the potion, taking off my clothes. Soon after, I slithered out to my waiting family. Harris's eyes got huge, but Lash reminded him it was just another form, like his own cougar one, and he calmed down.

I curled up in a pile, and began to sun myself, hissing in pleasure at how good the sun felt. I had never understood how good it could feel when I was human, not until I had been snake. *Ahh...*

"Want to swim?" Tryst Jr. offered.

Harris looked disgusted. "No! I hate water! I don't like to get wet."

"Tryst, leave him alone," I hissed in snake. "He needs time to adjust."

Tryst Jr. looked at him, shrugged, and made as if to walk away. Instead, he gave Harris a push off the rock, and into the water. But Harris wasn't going alone. He grabbed hold of Tryst Jr. and pulled him with him.

They hit the water with a splash, as Lash hurriedly pulled off his weapons, cursing. I was snake, and could do nothing but hiss anxiously at him. I hadn't learned to swim in that form yet.

Lash dove into the water amidst loud roaring, and yelling from Tryst. I peered over the side of the rock, but saw only churning water. Then Tryst Jr. appeared in snake form swimming hard for the other side. He had a claw mark on his back that was bleeding, but I didn't worry, as it was already healing up.

Lash surfaced in snake form, also swimming hard, his mouth dragging something. I slithered down from the rock as fast as I could, hissing my worry and fear. I got to the shore just as he was slithering from the water. To my utter shock that he was carrying another frantic young snake in his mouth, one who by its pattern was also a cottonmouth.

* * * *

Lash dropped the limp snake on the shore, and turned to Tryst, hissing furiously for him to get over here NOW. Tryst obeyed instantly, and then his father commanded him to change back and hold onto his brother. Tryst did and soon, there were two boys on the beach. The minute Harris had human lungs again, he let out a scream of fear and tried to run. But Lash had shifted back to human by that time and grabbed hold of him. "Shh!" he said soothingly. "Stay still, Harris. You are safe. No one is going to hurt you."

"I was a snake! He turned me into a snake! AHHHHH!"

"I didn't turn you into anything!" Tryst Jr. said angrily. "I shifted to snake because you were clawing me, and I had to, to get free of you!"

"Quiet!" Lash hissed sternly. "Control your fear! You will act like a male, Harrison, especially as you are snake."

"I'm a werecougar! I have been cougar my whole life!"

"Regardless, you are also snake," Lash hissed lovingly. "There is something of me in you, there has to be. Your form doesn't lie."

"Snakes are my enemy!"

"We are not your enemy," Lash hissed gently. "We are your family. Be calm and breathe."

Harrison breathed, as Tryst watched skeptically, rolling his eyes.

When Harrison had relaxed a little, Lash sat down next to him. "I want you to try to change to snake again, Harris," he said. "Tryst will help you. If you're successful, he and I will teach you how to swim."

"I don't want to!"

"Do it," Lash said flatly. "You must face this right now. It is not going to get easier. And I need to know for certain if the pattern I saw on your scales is the one I thought I saw."

Harrison swallowed, but he said he would try. He touched Tryst, and as Tryst turned to snake, he did too. They tried to go back to human, and again it worked.

"Now try yourself, son," Lash hissed eagerly. "See if you can do it on your own."

I said nothing in all this time, in too much shock to do more than listen and watch.

Harris tried, concentrated, and fell in coils to the rocky shore, hissing softly in fear, and worry. I went to him, rubbing my head on him, and told him that it was okay, that we loved him for who he was, and it was not a bad thing to be snake. I thought he couldn't understand my words, but hoped he understood the love and encouragement in my voice, and the nearness and comfort of his mother next to him. Some of the fear and tenseness left him, as he moved his body tight to mine, hiding his head under my chin.

By that time, Tryst Jr. had had enough of the family drama and had gone into the water in snake form looking for fish to eat.

Lash came up beside me, now also in snake form and asked Harris to come with him, that he would teach him to swim and catch fish. Harris said hesitantly in broken snake words that he liked fish, he always had. Lash gave him a gentle nudge toward the pond, and soon, Harris was following him awkwardly back to the water.

I slowly climbed back up the rock to sun myself, thinking it had been a very odd day.

* * * *

That night, I tucked in Harris and Tryst together in Tryst's room where we had moved in an extra bed. Surprisingly, Tryst had not minded sharing his room, in part because he'd had no one to play with that was like him, and now he did.

Lash and I sat for a while downstairs, talking and drinking wine. "He's partly mine, somehow," he said, downing his third glass and reaching for another. "He has my pattern on his scales. I've never heard of this before, Sar."

Tonight was not a night to remind him one glass was enough. One glass was not going to be enough for me tonight, either. "How can he have both forms?"

"I've heard of it with two kinds of wereanimal mating, like Serena," Lash said speculatively. "But not with a human mother and were father of only one type. It's almost as if Theo and I were both somehow his father. How can a child have more than one father?"

"I put in a call to Rene. She'll get here as soon as she gets it, I'm sure."

231

"You know what this means," he hissed softly. "It means I did get her pregnant, that time in New Orleans."

"I know," I said softly. "And she has some explaining to do to both of us, because she must have foreseen all of this and not told us."

"Maybe she didn't know?" Lash said tiredly. "I don't understand it, but Devlin says Rene should be trusted absolutely. Even putting aside her odd behavior these past two months, she can't have done what she did to hurt us."

"I don't think she did. We don't know what kind of potion Danial used," I said angrily.

"I can guess," a deep bass voice rumbled. Titus walked into the room, his eyes glowing red. I moved over a chair for him, and he sat in it.

"How do you know?" Lash hissed sarcastically. "Did you have a hand in that damn Danial's potion?"

"You ask me that, knowing how close I came to not knowing my own son?" Titus boomed at Lash, bearing his rows of teeth. "I had no part in that evil. Terian did not, either."

"Titus, please, we're just upset," I said, touching his arm comfortingly. "Please, tell us what you know."

Titus reached out and took my hand, and to my shock, Lash's also. "What I have to say isn't going to be easy for you to hear," he rumbled. "But knowing what I know of the pregnancy, and what Devlin told me of what happened today, I do have a theory—"

"Spit it out, Demon!" Lash said loudly. "Say it!"

"I'm guessing he's part your son and part Theo's, Lash. Originally, I'm betting he was your son."

Lash went still; on his face his anger and wild hope that he had not one son, but two.

"How could we prove it?" I said to Titus.

"His blood will tell if he has Lash's DNA or only Theo's."

"We need to get his blood tested immediately," Lash hissed. "I'll call Camlyn."

"He retired, remember?" I reminded him. "We'll have to call Dr. Brenda."

"For this, I'm betting he'll come out of retirement," Lash said,

232

rolling his eyes. "I need to know if he really is my son. Because if he is, he's living here with us, and not going back to Theo. Hell, even if he's not, knowing there is something of me in him, I'm inclined to have him stay here. Tryst loves having someone to play with."

"But he knows only Theo as his father."

"In the next weeks, he will come to know me as well," Lash hissed. "And if I am his father, I am not going to be shut out of his life."

* * * *

We took Harris to see Camlyn the next day. Stephen was intrigued, to say the least. "We never tested his blood at all," he said, checking over Harrison. "We just assumed when he was born cougar that he was werecougar. Theo took him so quickly, Harris wasn't here to test. But we'll check it now. Lash, I need a sample from you, too. The old one was thrown out long ago."

An hour later, Stephen came into the room where we were waiting and pulled Lash to the next room. I waited, looking with anxious eyes where Tryst and Harris were playing a game.

Lash came out to me a minute later. "He is my son," he hissed with emotion. "My weresnake DNA is in him. But there is werecougar DNA in him, too, Sar. Theo's DNA."

I hugged him, not knowing what to say.

"This is a whole new level of sharing," Lash grumbled good-naturedly.

"I'm sorry."

"Titus's theory might be right. Stephen doesn't know."

"What do we do?"

"Tell Harris the truth and try to make him see he'd have a good life here with us if he wanted to stay," Lash hissed. "Maybe we can get Theo to move back here so we can see more of Harris, if it comes to the worst. But I hope that Theo may not want him when he knows Harris is weresnake. You know how much he hates me. He may ask us to keep him."

"Maybe." *But unlikely.*

I teleported the three of us back to Hayden, and we spent the rest of the rainy afternoon watching horror movies.

233

Later, after the boys were in bed, Titus again appeared, and I told him what the tests had revealed. "I'm sure of it now," he said, looking at Lash a little sadly. "I know which spell was used. A witch in Australia who is half demon responded to my query on the alchemy website. She said she had made a potion for a man who could not have his own children, but was having his brother impregnate his wife, and they used this potion to make the child his own, and not his brother's. But the two different species of wereanimal were of course not mentioned to her." Titus paused. "Harris and Tryst probably would have looked very much alike, if all had gone well. But the potion Danial used let Theo's DNA into his cells as they were first dividing and growing, allowing him to look like his son and to be werecougar. But he was and is really your son, and so retained his snake form."

Lash was floored, and I wasn't sure what he was going to do. I grabbed hold of his hand, and squeezed it for support.

"Not all of your genetic material was deleted, so to speak. The baby had already started to grow before the potion was used on him. And so there will still be a lot of you in him, Lash, even though he doesn't look like you."

"I have another son," he hissed softly. "We have another son, Sweetness."

"He is Theo's son as well—" Titus started.

"He is my son!" Lash hissed in absolute fury, knocking over the table with a crash. "And I'll be damned if anyone will ever keep him from me again!"

* * * *

Rene arrived that night. She came to us both slowly, if a little regretfully. "Forgive me, if what I did hurt you," she said in her lilting voice. "I thought only of protecting Devlin's child and yours in Sar. I knew Danial, and suspected he might try to do something—"

"And what about our child?" Lash hissed, each word strangled and forced. "Did you care nothing for it, to risk it so casually?"

"I never expected one bedding to get me pregnant. I've slept with many weremen, Lash, including various snakes, and I didn't always use a birth control method. I never got pregnant, as I told Sarelle. Besides, it was taking you a while to get her pregnant, so I thought you couldn't impregnate me. I was thinking of my body as it had once been, not my new body that was part hers. It didn't even dawn on me it could be yours until you mentioned it the day I told Devlin. And even then, when it was cougar-shaped, I figured it was Theo's alone."

"But it is our child," Lash said, still in that strangled voice. "Yours and mine."

"It's no more mine than Theo's child would have been," Rene said gently. "It's your child and Sar's, with a little of Theo's DNA mixed in, according to Titus. Instead of tears and anger, you should look at this as a blessing." She took our hands and placed them together. "You have another child, one that couldn't have been born to you both any other way. Harrison is going to need his mother and his snake father, as he is part human and part snake. Take good care of him."

Lash and I looked at each other, then I hugged him tightly, and he was hugging me back, squeezing me a little too hard. Because Rene was right. And who knew how long we'd have until Theo showed up to try to take Harrison home?

* * * *

That first week passed quickly. The four of us spent many days on the rock, sunning ourselves in snake form. Titus was apprehensive about me using the potion so much, but when I explained to him that I was worried about Harris leaving, and not coming back, he said it would be okay, so long as it was only for these few weeks.

We went and saw movies most nights, and bought Harris some clothes, though again, Tryst Jr. seemed uncharacteristically willing to share his things with Harris.

But all was not well. I noticed Devlin was avoiding us, and even at night, he slept apart from Lash and I.

I confronted him about it the next day. "What is it, Oathed One?"

Devlin sighed. "I'm jealous, of course. V is almost grown, Sar. And you and Lash are there with your family, and your little dog, and I'm here by myself."

"Dev, you aren't alone. Even as V grows up, little Moon will be with us for years yet."

Dev smiled sadly and took his hand in mine. "Love, I always knew you loved Tryst more than you loved me. I used him to get your Oath, because I knew that."

"Be that as it may, my feelings for you have deepened from what they were," I said seriously. "We started in the wrong place, Dev. I did that with every single one of my lovers since meeting Danial, and it caused many problems. Believe me, I love you, and I'm happy to be here with you." I hugged him. "My sons will get older, and eventually leave for their own lives, and then it will be you, Lash, and I again."

"I know that, Love. I'm just bitter because I know we aren't going to be parents again, ever. We had the chance and it slipped out of our fingers like silk." He sighed softly. "Your scent has more vampire now than it used to, and I'm fairly certain that even if Titus hadn't acted as he had, you would no longer be able to give birth to another dhamphir. Rene's working on her experiments, but I understand that the balance is a delicate one." He forced a smile. "I must remember to be happy for the child I have, that we had." He kissed my cheek. "We are happy, happier than most couples ever are. That's not something to take lightly."

I gathered myself. "Dev, just because I can't doesn't mean you can't—"

"Yes it does, Love," Dev said with a sigh. "I don't want a child if he or she isn't your child too, not anymore." He paused. "But I cannot tell that to Rene. All I can hope is my feelings will change if she somehow finds a way."

I hugged him, not trusting myself to talk.

"Come with me to Anna's grave," Dev said tiredly. "I have not gone for a while."

We walked there, and sat on the cold stone. Devlin murmured some words of poetry to her, and then fell silent.

I was getting cold, even with my jacket, so I moved to get up. "Let's go, Dev."

He didn't move. "There is more to our separateness than just what I said," Devlin said awkwardly. "Part of me still feels guilty that I couldn't save you from Michael."

"Did Danial speak to you about this?" I said, sitting back down.

"No," he whispered. "Lash will not. You have not. Rene apparently saw what happened in a vision, but will not speak of it. And so everyone knows but me. I dislike that feeling, Oathed One. Yet the idea of asking you to tell me makes me feel even worse."

"I was asleep when it happened, dosed with a potion Cyrus made," I said softly. "I didn't feel anything, Dev. He snapped my wrist at the end, but that was the only violence he ever did to me."

"Can you forgive me for not stopping him?" he whispered. "I promised you I'd keep you safe. I failed you, Sar."

"No one failed me," I said. With a start, I realized I finally truly believed that. "It happened and it wasn't anyone's fault but Michael's. You did what you could."

"It's more than that, truthfully...I...I would not have been able to answer the questions you posed to Theo that day months ago, not even the one he answered. Likely Danial knows all the answers and to spare." His beautiful golden eyes were full of unshed bitter tears. "Lash knows them, too, and he met you a year and a half ago. I met you five years ago, we've been lovers for three years now, and I don't know them. That makes me feel like shit, Sar."

I took his hand. "My favorite song is 'The Dream of the Dolphin', Dev, by Enigma. The ending and beginning parts, with no words. It makes me happiest." I kissed his hand. "I like to think that in every bad situation, there's always opportunity for optimism and healing, even when it seems like there's no hope. That's what the song represents." I paused. "But it doesn't matter to me that you don't know that fact. The sum of love isn't in knowing everything there is to know about the one you love. It's just loving the person for themselves. Lash didn't answer correctly; I lied that day to Theo. Yes, Danial probably does know this fact about me, but that doesn't mean I love him more. Please don't feel badly about this."

"But I never asked you what you wanted out of life," Devlin said quietly. "And I take it that Lash did?"

"Yes, he did, but the conversation wasn't how I made it sound to Theo," I answered. "There wasn't altruism on Lash's part; he was just worried I was making a bad decision, when he asked if I was happy with my life. It was months later that I told him about wanting to be loved and happy after we were finally together, one day after we'd made love." I

237

paused, then leaned close, kissing him chastely on the lips. "You are loved for yourself, not the amount of facts you can recite about me."

"That's a relief," Devlin said, not sounding convinced.

"I can't answer the questions for you either," I said gently. "Not yet. But we have forever to discover each other, Dev. I'm learning what you like the more time we spend together. The difference is that I want to learn what makes you happy. I want to remember it so I can use it to make you happy. That's the key difference between Theo and you. You have tried to make me happy since you first loved me." I gave him a shrug, turning mock serious. "Danial did know all the answers once, but likely he's forgotten more than half, so you're on a level playing field."

Devlin burst out laughing, and then he was hugging me. "That's evil of you to say about my brother, but thanks for saying it and making me feel better, Love." He stood, and took my hand. "Now let's get home. Lash will be wondering where we are."

Soon, we were in the bedroom. I brushed my long hair, and then went in to Devlin. Lash was still in the shower, but he'd join us in a moment.

Devlin pulled me onto the bed, and kissed me vigorously. Wanting to bury all the strife of the last few days, I plunged my tongue into his mouth. He groaned, and then he kissed my neck, and moved his head down to my left breast, sucking hard. My head went back with a soft cry that intensified the longer he sucked. He moved to the other breast, as I jerked repeatedly in his arms, the feeling so good it was the edge of pain.

Abruptly, warm hands grabbed me by my hips and pulled. Then Lash was grabbing my neck in his hand, as he nudged my legs apart. With a loud groan of pleasure, he pushed in, thrusting hard and deep, his hands holding me tightly, moving me to receive him. He kissed my right shoulder blade. Without a sound I felt his fangs brush me, and then slip in, and his sucking gently, still hammering into me. With a kiss, he slipped his mouth off me, and grasped my breasts, kneading them roughly as his thrusts got faster and more frenzied. With a loud cry he came, his spurting manhood so thick and good inside me. With a last kiss, he withdrew, then Devlin was settling me on him, his eyes red with lust from watching. I let go a long moan to feel him stretching me, opening me up so completely as he eased inside.

"There's a blush for shan't, and a blush for can't, and a blush for having done it," he whispered, sliding up a hand to cup my face. "There's the blush of your skin, the blood underneath that is begging me to set it free, that fire and warmth I love to consume. You are beautiful, My Love. And you're mine. Hold her, Lash. Move her."

Lash's hands grabbed my hips, and then he was moving me purposely on Devlin. Devlin's arms held me tight as he nibbled gently down my neck. As I felt my orgasm flood my senses, Devlin sank his fangs completely into me. I gasped, and Lash was there to swallow my breath with his kiss, his hands still moving me. I went rigid from pleasure and then limp as cooked spaghetti. Lash kept kissing me, kept moving me, and I came again, as Devlin drank me down, his organ spurting into me as I felt his muffled cries against my throat.

Lash gently helped me off Devlin to lie beside them.

"God, that was good," I said happily.

"Can I slip inside?" Lash hissed, moving against me. "I'm not done, Mate. I'd like to give you an orgasm or two, if you'd be receptive."

"Sure," I said, laying back. "But be gentle. I'm out of practice."

"So are we," Devlin said, moving closer. "And there's only one way to remedy that. Come here, Love."

* * * *

The next afternoon, I lay on the rock as snake, and thought about how one week was already gone. It slipped by so fast. I looked over at Tryst and Harris and wondered how I was going to let him go when the time came.

"I'm cold," Tryst hissed, curling up close to me. "The wind's getting me, Mom."

"It's November," I replied. "Winter's around the corner. It's only with Titus's magic we're even able to still use the pond. He said this is the last day he'll be able to give us this kind of sun, so enjoy it."

Sudden coils wrapped around us and squeezed gently. "Is that better, Sweetness?"

Lash had coiled around me and Tryst a few times, and was blocking the wind with his thick body. Sun directly above us shone down, and we were deliciously warm.

239

"Much better, Dad," Tryst said happily.

"What about me?" Harris hissed hopefully from outside.

"There is room for you, too, son," Lash hissed lovingly. He picked Harris up with his mouth, and dropped him in on top of us. With a little wriggling, we got ourselves comfortable, enjoying the last day of Indian Summer.

* * * *

"Do you like being with us?" I said to Harris that night at the movies, when Lash and Tryst had left to go grab the men's room.

"I miss Dad," Harris said sadly. "He doesn't call every night, like he said. He didn't call last night or the one before it."

"You can call him when we get home, alright?" I said, secretly pleased and guilty about it. "We can call right when you get back."

"Thanks," he said smiling at me. "You're a good mom."

"Ready to go, Sweetness?" Lash hissed at me, returning with Tryst Jr.

I nodded.

We went home, and Harris called Theo, but got no answer there, which gave me a dilemma. Titus could not teleport there, having never been there before, and he was watching Leri anyway, as Rene was out with Mad. I couldn't go alone, and there was no way I was taking Lash; he was sure to let slip he had been there before, and even if he didn't, Theo would go ape shit just smelling he had been in his house. Devlin would only cause problems too, especially as there it was still daytime. Shaker could've gone, but told me that Titus has passed onto him that Terian had put a multitude of spells on the house that would allow no pure demon access. So I called Terian, and asked him to go with me.

Lash had a good deal to say to me about going without him and with only Terian, but I told him I was going anyway. Finally, he said that he would stay with the boys, and to call, if I needed him, that he would have Titus use the tracking spell on me, and be there a half second later.

Terian came to Hayden in a few minutes, and then together, we teleported to Theo's house. The place was in shambles, but at least it was not burned. There was blood on the floor, but Terian said it was not Theo's. He told me to stay inside, and to teleport immediately if there was any sign of trouble. He went out to search.

I busied myself cleaning up the house. Really, not much was broken, save a chair or two. I felt bad though, as they were the ones Theo had carved for us years ago, and it hurt to see they were splintered beyond fixing. I piled them outside on the burn pile with other dead branches, and then went in to make a pie.

I felt somewhat ludicrous making a pie for my ex-husband after all that had happened between us. But I knew Theo would like it, and the truth was I had nothing else to do but wait and worry. I found all the ingredients where I had found them so many years ago, and set about making both apple and banana crème, as there was no pumpkin in the cupboard or limes in the fridge.

After they were baking, I looked around for something else to do, and found Harris's baby book. It was astonishing to see how small Harrison had once been, and how much like Devon he had looked. I cried for a while looking at the pictures, feeling some measure of forgiveness for Danial. He had given me something of the child I'd lost, even if he hadn't done it for any reason save revenge.

Terian came in, walking quickly to crouch in front of me. "Sar," he said softly. "I found a lot of blood, and its Theo's. I also found two men dead, and they had identification on them with their names. They were the sixth and fifth best in the Ranking." He paused. "He was supposed to fight the third and fourth best first, then these men who are dead after them. From the tracks and blood trail, I think the first two took him. If they did, he may still be alive, but not for much longer." Terian took my hand. "You know what I'm going to ask you."

"No," I whispered, taking my hand back. "No, Terian. I always say yes, I always say that I'll risk everything to save someone I care for. It's only ever brought me grief and pain to those I love. I'm not going to dream of him, not even to save him."

"Please, Sar, he's my best friend!" Terian begged. "You know what he's been to me, after I went demon; he was the only one who forgave me completely! Please!"

"No," I said, turning from him.

"I have never asked you for anything," he said bitterly. "Not anything, in all the years I've known you."

241

"You asked for my body in the guise of my love," I said coldly. "And you feel no remorse. Anything I owed you is paid in full, Tears."

"I've given you everything you ever asked me for and it's been a lot. I am asking this one thing of you. Damn you to hell if you let him die because you're too much of a bitch to see he always loved you, even when it drove him half mad with pain, and he had to come all the way out here to forget you."

I asked Terian to leave, and called Lash. A minute later, I teleported to Hayden, and then back with him to Theo's home.

Lash stood there for a moment looking around, and then recognition registered on his face. "That night with you," he said, giving me a loving look. "That first night, years ago."

He came over to hug me, but I pushed him away gently. Then I explained why I'd brought him here. I hoped he would just be angry, but instead there was sadness, resignation, and more than a little disappointment on his face when I'd finished. "Don't ask me to tell you it's okay, if you do this," he said finally. "It's not, no matter the reason."

"I'm not asking," I said. "I don't want to do it either."

"Don't lie to me," Lash hissed bitterly. "You want to do this, at least part of you does, the same part that loved saving Danial, and loved saving me."

"No, I don't," I replied. "I told Terian that. But he made me feel guilty enough I decided to ask you. You tell me not to do this, and I won't. I'm your mate, and I'm not going to go against your wishes." I took his hand. "I want you to say no, Lash."

"You mean it?" he said, disbelieving. "You won't take the potion, and dream of him?"

"No, not without your permission. I'm not going to Hell for Theo. We'll go to Titus. There must be another way."

"Let me see the trail first," Lash hissed, resigned. "I don't trust that half-demon as far as I could kick him. This may be a trick, or a trap."

* * * *

"There isn't another way," Titus rumbled, looking at Lash and I, and Terian.

After Lash had concurred with Terian's assessment of the blood trail, we'd sought Titus back at Hayden. We were in his workshop.

"There must be something else," Lash hissed at him. "Something to locate him."

"How?" Titus said in irritation. "He doesn't have a tracking spell on him. His phone was found with the two dead men. He's not wearing any charm I know of, or anything to trace him by magically. He could be in another country by now; I have no idea where the other assassins hang their hats—"

"They were from Arizona," Terian supplied. "But where in that state, I don't know."

"I can ask Frederick, Arizona's Ruler," Devlin said from the doorway. "But a whole state is too big; he could be in the desert or hidden in a cave."

"The point is, we don't have time!" Terian said angrily. "Theo's got to be close to death, with losing all that blood!"

"He may be already dead," Devlin replied. "Lash reported there was a lot of blood. You need to face facts, Terian."

"I should've killed you years ago," Terian hissed, his teeth becoming long and pointed. "If I'd have killed you, none of this would've happened."

"Even if you had, it wouldn't be you in her bed," Devlin sneered, baring his fangs back.

"Stop it," I snapped.

"This isn't about her," Lash hissed angrily. "So don't bring her into it, either of you."

"You're right. Theo needs me, and I'm his friend, like you're Devlin's! Please, Lash, let Sar take the potion! Titus can break the bond after, like he did before—"

"No," Lash hissed with narrowed eyes. "I'm not having them bound together again! I've had Theo like an albatross around my neck for years! He took one of my sons for his own, raised him to hate me! He tried to turn my mate into a werecougar! I saved his ass last time with Satar and his men, and it got me my death wound! I'm not saving his ass again, or risking Sar!"

Most everyone was quiet after his outburst, but most of them hadn't known about any of that, or at most, had known only part.

243

Terian alone was not cowed. "There is no risk to her in dream form! She isn't doing this so they will have sex, only to locate him!"

"Is that true?" Lash said, looking at Titus. "Can they dream together, and not have sex?"

"Of course," Terian said, giving Lash red eyes full of defiance. "What happens in the dream is what Sar and Theo want to happen. He cannot have her unless she submits to him."

"What if he tries to force her?"

"He is not going to do that, we just want to find out where he is, jackass!" Terian said.

"What if he tries to force her, Titus?" Lash asked, as if he had not heard Terian's words.

"She would wake," Titus said to Lash. "They can only dream together if they want the same dream. The other times, they both wanted to make love, and so they did. Some of that was the bindweed Terian used that first time that made Sar want Theo, as he wanted her naturally, though my son didn't know that. Frankly, with Sarelle not loving Theo, and loving you instead, she may not even be able to dream of him at all." Titus turned to me. "It was you who chose the dream, Sar, from what you told me; chose how it began, and had the power to alter it. You who had most of the power over what happened in it, from the demon/faerie blood in your veins from Terian. By logic, you should have more power over the dream than before from the additional demon and faerie blood. But I can't say if you'll have the power to alter it this time, or what will happen, other than it is at least half under your control."

We were silent.

"Let me think on it," Lash hissed. "Give me ten minutes, everyone. You, too, Sweetness."

I went out and to Rene. She was working in her study. "How is it going?" I asked.

She turned to me with a triumphant smile. "I've been an idiot, Sister. After much searching, I found the missing ingredient to duplicate your summer blood."

"What was it?" I practically demanded.

"Faerie blood, in a very minute quantity," she said. "I added just a bit, in desperation, as it would be necessary anyway to alter your DNA in

244

the eggs to replace them with mine. I decided to work on that issue, because I couldn't get anywhere with duplicating your blood. Suddenly, the scent of the potion changed from citrus and melons to overripe flowers and rainswept fresh earth."

"From my exposure to Terian's blood, from his long ago fight with Danial," I said slowly, surprised I hadn't thought of it myself sooner. "I always forget he is part faerie, half faerie, really."

"Yes," Rene said with a nod, stirring her concoction. "That's why it has been so difficult. Terian's blood was and is very hard to replicate, because he's not just demon and faerie; Titus used a major spell to impregnate Leri, who is also faerie. But I am almost certain I can get the spell to work now."

I hugged her. "I'm happy for you. I truly hope it works!"

"I will not tell Devlin unless it works," she said darkly. "I don't want to get his hopes up for no reason."

"I think that's best." Happy though I was for her, I hadn't come here to congratulate her. "Tell me the truth," I said wearily. "How much did you know of what would happen?"

She stood still, and then sagged. "All of it, Sar. My visions have played out as they had to."

"Couldn't you have done something?"

"No," she said bitterly. "I've tried many times over the years to stop things from happening. I tried to stop Anna's death and failed; she just died another way. Bad things can't be adverted; they can at most be delayed. I've found interfering only works if you're willing to do whatever it takes for the greater good. That meant my death once."

"How do you determine what matters most?"

"You do the best you can," she said wearily. "There's no one answer, Sister." She paused. "But that was the reason that I asked you not to come and get me immediately, when you first returned from your captivity. And why I have been absent so much from Hayden, also. I did not trust myself to stay my hand." She smiled bitterly. "My heart is not made of stone, Sar."

"Should I go save Theo?" I asked quietly.

"Do you want to?"

"No."

"Then don't."

"I've said I would try if my mate agrees. Lash is deciding now. What will he decide, Rene?"

"To let you do it," she whispered. "And you will save Theo, Sar, one last time." She turned to me, crying hard. Despite everything she'd done, I went and hugged her.

"It's not a blessing to know what's going to happen," she sniffled. "I do it because I have to, because only I can, Sister." She gave me a wan smile. "That's why I carried Harris. I foresaw it was the only way to give you and Lash another child."

"I'm thankful for him," I said, wiping away tears. "So is Lash."

"I would never betray you," she said softly. "But you had to believe I could, to doubt me, so when Valerian played his hand you would fight back. He'd have killed you, Sar. I saw him kill you in vision after vision, saw you die at his hands as you cursed me with your last breath."

"I love you," I whispered fiercely. "You have my trust, Rene. No matter what."

"Good," she said, releasing me. "Go back, Sister. Your real hour of being brave is finally here."

I ran back upstairs, just in time to stand with the others when Lash came out, resigned. "Go ahead and do it," he hissed. "But I'll be there beside you, Sar. If I see any sign of Terian or him doing anything to you, I'll wake you."

"Will he be able to wake me?" I asked Titus. "You told me that the dream must play out."

"I can't say. You have a lot of power in dreams, even ones given to you." Titus shot a glance at Terian. "You may be able to wake yourself after you find out where he is. Terian can link to you as you dream. With his faerie blood, he can do more than I in dreams. He can see what you see. Once he sees the place in his mind, he can teleport there."

"I don't want Terian dreaming with her," Lash hissed angrily. "I will go."

"You can both be there," Devlin said, placating. "I will wait with the children. I do not want to be there."

I thought that odd, but Terian was already moving with Titus to prepare. "Give us ten minutes."

Nervous, I went with Lash to his bedroom, where we lay down and hugged. "I feel jealous of him already," Lash hissed bitterly. "I want to be the only man in your dreams, Sweetness."

"You are," I said, breathing in his comforting scent of autumn leaves, earth, and leather. "It won't change anything."

"It will," Lash said with a note of resignation. "I said the same thing about Danial finding out who you were, and look at everything that caused. If you had not gone to Theo and Danial that night, Harrison would be the twin of Tryst. He would have only known me for a father." He cut off my breath with a squeeze. "And that's my fault. I let you go, because I trusted that nothing bad could happen. But it did."

"I'm sorry."

"It's not your fault, it was mine," Lash hissed. "I should have trusted my instincts, they told me not to let you go that night. Just like they are telling me not to let you do this tonight."

"Then I won't do it."

"You need to do it," Lash hissed softly. "He is part father of Harris, and much as it would be easier to let him die, it would be wrong. Part of you would always blame me, that I refused to let you help him. Our son would blame me. We will deal with the consequences as best we can."

Seth appeared at the door. "Sar, it's time. They've got everything set up in the silver room."

A few moments later, I lay down on the guest bed, Lash on one side and Terian on the other. Titus was also there, though once he'd given me the potion, he left, asking them to call out if anything happened.

"How does it start?" Lash hissed softly. "Can I touch her? I want this to work, but I also don't want her to feel like I'm not right here with her."

"Shut up, hold her, and wait," Terian said, his eyes red. "She will fall asleep shortly."

I opened my eyes to find I was in my same clothes. Lash and Terian were nowhere to be seen. I was alone.

I got up, and tried the door, but it was locked. I closed my eyes and imagined my set of lock picking tools. It appeared on the floor. I used it to pick the door lock, and found myself in a hallway.

Every door was locked, all ten of them. So one by one, I picked them.

In the first, I found my life if I had lived it with Danial, if I had gone back to him that night after Flora's funeral. We were married, and lived at his house. We had four sons, one of them Theoron, and two daughters. Theo had left us and married Tawny, when she came to him pregnant, and now lived in Europe. They had split up in a few months, and he and Therese, his daughter, lived in France. He worked for Samuel. I was pregnant with Devlin's first child, a girl, and Oathed to them both, and partial vampire, thanks to years of blood from Devlin. He had finally won me over, after years of romancing me. Lash, I knew only as Devlin's good friend, and he had never treated me with anything but distant coldness, though I'd seen him be tender with his steady girlfriend Lyssa on some rare occasions. Devlin was Ruler of the States and had never been dethroned, and Danial still Ruled New York. And the three of us were discussing if Danial's home should be sold, as we spent most nights in Devlin's bed at Hayden, when I closed that door, and went on.

The second door held my life, if I had lived it with Theo, if he had not been taken, having never returned to Europe. I worked at the metal fabrication shop, and he worked for Danial. I had two baby sons by him, twins. Tawny had died in Europe, and so had his baby daughter. Danial I never saw, save once in a while. He was with Monica now, and she had Oathed to him, and was expecting his child.

This life turned nasty suddenly. Monica died in miscarriage. An angry client with the help of vampire hunters killed Danial, as Terian had never become his bodyguard, and Theo had been with me and our sons at our home that night. Lash arrived at our home on a steaming August night a week later with ten bears, killing Theo and taking me to Devlin, where I promised to be his forever, in exchange for my sons' lives. I closed that door and locked it before I saw any more, and moved on.

The third door was a surprise. It held what would have happened if I had asked Terian to stay, to give him a chance to be more than my friend. I was surprised to see that it was a good life. I had married Terian, and had never had any children at all. Danial had come to me and released me from my Oath and my choker when Theo had told him Terian had been with me, and I had never seen him again. Theo had also never come to me. Titus had never learned Terian was his son, and we had never met him. Devlin showed up to take me as he had in life, but Terian fought him and his bears off alone, wounding him so badly that he renounced all claim to me. Lash, I never even met. I continued to work, and Terian ran his online business from our home. We planted gardens, shoveled snow, watched movies, and for the most part, kept to ourselves. The years passed, and I grew older, but Terian did not. And when I was sixty-seven, and Terian still looked twenty-five, I softly closed the door on that future, and locked it. Because I saw in his eyes as they looked into mine that he loved me, even then, and that in the years we had spent together, I had grown to love him.

The next doors were the same, all possible futures. Some were not surprising, like if I had not broken Theo out of his love spell (again, children with Devlin and Danial, and a life with them), or if I had not saved Terian from death that night (again a life with Danial and Devlin, and children, and being part vampire), or if I had refused to give up Danial and gone to him when my body began to demand it of me (again, the same, though in this one, I bore twins twice, and both times, each brother was the father of one). In all those lives, Theo was never with me, or he left me. Also, I met Lash only briefly, if at all, and then he died. Terian also drifted away, sometimes alone and sometimes with Sundown, when he wasn't killed.

Some lives were terrible. I went with Devlin to Rio in one of those, leaving Theo. We were happy for a short while, but Devlin turned bitter shortly after, as Danial broke all ties with him, and petitioned the Rulers to bring his Oathed One back to him. It was lie, but they believed it. We ran from country to country, hunted. Lash was killed defending us in six months, when a poisoned bullet struck him, and he could not heal it. A week later, Samuel killed Devlin by fire, and dragged me before Danial and the other Rulers, six months pregnant by Devlin. Theo refused to take me back, but Danial did, though he would not touch me at all. I gave birth to Devlin's child, a beautiful girl, but Janice took her after I birthed her, and soon after, Samuel arrived to take possession of me for his own, as he was to be first to have his own dhamphir, according to the deal he had struck with Danial, in return for giving him Devlin's child.

In another, I didn't open the package with Lash's knife with its cryptic note until I returned home from Danial's house. I teleported to the Everglades as I had in life, but when I came to Lash's tent, I was too late and he was dead. I held his body for a long time, and told him I loved him, but my blood would not bring him back to me, and eventually, I called Devlin. Devlin sent Titus back to Hell as punishment for letting Lash die, and when Ulysses came for his vengeance that Fall, there was no one to protect us. Danial was in his coma when Jerry opened the gates and Devlin died screaming as he burned. I died at the hands of vampire hunters who had already killed Venus, as they set fire to Hayden around us.

In another, Danial took my blood, reviving from his coma but killing me in the process, and Lash killed himself at Davy's, as Devlin didn't get there in time to stop him, because he was so busy grieving me.

But the worst was seemingly innocent. That day at my house, when Lash had told me he wanted me, that he would take me to a hotel, I gave into him, not knowing Theo was there watching us. Lash never hesitated when I told him to please have me there, right there, that I couldn't wait to go to a hotel. A minute later he was pumping into me against his truck, crying out loudly that I felt better to him than anything, that he was so glad Devlin had given him permission to bed me, and that he didn't give a fuck who knew that we were lovers again, that if Theo didn't like it I was welcome to come and live with him at Hayden, because he wanted me to be with him. He lasted only seconds. Just as he finished coming, he whirled around to be shot five times in the chest, and collapsed. I collapsed too, as the fifth shot had missed or gone through Lash, and hit me in the lung, and I couldn't get any breathe to breath. I looked up desperately to see Theo holding his regular gun, looking down the barrel at me. As I put up my hands for him to stop, he fired again, and I felt the bullet hit my chest like a load of bricks. Everything started graying. I saw Lash kill Theo, blowing his heart to ribbons, and then he was holding me, crying, begging me to hold on, to please hold on, he would change me, save me, as he changed fast to snake. Yet I died in his arms before he could.

But there was one that was sweet and good, one I considered staying in, the only one. In that one, I saved Lash with my blood, but instead of calling Titus as I lay dying, he changed me, as I had told him to. Much as he had that night at the hotel, he coiled around me and then he bit me.

When the sharp pain faded, I felt my body becoming snake, Lash's body still wrapped around me, his loving voice hissing gently that I was safe now, and to not worry, that he would take care of me. I heard in his voice how much he cared for me. I told him that I knew he would, and it was in my voice as snake that I loved him too, because I could not hide my emotions in my garbled words. He said nothing for many minutes, and then he helped me become human again, and held me. A few minutes later, he asked me hesitantly if I wanted a life with him, that he would give up all he had been, and go with me wherever I wanted, if I would only stay with him, and be mate to him. I agreed, because I'd known when I felt him change me that now I was weresnake, my old life was finished anyway.

We left a trail from his campsite into the swamp, he as snake and I as human, and when we were deep in the midst of murky water and trees, I teleported us out to Orlando, leaving all of his gear there, and his truck, and my bag and rings in the swamp, so it would look like we had both died. We used the rest of his cash to rent a car in Orlando, and headed West, settling finally in Louisiana's rural southeast, a place he said he had known many years ago. He looked younger, and no one knew who he was, so no one found us. He accessed some people he knew from his old life, and got us new names and identities. I got a job in an office, and he got a job doing construction. We worked hard, and didn't have a grand house or many things, but at the end of each day, we would shed our clothes, and lie together as snakes under the covers or make love as humans, and I knew I had never been happier. After a month, when I had completely mastered being snake and he said it was safe, we became lovers again in both forms. Nine months later, I had the first of our children in human form. When he held our son, he told me for the first time that he loved me, and we were married the next day.

I wanted to stay in that life with him. In that life there was no struggling to stay pregnant with his child, I had them easily, often in those early years with him more than one. He made love to me as often as possible, and never nightmared, felt jealous, or had to kill again. His smiles were easy, never sarcastic or bitter. In the twenty years I watched, we had ten children, all healthy, all with his darker hair, and eyes, though some had lighter skin like me. They grew up and had children of their

251

own, and we were grandparents.

Lash aged a little faster than I did, but not much. In twenty years, we both looked fifty-five, though some days he looked a little more like sixty. But his body was still strong, and it still brought me the same pleasure every night, as he loved me in human form. When ten years had passed, and I turned forty and him what looked like fifty, the animal side of us lost the urge to mate as our fertility dwindled. But we still held each other as snake, as we had in those first days, and I did not feel bereft, that we were no longer lovers in that form. Every night he whispered to me how happy he was that he had changed me, that we were together, that he had left his life of killing, and that we had a family, that this was all he had ever wanted in his life, and that he loved me more than anything. And I told him that I felt the same way.

I was sobbing as I closed the door on that life, because I wanted more than anything to go back there, to take that road I had not, to share that with him, to grow old with him, to never have gone through Michael's captivity, or Ulysses' torture of everyone I loved, or Danial's forgetting of me, and his revenge, when he came back to himself. To be just with Trystan, love him, and be everything to him, the way I could not be to him in my life now. But I knew that it was too late, that the chance had passed, and even if it hadn't, I would never have been free of my conscience enough to leave everyone behind that I cared for, with no explanation or reason to Danial, to let my two twin babies of Theo and Devlin grow up without their mother. There was nothing in that future about what happened back home, because in that life, I never knew what happened. It was thought by Lash and I that Devlin and Titus and the rest had assumed I had gone to Lash, and I had died trying to save him, and he had died as well, but we never tried to find out what had happened, for fear someone would come to try to separate us. For some men did come searching in that second year on behalf of the Vampire Ruler of Louisiana, bearing pictures of Lash and I, but when they came, Lash was not recognized in his changed youthful appearance, and I was in snake form, pregnant again already with twins, and surrounded by my two older children. And they believed that we were who we said we were, and left, thanking us for our help.

I turned my back on the door and found myself in another room.

This time, Theo was there.

* * * *

I crossed to him immediately, taking him in my arms. He was bleeding from many cuts, and unconscious. I didn't know what to do, and there were no windows. I thought about picking the lock, but wondered what was outside that door. *What if I came into another hall, and had to open doors again?* Theo looked in bad shape, too bad to go another hour without help.

Thinking that, I grimaced, and brought my wrist to his mouth. I imagined Lash's knife, and when it appeared in my hand, I slit my wrist, and gave it to him. In a second, Theo was drinking my blood, lapping it up like cream. In a minute, he had healed. He was shocked at first to see me, and then rolled his eyes. "Another dream?" he rasped. "Haven't you dreamed with me enough to last you the rest of your life?"

"Tell me where we are," I said urgently. "I need to know where you are, so I can send Terian to you. He is with me, watching this dream, and waiting. We did this to save you."

"Don't save me," he said wearily. "I'm tired, Sar. I'm ready to die."

"You have a son waiting for you—"

"He's not my son, he's Lash's," Theo said bitterly. "No true cougar could like snake scent, it's hardwired into us, even those like me that aren't born cougar. That's why I let you take him. He can't be mine, though the trick Danial did fooled me good, and I loved him like my own—"

"He loves you as his father! It was his wanting to talk to you that led us to find out you'd been ambushed! Now tell me where we are!"

"No," he said, settling down again on the bed. "I'm badly hurt, Sar, too bad to recover. I can't go through months of pain again, trying to be able to be how I was. They're going to kill me very soon anyway. I've had enough of this life. I've had enough of dreams that linger and seem so real and never come true."

"Please, tell me where they have you!"

"No," he said, closing his eyes.

I went to the door, and looked out, seeing nothing. And it came to me that Theo was doing this. He was deliberately doing this, thinking of a room in no place, where nothing existed, to give me no clues. I hated him in that moment, because I knew what he wanted me to do. I knew I had to do it or he would die, and I hated him more. He knew me, knew that even though I myself could leave him here to die I could not leave the father of my son here to die, not and ever face my son again.

I went back inside the room, and locked the door. "Do you want me, one last time?"

"You have to ask?" he rasped. "Did you ever know me?"

"I always knew you," I said bitterly, lying down next to him. "I know you are doing this on purpose, because you know Lash lies next to my body that is dreaming, and you want to hurt him. And this is an easy way to do it—"

"I don't give a fuck about him, or if anyone is watching!" Theo growled, sitting up and looking spry all of a sudden. "But yes, if this is the end, and there aren't going to be any more dreams, or hopes of anything, I want one last one with you. And I want it to be as our dreams always were, with us making love to each other."

"Tell me where you are," I said softly. "Then come here and say it to me one last time."

"I can't," Theo said, pulling me close and grinning for the first time. "We have to do it at least once before I can ask that."

I felt him slipping my clothes off. Then he embraced me, though he wasn't hurried, as we had always been before both in life and in dreams. "You're going slow," I said sarcastically. "Must be your age."

"I want to take my time," Theo said seriously. "So many times with you I didn't, and I regretted that. I didn't know much about women, when I was with you. I hadn't had experience. You should have told me that I needed to build up to sex, that it wasn't good to jam myself in, without kissing you and touching you, so you were ready." Theo swallowed. "Jenny and I fought one night when she refused my advances, and she told me I had the finesse of a drunken ape. She told me what you said, that I wasn't very good in bed, at least not next to your other lovers." He swallowed again. "I'm sorry I wasn't better, Sar. Please know I always wanted to be good for you. I wanted to feel wonderful to you and I'm sorry if…if I wasn't."

I felt more awful then than I had in years, and flushed beet red. "I'm

254

sorry," I whispered. "She was pissing me off that day I said that."

"It was still true, wasn't it? Tell me the truth."

"Yes. But I didn't leave you because of it. It was good, what we had, Theo. I wouldn't go back and make you other than you were, in those times we had when we were both happy."

"Kiss me," Theo said softly, laying his body on mine. "And tell me you still love me."

I couldn't make love with him. But what he really wanted wasn't that. "Tell me where you are," I whispered, kissing him. "I can come to you, if you only show me a picture in your mind. I'll bring you home, teleport you. I can't lose you, Theo. Harris and I need you. You want a life with me, give me this first."

He kissed me gently, more gently than he ever had. "Tell me you love me first."

I cast my mind back to the years I'd loved him, when we'd been married. I gathered the feelings I'd once had for him, wove them together, and put them into the three small words.

"I love you."

In that moment when he was happiest, the room defined itself clearly. We were in a hotel room. The address and phone number of the hotel was on a notepad on the dresser. Theo was bound to the bed, and dying, his throat steadily leaking blood. He'd been mutilated with both knives and burns. Both his legs were broken, too, and had healed badly so he couldn't walk.

Theo blurred the room with a snarl, as I kissed him quickly and then woke.

I sat up gasping, to find Terian beside me in a chair, writing down the information he had seen in my head. Lash was beside me.

"I'll go now," Terian said without looking up, pocketing the address. "Thanks, Sar. I'll call, when he's safe." He winked out of sight.

I snuggled down next to Lash, exhausted and drained. He held me contentedly. "I saw it all, what was behind those doors," he said softly. "Terian said I might, if I closed my eyes, and concentrated." He paused. "I loved that last door, Sar. Even though we both could not have walked away from our lives, it makes my heart glad to know we would have been happy with only each other. I felt what you felt, how good it was to

255

you, how much you wanted that life with me. It made letting you dream with Theo again bearable. I'm glad we did this, if for no other reason than to see what it might have been like if I'd turned you."

"Part of me wants to tell you it's not too late," I said seriously, grabbing his face in my hands. "To tell you right now to do it, to make me snake for real. Because it's not too late, if we go now. I'm not too old, we could still have that life, and it was so good—"

"No," Lash hissed in longing. "We have a good life, Sar. I'm not going to take immortality from you by making you snake. I am however going to get a potion for you tonight, because after that, I need to coil with you, and make love with you in both forms. I'll tell you after that I love you, and that I am happier with you in this life that I ever thought to be, because that is true for me in this life too. Everything I said in that other life is true in this one, too."

"We just made love—"

"That was not today," Lash hissed firmly. "I also need intimacy just to have reassurance. Those other lives, I always died without knowing you at all. And it was horrible, what happened when we were at your house, when you died in my arms. I nightmare about that sometimes, Sar, about you slipping away, dying in my arms, and I'm not fast enough, and I can't save you." He turned colder and darker. "I also saw Theo's gun that day at your house, and that it wasn't one with explosive bullets. I know if you had not refused me, that future might have come true, because he didn't grab that gun for me that day, he grabbed it for you."

I shuddered. He held me, and we said no more.

* * * *

Sun called that night looking for Terian. She was both worried and scared for him. I did my best to alleviate her fears. Then she said out of the blue, "I'm thirty-five, Sar."

"That's not that old," I said, knowing she was upset because she was getting older, and Terian wasn't.

"He's not getting older."

"I know," I said gently. "Talk to him, Sun. There are things he can do magically to slow your aging. If he can't do them, Titus or Rene can."

"Leri mentioned something, but she said it won't keep me young. I don't want to turn, um, demon-like."

Good time to change your MO and tell her absolutely everything, Tears. "Sun, Terian loves you. You—"

"I'm going to get old and he'll be young!"

"He'll still love you," I said firmly. "You have to trust that he means what he says."

"How can I?" Sun said in a whisper. "Would you, if you were in my shoes?"

"Yes," I said, remembering my dream. "Yes, I would." I hung up before she could ask me anything more.

* * * *

Later, Terian called Hayden. He told us that he'd found Theo, but he hadn't been in time.

"I killed them," he said drunkenly, sobbing. "I slaughtered them! But they hurt him too badly."

"He's dead?" I whispered, feeling terrible.

"He's in stasis," Terian said. "If I bring him out of it, he's sure to die. Keeping him frozen in time is keeping him from dying, but that's all it can do."

"Can't Titus do anything?"

"He said for you to come and talk to him, Sar. That there was something that could be done, but he'd need your help—"

I hung up on him, and went outside for a walk. *Why is it always me? I am so sick of this!*

"Love, you should not be outside by yourself at night," Devlin said in my ear.

"Ass! Why must you sneak up on me?"

"Because I'm me," he said, smiling, and baring a little fang. "I was worried. Titus is asking for you." He held out his hand. "Come."

I took it reluctantly, and we walked to Titus and Leri's home. As always, Leri welcomed us in, and told us to go ahead downstairs. Titus was waiting for us. As soon as we sat down, he began. "There is something that I can do," he rumbled. "I'll need your help, Sar."

"I am not rebonding to him."

257

"On the contrary, I need you to help me break the bond that dreaming with him has placed on you."

I nodded. "What do I have to do?"

"You hold still, and I'll do it," Titus rumbled softly. "The stasis is holding him, but you are, too, Sar. Once you are no longer bound to him, he will be free to move on."

He means die. Theo is going to die. "I thought...I thought you wanted me to save him."

"You cannot save him, Sar. He is past salvation, at least from you."

"Is there nothing else you can do?" I rasped.

"He does not want to live," Titus said. "He said this when I had Leri patch me into his stasis. With the best of healing magic, he could not expect to be what he was."

"Why? You can heal all things, and what you can't, Leri can."

"He is forty-five, Sar. For a werecougar, he is old enough that his regenerative power is fading, much as Lash's did—"

"But he was older than Theo is now when—"

"Theo does not want a potion, Sar. He does not want to live. The truth is if he lives, he will only have more attempts on his life."

"I don't want him to die."

"It isn't your choice, it's his." Titus was gentle, but firm.

"But I went to save him—"

"And you did, Sar. He is not in pain, and he'll slip away gently, when he goes, not screaming. You saved him from dying alone. You gave him what he wanted most, a last dream with you, and that is worth a great deal to him." Titus gave me a sorrowful look. "Stand there, please."

I felt a blaze of heat from him, my body instantly sweating hard. Titus said some words, the Hellfire suddenly searing me. Then there was a cool wind, and I came back to myself.

"It is done." Titus took my hand. "Come, Kin-daughter. It's time."

I took his hand, and he teleported me to Devlin's cemetery. I looked around with surprise, realizing we were there to pick up Devlin. He was dressed in a black silk suit. Rene was with him, in a long black dress and cloak, V dressed in black as well.

We arrived at Danial's cemetery. T was there. I immediately looked

258

around for Theo, and then realized that he would never be in the crowd again, because he was dead. I burst into tears, Devlin's hand squeezing mine. Everyone was there and we were all crying.

Danial, his eyes red from crying, took an urn and scattered its contents into the ground, into a hole in the earth beside Devon's grave. "You were a good friend," he said brokenly. "Rest well here, and know you are safe, finally. No one will ever hurt you again, or take you from us."

Devlin went to him, and led him back to the group. Harris and Tryst Jr. had also joined us, Harris clutching me around my waist tightly, Tryst Jr. watching intently.

Terian moved the earth over the ashes, making a slightly curved mound, then moved a large rock to mark the spot.

"Good night to you all," a hissing voice said. I looked up with shock to see Lash at the podium. "Thank you for coming here."

Even in my grief, I did a double take. *He's going to say something? Him?* God, Theo had to be cursing from the afterlife…

"You all know Theo was my enemy," Lash hissed. "It was well known that there was no love lost between us, and that when we began to love the same woman, things got worse." He paused. "I have no idea why he asked that I say something at this time and place, instead of Danial." He cleared his throat. "In spite of what he was to me, I look out, and I see all of you here. And no matter what I thought of him, it's easy to see you all loved him and called him friend."

He stopped and closed his eyes. "I know I would not have so many at my funeral," he hissed softly. "Because Theo was a better man than I. That is not saying a lot, I know. The truth was, he was a better man than most." He looked down at Harris and me. "He was a good husband to his wives, and a good father, even to children not his own. And there is nothing in this world more important than those things." He paused. "I will do my best to do as he would have done by Harris and Sar. Believe it or not, I will miss him. He was my favorite adversary."

Lash moved to go, and a fox shouted, "What of his killers?"

"They are mutilated and crucified," Terian said gruesomely, coming forward. "I have taken care of them. I will be assuming Theo's position in the Hierarchy, as second Ranked. I'll also be assuming Theo's role at

259

Danial's, for good. I will become full partner with Danial, and T—"

"'Theo'," T said in a cracked voice. "From this moment on, everyone is to call me 'Theo', please, or 'Theoron'. But I'd prefer 'Theo'."

There was a hushed silence.

"Harris may join us, when he is of age," Danial said suddenly. "Trystan, his brother, the invitation extends to him as well."

"Cool," Tryst Jr. hissed. Lash cuffed him lightly, telling him to hush.

"Everyone is welcome at Hayden," Devlin said, his voice not loud but carrying. "We are going to drink to excess. There will be guards, so any and all are welcome."

"We are going to run for him in the forest, as is tradition," Cia said, her eyes red from crying. "Theo was not one of us, but he was still family. We will come after."

Without words, the foxes changed in mass and shifted, running into the forest. Brian and Demi followed as bears, Elle and Harris bounding after them, roaring.

Tryst Jr. made a move to go too, but Lash grabbed hold of him. "No," he hissed. "You will not be able to keep up as snake. You can wait for them at Hayden."

Tryst Jr. swore angrily, but when Lash looked hard at him, he stalked over to Titus and teleported home.

"Come, Sweetness," Lash hissed. "It is time to go. Danial and Devlin have already left with V and Tears."

He was right. We were alone. And a heavy snow was starting to fall.

"Did I do the right thing?" I said, walking to the grave, and sinking to my knees in the fresh snow. "We hurt each other so much, Lash. So many times—"

"You loved him, and he loved you," Lash hissed softly, coming to stand beside me. "There is nothing wrong in that. You were a good wife to him for as long as you could be, with what happened to you."

"Was I?"

Lash pulled me to my feet, grabbed me up in his arms, and walked away carrying me. I hugged him, but looked back over his shoulder at the fresh grave, and the mound of new snow already covering the fresh earth.

* * * *

I don't remember much of the scene at Hayden. Everyone was there, but I couldn't remember later what was said. I spent most of it sitting in the chair, looking at the fire, as people milled about the ballroom. Before long, Devlin was taking me to bed and helping me get undressed. "Rest, you've had a trying day, Love," he said in my ear. "Please, rest?"

"Where is Danial? V? Tryst and Lash? Harris—?"

"V is with Harris and Tryst, watching some movies in pay per view. T... um, Theoron is with Lash and Danial, getting drunk in the ballroom. Titus is watching over us all with Leri, Shaker, Rene, and Rip, so no one attacks."

"And Elle?"

"Elle is with Elijah. He came in late last night, when she called him, and told him her father had died. He took her home. Their wedding is going to be put off until the weekend."

"I can't believe he's gone."

"Shh, rest, Love."

"I never thought of him as going to die," I said haltingly, wiping away tears. "I knew he was mortal, I knew he was getting older. But I thought it would be a while off."

"Shh." He wiped away my tears gently. "I've lost many that I was sure I'd see again at least one more time. Life is like that."

"It makes me afraid, Dev. How much longer am I going to get? How long do any of us have?"

"Don't be afraid," he said staunchly. "In four hundred years I've learned a few things about how to stack the deck in my favor to keep myself and my loved ones safe. If you ever do die it will be of old age, Love." He kissed me gently. "And I will be there by your side."

I twisted my Oathing band, the swirled colors shimmering in the light. "Forever."

"Forever is so limiting," Devlin said seductively, taking my hand. "Just as life is limited and measured in days and hours and years. What we have is eternal, Love. It will last not just forever, but a thousand, thousand forevers."

261

"Will you sing to me?" I murmured.

"Of course. What would you like?"

"'Fire and Rain', please."

"Ah, of course." He cleared his throat and began.

Before he'd reached the second stanza, I was asleep.

* * * *

I dreamed then, and my dream was of Theo standing in mist, looking at me wistfully.

"Is this real?" I said, reaching out for him.

"As real as our dreams ever were," he said, giving me a smile.

"Are you—?"

"Yes," Theo said, hugging me. "But it's not the end, Sar, it's another beginning. Titus said I might be able to visit you, in your dreams."

I gave him a smile, but it slipped, his face was so sad.

"It's not forever," he whispered. "I'll only be able to focus enough energy for a short time, and then I'll have to let go. I can already feel a pull. Soon, I'll have to leave."

"I don't want you to leave," I said, crying, and holding onto him. "I didn't want you to die!"

"It's too late," he whispered. "Shh, Sar. Be with me, while it lasts. Please?"

"Come here," I mumbled, trying to talk, while my eyes kept filling and my voice broke. "Say it to me."

"I love you," Theo said, his storm cloud eyes full of emotion and longing. "I've loved you since the moment you comforted me on our first walk at Danial's house all those years ago. I could make love to you forever and it would never be enough. There would never be a time I wouldn't want you again. There was never a time I didn't want you. There was never a time when you weren't beautiful to me. And I'm sorry that I hurt you so much, when all I really wanted was to be happy with you and for us to live out our lives together."

"I love you, too," I said, weeping. "I always did, I lied when I said I didn't. I loved you from the moment you dreamed with me, and I never stopped, not even when Titus broke the spell."

"I know, Soulmate," Theo said, smiling at me happily. "Now come here."

I went to him, and he began kissing me. Abruptly, I pulled back from him, and concentrated, and suddenly, we were in Wyoming again, back at the red rocks.

Theo looked around in confusion. "What—?"

I concentrated again, and felt myself shifting. But this was not the snake I had been so many times. This time, I became a lioness.

I looked at Theo from all fours, saw his intake of breath, and then he was shifting fast, roaring, his feet flying as he tackled me. His fangs gripped my neck as he moved into position. He slid in with a growling purr, and then he was thrusting fast, guttural roars coming from him. I felt him come and came myself, roaring loudly, our loud cries echoing down into the valley.

Theo made love to me for an hour frantically as a mountain lion, and then we collapsed, panting. I shifted back to human, and he followed me.

"Thank you," he said brokenly. "I love you, Sar."

"Theo—"

"Say nothing," he purred. "Please, just lay with me. Lay with me here at long last, as I always wanted to again with you."

I hugged him and the dream ended.

I awoke smelling of sex and of mountain lion, and then realized I was alone in Devlin's bed. *Shit.*

I threw on a robe, and went downstairs toward voices.

"Fuck, I knew it seemed too easy," Lash hissed angrily. "She's going to dream of him every night! How can I lie next to her and think of her and that Cat—"

"He is dead," Devlin interjected, also irritated. "Titus said it would pass, but to expect this might happen."

"When?" Lash said nastily. "I hate the scent of lion on her." He paused. "But the worst is, I can see it, Dev, all of it." He swore. "Every time she dreams of him now and I'm touching her, I see what she sees, feel what she feels. I feel how much she loves him still."

"He is dead and you are alive," Devlin growled. "Theo will have to move on, Lash. Be patient."

"Easy for you to say! You'd be more upset, if you heard her joyful roars, felt how much she wanted him, felt her feeling him inside her."

"She loves you."

"She was his soul mate," Lash hissed sorrowfully. "And she isn't mine."

"You don't know that."

"Because I'm too much a coward to find out for sure," Lash spat. "I can't face taking the potion, kissing her, and not dreaming with her."

"You aren't alone in that," Dev said quietly. "Danial and I feel the same. We don't want to know if we could dream with her, because finding out is like finding out we aren't good enough. What if one of us could, and the others couldn't? When we all knew that, would she not love that man more than the others? If none of us could, and Sar knew it, would she still stay?"

"You are good enough," I said, going over to them. "We don't have to make love in dreams. You have me in the waking world for the rest of our lives. Don't envy Theo."

"We are sorry," Dev said quickly. "It's just jealousy talking, Love."

"I'm sorry, Sweetness," Lash hissed, not meeting my eyes. "I didn't mean for you to overhear what I said. Not any of it."

"It's okay," I said, hugging him. "I understand. I'd feel the same way, if our roles were reversed."

"The boys are outside, playing with V," Lash said, changing the subject. "Come outside with me, Sweetness. It's going to be a gorgeous day, even if the temperatures are colder."

I looked over at Devlin. "Go ahead," he said, grumbling a little. "I have conference calls with a few Rulers, and also with Tony and Thane."

"Trouble?" Lash hissed immediately.

"Maybe," Devlin said wearily. "You know how it is. As soon as one problem resolves, another develops."

"Then I'll stay for those calls," Lash said firmly. "Sweetness, you go and get some sun. Harris has been asking for you this morning, he's still very upset. I'll be out after to join you."

I nodded, gave them each a kiss, and headed out into the day.

EPILOGUE

The moon shone down, bathing the path ahead in stark tones of black shadow and pale illumination. Only a soft wind stirred the leaves.

"This way, Sar."

Danial had my hand, as he led me through the trees. When I'd asked him to show me the way, he'd been reluctant. But when I told him why, he'd nodded, and said to meet him at his cemetery at nine.

Danial stopped suddenly, and turned to me. "Do you see the large rock, and the small pine tree?"

"Yes."

"Angelica is buried between them. In summer there are small blue flowers to mark the spot, but there is nothing there now."

"Okay. I'll only be a minute."

"Take your time."

I walked closer, and saw the remains of a patch of dead flowers. In addition, I saw the beginnings of green sprouting, the perennial flowers breaking through the dead remnants. I gently pulled the old away, and put it aside, making room for the emerging flowers to get all the light and water they needed.

"I know you hated me," I said very softly. "And the feeling was mutual, from the first time I saw you with Danial. But the truth is I owe you too." I paused, gathering myself. "I got to know Theo because of you, and to be mother to Elle. I know you didn't do me any favors to be kind, but that's the truth of it. So I hope you're at peace, and wherever you are, they're letting you wear those high heels and strapless dresses you liked so much."

I got to my feet, and walked back to Danial. He took my hand, and led me on.

265

A minute later, he stopped again. "See the rosebush? Monica is under that."

The five-foot high and three-foot wide one? "It's big."

"I had Terian give me a spell to make it grow quickly. I was afraid I'd forget where she was if I didn't, because I was so angry at her I couldn't bring myself to visit. I didn't come here again until I'd heard from you the truth of why she'd betrayed us to Manir." He paused. "It was only then I forgave her."

"I'll need longer this time."

"As I said before, take your time, Love."

I walked to the rosebush, and looked it over. As the other flowers had been emerging, the bush was blooming here, too.

"I'm sorry. You loved Danial and I hated you for it. I did what I could to make you jealous. And it worked so well you tried to kill me." I paused, gathering my thoughts.

"I'm not sorry I killed you, or how I did it either. I came here to tell you I was sorry for hating you, and to tell you thank you. For all I hated hearing your name, and remembering you, it's you and the formula you designed who've given me freedom from the other Rulers. And it was your plan that led to me loving Devlin, and being Oathed to him, and then falling for Lash, and mating to him. So thank you for that." I paused, taking a breath.

"I can't bring you back, not that I'd want to. But you will be remembered. Dr. Brenda has synthesized your formula, and written a paper on it. Originally, she wanted to name it after me, as it needed my blood to work. She's been able to produce a substitute for that, which is good as my blood is too vampire-tainted anymore to let me remain fertile. So instead, we're naming it after you. Monica's formula, it'll be called. You've given the vampire race something they've wanted for centuries. You'll be remembered forever as their benefactor." I paused.

"I forgive you," I whispered. "Be at peace. I won't return, but Danial will, and he'll tend your grave."

"Yes, I will. I give you thanks, too, Monica, for what you've given to not only me, but also my race. Most of all, I give thanks to you for giving Sar's life back to her. You saved her in a way that I and no one else could, not even Dev, no matter what we tried. Most of all, I thank

266

you for loving me, as it was because of that love that you created your formula. I'll be grateful for that for the rest of my life. Be at peace."

I got to my feet, and took Danial's hand. "Ready to walk back?"

"Not yet," he said in a low voice. "Do you feel like walking with me? I am too emotionally wound up to sleep or even make love."

"Sure. Which way should we head?"

"We'll skirt the cemetery and head over past the firing range. There are some deer paths to take."

"Sounds good."

"Come on then."

"You sure you're alright?" I asked, concerned.

Danial turned and faced me. "Are you ever going to leave me, or tell me you want out of our Oath?"

I smiled at him. "No."

"Do you love me?"

"Yes."

"Forever?"

"Yes." I let all my emotion flood my eyes as I looked at him, and watched his eyes mirror the love I was feeling for him. "That's a promise, Danial."

He kissed me gently. "Then I'll be all right no matter what else happens, Oathed One. We both will." He slipped his arm around me, and together, we walked off into the moonlight.

The End

About the Author

Tara Fox Hall's writing credits include nonfiction, horror, suspense, action-adventure, erotica, and contemporary and historical paranormal romance. She is the author of the paranormal action-adventure *Lash* series and the vampire romantic suspense *Promise Me* series. Tara divides her free time unequally between writing novels and short stories, chainsawing firewood, caring for stray animals, sewing cat and dog beds for donation to animal shelters, and target practice.

www.tarafoxhall.com

Other works by the author with Melange Books, LLC

Return To Me
Surrender to Me
The Origin of Fear in Spellbound 2011 Anthology
Night Music in Midnight Thirsts II Anthology
Partners in Midnight Thirsts II Anthology
Kink in Wicked Christmas Wishes Anthology
The Oath in Wicked Christmas Wishes Anthology
Bedtime Shadows Anthology
Make Me Behave Anthology
Latham's Landing, An Anthology
The Oath
Her Frozen Heart, in Frozen Anthology
Night Music, a Novella

The Promise Me Series
Promise Me, Book 1
Broken Promise, Book 2
Taken in the Night, Book 3
Taken for his Own, Book 4
Promise Me Anthology, Book 4.5
Immortal Confessions, Book 5
Her Secret, Book 6
Point of No Return, Book 7
Lost Paradise, Book 8
Dark Solace, Book 9
Eye of the Storm, Book 10

Tempest of Vengeance, Book 11
Sundown-Serena, Book 12
Hope's Return, Book 13
Fate's Prison, Book 14
Web of Memory, Book 15